Mad

Doctor Sean

For my family and friends.

Acknowledgments
◆◆◆◆◆

There were many people who were helpful and supportive of me while I wrote this book, and eventually brought it to publication. Perhaps too many. First, I'd like to thank my brother, James. He helped me develop a compelling plot, and characters that were believable enough to drive this story. My mother, who was an indispensable critic and proofreader. My sister and my father, for their never ending support and love. Jeff Herman, a fabulous literary agent who truly believes in his authors. Paul McCarthy, whose literary insight is second to none. Cathi Stevenson for her wonderful work on the cover. Angela Adair-Hoy, and the rest of the staff at Booklocker.com for making this book a reality. I'd also like to credit New York Medical College for my phenomenal medical education. The wonderful doctors, nurses, and staff at Long Island Jewish Medical Center for their friendship and support. All of my friends who have shared their love, their laughs and their lives with me. Sr. Mary Healy for her eternal support. And special thanks to Jennifer, who thoughtfully read every word of this manuscript, several times, until I got it right. Thanks.

There is no great genius without a touch of madness.
-Lucius Annaeus Seneca   *circa* 30 A.D.

CHAPTER ONE
♦♦♦♦♦

"Watch where you're going asshole!"

The chrome coffee cart rattled over the curb and onto the sidewalk, nearly running the man over. An obviously unshowered man pushed the cart awkwardly from behind. It was early morning, perhaps a hair past sunrise, and the desolate streets were punctuated only by an occasional yuppie. Along the curbside dampened leaves mixed with the street sludge and trash, and the cool morning wind created a steady stream of ripples in the usually stagnant puddles on East Eighty-fifth Street. There were several lipstick-stained cigarette butts peppering the stoop of a small brownstone nearby, and a passing cab splashed muddy water onto the concrete steps. A drunken tourist staggered limply up ahead, and then discreetly began to urinate against the brick facade of an apartment building. It was fall in New York City, and it was ugly.

Suddenly Eighty-fifth Street fell silent. One of the coffee cart's wheels had gotten crammed into a crevice between the concrete slabs of the sidewalk. Swearing in what was probably Greek, the coffee man stopped and reflected upon his situation. For the past eleven years he has made this same trip. Each weekday he awoke at five a.m., brewed his coffee shortly thereafter, and then stocked his cart with the donuts, rolls, and bagels that he had purchased the night before. By five-thirty he was en-route to perhaps the busiest corner in all of Manhattan, Eighty-sixth Street and Third Avenue. Several buses and the Number Four, Five and Six subway lines provided a generous patronage here. The money was great, some days he took home a thousand dollars in cash. But the people were cutting him to pieces. The snooty business types, the religiously ungrateful homeless, and the indignant punks who wear their pants three sizes too big were giving him an ulcer. Day after day he wheeled this mobile caffeine crackhouse to the same corner, at the same time, for the same people: Anorexic models, junk-bond junkies, and fat hyper

1

children. He wiped a fly from his oily forehead and wondered how his American dream had become such an awful Manhattan nightmare.

Heaving the cart from the front, the man successfully maneuvered his livelihood over the crevice. He navigated his cart between the traffic and the trash until he arrived at his destination. As always he situated himself at the downtown entrance to the subway and placed the break firmly down. With one last survey of his goods he climbed inside. He opened the donut smudged *Plexiglas* window, and the rich aroma of his coffee poured out onto the street and down the blackened steps of the subway station.

A jogger wearing beaten up *New Balance* sneakers huffed his way toward Central Park. He was nauseated by the passing smell of car exhaust as he darted past the coffee man's cart. There were too many cars in this city, and the air at street level was simply suffocating. For a moment he thought of holding his breath until he reached the relatively fresh air of the reservoir. But it was still far off. Reluctantly he took a full breath of the dank city.

For a man in his late forties, Jack was in excellent shape. Running thirty miles a week, hitting the weights and strict adherence to diet have served him well. And while his placid demeanor allowed him to avoid confrontation, there was little doubt that he was a man who could take care of himself.

Upon entering the park, he noticed a bustling in the leafy woods up ahead of him. A curious looking homeless man finally stepped out of the bushes. He was apparently talking to someone, and as Jack approached him, he tried to ignore the man. Jack felt uneasy about this person, and he inconspicuously picked up the pace. From a distance, the homeless man leered at Jack with a vague sense of familiarity. Jack grew more uncomfortable, but refused to break his stride. In New York City, a scene such as this was not uncommon, and Jack tried to swallow his concern. As he ran past the homeless man, he was greeted with a toothless smile.

"Have you seen her yet?" he asked.

"Huh?" Jack slowed his stride, and looked back over his shoulder at the indigent, bewildered.

"Huh?" the homeless man repeated. "He knows you, man! He will freakin' destroy you!" Now attracting the attention of several other runners.

A little flustered, Jack turned forward again and continued his run. For a few steps he imagined several gruesome scenarios that could follow such a meeting in this city, in this park, at this hour. A bullet or two in the back, a knife across the throat, a dull thud over his head followed by complete blackness. The possibilities were limitless.

Jack's fear ultimately dissipated in a cool sweat. And with each muffled step on the dirt trail, his anxiety retreated further. Once calmed, Jack began to intellectualize his reaction to that seedy man.

Jack Benedict, M.D. was fortunate amongst his medical school colleagues in that he received his calling early. The only son of a narcissistic investment banker and a depressed housewife, his choice of psychiatry was both a search for answers and a framework for solutions. It was truly a rare occurrence when a person's vocation and avocation were one in the same. This was true for Jack. He loved the clinical aspects of psychiatry, and he devoured texts on historical psychiatry. He was well regarded in the psychiatric community as one of the last bastions of psychoanalysis, often defending the indefensible like Sigmund Freud.

After attending Dartmouth as an undergraduate, he went off to medical school at Columbia, the School for Physicians and Surgeons in New York. Subsequently he completed his residency in psychiatry at New York University. Jack felt that working in Bellevue Hospital was the best education in psychopathology in the world. According to him, even the staff had 'issues'. He currently held many teaching posts both at his *alma mater* Columbia, and NYU. Renowned for his knowledge, he was long considered the authority on the diagnosis and treatment of schizophrenia and the related psychoses. In fact, he was so well versed in the esoterica of medical life that he was affectionately referred to as 'The Benedictionary' by generations of medical students.

Jack had now been in practice for nearly twenty years, yet there were times that he felt like he had never worked a day in his life. Nowadays the more he looked, the more insanity he saw. It was virtually impossible to walk down any New York City street, or ride any subway car without seeing someone who was actively hallucinating. Was it this city, or just the people who preferred to live here? Jack was never sure.

Lately Jack's life had been plagued with uncertainty, particularly in his professional life. There was a lot of uncertainty in psychiatry. Uncertainty about diagnosis, uncertainty about therapy, and uncertainty about theory were the major criticisms about his beloved profession. In fact, Jack was certain about only one thing...he had never cured a patient. It was Jack's contention that no psychiatrist ever had. Sure they could provide insight and mechanisms for dealing with mental illness, but this is a far claim from cure. Pharmacological therapy could alleviate psychotic features, depression, and mood swings, but not make them leave. Jack could even make the functionless functional, but he could not make them well. This was the life of Dr. Jack Benedict, noted psychiatrist.

The morning sun finally appeared between the high rise apartment buildings of the Eastside. Ephemeral beams of light ignited the surface of the lifeless reservoir. Like most runners on the reservoir trail, Jack ran counter clockwise. This was the convention. Uptown on the Eastside, downtown on the Westside. It was a simple enough concept, yet there were many who did not comply. Jack was always resentful of these clockwise runners, especially those who gave him a friendly wave, a subtle nod 'hello', or an irritating 'Good morning' with each and every lap.

"Hey." huffed a passing clockwise runner.

Jack returned with an exasperated wave.

About one-tenth of a mile later, Jack received another runner's nod, and he promptly nodded back. They were all regulars on this trail, and Jack felt painfully obligated to return their greetings. A young woman approached him. She was perhaps twenty-one years old, and Jack had never seen her before at the reservoir track. She was wearing an inside-out *Champion* sweatshirt that did not even come close to concealing her large breasts. Jack was mesmerized as he watched her breasts bounce a little to the left, then a little to the right. She wore black Lycra leggings that outlined her steely calves and thighs.

As Jack and the girl continued to approach one another, he again picked up his pace, and puffed out his chest. When close enough, he could see her pouty lips, olive skin and long dark hair held cutely in a ponytail. Their eyes met.

"Good morning!" Jack said, with a ghoulish wave and a nod.

The girl did not even acknowledge him. She didn't even give him a passing look of unfamiliarity. Jack was completely non-existent, a total zero to this young hot woman. Jack then recalled something that a close friend had once told him. The single biggest hallmark of middle age was a complete invisibility to young women. Jack had never noticed it until today, and for the duration of his run he amusingly reflected upon this eye-opening encounter.

He was beginning to cramp, so he decided to head home early. He began to walk about a block and a half from his brownstone on Eighty-fifth Street and Lexington to cool down. Once he caught his breath, Jack visited his favorite coffeehouse.

"Good mornin' Doc, what'll you have? The usual?" asked Kylie from behind the glass counter.

"Good morning Kay. I think I'll break with tradition today and have an iced hazelnut, please."

"Sure thing Doc. Did you have a good run?"

"Is there another kind Kay?"

"You're asking the wrong gal, Doc. Do I look like a marathoner to you?" quipped the modestly overweight Kay.

"I guess that would depend on the length of the race Kay, I guess it would all depend on the length of the race."

Kay and Jack both chuckled congenially, and said their goodbyes. Jack spied the mini bundt cakes on his way out but managed to resist this temptation. As he exited the coffee shop he was struck by the sudden commotion on Lexington Avenue. When he had entered the coffee shop there was hardly a soul on the street. Now, just a few moments later, the streets were jamming with pressed suits, and sharp *Ann Taylor* outfits. Jack glanced at his watch. Nearly seven o'clock, better hit the shower.

○○○○○○○

Across town on the Westside the music had been playing all night, and Casper Lolly's neighbors were planning to move out. The landlord and a small crowd of irate tenants gathered outside of his door, and despite repeated attempts to gain entrance, the punk band *Prodigy* played on, and on.

Behind the door, several deadbolts and their chains rattled to the raging base coming from Casper's stereo. The music inside the apartment was deafening. Even Casper's fish, Pontius and Pilot, were distressed.

His apartment was lofty and upscale. It had a great view of the park, and a large balcony off of the living room. There were clothes scattered all over the floor, both male and female. A garter and stockings were carelessly tossed on the stone kitchen tile. Inside the bedroom the morning sun slipped through a crack in the venetian blinds, revealing two bodies on the oversized oak bed. Both were tone and lithe. She was lying on her back with her legs over his shoulders. Her toes curled upwards in the steamy air. Sweat dripped off of Casper's beaded chest, and onto the woman's breasts. A blindfold hid her deep brown eyes, and Casper occasionally took the time to pull on her long blond hair. His thrusts were echoed by her spine tingling moans, and together their passion resonated throughout the apartment.

Like most weeknights Casper had been out partying. Last night he was downtown in a restaurant in SoHo at a party for a wealthy friend. As usual he had more than a few drinks, and he was not enjoying himself. The crowd was uptight and pretentious. Casper had his eye on this woman as soon as she entered the party. She was dressed in a short black party dress, and attached to her sleeve was some tuxedoed meatball named Vito. Naturally, Casper chose the bar to make his move.

"I've heard of people bringing their own Italian dressing to restaurants, but you're the only person I've seen bring her very own dressy Italian."

She was apparently the type of flit who found Casper's impudence refreshing. Women in general adored Casper. In truth he was a stellar looking man. He stood only five-foot eleven, but his presence was much more commanding. He had a chiseled body and sculpted face, and despite the fact that he had a rabid streak, his intellect was second to none.

Doctor Casper Lolly was born into a blue-collar family thirty-five years ago. He had rather inauspicious beginnings, working part time in his father's garage to pay for college at New York University. At NYU he majored in biology, with a minor in physics. He was also a track and field star. As a junior, he even set the school's indoor record for the long jump. It was a record that still stood today. He was twice voted NCAA division III All-American in this event, and he was a competitive sprinter as well. He scored in the ninety-eighth percentile on the MCAT, the admission test for medical schools, and subsequently attended Yale University, School of Medicine.

Unlike Jack Benedict, Doctor Casper Lolly did not feel predestined to become a psychiatrist. Most of his medical school classmates felt that he was a natural surgeon. He always had an uncanny grasp of anatomy and physiology, a gift he credited to his deceased father and his experience as an auto mechanic. Academically he stood at the top of his medical school class, and frankly his choice of psychiatry was a shock to classmates and professors alike.

"Why psychiatry?" they would ask.

Casper always responded similarly, "The single biggest contributing factor to my choosing psychiatry, is my hatred of the kidney. I simply hate the kidney. Sure, it's a phenomenal and interesting organ, and I'm thankful that I have two of them...but when the kidney gets disordered, everything else gets fucked up. Renal tubular acidosis? Glomerulonephritis? Who gives a shit?"

Casper stayed on at Yale to complete his residency in psychiatry after his graduation. After an uneventful four years of treating rich folk for depression and outlandish phobias, Casper decided to return to New York City. His candor and disdain for tradition enabled him to quickly garner a flourishing practice. New Yorkers loved his eccentricity. Casper also held an academic post at the New York Hospital, Cornell Medical Center, where he eventually became the director of the psychiatry residency program. Now at the age of thirty-five, Casper was affluent beyond his wildest dreams.

Casper had no role models, and only a few confidants. He was frequently contemptuous to his colleagues, even to the point of public beratement. In his editorials for psychiatric journals, Casper would routinely dismember the time-honored conventions of orthodox psychiatry. He had an unabashed disdain for the current practice of his profession, and Casper truly deserved his reputation of being a self-hating psychiatrist.

Professionally, Casper chose to work exclusively with the sickest of the sick, the schizophrenics. And while his theories on the etiology and evolution of the psychotic state were largely considered radical, he was regarded by all to be an exceptional physician.

The music was still vibrating in the apartment, and Casper and the woman tumbled to the floor. She had been getting sexed all night. Perhaps four, maybe five times. She was on her belly and Casper was taking her from behind. The clock flashed 7:30am, and Casper could not recall the party, the place, nor the name.

Casper's dating habits have always been predatory, and his sexual appetite was insatiable. His social life was a virtual celebration of the female form, yet he showed a profound indifference towards these women. He had a few relationships in the past, but he always kept them purposely unstable. He was decidedly alone, but he was far from lonely. He was also rude and obnoxious. But despite all of this, people were inevitably drawn to him. They admired him. Some worshipped him. He was recklessly honest, and he possessed the brutal confidence of a prizefighter.

The woman's face twisted into a bizarre marriage of exhaustion and pleasure. Casper finished in a crescendo of grunts and groans, and then limply flopped beside her on the shag carpet. After several minutes, without saying a word, he loosened the blindfold to reveal the woman's sultry eyes.

"I'm Casper," he said as he extended his hand.

"Cathy...Nice to meet you." she loudly returned.

Casper jumped to his feet and crossed the floor. Cathy discreetly admired his build through her manicured fingers. She was mortified, and she buried her face into the palms of her hands. Casper finally turned down the stereo.

"Listen Cathy, I have to go to work. But make yourself at home, there is coffee in the kitchen…and why don't you give me your number so I could…"

"Do you have a pen and paper?" she interrupted.

"I have a good brain. A memory like an elephant. Just tell me."

She told him the number as he climbed into the shower. Suddenly there was a banging at the door that startled her.

"Doctor Worry, I know you there!" screamed an angry Asian neighbor.

"Who is that?!" asked Cathy.

"The neighbor." Casper said, and climbed into the tub.

Casper's shower was brief and cold. When he finished he wrapped a large towel around his waist and finally attended to the escalating commotion at the front door.

"Who is it?" he sang.

"Doctor Worry! Open up, this is wast time!"

After unlocking several deadbolts and chains, Casper creaked open the door, and peered outside. Tommy Wu, a wealthy electronics executive, was outside of Casper's door in a bathrobe, and he was fuming mad.

Retreating back into the apartment a little bit, Casper turned toward his bedroom and yelled, "Honey, did you order the Chinese?"

Tommy Wu lunged at Casper through the half-opened door.

"Whoa, Tommy! Whoa! Slow down! What's the matter?"

Casper fended him off and managed to step out of the apartment. He closed the door quietly behind himself. Six restless neighbors and his landlord were waiting for him.

"Ssshh…You're gonna wake the entire building, Tommy." Casper whispered.

Tommy Wu lunged at Casper again. Casper defended himself, almost playfully, and awkwardly struggled to keep his towel from falling from around his waist. Several other tenants had to separate the two men.

"This is your last warning Casper. Next time you're out." the landlord said.

Casper looked forlorn and feigned ignorance. He leaned against the wall of the hallway, and clutched his chest. The crowd slowly dissipated in waves of sneers and mumbles, and each tenant shot a venomous look at Casper as they passed him. Then, with a subtle smirk of satisfaction, he crept back into the apartment and shut his door.

OOOOOOOO

Jack Benedict wiped the steam off of the bathroom mirror to reveal a distorted image of his rugged face. He surveyed his stubble for a moment, then methodically brushed shaving cream in small concentric circles along his jaw and mustache. At first he was cautious and systematic. But then his beeper began to go off in the bedroom. Hastily he finished his shave and removed the remaining shaving cream from his face with a damp towel. He threw it in the sink and ran silently into the bedroom.

Caroline Benedict was already awake, and slightly disoriented. She was rustling helplessly under the down comforter.

"Jabes? Your beeper is going off."

Only Caroline called him 'Jabes', which was an expansion of 'JB', which in turn was what Jack's close friends called him.

"I know sweetheart, I'm sorry, go back to sleep."

"What time is it?"

"Seven fifty-five. That's the office. I'm supposed to deliver a lecture to the medical housestaff this morning, and I need to pick up..."

Caroline was back asleep already, snoring softly.

"My...uh...slides."

Things between Jack and Caroline have been improving over the last several months and lately he has been working hard at reviving the excitement in his marriage. Like many other marriages, a romance fizzled as a friendship blossomed. After many years of contented marriage, Jack began having an affair with a much younger psychology graduate assistant. He had suddenly lost site of the important things in life. And while this affair was gratifying from the sexual point of view, it was devastating to Jack from a spiritual point of view. He had tremendously strong feelings for this other woman, perhaps uncontrollably strong. But Caroline was his best friend, and if needed, Jack would take a bullet squarely in the chest for her. How could he? How did he do this to her? He simply had no good answers.

He ultimately faced the consequences, and was forthright with his wife. He told Caroline of the affair, and pleaded for her forgiveness. Her heart was broken, and this still tormented Jack. Together they sought professional help, and began to rebuild a romance.

Jack finished the knot in his necktie and gave it one last tug and tuck. He closed the closet door and looked at his watch. It was a little after eight o'clock. He scurried over to Caroline, and gave her a small kiss on the forehead. She barely flinched. He grabbed his sportcoat, and swiftly left the brownstone.

CHAPTER TWO
♦♦♦♦♦

The streets of the Upper Eastside were bustling with people. The concrete shook underneath Jack's feet as the subway roared into station on the tracks below. He waited on the street corner and mentally rehearsed his lecture, 'A Review of the Diagnosis and Therapy of *Dementia Praecox* (Schizophrenia)'. The traffic light turned green, and in a swarm of pedestrians Jack scampered across the street. Like most New Yorkers, Jack closed his sport coat slightly as he descended the gum-studded steps of the subway station. He had been pick-pocketed once before, and he was determined to never let it happen again.

Jack swiped a *Metrocard* through the turnstile, and then gingerly pushed through it with his groin area. They occasionally got stuck. He followed the bulk of the crowd and descended all the way down to the express platform. He looked aimlessly uptown for the approaching train. He was planning to get on the express and then take it to Forty-second Street. Then he would either transfer to the local, or perhaps just walk the remaining distance to work.

Overhead he heard the downtown local train as it lumbered into the station. Many of the commuters frantically darted back up the steps in a stampede of loafers and heels to catch the local. Jack was patient, and before the local even pulled out, the express suddenly appeared and screeched to the platform.

The inside of the subway car was a microcosm of New York itself. A variety of nationalities were crammed into every corner. At the front of the car a group of Latina catholic schoolgirls were dressed in their uniforms. They talked to one another as if they were alone on the train. They were talking about boys, classes and parties. Behind them sat a bearded white man who was trying desperately to be inconspicuous. His gaze alternated between a nonchalant glance at the other riders and a blatant leer at the ass of one of the girls. She had hiked her skirt up once again, a practice they called 'cinching', and the result was honestly alluring.

"Lokie says you been cold, an' that you an' his brother be gettin' a little freaky, Maria." one of the girls said to the girl with the short skirt.

"He's crazy." Maria coyly responded.

Maria gently swayed her ass back and forth as the subway rumbled down the tracks. She was softly mouthing the words to a song that was in her head, and the bearded man was fixated. Other passengers began to notice this impropriety, and they shook their heads in embarrassment. The lights flickered and everyone fell silent for a moment.

Next to the bearded pervert sat two unattractive women in business outfits. Neither one of them wore makeup, and their faces were a ghastly white. Both had their hair tightly pulled back in a bun. The fluorescent lights cast shadows across their faces, and colored every blemish on their skin in a pale city blue. A dried coffee stain decorated the floor, and a cardboard blue cup, the kind with the Greek writing on it, rolled underneath the communal bench. Against the doors stood two large black men in street clothes. They were obviously dressing for intimidation, and Jack was unsure if they knew one another. They impassively stared straight ahead, with a complete vacancy of expression in their faces. As usual the bulk of the subway car was occupied by straphanging suits and skirts of all colors, who jiggled in synchrony as the car waddled its way downtown.

"It's time. She's near." someone said, or so Jack thought.

Jack turned around, holding firmly onto a metal pole, but nobody was addressing him. Behind him there was an old woman reading a book, a few suited men, and a sleeping homeless man. Jack received a few blank stares in response to his non-verbal questionnaire, and he slowly turned back around.

"This is Forty-second Street, Grand Central Station, *Fooorty*-second Street. Transfer for the..." the conductor cracked through the intercom.

The platform was crowded with commuters who gathered around the doors as the subway pulled into station. They parted to make a narrow passage for those who were exiting the train with Jack. The doors slid awkwardly open and a flood of straphangers poured onto the platform. Jack moved quickly and uncomfortably along with the crowd. There was a momentary slow down as the crowd filed through the revolving doors. These 'doors' always reminded Jack of meat grinders. In fact they were not doors at all, rather they were a rack of menacing horizontal rods that swung by, and interdigitated with a rack of stationary rods. They were truly frightening to watch. Jack always imagined someone getting caught in this pedestrian powered *Cuisinart* and getting chopped to pieces. He took a deep breath and shoved through the exit.

He picked up a copy of *The New York Times* at an underground kiosk, and stuffed it securely underneath his left arm. He was heading past the token booth when he heard his named called by a familiar throaty voice.

"Jack...Jack!" Quizzically, Jack searched the crowd before him.

"Yo, over here Jack." Ellen McCormick stepped out of the crowd with an impatient wave.

Jack's heart sank for a moment and his face turned pink and warm. "Hello Ellen. What are you doing here?"

"What the hell do you think I'm doing here?...Stalking you!" she returned. "I'm going to work, of course."

"Oh hey, that's right. How's work going, Ellie?"

"Fine, I'd rather be a grad student again, if you know what I mean." She nudged him with her elbow.

Ellen had been Jack's graduate assistant while she was pursuing her Ph.D. in psychology. She was industrious, smart and frighteningly sexy. She was more than twenty years his junior, and he had a difficult time connecting with her at first. However, the long hours and intimate working conditions ultimately pushed them together. Before either one of them realized it, they were enveloped in a scandalous affair. Despite his strong feelings for her, Jack broke it off with Ellen abruptly. The guilt was destroying him and he could no longer betray his devoted wife. Ellen was simply devastated, and even now she continued to perseverate on her brief but intense relationship with Jack.

Jack still had feelings for Ellen too. They had a tremendous amount in common, and he was probably physically infatuated with her. She was thin and tight, with long blond hair and a magical smile. The conversations they had were deep and insightful, and the sex was always athletic and wild.

Jack was clearly uncomfortable with the implications of Ellen's last remark. He nervously fidgeted with the newspaper under his arm, and avoided her warm stare.

14

"I'm sorry, Jack." she said, "I just thought that we..."

"We did! Ellen, we did. We do, I mean. We have a beautiful friendship and memories of a wonderful time together, but that's it, Ellie. That's all it could ever be." Jack paused, "C'mon, let's go. We're holding people up."

"Where you headed, JB?"

"I have to lecture the medical housestaff today, I'm already a little late."

"Let me guess...schizophrenia, right?"

"Very funny, Ellie. Amateur night is Thursday." he wisecracked as he led her through the crowd.

The two former lovers walked closely side by side down Lexington. She resisted the urge to take his arm, and he resisted the urge to just take her. Heading east on Thirty-eighth Street, they made a lot of small talk for this big city.   •

○○○○○○○○

Casper shook off an irate cabby, and he flipped him the finger. He was in a xenophobic mood today. Damn foreigners. He crossed the street at the signal, strutting his way past the nurses of the nightshift. He greeted several of them, and turned back to look at their rears as they passed. He was pleased with what he saw, and he jumped spryly up to the curb.

The entrance to New York Hospital was jammed with reporters and cameramen. Casper loitered curiously around the scene for a while. The reporters were discussing another hospital merger. Casper was immediately disinterested, and he entered the hospital. He placed his identification tag on his jacket as he passed the carelessly chatting security officers. He turned down the long corridor and waited for the elevator. As usual, the wait for the elevator was a lengthy ordeal. Casper could never understand this elevator paradox. It seemed to him that the elevators were always horrible in great hospitals, but they were always great in horrible hospitals. The reason for this was beyond his comprehension.

As usual, he was waiting with a large group of people. It was the same group each morning. None of them ever talked to one another despite working in the same hospital. Casper found this odd, but he preferred it that way. He didn't need extraneous people cluttering his life. He wasn't interested in small talk. The elevator doors finally opened and some of the night staff filed out while the morning crowd filed in.

The elevator stopped at nearly every floor. This annoyed Casper, and he did little to hide his aggravation. He especially detested the fatties from housekeeping who consistently took the elevator only one flight. Up or down. He took a deep breath, and calmed himself. The ride was always interminable for him.

Casper's office was located on the fifth floor. It was near, but not inside the more formal Department of Psychiatry. For reasons that were obvious to both the department and Casper himself, this distance was desperately necessary. From the elevator Casper noticed that the office was packed with his psychotic patients, their aides and family members. It was truly a wild scene. He charged down the corridor and swung open the glass doors of his office, fanning the psychotic firestorm. Stepping heroically into the waiting room, mental patients and hospital personnel instantly mobbed him. Most psychiatrists would be overwhelmed by this situation, but Casper relished this mayhem. With a grateful sigh, he finally relaxed. He was home.

Opening his arms as if to embrace the crowd, he asked, "Who here is the craziest? Raise your hand and I shall see you first."

In a wave of "Me, me, me and Ooo me!" nearly all of the patients responded.

"Doctor Lolly, I feel like my heads gonna explode!" implored one patient.

"La, la, la, la, la." sang another.

One patient covered his ears and began to scream. "Doctor Lolly, don't leave me here with these psychos! Please! Please! I beg you Doctor, see me, see me!"

Casper surveyed the waiting room. 'Bedlam West', he liked to call it. This was his home, his sanctuary.

Most psychiatrists decorated their walls with placards and portraits of famous psychiatrists. Some hung advanced degrees and medical citations. The walls of Casper's office were adorned with portraits of infamous psychopaths and photographs of grisly crime scenes instead. Adjacent to the doors, pictures of mass murderers Ted Bundy, Charles Manson, Joel Rifkin, and Jeffrey Dahmer were hung with reverence. Tormented Eastern European writers, like Dostoevsky and Tolstoy, shared a wall with cult leaders Jim Jones, David Koresh, and that whacked-out bald guy from the Heaven's Gate doomsday cult. The oversized photos were all black and white glossies, and were framed in an austere black lacquered wood. This imparted a clinical quality to these otherwise tasteless photographs. While most of his colleagues found the room appalling, Casper considered his office a monument to mental illness and an artwork in development.

In the corner, underneath the aged photograph of Rasputin, sat Roger Finnegan. He was classified as a Catatonic Schizophrenic and was a relatively new patient of Casper's. Roger seemed threatened by all of the commotion and cowered slightly into his seat. It was and odd posture for such a mammoth of a man. His hair was closely cropped to his lumpy skull, and his deep green eyes darted rapidly behind his jutting brow. He continuously fiddled with his clothes, anxiously knocking his knees together.

By all standards Roger was profoundly psychotic. Flight of ideas, loosening of associations, auditory command hallucinations, and visual hallucinations were all manifested in his disordered thinking. Yet despite the profound disorganization and psychotic features, Roger managed to impress Casper with a bizarre intelligence. There was a purpose and a subtle structure to his madness. Casper wanted to interview him last. He found Roger extremely interesting, and he was going to need a lot of time.

OOOOOOO

There is a well-known phenomenon often cited by psychiatrists, called 'Aberrant Perception'. During the course of a psychiatric interview, a psychotic patient may say something that borders on clairvoyance. Perhaps the patient accurately predicts an earthquake, or a severe snowstorm. At times they may say things that are pertinent to the psychiatrist's personal life, like the death of a child, or the infidelity of a spouse. Oddly, there is often mention of the personal lives of other patients. There are even times when patients appear to be sharing information with one another, despite never having met. These episodes were usually dismissed as coincidences by most reputable psychiatrists, with the notable exception of Dr. Casper Lolly.

Shortly after he returned to New York City, Casper began to have multiple encounters with this yet undefined subgroup of schizophrenics. To Casper, many of them appeared to have exquisitely sensitive perceptive abilities. Furthermore, not only were some of his patients keenly aware of their immediate physical surroundings, some of his schizophrenics were downright prophetic. It was Casper's contention that these patients may not be mentally ill at all. In fact he was convinced that they were gifted. He hypothesized that somehow this small group of schizophrenics were 'perceiving' clues from another dimension. Perhaps they were witnesses to another aspect of space-time, which most physicists believed to be the fourth dimension. Perhaps they were operating in a different dimension altogether. A dimension that was unseen by the majority. Casper believed that the subsequent misinterpretation of clues from this super-dimension might have lead to symptoms that were clinically indistinguishable from the common psychoses.

Casper's research with these insightful schizophrenics quickly became both his opus and his albatross. The long hours and lack of professional regard for his work plagued the first years of his research. His first paper describing this cohort of psychotics was rejected by no less than fourteen scientific journals. Casper was openly laughed at during lectures and society meetings. Knowing that his professional reputation may be on the line, he lobbied editors across the country until his paper was finally accepted for publication.

Lately, his theories have been gaining acceptance within the psychiatric community, though his critics still greatly outnumbered his followers. This burgeoning scientific interest was partly due Casper's refusal to yield to adversity, and partly due to the growing belief in 'Perception' as a clinical entity. Today Casper was not only considered the authority on such patients, but he was the guru of a growing body of scientists who believed in their existence. His unpublishable paper was now considered by some to be a landmark article.

"Okay Misses Cravitch...Let's go!" Casper picked his first patient.

Misses Cravitch was a fifty-six year old narcissistic, paranoid schizophrenic who has been seeing Dr. Lolly for the last two years. She was wearing tight pink leggings, and a flamboyant sweater that covered her cellulited rear. She flipped her hair almost disdainfully at the others as she entered the conference room. Casper shut the door behind her with a nod.

ОООООООО

The atmosphere at Doctor Benedict's office was subdued and quiet. His waiting room was painted in a reserved shade of forest green and trimmed with a decorative oak molding. The lighting was intentionally dim and his secretary was an unassuming middle aged woman named Gladys. His patients appeared to be well to do, wearing stylish European suits, expensive jewelry and impressive overcoats. Jack entered the office, and was greeted with whispered 'Good mornings' from his patients.

"How'd the lecture go Jack?" asked Gladys from behind the desk.

"Superb Gladys," Jack said, "It went quite well, thanks."

Jack turned toward his waiting room. The patients were quietly sitting with their legs crossed. A few were casually flipping through copies of *The New Yorker* and *New York* magazine, while others admired the placid serenity offered by the Ansel Adams portraits on the wall.

"What's the rest of the day like for me, Gladys?" asked Jack, as he turned his attention away from his patients.

"Ten-thirty to two-thirty you have private patients. Then at three, you have to preceptor the medical students. And at..." Gladys paused as she flipped the pages of the appointment book. "...four o'clock you have teaching rounds with the residents. Oh! I have scheduled two emergency patient appointments, here in the office, at five and six o'clock."

"Who are they again?" he asked.

"Mary Mitton, and that guy Lipton."

"You mean Lepton?"

"That's the one!" Gladys smiled.

"Just pull their charts for me before you leave, would you Glad-Bags?"

"Did it already, they're on the desk."

Jack turned to enter his office. The decor was quintessential nineteenth century psychiatry with an oversized antique mahogany desk, leather couch, tiffany lamps, and a comfortable sitting chair. The bookshelves were packed with bound editions of classic psychiatric texts, and a bust of Sigmund Freud cast a shadow onto the far corner of the room.

Jack placed his briefcase on the leather blotter of his desk. He flipped the latches and it opened with a soft creak. He removed the slides from his presentation this morning and put them in the fourth volume of his slide albums. He carefully examined all of the slides before placing them back into their appropriate plastic slots. Disorganization drove him batty. He placed the album back on the bookshelf and then returned to his briefcase. He searched the pouch aimlessly, then the other pockets, then looked under the manila folders. He was suddenly frantic. *Where were his reading glasses?* A sudden sense of doom welled up in Jack, and he desperately patted his chest. After several worrisome taps he found them in his breast pocket.

Relieved, Jack carefully removed the remaining contents of his briefcase and placed them onto his desk. He slid his glasses to the bridge of his nose, and sorted through the files and periodicals. He glanced at the cover of this month's *Journal of Clinical Psychiatry*, and scanned the titles of the articles. He flipped over to the back cover. There was a tacky advertisement for a CME lecture on schizophrenia at New York Hospital this week.

The caption read:

PERCEPTIVE SCHIZOPHRENIA:
Psychos or Psychics?
Presenter: Casper Lolly, M.D.
Saturday October 3

Jack shook his head and snickered. "Fucking idiot."
"Gladys?" Jack buzzed his secretary through the intercom.
"Yes?"
"You can send in my first patient now."

CHAPTER THREE
◆◆◆◆◆

Casper chewed on his pencil intently. Mrs. Cravitch was jabbering on and on about these men who keep looking in her window at night. She told him that these men were sending her electronic signals through her television set, and kept asking her to provide them with oral sex.

"What do you do then, Mrs. Cravitch?"

"I put a cucumber in my mouth to stop me from doing it."

"Uh-huh, I see."

Renee Cravitch was referred to Casper two years ago when she thought that Peter Jennings from *ABC News* was sending her similar electronic suggestions. She believed that the anchorman even proposed to her in this way. Excitedly she then visited the glitziest bridal boutiques in all of Manhattan and tried on several glamorous dresses. She finally decided on an exquisite satin gown by *Jessica McClintock*. It had a flowing ten-foot train and a cathedral length veil. When the owner of the boutique asked her how she intended to pay for the expensive dress, Renee told him to put it on the expense account of Peter Jennings, her soon to be husband. The police arrived shortly thereafter.

Renee was incessant about these voyeurs. "I can't even bend over in the comfort of my own home!"

"What does Peter have to say about all of this?" asked Casper.

"Oh..." Renee softened her voice and suspiciously stared at the computer monitor on Casper's desk. "He doesn't know. He gets very jealous. He's liable to hurt someone if he finds out."

"Peter can get out of control, huh?"

"Oh, yes." Renee nodded.

"He looks the type. I wasn't aware that you and Peter are still talking, Renee."

"Sure we are, almost every night. Six o'clock p.m. Every night except weekends."

"Well, how do you explain that Renee?"

"Explain what?"

"The fact that you and Peter Jennings talk only when he's broadcasting the nightly news."

"Well, he has to wait until Barbara leaves of course."

"Barbara?"

"Streisand, Barbara Streisand. She knows nothing about us."

"Barbara Streisand and Peter Jennings are having an affair?! They're both married!" Casper feigned astonishment.

"Oh yes, for a long time now."

Casper reclined in his mock disbelief, when suddenly the chime of the alarm on his wristwatch went off. The half-hour was up, and it was time for Renee to go.

"Well Renee, I think we accomplished something good here today. C'mon, upsy-daisy."

Casper fixed his tie and gleefully bounded to his feet. His genitals were now in close proximity to Renee's face. She looked up at her psychiatrist seductively.

"Excuse me." Casper cleared his throat and pardoned himself.

○○○○○○○○

There was a long silence in Jack Benedict's office. It was an intentional silence that compelled Josey to continue speaking. "So that's when I first began to realize that I was worth something…that I was not a stupid, thoughtless, worthless, speck of nothing in this universe."

Josey Cartwright was having a catharsis. Jack quietly observed her and listened patiently from his comfortable armchair. Occasionally he jotted down notes on a spiral notepad with a *Cross* pencil that was given to him by his wife.

"Go on." Jack facilitated the conversation.

Josey continued. "Everything that I learned as a kid is wrong, completely wrong…about myself…about my brother…about my father…about the whole damn mess. It was not my father who did the beating, nor the cheating. It was alcohol, and human weakness. We all have weaknesses. Alcohol, drugs, and violence are predators that exploit these weaknesses. And pain is the parasite that lives off of them. That's all. I have come to learn that pain whether it be emotional, physical or spiritual, is intimately connected with human weakness. I just realized it last week."

Intellectualization. Jack wrote this word twice, retraced it and underlined it several times on his notepad. This was one of the classic neurotic defenses. Unfortunately it was only a small portion of Josey's arsenal of defense mechanisms. Classic psychoanalysis taught that intellectualization was a systematic excess of thinking, devoid of any feeling, in an attempt to defend against anxiety. Essentially Josey was delving too deeply again. She was pathologically introspective, and Jack had been tirelessly working with her for years on developing more effective coping strategies. Her psychological problems were legitimate, and Jack did not doubt this. It's been difficult for both of them, but he promised her that they would get through this together. No matter how long it took. It was a promise of partnership that Jack made to all of his patients.

"For once in my life, I feel good, Doctor...I feel healthy." Josey turned back toward Jack, her voice was wet and tearful. "...I really do."

"That's all that matters to me." Jack took her hand sympathetically, and then noticed the time on the grandfather clock against the wall. He quickly double-checked this with the vintage *Rolex* wristwatch that his grandfather had given him. He discreetly told Josey that their time was up, and they made arrangements for her next visit.

OOOOOOOO

"So you feel that your family, your friends, and me, your psychiatrist, have all been replaced by imposters? Am I correct in that Mr. Winston?" Casper asked, confronting his tense patient.

Casper was hunched forward in his chair like a baseball catcher. His face was just a few inches from Simon Winston and he breathed heavily into his psychotic patient's ear. Simon appeared distressed, nervously peeking at Casper from the corner of his eye.

"Yeah all that's true. Yep. Uh-huh. Okay then are we finished?" Simon attempted to get up from the couch but Casper forcefully pushed him back down.

"Hold on, hold on!" Casper said. "Before you go I need to know one thing." He glided to the door and locked it.

"Huh?" Simon swallowed deeply and eyed his doctor.

"Who gave us away, Simon? What gave us away?" Casper stuck his tongue between his teeth and hissed like a snake at Simon. Simon became hysterical. He dove off the couch and crawled away on the floor. Casper chased after him, jumping over the arm of the couch.

"Simon! Was it my curly tail?"

"No!" Simon was crippled with fear in the corner of the office. He tightly covered his ears.

"The horns on my head? Did you see the horns on my head Simon?" Casper straddled him. "Tell me it wasn't the horns!" He ran over to a mirror on the wall, and fixed his hair wildly in an attempt to conceal make believe horns.

"No horns, No horns!" Simon cried.

"Then it must have been the…" Casper was interrupted again by his alarm. "..the mother…ship."

Casper was upset. He was just starting to have fun. He called it 'Confrontational Therapy' but in reality he was just trying to have a few laughs. He dragged himself over to the door and sadly unlocked it. "Okay Simon, we're finished for today. I'm increasing your medication again." Casper opened the door and fanned Simon out with his hand. Simon scampered out of the office as fast as he could on his hands and knees.

"Next!"

ОООООООО

"Anger is something we all experience, Tom. It's a fundamental human emotion, and it's a healthy one to have." Jack touched the pencil to his lips and was momentarily lost in thought.

"Yeah, I guess. I just think that I get angrier than most, Doc." Tom was clearly frustrated. He voluntarily placed himself in therapy after striking his wife and child.

"It is not the amount of anger that you have, it's your inability to cope with it effectively, Tom."

Tom did not respond. He sat on the couch and he began to fiddle with the buttons of his oxford shirt. There was a long pause. After a deep breath he began to whimper. "Can you help me, Doc? I love them so much. I hope I haven't lost them…Can you help me?"

"Yes Tom…" Jack took the glasses from his nose. "I can, and I will."

○○○○○○○○

Mickey Manning was energetically pacing the floor. He wore a pair of latex surgical gloves, and a football helmet that he had lined with aluminum foil. Every few minutes he stutter-stepped and then drastically changed his direction as if he was dodging invisible tacklers. He spoke quickly and simply as he paced. He repeatedly picked up the phone, unscrewed the receiver and looked for electronic bugs.

"They'll be here after I leave, I just want to warn you." Mickey informed Casper.

"Over there Mick!" Casper screamed and pointed. Mickey jumped back and again changed his direction. Casper was wearing a foil lined *Yankees* baseball cap and his attention was focused on an electronic gizmo in his hand. The office was again silent except for the hum of the fluorescent lights. The two foil hatted men concentrated on the flashing lights on the device in Casper's hand.

"It's a good thing you brought this brain theft detector. I had no idea how many of my thoughts were being stolen." Casper thanked Mickey.

"Yeah…" Mickey acknowledged him briefly. "They're all over. You can't get away. Our best offense is a good defense." Mickey tapped the helmet on his head.

The machine whirred uncontrollably. "Over there Mick!" Casper pointed at his feet.

Mickey jumped back again, and then abruptly changed direction. "Jump Mick! Higher Mick! Again Mick!" Casper pointed again, and Mickey jumped and jumped, and jumped to the point of exhaustion.

OOOOOOO

"Now Tara, I want you to tell me what you are experiencing right now?" Jack's voice was calm and soothing. He hypnotized Tara Martin in an effort to free her of her 'ego' defenses.

"I'm hurt, I'm worried, and I feel helpless."

"Talk to me about helplessness Tara, what is making you helpless?"

Tara talked about all of her hidden insecurities, and Jack skillfully guided her through a liberating hypnotherapy session.

OOOOOOO

Sophia Pratt was a rambling mess of sniffles and blubber. "I'm a terrible, terrible daughter. I'm a lousy wife. I don't cook, I don't clean...I don't take care of myself. My kids hate me. I'm a terrible mom. I have no skills. I'm probably gonna be fired. I have no friends. I am..." She blew her nose. "...I'm a horrible friend, and a horrible person.."

Casper interrupted her. "Sophia?" He looked at her compassionately. "You're forgetting one thing."

"Yeah?" Sophia held a handful of drenched tissues under her reddened nose.

"You're also fat."

Sophia exploded, sobbing uncontrollably. "I'm a fat whale!"

Casper responded by stroking her hair in a feigned gesture of sympathy. "There there, Sophia. You're a good whale though...a very good whale."

○○○○○○○○

After seeing the full caseload of patients, both exhausted psychiatrists reclined to start their daily dictations. Jack pulled the pile of charts across the blotter on the desk. He opened the first file, and carefully compared his hand written notes with those of the last visit. He mentally constructed an appropriate dictation, then rewound the machine.

Jack always started with the date of dictation, the patient's name and the medical record number. This was followed by a brief summary of the patient's psychiatric history, and then he identified any ongoing psychiatric and medical issues. The bulk of his dictated record was dedicated to the therapeutic session itself and the events that transpired during it. Jack finished with a short summary, a complete five axis psychiatric diagnosis, and a coherent plan of treatment.

○○○○○○○○

Casper rewound the *Dictaphone* and intermittently stopped the tape to hear the dictations of the previous patients. He thrusted his feet upon the desk, and leaned far back into his chair with a groan. Casper hated keeping records. To him, all the paperwork was a cowardly acquiescence to authority, and an unwelcome legal intrusion into his practice.

"Start dictation dated October second, Doctor Casper Lolly dictating..." Casper clicked off the *Dictaphone* and groped for the files on the desk. After opening the first file he restarted.

"Patient name is Cravitch, Renee..C..R..A..V..I..T..C..H, first name Renee. Medical record number is 112875...Mrs. Cravitch is..." Casper paused the machine, and bit his lower lip as if he was searching for the proper word. "...She is still crazy. A real whacko. Increase *Haldol* to five milligrams P.O. B.I.D. Period. End dictation."

"Next dictation dated October second, Doctor Casper Lolly dictating. Patient's name is Winston...W..I..N..S..T..O..N, first name is Simon. Medical record number is 128926. Mr. Winston is also...still crazy, and is probably a full-blown lunatic. Increase *Clozaril* to fifty milligrams P.O. Q.H.S. Period. End dictation."

Casper removed his feet from the desk, and spun in his chair to face the window. "Next dictation, dated October second, Doctor Casper Lolly dictating. Patient's name is Manning...M..A..N..N..I..N..G, first name is Mickey. Medical record number is 367465. Mr. Manning is still paranoid, delusional, and psychotic. This triad of symptoms leads me to believe that he, in all probability, is a little bit crazy. Quite possibly a basket case. Will increase *Resperidone* to three milligrams P.O. B.I.D. Period. End dictation."

Casper then came to the file on Roger Finnegan and he paused for a moment. He turned on the computer and waited impatiently for the system to boot up. After inserting a new diskette into the 'A' drive he began to type.

Date: October 2   Dr. Casper Lolly
Finnegan, Roger   176871

This represents my third meeting with Roger and like the others, he appears to be Perceptive. He reportedly predicted the death of a "royal princess" in August 1997, followed by the death of a nun. This was just about one month prior to the fatal car crash of Diana, the Princess of Wales, and the subsequent passing of Mother Theresa.

During his visits with me, he knew my phone number, my home address, and my middle name. He appeared to read my thoughts at times, and accurately foretold the death of my father. His Perceptive abilities seemed to dramatically increase as I continued to taper his neuroleptic medications.

Today, I have Roger off all medications. Although he has had a dramatic increase in his negative symptomatolgy, he has become floridly Perceptive. He commented on several of my sessions with other patients today, yet he was not present during them. Again he seemed to read my mind on several occasions, answering questions before I could ask them.

He predicted a severe storm, an unexpected celebrity death, and a scientific experiment gone terribly wrong.

When leaving my office today, Roger turned to me and said, "He raped and killed those two precious children, you know." I asked him 'who?' but he did not reply.

To date Roger Finnegan has not had any suicidal gestures or attempts. If he develops any signs or symptoms of homicidal or suicidal ideation (as many of my perceptives do), then I would feel compelled to hospitalize and restart Roger's antipsychotic medication.

-Dr. Casper Lolly

Casper saved the file onto the diskette and then shut down his system. He placed the diskette into a packed diskette storage box. After finishing the rest of the dictations, he banged the eject button on the *Dictaphone* and the miniature cassette popped out. He tossed it into the air and then snatched it snuggly into his fist. He flipped his sportcoat over his shoulder and strutted into the reception area.

"Hey Sara..." Casper flipped the mini-cassette tape at his twenty-two year old receptionist. "Think quick!"

"What?" Sara aimlessly threw her hands up in front of her face. The tape crashed onto her desk, ricocheting into a picture of her with some sorority sisters on spring break. Sara clumsily followed the cassette and inadvertently knocked over several items on the desk. After fixing things, she turned to Casper, placing a hand on her hip.

Sara was not too bright, but she was sure pleasant to look at. Casper knew that he could have her. She made this obvious. She was the no nonsense, no underwear, and no inhibitions type. Casper had thought about it many times, but so far he had not sexually exploited the situation.

"Where are you going?" Sara pouted.

"The Jerry Springer Show called. It seems that someone that I work with has a secret crush on me. Can you imagine that? Me!" Casper took a step backwards, outstretched his arms, and checked himself out.

"Well loverboy, after you're done dreaming go down to the thirty-fourth precinct."

"What?" Casper was snapped from his little fantasy. "I have a DOCI today?"

"Uh-huh. Sergeant somebody called."

"Sergeant who?"

"What's his name...Warren, Sergeant Warren. He called at five-thirty." Sara handed Casper the message slip.

Like many of the city psychiatrists, Casper often did these brief psychiatric assessments for the police. They were called DOCIs. It was an acronym for Determination of Criminal Insanity. Basically they were curbside consultations. A quick psychiatric examination that was performed on violent offenders, sexual offenders, and those criminals who appeared overtly psychotic. They were given under the auspice of prisoner safety and suicide assessment. While there was no official credence given to these exams, they often helped the police and the District Attorney develop an effective strategy for prosecution. Casper always enjoyed these exams despite the modest pay, and he willingly accepted invitations from precincts throughout the city.

"Get me my things." Casper told her.

CHAPTER FOUR
◆◆◆◆◆

Roger Finnegan sat in an armless vinyl chair in his apartment. The aluminum legs were twisted out of shape, and they etched a jagged groove into the parquet wood floor. He slowly ate soggy *Cheerios* from a bowl that was precariously resting on his enormous lap. With each spoonful, some sugary milk dribbled down his chin and plopped onto his turtleneck sweater. The smell of greasy pizza oozed in through his open window and a Spanish soap opera was blaring on the television set.

Hector Figueroa sat on the couch engrossed with the soap opera. Hector was Roger's Home Health Attendant, and he had been with Roger for three years now. As Roger's psychosis progressed to the point of near total disability, Hector voluntarily moved himself into Roger's apartment. This was a mutually beneficial arrangement. Roger received the help that he desperately needed, and in return Hector got a free place to stay in the Village. This situation was actually a large sacrifice on behalf of Hector, who under ordinary circumstances would have been much happier pursuing the bohemian gay lifestyle offered by Greenwich Village.

"Go ahead girl! You tell him. You're too good for him anyway. Damn Latino men, freakin' macho pricks!" Hector commented to an actress in a short skirt on the television.

Roger looked briefly at Hector, then quickly turned his attention back to the bowl of *Cheerios* in his lap. A few runaway *Cheerios* managed to elude Roger's spoon, evasively floating away from him in the warm milk.

"No, No, No!" Hector shrieked, and sprang out of his seat. He skipped and bounced around the living room as if he was on the verge of urination. After all the theatrics were finished, Hector fell to his knees exasperated in front of the television set. He shook his head disapprovingly. "You stupid, stupid slut." The actress was now kissing the 'macho prick' with smoldering Latino passion. After a few startled blinks, Roger reverted back to an empty stare, and continued to dribble his mushy dinner until all of the *Cheerios* were eaten.

There was a suspense building interruption in the program for a commercial break. Hector leaned onto his elbows, putting his rear into the air, and tried to forward the VCR. He had videotaped his favorite soap opera today because Roger's appointment with Doctor Lolly conflicted with the show. Whispering Spanish obscenities, he attempted to locate the resumption of the soap opera by employing a nonsensical cocktail of forward, reverse and pause. Hector was having a considerable amount of difficulty with this, and somehow he found himself back at the kissing scene. He shifted back onto his knees momentarily, looked confusingly at the picture, and with a brief scratch of his crew-cutted head, he was on all fours again.

Hector shaved his entire body this morning and then liberally applied a banana-butter skin lotion afterwards. He still stank, and his hairless legs shimmered in the light of the flickering television set. He was wearing tight jean shorts, a white tank-top and shiny black combat boots. Roger was beginning to feel nauseous. The visions were coming. He dropped his spoon into the empty bowl, and Hector quickly snapped his head around.

"You finished already, Roj?" he lisped.

Hector suddenly realized that he had forwarded the VCR too much. "Ay!" he shrieked, and haphazardly pushed buttons to stop the tape. After a series of dainty pokes, the television set crashed into a deafening snow pattern. He fumbled with the buttons on the television set, and finally found the volume control. He lowered the volume with repetitive taps, and then turned to look at Roger. Roger had made quite a mess of himself.

"Roger Finnegan...My little dribble-puss."

Hector swaggered over to Roger and removed the empty cereal bowl from his lap. Roger's dungarees were dampened with overspilled milk and fragmented *Cheerios.*

"Is that your dinner, Roger...Or are you just happy to see me?" Hector pointed to Roger's groin, and Roger listlessly looked down.

Hector took the bowl into the kitchen, and tossed it into the sink. He turned on the faucet, and ran a dry towel under the cold water. After twisting the water out of the dishrag, he returned to Roger with the cold damp cloth.

"Roj, what are we gonna do about this?"

Roger offered no response and Hector continued. "I wear my most fabulous outfit today, and your handsome doctor didn't even notice me. What's a girl to do, Roger? Should I use more banana butter next time?"

The visions were mounting in Roger. "Maybe you should stop, Hector. Just stop." he said, and turned his head away from Hector.

"Stop what, Roger?"

Roger turned to look squarely into Hector's eyes. He saw the unmerciful face of death again. Hector was dying, but he was completely unaware of this. Images of Hector in a leather G-string, kissing men much older than himself flashed through Roger's mind. There was an indoor pool. The pool was infested with naked men, and their cheerful voices echoed off the sweating walls. Hector was intoxicated by their exuberance, and he unwittingly dove into this chlorinated soup of disease. He paddled around for a while, and playfully splashed some of his friends. Holding his nose, he dipped his head back and then pushed the hair off of his face. He wiped the water from his eyes, and swam to a ladder at the side of the pool. He climbed up the slippery chrome steps, and grabbed a towel from the bench. The men in the pool were no longer smiling and chatting. There was only silence and water. Hector was covered with a vulgar film, and he could not scrub it off. He asked for help, but most of the men swam to the other side of the pool and watched. Then there was blood. Hector began bleeding from the rectum, and a thin crimson river of blood streaked down his thigh and onto the tiled pool deck. Hector started panicking. A growing purple cancer spread across his face and then down his throat. The cancer quickly choked him, and soon his entire face was eggplant purple. His eyeballs began to swell.

"Your face is changing Hector. Don't go in the pool! Your eyes are gonna get big, and you need help now Hector! Stay away from the pool." Roger begged his only friend.

"There's no pool here, Roger. You see a pool? I can't even swim, Roj..." There was no response. "...Roger?" Hector waved a hand in front of Roger's eyes.

There was something growing in Hector's head. It was still small, but it was indeed something sinister. Roger closed his eyes again in an attempt to abort the disturbing imagery, but the malignant visions continued. Suddenly, Hector was lying in a hospital bed, alone and unshaven. His eyes were bulging, and they no longer moved in concert with one another. He was emaciated, and there was only a thin layer of parched skin covering his skeletal body. He turned his head slowly to the right, and pursed his lips. His face began to twitch, then his arm and then his leg. This progressed to frank convulsion. Hector's eyes became huge and tight almost popping out of his skull.

"Okay Roger, if you're gonna play nonsense with me all day, then you'll get no dessert after dinner. I'm gonna go shower now...okay?" Hector wiped Roger's mouth one last time and headed back to the kitchen. He turned the faucet on and rinsed the *Cheerios* and milk into the sink.

"Please, please..." Roger softly cried as the visions of Hector's death receded.

Hector turned the faucet off. "Roger?...Did you say something?"

"Please...please help me."

Hector did not hear him, and he laid the dishrag over the faucet, and left the kitchen. Walking toward the bathroom, he affectionately rubbed Roger's prickly head as he passed.

The bathroom was small and cramped. Hector looked into the mirror, but he did not notice the small patch of purple skin that was hidden in his hairline. There was a radio on top of the toilet tank, and he flipped it on. It was tuned to a local Spanish station, and there was an advertisement for *El diario* playing. A fast talking Spanish deejay soon returned and spun a festive salsa tune. Hector started to dance, turned on the faucet and wet his face with the warm water. He picked up the shaving cream, and turned the volume up on the radio. Using the can of shaving cream as a makeshift maraca, he rhythmically shook it to the distinct Latino beat. He closed the door and began to howl the lyrics as he shaved.

Roger sat motionless for a few moments, then he rose and shuffled over to the open window. The dusky street was littered with people. A woman who lived across the street was parallel parking her *Toyota*. Her back and her buttocks hurt, and she cringed as she turned in her seat. Her husband beat her horribly last night. She feared for her children, and she feared for herself. Her back was covered with bruises. Some old, some new. One of them was weeping a clear fluid, and Roger knew all of this, but he couldn't understand why.

Two men were walking closely together on the sidewalk. One of the men was very sick like Hector. The other was sick also, but to a much less degree. Both men had ghostly shadows following them. The shadows were primitive and violent in nature, and they savagely climbed all over the two men. A few buildings up ahead, there was a man exiting a taxi. He had a new job, and he was very uncomfortable in his new suit. There was a small girl rollerblading on the sidewalk, and she zipped by the man in the suit. Her skates occasionally got stuck on pebbles and cracks in the concrete, and she came close to falling several times. Her knees had small scrapes on them, but they stung her only a little bit. Roger closed his eyes and began to weep. In a few years this little girl will be raped and beaten in Central Park. The story will become a media sensation, and receive national attention.

"The Central Park Rollerblade Rape" Roger mumbled.

He placed his hand on the window screen and watched the girl skate down the block until she turned the corner. There was a brown sedan waiting at the red light. The two men inside watched the girl while they chatted casually about pornography. Around the block, two young boys were just molested in a seedy studio apartment. They each clutched a few candy bars in their small hands, standing only in their underwear. They huddled closely to one another, feeling cold and violated.

"Now take your candy, boys." Roger said.

Roger pulled the canvas shade down and pushed it firmly into the window. He turned back into the living room, and it was much darker now. He could no longer take these visions, and tears poured down his pimpled cheeks. He heard strange voices talking to him. They talked to him and about him. There were two demonic shadows hiding in the corner by the bathroom. They were waiting for Hector to get out of the shower. Roger was distraught and frightened, and for the first time in four years he fled the apartment alone.

Hector was almost finished shaving when he heard the apartment door slam. He turned the volume on the radio a little lower, and drained the frothy water from the sink.

"Roger?..." There was no response. He wiped the shaving cream residue from his face, and turned the radio off. He listened carefully, but there was no sound from the apartment. Hector wrapped a flowered towel around his waist and opened the bathroom door. He peered into the darkened living room.

"Roj?"

Roger was gone.

〇〇〇〇〇〇〇〇

Casper stepped out of the taxi at the thirty-fourth precinct, and looked up at the setting sky. It had become very cloudy, and the air was now cool and wet. He was carrying a large black leather satchel, and there was something heavy inside of it. He generously tipped the driver this time and bounded up the concrete steps of the police station. A curious metallic rattle escaped from the leather sac as he ascended. He yanked open the glass door and walked across the shallow lobby. There were two uniformed policemen and a civilian woman talking behind the desk.

"I'm Doctor Lolly. I was asked to perform a DOCI today. Is there a Sergeant Warren here?" Casper asked, placing the heavy satchel on the floor by his feet.

"Yeah, right here Doc." Sergeant Warren identified himself from behind the desk. He was a thick black man of imposing stature. "I have the folder right here." He tapped a neat manila folder in his hand.

Casper raised his hand in a polite wave. "I would prefer not, Sergeant."

"You don't want the folder?"

"I'd rather examine the subject first, so I can form an unbiased psychiatric opinion. Then I would like to look at the file to construct my profile."

"Suit yourself, Doc. But this case is a no-brainer." Sergeant Warren took two giant steps to the desk and he leaned over it. He signaled Casper to come closer with his index finger, and Casper leaned toward him.

"You got kids, Doctor?"

"Kids? Uh...no, no I don't."

"Well, I do, two of 'em. A boy and a girl. Anyway, two little girls were raped and murdered this week."

Casper raised his hand to stop the Sergeant but then he hesitated. "Did you say raped and murdered?" His stomach cramped as he recalled the parting words of Roger Finnegan only hours earlier.

"Yeah, uh-huh that's right, butchered would be a better choice of words. This man in the IR, he's the neighbor of the two dead girls. We collected an extraordinary amount of material evidence on that scumbag. Blood, hair, semen...you name it, and we found it."

"I see." Casper sighed and looked down at his shoes. He lightly kicked the black bag on the ground and then looked back at Sergeant Warren. "Can I see that folder?"

Sergeant Warren handed Casper the thin folder, and with a brief nod of his head, he walked away from the desk with the other officer. Casper opened the folder and reviewed its contents in detail for several minutes.

"Where's the Interrogation Room?" Casper asked the civilian woman behind the desk when he finished.

"The IR? It's the first door on the right." She turned and pointed down the hallway.

Casper closed the folder, and slid it across the desk to the woman. With an exhausted grunt, he lifted the heavy leather satchel and headed towards the IR.

"Hey Doctor, you don't wanna take this with you?" the woman asked, holding the folder.

"I've seen enough, thanks." Casper smiled and looked for the IR.

The door to the Interrogation Room was made of steel and painted in a dull gray. The white letters 'IR' were stenciled into a black piece of plastic that was bolted to the door. There was a video camera pointed at Casper's face, and a red light shined underneath it. He tried the metal doorknob but it was locked, and did not budge. Noticing a small white button to the left of the door, Casper pushed it twice. After a brief pause, there was a long buzz and he turned the knob.

The observance area of the IR was dimly lit and two police officers inside watched the suspect's interrogation through a transparent mirror.

A detective in plain clothes questioned the suspect. Their voices were heard over two small speakers under the mirrored wall and the man vehemently asserted his innocence. There was a closed circuit television monitor suspended by chains in one corner of the observation area, and a row of eight comfortable seats. The two officers turned to greet Casper.

"You the Doctor?" asked a moderately overweight officer.

"Yes."

"Detective Ganzi is just finishin' up in there. Have a seat, Doc."

Casper sat on the theater style chairs and crossed his legs. Through the mirror Casper watched the remainder of the interrogation. The suspect was sitting in a chair, resting his hands on the cold steel table. The table was bolted firmly to the floor, and a single light swung overhead. There were scratch marks all over the suspects hands and face, and he picked at the scabs as he was being questioned.

"How do you explain the blood in your bathtub, Mister Henson?" asked Detective Ganzi.

"I don't know."

"Well, we'll see how much talkin' you do on Riker's Island." Detective Ganzi poked the suspect in the chest with a stubby index finger, and then took a long painful drag of his cigarette. Like an untalented drama school student, he was overacting the 'bad cop' role again. He paced the floor and smoked the cigarette almost down to his fingers. He puffed a swirl of smoke into the air, and mashed the remainder of the cigarette into the floor. He pulled a chair around the table and placed it backward next to the suspect. He sat down, straddling the backwards chair, and looked into the eyes of Tremain Henson.

"How about the panties? Do you recall these bloody panties, Mr. Henson?" Detective Ganzi held up two evidence baggies. Each held a small pair of cotton underwear. There was no response from the suspect, so the detective continued with his questioning.

"Are they yours?" He pulled himself closer Henson's face.

"No, I've never seen them before." Henson said defiantly.

"You were holding them in your hand when we arrested you!" The detective slammed the palm of his hand down onto the table, then jumped to his feet and threw the chair against the wall. It bounced off of several walls before it came to a stop. Casper smirked at the theatrics of the detective, and the two officers in the observation area started to giggle.

"I'm finished here." Detective Ganzi turned to the mirror and walked to the door of the observance area. He jerked open the door that separated the observation area and interrogation room, and stepped inside. The door shut behind him, leaving Tremain Henson alone at the table. Without a word, Ganzi lit another cigarette and took a long cancerous drag. One of the officers broke the awkward silence.

"Couldn't get him to talk, huh Detective?" Both officers started laughing.

"Fuck you flatfoot."

Casper rose from his seat and walked over to Detective Ganzi. Slapping him on the back.

"Um...excuse me, Columbo? Don't you think you've been watching too many police movies?"

The two uniformed officers tightened their lips, but intermittent laughter managed to spurt out. Ganzi shot them a hostile look.

"Who the hell are you?" Ganzi asked, turning back toward Casper.

"I'm Doctor Lolly, the psychiatrist."

Ganzi chuckled. "The shrink, huh?" He looked Casper up and down. "Let me ask you something Doctor."

"Go ahead."

Ganzi moved his face closer to Casper's. They were almost nose to nose. "Why are all you shrinks more fucked up than the psychopaths?"

"All of us? Wow, I thought it was just me! What a relief! Thanks Detective."

"You think you're funny asshole? Well then be my guest Doctor Freud. He's all yours. I've had more than enough bullshitting assholes for one day." Detective Ganzi flicked the burning cigarette to the floor, and smushed it with his foot. He pushed the button on the wall, and stormed out of the observation area into the hallway.

Casper walked over to his chair, and hoisted his leather bag. He turned to the remaining officers. "He's a little uptight, huh?"

"He's alright once you get to know him." said the heavy officer.

"I'll pass, thanks."

Casper lugged his bag into the interrogation room. Tremain Henson was still sitting at the steel table. He was a forty year old white male, balding, overweight, with piercing green eyes. Although he was unshaven and bruised, he appeared to be comfortable and refreshed. Behind Henson there was another monitor with a view outside the door in the hallway. The Interrogation Room was cold and quiet, and the walls were painted in nondescript beige. Casper picked up the chair that was thrown across the room by Detective Ganzi, and he slid it to the table.

"Mister Henson?" Casper always approached the suspect very formally.

"Yep."

"I'm Doctor Lolly. I'm a psychiatrist. I'm here to assess you, and whether or not you pose a risk to yourself, and others. What we do here will not affect your defense, and I'm still bound by the laws of patient-doctor confidentiality. And as you know, in the absence of your court appointed attorney, anything that you say, cannot and will not be used in a court of law."

This was not entirely untrue. The DOCI did require the administration of a brief Suicide Probability Scale (SPS), as well as a modified Depression Rating Scale (DRS). A battery of other modified psychiatric tests were also employed. These constructed a preliminary psychiatric profile of the suspect. Cognitive abilities were usually tested with a modified Wechsler Adult Intelligence Scale (WAIS), and personality disorders were identified by an abridged version of the Minnesota Multiphasic Personality Inventory (MMPI-2). Affective disorders and the psychoses were evaluated in the Schedule for Affective Disorders and Schizophrenia (SADS), and the remainder of the DOCI proceedings were usually dedicated to a brief but directed psychiatric interview. Altogether, the tests took a little less than two hours to complete, and there was a considerable amount of variation in the administration of the modified subtests. Casper routinely exploited this variability.

Casper placed the satchel on the steel table and it landed with a heavy 'thud'. "Shall we get started?"

Tremain Henson shrugged his shoulders and frowned. Casper began the lengthy assessment. As usual he started with the customized intelligence test, and followed this with the personality inventory. Casper abandoned formal tests of insight and judgement in his assessments, but he usually attempted to evaluate these parameters during the psychiatric interview.

After administering the first two conventional tests, Casper and the suspect were consumed with boredom. The officers behind the mirror were no longer paying attention either, and they chatted about the not so mindless nature of their jobs. Casper quickly graded the tests, and then rose from his chair. He walked over to the door of the observation area and opened it.

"Gentlemen, it's time for the psychiatric interview."

"Okay, Doc." The two officers were confused, unsure of what they were being asked.

"Patient-Doctor confidentiality? I'd like to be alone with the subject."

"Uh...Okay. Sure Doc, whatever you say." The two relaxed officers collected themselves and headed toward the exit. Casper pressed the exit button on the wall and they left. The door shut behind them, and Casper watched the officers step into the hallway on the monitor. They continued their conversation just outside the door. Casper turned back toward Henson with a crazed look in his eyes. He shut the door. Casper and Henson were now alone in the IR.

Casper rushed over to the mirrored wall and pulled down the large shades. Once the mirrors were totally obscured, Casper checked the camera and the observation area again. They were still alone.

"What?" Casper asked, looking at Henson.

"Who me?" Henson said, pointing at himself.

"Yeah you."

"I didn't say anything." befuddled.

Casper then dropped to his hands and knees and began crawling all over the floor. He banged his fists on the floorboards as he crawled.

"What the hell are you doin'?" asked Henson.

Casper sprang to his feet, and ran over to him. He quickly shushed him. "Shut up, shut up! They're gonna hear you. You're probably one of them, aren't you? Beady eyes, pointy head. What do you want, already?...Oh god, what do you want?!" Casper pleaded with the suspect.

"What's your problem? I don't know nobody."

"Are you sure?" Casper asked suspiciously, but then composed himself.

"Am I sure what?"

"That you're not one of them?"

The suspect Henson sat back in his chair, and didn't say a word. Casper turned to the table, and ripped open the satchel. He pulled out a triangular foil hat. It was crumpled and folded upon itself. He unfolded it and smoothed it out on the table's surface.

"Here, put this on! Quick!" He handed the foil hat to Henson. "They got thought detectors all over this place. We've wasted a lot of time already, and they're probably onto me. I think those two bought it, though...Don't you?" Casper looked at the video monitor and the two officers were still chatting.

"Who?" Henson placed the hat over his balding head.

"The so called Police Officer's Union. The POU, in other words." Casper gave Henson a sly look of understanding.

"What are you talking about?!" Henson was confused and irritated.

"POU...Protect Our Universe, the multinational effort to smother insurgents like us! They're trying to extinguish the revolution. They've got intelligence and counter intelligence everywhere. They even have counter-counter intelligence. Have you ever encountered counter-counter intelligence? It's some heavy-duty shit, man! Now...countering the counter-counter, you see? That's where I come in. I'm what you call...a specialist. Specializing in countering counter-counter. I know, it's real difficult to figure out sometimes." Casper started slapping himself in the head. "Stupid microchip."

"What the *fuck* are you talking about?!"

"What the fuck are *you* talking about? You're not one of the rebels?"

"No! What are you, some kinda freak? Fuckin' psycho?"

Casper laughed. "That's exactly what they want you to think...See? They put this chip in my head..." Casper pointed to the top of his skull, parting his hair. "...And at times they just zap the thoughts right out of my head. I got a lot of good ideas, you see? They want 'em. It's all part of the big plan, brother...The Great Takeover."

"There's no fuckin' takeover you nut job!" the suspect fumed.

"C'mon, don't be naïve. *Microsoft, IBM, Dell Computers*...Why do you think they're miniaturizing everything?"

Henson was getting angrier. He shook his head and shrugged his shoulders.

"So they can fit the chips inside your brain, man! Little noggin dwellers! Brain Burglars...Whatever you wanna call them."

"You're nuts! I've had it with this freakin' shit." Henson attempted to get out of his seat, but Casper forcefully shoved him back down into his chair.

"Wait one minute." Casper ran to his satchel and pulled out a belt and eyeglasses. The belt had several D-cell batteries attached to it, and electrical wires joined the glasses to the belt. Casper placed the glasses on his face and stumbled over to Henson.

"It's too late for me but maybe it's not too late for you." Casper went behind Henson and removed the foil hat from his head. He placed his hands on the suspect's shiny scalp and examined it thoroughly.

"Lemme see...There's nothing in either of the frontal or parietal lobes..." Casper continued to inspect Henson's entire cranium. "...Nothing in the temporal lobes...and nothing in the cerebellum...Hmm, that's funny."

Coming around to the front of the suspect, Casper firmly gripped Henson's right hand. "Let me see your arm. Sometimes they hide them in the arm."

Henson attempted to pull his hand away, but Casper was too strong.

"Ah-ha!" Casper screamed, staring at Henson's wrist. "Fucking eureka!"

"What?" The suspect wrestled with Casper.

"I found the chip! Sneaky little bastards. Wow, It's quite sophisticated. I've never seen a model like this before. I don't think I'm gonna be able to do this."

"Do what?!" Casper let go of his hand and Henson quickly withdrew it.

"Deprogram it." Casper took off his glasses and the belt. He shook his head in dismay. "It's gonna have to come out. I'm very sorry." Casper placed his hands on his hips for a thoughtful moment, and then returned to the satchel. He reached deep inside the leather bag, and lifted out a portable meat grinder. It was bloody and rusty, with bits of meat hanging from the press. After plugging it in, Casper flipped the corroded switch and the machine began to clatter wildly.

"What the fuck is that for?!" Henson climbed backwards over his seat, and far away from Casper.

Casper chased him and grabbed him firmly by both wrists. "C'mon, put your hand in the grinder! It's our only chance!"

"No way, what are you fuckin' crazy? Help guards! Guards!" The guards could not hear his pleas, and he sank to his knees. Casper kept dragging him over to the grinder. It was making a tremendous racket, vibrating on the steel table.

"Guards!" he cried again, and started to weep.

"Get up, and put your hand in the grinder or we will all die!"

"Guards! Help! Help!"

"Do it for the revolution!" Casper almost had Henson's hand in the grinder.

"Guards, please! Help me!"

Casper released Henson, and he scrambled away on the floor. Casper followed him to the corner, crouched down and grabbed the suspect's fat face. "Listen you worthless piece of shit. You're far from crazy. If you were crazy, you would have stuck your hand in that grinder. But you didn't, did you?"

Henson, fearing for his life, could not respond.

Casper continued. "You knew it was wrong. You knew it would hurt, didn't you? Didn't you! Well fatso, that establishes sanity for me. I've been doing this for a long time, and I've never seen one of you cowards put a hand in the grinder. You're not insane, you're just a sick fuck. If you think of pleading the Insanity Defense, I'll kill you myself. I'll kill your friends. I'll kill your family." Casper let go of his face and Henson cowered further into the corner. "You're gonna fry...You sick fuck."

Casper picked up the foil hat from the floor, and packed it with the grinder and the glasses. He closed the satchel and left the observation area. The attorney for Tremain Henson had just arrived, and Casper greeted him in the observation area.

"Good luck Counselor." Casper said smugly as they passed one another. "I'll warm up the chair." He stepped out into the hallway.

The two uniformed police officers were still standing just outside the door. Casper passed them without a word. From the hallway he heard Tremain Henson complain about the DOCI to his attorney. "He threatened my life!"

"Hey Doc, what'd ya think?" one of the policemen yelled.

Casper was almost through the glass doors. He turned to them and shouted, "He's not crazy."

CHAPTER FIVE
♦♦♦♦♦

The setting sun finally sank below the looming Manhattan skyline, and a cold wind dashed through the shadowy trees of Union Square Park. The rambling gusts of air lifted dead leaves off the ground and swirled them around in small tornadoes, while in the shadows a pack of young drug peddlers boldly propositioned potential clients. In the northwest corner of the park, merchants from the farmer's market were packing their goods, as a trainload of commuters surfaced from the subway. Roger Finnegan watched the crowd, but the visions were overwhelming for him. Death and birth, pain and pleasure were tossing in his mind like a nightmare salad. He closed his eyes but the visions persisted.

A young black man passed conspicuously close to Roger, and quickly glanced at him. He soon returned. This time coming closer, he quietly asked Roger. "Buy some smoke? You want some smoke?" The man was now within inches of Roger's face.

Roger looked at the man and was immediately overcome by a horrific scene. The man was on his knees in an abandoned building far uptown. There was a gun to his head. He was crying, and begging for his life. Three other men in flannels and sunglasses surrounded him.

"Where's the rest?" A man with a large scar on his face asked him.

"That's all I got, I swear...I swear!" The drug peddler pleaded.

The man with the scar nodded to the man with the gun, and a bullet was callously shot through the back of the dealer's head. He flaccidly slumped to the ground, while pieces of his brain dripped out of the gaping hole in his forehead.

Roger pounced on the unsuspecting dealer, desperately grabbing him by the zipper of his *Timberland* jacket. "Stop what you are doing! Stop tonight! Please! Please, you're gonna get killed! Don't you see it?!"

"Get the fuck off me! You wanna get stabbed, motha fucker?!" The dealer forcefully pushed Roger away, and quickly walked off. "Goddamn psychopath!"

Roger stumbled, almost hitting the ground but then regained his balance. He watched the dealer hurry off to his grisly death and he suddenly felt a mind-numbing chill. Without his jacket, he was somewhat underdressed for this cool evening. He shuddered and quickly descended the steps of the subway station.

The underground air was warm and stale. Roger rummaged through his pockets, turning them inside out. He had no money. He circled the token booth several times, searching the spit stained ground for stray coins, *Metrocards* and tokens. Roger was careful not to make eye contact with anyone, but many people took notice of his peculiarity. A man in a brown overcoat stepped away from the token booth after purchasing a few tokens, and approached Roger.

"Excuse me, do you need a token?" the man asked, extending a token toward him.

"Yes, thank you." Roger looked up at the man, and he saw mostly goodness. The man was a good provider for his wife and child on Long Island, and although he had many sexual urges, he did not act upon them. Roger took the token from the man and briefly touched his hand. Roger suddenly saw a vision when they touched. The man was in the bathroom stall at his place of employment. It was only a few hours ago. He was masturbating to the mental image of a young female employee. He still had a water stain on the back of his shirt from where he leaned against the toilet pipes. Roger pinched the token tightly between his thumb and index finger, and tried not to vomit. He headed toward the turnstile.

"It's not real...It's not real...It's not real..." Roger told himself.

The express platform was crowded with people waiting for the trains to Grand Central Station. A group of Jamaican musicians were playing contemporary tunes on kettledrums, salting a little reggae spice into the otherwise lifeless Michael Bolton music. A commuter threw a dollar bill into the hat on the ground in front of the musicians, and two of the drummers nodded in appreciation. Passing them quickly, Roger fiddled with his turtleneck collar with one hand, and wiped the other on his pants. He could still feel the man's fluid on his fingers. He talked to himself as he walked, and he found a wooden bench and sat down.

Roger, what are you doin' down here? A voice asked him.

"Just sitting, leave me alone please!" Roger begged, and a few surprised commuters turned to look at him. He was sitting alone on the bench. "It's not real…It's not real…" he said, over and over again.

Where are you going to go? You can't do anything by yourself, Roger.

"Shut up." Roger covered his ears, and more people on the platform were noticing him now. Roger looked around at the crowd. There was a strikingly attractive woman a few yards away from him. She was wearing a garter belt, and a lace bra underneath her clothes. She was screwing her boss at work. He was married with two small children.

That's it Roger…you like her? Go get her Roger.

She'll never give it to someone like you.

You're pathetic, and stupid.

Roger licked his lips and looked at the woman. She was a little uncomfortable, and she slowly walked down to the other end of the platform. There was a man waiting on the edge of the platform for the train, and he was smoking a cigarette. As he inhaled it, Roger could see the smoke swoosh into his blackened lungs, and circle around the tumor that sat there. The man looked impatiently downtown, as the train approached from deep inside the tunnel.

You should have never been born. One voice said.

"It's not real…It's not real…It's not real…" Roger tried desperately to convince himself. He covered his ears and squeezed his head tightly.

There's no love for you here. Confirmed another.

Roger removed his hands from his ears, and answered them. "I've tried, I've tried! Can't you understand that?" He began to cry, as the rattle of the approaching train grew louder. People slowly shifted away from him on the platform, distancing themselves from his bizarre behavior.

You see Roger?…You're a freak.

We told you so.

Nobody wants to be near you.

"Leave me alone!" Roger screamed, and jumped up from the bench. He rushed to the side of the platform, and stopped at its edge. Several nervous commuters pointed at Roger, but all were afraid to approach him. The train sped toward the station, and the conductor sounded its horn. Roger looked down onto the tracks and saw a few dismembered bodies. He rubbed his eyes, and looked again. There was a bloody woman with no legs waving at him. She stood on the stumps of her severed thighs and signaled him to come onto the tracks.

"It's not real…It's not real…It's not real…"

A blood soaked man with a broken back slithered a few feet away from the legless woman. Broken arms, battered legs, and severed heads were scattered all over the tracks, and blood dripped from the rails onto the blackened floor.

Go ahead Roger…We don't want you here.

"It's not real…It's not real…It's not real."

The train pulled into station, and bright white sparks flew from its wheels. It bellowed its horn again.

Come on Roger! My legs hurt. The woman on the tracks coaxed. *Come join us.*

Do it! You coward.

Roger looked again at the people on the platform. Some kids were laughing at his confusion, but most of the commuters were horrified for him. Nobody else on the platform seemed to notice the mangled people down on the tracks.

"There's people down there!" Roger screamed and pointed as the clatter of the train filled the station.

Do it! A voice commanded Roger.

"Tell them to stop!" Roger begged the other people on the platform.

Do it!

The train barreled towards Roger.

"Tell them to stop!" he screamed and jumped headfirst onto the tracks. The train sounded its horn again, but it was too late. In a blaze of sparks and steel, the train screeched to a halt a few seconds after killing him.

○○○○○○○

Jack Benedict slowly shuffled up the crowded steps of the Eighty-sixth Street subway station. He was sandwiched between a large woman, and a group of street kids. His briefcase accidentally hit the woman in the heels several times, but she did not complain. He looked at his watch, it was seven o'clock. His rounds at the hospital went a little bit longer than expected, and he was already late for dinner. Caroline was probably going to be angry.

The restaurants on Lexington Avenue were filled with people, and Jack headed quickly downtown toward his brownstone. At the corner of Lexington and Eighty-fifth, a man was selling floral arrangements from a wooden cart that he built himself. Although he owned a small flower shop a few blocks downtown, he preferred to be out on the street, mixing with the people. His brother in-law usually ran the busy shop while he was out, and they both did quite well. He was an industrious Italian man with two beautiful daughters, and a handsome son at home. He was a reliable source of great flowers and sound advice, and Jack was a generous and regular customer. He stopped and browsed through the colorful bundles of roses.

"Hey Doc, what's cookin'?" asked the smiling flower man.

"Not much Vin, how about you?"

"Oh, the gout's got me bad today, Doc." Vin shook his leg in mild agony. "I took four *Naprosyn* today, and I still feel like crying."

"And Bernadette? How's she?"

"She's worse than the gout, Doc." Vin joked. He was still enamoured with his wife after thirty years of marriage.

Jack nodded his head in amusement, and picked at some of the bouquets. He pulled out an arrangement of red and cream colored roses and asked Vin. "How much for this bundle, Vinny?"

"Eight dollars...Say Doc, which hospital do you work out of again?"

"NYU...and sometimes Columbia Presbyterian, but mainly NYU."

"My youngest daughter is dating a doctor from Long Island Jewish. You know anyone out there?"

"LIJ? Sure, I know several people. It has excellent departments of Neurology, and Medicine. Hillside Hospital is the psychiatric affiliate out there. I know most of the attending physicians at Hillside as well." Jack handed Vin a ten-dollar bill.

"He's the Chief Resident of Neurology over there, another half a year to go, I think." Vin gave the flowers to Jack, along with two folded dollar bills.

51

"That's fantastic, Vin. Wish him my best."

"I will Doc...Hey I hope your wife likes the flowers."

"She will Vin, thanks."

Jack walked down the block to his brownstone. He turned through the cast iron gate and walked up to his door. He unlocked the oak door to his foyer, and the glass panes rattled as he closed it. He twisted his arm and the flowers behind his back, and continued into the hallway.

"Caroline?"

"In here Jabes." Caroline called to him from the kitchen, and she did not seem angry. Jack was pleasantly surprised, and he walked into the room. Caroline was sitting at the table, casually reading a magazine when he entered. The kitchen was immaculate, and the table was bare.

"I cleaned the kitchen today. I had a bad case of writer's block. I guess I got a little overzealous." She looked up at Jack and chuckled.

Jack looked around the kitchen in amazement.

"So..." Caroline continued. "I thought we'd go out for dinner?"

"Well, I thought I'd buy you some flowers." Jack took the flowers from behind his back, and showed her the cheap but beautiful bouquet.

"Oh Jabes, they're beautiful...Let me get a vase." Caroline's face went flush. She stood up and looked through the cabinets for a vase.

Early in their marriage, Jack used to bring her flowers and random gifts quite frequently. But as the years went on, these times became few and far between. Then came the affair, and this put their relationship into a tailspin for some time. Things were much better now however, and lately the more romantic aspects of Jack Benedict had resurfaced.

Caroline filled the vase with cold water from the sink, and took the flowers from Jack. Removing the cellophane from them, she cut the stems on an angle with scissors, and placed them in the vase. After briefly arranging them with her hands, she took the vase of flowers and placed it on the table.

"They're really beautiful Jabes."

"So are you, babe...So are you." Jack grabbed his wife and hugged her from behind. He softly kissed her neck, and she closed her eyes. "Where would you like to eat?" Jack whispered seductively, and nibbled on her ear.

"Anywhere Italian." she moaned.

"*Il Basilico* sound okay?"

"Mmm...It sounds great." The two parted, and Caroline skipped happily to the next room to get her coat. Jack placed his briefcase on the table, and admired the spotless kitchen. He wiped the counter with a finger, then examined it. There was not a speck of dirt on it. He opened the oven, and it was spotless as well. He looked about with genuine surprise. Caroline hated to clean.

"Jabes?" Caroline called from the closet.

"Yeah."

"I was speaking to Wendy and Steve today, they're coming for dinner tomorrow. Is that Okay?"

"Tomorrow is Saturday?" Jack thought. "Sure it sounds okay...Whoops, wait a minute. There's a lecture I wanted to attend at New York Hospital that night." Jack yelled to Caroline. She was coming toward the kitchen.

"What lecture?" she asked, returning with her coat and her handbag.

"Casper Lolly is talking about Perceptive Schizophrenia."

"Oh, Casper is? Is it gonna be a good one?"

"They're usually interesting."

"What time?"

"Eight o'clock?" Jack asked, boyishly looking for approval.

"Can you go a little late? We have not seen them in a long, long time, Jabes."

"Uh...sure. Sounds good." Jack compromised a bit, but it made Caroline happy. He put his arm around her trim waist, and the two strolled out the door to eat supper.

CHAPTER SIX

◆◆◆◆◆

The Bergen Auditorium was dim and crowded, and Jack stood in the open door squinting as he scanned the crowd for a vacant seat. He had a rolled up issue of the *Journal of Psychiatry* in his hand, and he lightly tapped it against his lips. He quietly burped, and the smell of grilled eggplant casserole seeped out of his mouth. The cheesy dish was one of his weaknesses, and he over indulged himself at dinner with Steve and Wendy.

A beam of light dissected the darkness, and it fell upon a large screen at the front of the auditorium. Doctor Casper Lolly was speaking enthusiastically at the podium. His youth and exuberance were frankly magnetic. He highlighted the salient features of his colorful slides with a small, hand held laser pointer. There was a large pie chart cast upon the screen. It compared the incidence of the 'Perceptive' subtype of schizophrenia to the other known subtypes. Casper reported it to be far less common than the Paranoid, Catatonic, Undifferentiated, or Residual variants.

"Lifetime prevalence of schizophrenia is about one percent in the general population. Among those afflicted, I estimate that only about 0.6 percent will fit all of the criteria for Perceptive Schizophrenia." Casper traced the smallest slice in the pie chart with a laser red dot.

Jack looked at his watch. It was eight-thirty five, and he had already missed a substantial portion of Doctor Lolly's lecture. He painfully considered his seating options. It was going to be very difficult not to distract the volatile speaker. Stretching his neck, Jack noticed a few empty seats in the middle of the auditorium, and an unoccupied chair near the end of the second row. He would have to climb over several people in the back of the room, or climb over a few people in the front, just to get to an empty seat. He was uncertain which option would be less disrupting, and he spent a considerable amount of time debating this.

With a deep breath, Jack pardoned himself, and clumsily headed for a seat in the middle of the room.

Casper continued onto the next slide. "Like the other subtypes of schizophrenia, Perception is treatable...but not curable. With current neuroleptic medications, Perception can be markedly diminished. I believe that this is the result of a generalized cognitive blunting that we often see with the antipsychotic agents. Furthermore, Perceptive abilities dramatically increase when the patient is tapered off of medication."

Casper stopped for a moment. There was a small commotion in the audience. Shielding his eyes with one hand, he peered into the dark crowd. He noticed Doctor Jack Benedict awkwardly climbing over a row of disgruntled psychiatrists. He pressed the button on the laser pointer, and focused the beam into a small red dot on Jack's forehead. Jack cringed. He was trying to avoid this, and he politely excused himself to the speaker and his audience.

"Please make room for Doctor Benedict, ladies and gentlemen. He desperately needs to learn something." Casper wisecracked, as Jack stumbled on a few more toes.

"Sorry." Jack offered quietly.

Jack Benedict and Casper Lolly were polar opposites. As psychiatrists, the two men were water and fire. Jack was a soothing and pacific force, while Casper was wholly cataclysmic. They disagreed on just about everything, and the two had made this professional disdain for one another rather public. The editorial pages of nearly every respectable journal had been a battleground for these two men. In the current issue of the *Journal of Psychiatry*, Casper again lambasted Jack. It was an absolutely scathing response to a book review that Jack had done a few months ago. The audience was clearly not expecting a personal appearance from Jack Benedict tonight.

Jack finally plopped himself into a spongy seat, and wriggled his coat off. Casper shook his head twice and then continued his lecture.

"As I was saying...the neuroleptic medications will diminish Perceptive abilities, but is that a reasonable end point in the treatment of these patients? Are we not treating a phenomenon that perhaps should be studied instead? It's a difficult question...more difficult than you can imagine."

.

Casper flipped the projector to a new slide. On the top of the slide the word SUICIDE was written in bold letters. "Suicide...Suicide...Suicide. My studies of the Perceptives indicate that they are four times more likely to attempt suicide, and five times more likely to complete it, than are their schizophrenic counterparts. This is truly a scary statistic." The audience audibly whispered to one another.

"I believe that this high rate of suicide is the result of the disturbing, and prophetic imagery they experience." Casper focused the laser red dot on the bottom line on the slide.

"So, why do I treat the Perceptives with traditional antipsychotic medication?" Casper flipped another slide. It was a graphical comparison of the dose of antipsychotic medication and degree of suicidal ideation. It was apparent from the graph that suicidal ideation markedly decreased, as antipsychotic medication increased.

"As you can see here, the suicidal tendencies are dramatically attenuated when on conventional neuroleptic medication. In fact I have never had a Perceptive commit suicide while on therapeutic doses of antipsychotics." Casper flipped to his last slide, the massive face of Roger Finnegan appeared on the screen. The audience jumped backwards at the sight of him.

"This unfortunate man was a patient of mine. Some of you in the audience may recognize him. Some of you have treated him. He was in and out of psychiatric day programs for the past several years. He was felt by most to be profoundly psychotic, refractory to all conventional treatments. He was subsequently sent to me by a colleague who noted some abnormal abilities." Casper took a sip of water from the glass at the podium. "Although I had only three sessions with him, I found him to be profoundly Perceptive. He was malignantly prophetic, predicting the death of my father, the death of Princess Diana and Mother Teresa, as well as other events of the future. He was also keenly aware of past events. He was not, and could not have been witness to these events. When he was taken off of medication, he became a prisoner to these visions. When on medication he was an absolute zombie. As I tapered him off the medication, his Perceptive abilities grew. He was clearly witness to more than I could appreciate. That's for sure... and shortly after his last visit with me, he jumped to his death in front of a speeding Number Four train. That was yesterday."

The audience stirred nervously in their seats. Jack also fidgeted, wrestling with his crumpled slacks. Like most people, Jack was a little uncomfortable with this subject matter. Seeing the past and predicting events of the future. It was difficult to ignore the implications. Were these events predestined to happen? Was the remote past being recorded on some surreal astro-plane? Life, death, and suicide, frankly Jack found this all a little spooky.

Casper turned off the projector with a remote, and the imposing head of Roger Finnegan faded into the screen. Jack closed his eyes for a moment, but the negative image of the Perceptive Schizophrenic lingered on his retina. Casper cleared his throat and turned up the lights. Several hands in the audience initially shot up but Casper wasn't taking any questions yet.

"Ladies and gentlemen, before I take any questions, I would like to show a brief video." He pressed a button on the console at the podium and the videotape started on the screen. After the electrical snow, the screen turned black. The words 'Patient One: AC' appeared in bold white lettering.

The camera focused on a scrag of a woman. She was wearing a pink dress, and a long pearl necklace. She had her arms folded across her chest, and she was holding a cigarette between two tar-stained fingertips. Someone shooting the footage was focusing and refocusing the camera. It bobbled once or twice, and the distorted figure of AC grew larger then smaller on the screen. Finally the camera was still, but the patient was not. She smacked her lips and projected her tongue involuntarily, manifesting the hallmark signs of Tardive Dyskinesia. This is a well-described, and often irreversible side effect of the antipsychotic medications. Following a series of facial tics and twists, AC took several protracted drags of her cigarette. She talked aimlessly about skiing and snowballs, hot tubs and youthful fun.

"What about the snow?" Casper was not seen on the screen but he was conducting the interview.

AC shrugged her shoulders and shivered. "It's gonna fall all over them. They'll be frozen in the ice. Those good clothes she got for

Christmas ain't gonna help her. No sir." AC twisted her face to the camera and dribbled as she greeted the audience. "Hello there in TV land." She said with a bizarre wave.

"Who will be frozen?"

AC smiled blankly into the camera and waved. "Wow, look at all those people. They came to see you and me Doctor Lolly?" She turned back toward Casper.

"There's nobody here but us...Now, can you tell me about the frozen people? Who will be frozen?"

AC quickly shot one last look at the camera then turned again to Casper. "Oh yes, the kids on the mountain? They're students ya' know." She blew a long stream of curly white smoke out of her nostrils. "They're not gonna be able to breathe underneath all that snow, and they can't climb out because the snow is frozen around them. Their muscles stiffen up pretty quick in the ice like that. The little one...Well, she's missing her gloves. She's very cold. She gives in first." AC took another drag.

"Which mountains are you talking about?"

"They're in Vermont of course." AC nervously chuckled but then stopped abruptly and attended to the ashes that were building up on the end of her cigarette. Casper paused the tape as her image disappeared from the screen.

Casper addressed the audience. "I videotaped this meeting with AC last January. The excerpt you just saw was taped just eleven hours prior to the avalanche that killed fourteen students on Mount Snow."

Several gasps escaped above the whispers. Jack also was somewhat stunned by the tape and he rubbed his stubbly chin in amazement. Casper pushed the button on the console and turned back to the screen.

Patient number two was an Indian man named PB. He was also smoking a cigarette. He was clearly very anxious, and several times he got up from his seat and restlessly paced the floor. Casper, again off camera, urged him to sit down. After a fair amount of reassurance, the patient did so. PB sat on the edge of the chair, shaking his legs. "Okay Doc, you must let me go." He took a long drag of his cigarette.

"In a few moments, why are you so nervous?" Casper asked.

"Doctor Lolly, there are bad waves coming from India. Earth rattling waves. They'll be buried alive! Thousands of 'em. They're all dead!

We've got to warn them. We gotta tell the authorities! Do you know any of them?"

"Who? Indians?"

"No! The authorities! C'mon let's go." PB twisted his cigarette into the ashtray, and hopped to his feet.

"Where are you going?"

"I've got to get to Gujarat."

"Guja-what?"

"Gujarat!" A droplet of sweat dangled from PB's nose. He turned toward the camera, and it flung onto the lens. "Can we bring the camera?" The screen went black, and Casper again paused the tape.

"This was taped only hours before a massive earthquake hit Gujarat, India, in January. The quake killed twenty thousand Indian citizens. He made it down to the Indian embassy here in New York in plenty of time, but security personnel summarily removed him. I do not know where he is today, or if he is still alive."

Casper continued the tape. Patient number three spoke quietly about Casper's father. The patient revealed minute details about Casper's childhood, and his father's long battle with cancer.

"He loves you very much, and he is going to miss you terribly." The patient finished, and dropped his head. He avoided eye contact with Casper.

Casper paused the tape. A large blurry image of the patient remained on the screen. "My father was dead by the end of this day. This patient, and RF, both warned me of his passing."

Patient number four predicted the crash of flight 800 over Long Island in the summer of 1996. Patient number five elaborated on details of a recent rape and murder that had been unsolved by the NYPD for fifteen years.

"This videotape actually helped the police apprehend and convict the perpetrator." Casper told the stunned audience.

Once all of the extraordinary videotape was shown, Casper turned off the VCR, and invited questions from the audience. A veritable sea of hands rose simultaneously, and many resorted to shouting their questions at him. Jack sat quietly in the turbulent crowd. Some psychiatrists turned to one another and discussed similar experiences in their own practices.

Others discussed the remarkable video footage. Jack thought for a moment. He recalled several instances of probable Perceptive Schizophrenia during his lengthy career. He hated to admit it, but Casper was truly onto something big.

Casper pointed through the crowd and called upon Doctor Tom Jenson first.

"Okay, Doctor Jenson?"

"Thank you, Doctor Lolly." Doctor Jenson shouted above the impolite crowd. "In your population of schizophrenics, how many have you identified as being 'Perceptive', and how many of those have attempted or completed suicide?"

"Those are both good questions, Tom..." Casper started. "There are approximately two-thousand three hundred schizophrenics in my hospital based and private practices. Of course they are not all patients of mine, but I have assessed all of them...And of these I have identified only fifty-one Perceptive Schizophrenics. You may notice that this is considerably higher than my estimated prevalence, but I have a strong selection bias in my practice."

Casper continued, "In regard to the second part of your question, eight of these fifty-one have completed suicide, thirty-three of them have attempted it."

Casper invited more questioning from the floor and the audience jumped at the opportunity. He methodically clarified his novel theories on the common psychosis, and the evolution of Perception to the eager conference attendees. Most of the audience was boiling with enthusiasm, but there were also a few skeptics in the crowd. Casper convincingly extinguished any doubts with a litany of evidence and examples. After a half an hour of questioning Casper was mentally exhausted. But understandably, the questions were still coming. He hushed the crowd by waving his hands at them.

"No more questions please."

The frenzied crowd reluctantly fell silent, when a voice cracked a question from the center of the room. The other members of the audience turned in their seats to see who was bold enough to ask the uninvited question.

"Excuse me?" Casper asked, searching the crowd. The room was silent.

Jack Benedict stood up and fixed his trousers. Giggles and whispers surrounded him. He cleared his throat and repeated his question.

"I asked, if you have formulated a psychoanalytic theory for Perceptive Schizophrenia?"

Casper attacked, "Doctor Benedict, your continuous efforts to apply archaic psychoanalytic constructs to something as organic as schizophrenia...lead me to believe that there are more holes in your head, than there are in Freud's theories."

Despite the snickering the atmosphere in the auditorium was wickedly tense. Few psychiatrists have been witness to a public showdown between these two opposing psychiatric superpowers.

"Are you implying that I have an open mind, Doctor Lolly?"

"That would be a flagrant misinterpretation of what I said, Jack."

"Frankly, I have been having a lot of trouble understanding you lately, perhaps you can help me?" Jack asked, and slowly unrolled the journal in his hand.

"Go ahead, shoot."

"For instance..." Jack licked his fingers and flipped through the pages of the journal. "Aha, here we go, on page eleven twenty-seven of the *Journal of Psychiatry*, you referred to me as a psychiatric dinosaur, and that the only thing on Earth more antiquated than psychoanalysis, was the primitive architecture of my brain."

"Yep. That was me." Casper acknowledged him smugly. "What's the question?"

"Well, I'm not sure what this means, Doctor Lolly. Perhaps you could clarify this for me?" Jack shrugged his shoulders, intentionally backing the speaker into a corner.

Casper stepped to the end of the stage. He was obviously unaffected by Jack's attempt to humiliate him. "This isn't *Sesame Street*, Jack, so I hope you can follow me." He paused for a moment, then continued. "There was so much cocaine in Sigmund Freud's nose, he could have been a Colombian jumbo jet." Casper shot a piercing look at Jack. "Your inability to abandon his theories is nothing short of malpractice. In fact, by embracing his psychedelic theories, you're putting the mental health of your patients in the hands of a coke snorting, sexual deviant." His expression was both frigid and self satisfied. "Yeah," Casper chuckled to himself, "you say that Freud was ahead of his time. Well let me tell you something Jack. He was ahead of his time, but unfortunately he got stuck in the sixties. His theories are no longer groovy. This isn't Woodstock, Jack." Casper glared at him. "And you're no hippie. Can you dig that, Daddio?"

Jack felt like crawling out of the auditorium. He was thirsty for friendlier air, rendered mute and motionless by Casper's quick wit. He had been publicly flogged again.

Casper waited patiently for a comeback, but Jack did not offer one. He frowned, and shrugged his shoulders. "I guess if there are no more questions, or comments, I'd like to adjourn for a small cocktail party sponsored by our friends at *Parke-Davis Pharmaceuticals*."

Jack gathered his things from his chair and joined some sympathetic colleagues. They discussed the rudeness of Casper's comments and slowly shuffled down the aisle toward the door.

CHAPTER SEVEN
◆◆◆◆◆

Many of the psychiatrists and psychologists discussed the electrifying lecture, as they were lead into the Cohen Memorial Conference Room by a pharmaceutical representative. The room was distinctly opulent with a peaked cathedral ceiling and several glittering chandeliers. Along the walls, aged oil paintings of physicians and generous benefactors were hung in tasteful reverence. There were several waiters and waitresses dressed in formal attire. Some of them were attendants at various hors d'oeuvre stations, while others circulated the floor with drinks and snacks upon twinkling silver trays.

Jack's ego was slow to recover, but he managed to maintain an idle conversation with several colleagues as he entered the cocktail room. Like most of the psychiatrists at the lecture, Jack too had many stories of possible Perception. He discussed the case of Barry Fierstein with those around him. He was a former patient of Jack's, and he was probably a Perceptive. Like the Perceptives in the video, Barry was also able to prophesize. There were even times when Jack felt that this patient was reading his mind. During one visit, Barry suggested that Jack was soon to lose a large sum of money. The visit was one day prior to the stock market crash in 1987, and Jack did take quite a financial beating. Interestingly, Barry Fierstein committed suicide shortly after his last visit with Jack. He was found hanging by a shoestring from his shower nozzle.

Doctor Ryan Forbes, and Doctor Sharon Gardella shared similar stories with Jack, and these were likewise remarkable. Jack then recalled a patient by the name of Harry Landers, but this time he did not tell his colleagues. He has almost conveyed this story several times. In truth, he was dying to share this story, but he could never do it.

In Jack's opinion, Harry Landers was undoubtedly a Perceptive Schizophrenic. During one session, Harry described Jack's illicit affair with Ellen McCormick. He knew where, and when they made love. He knew the exact age difference, her hair color, and her nickname. He condemned Jack as an infidel, and spoke frequently about the sanctity of marriage, and the holiness of matrimony. Of course, Jack passively denied his accusations. Despite the fantastic nature of Harry's visions, Jack could never tell anyone about these sessions. It would certainly have created an unwelcome scandal at the hospital, and probably would have destroyed his pristine reputation.

Like Casper's Perceptives, Harry Landers also attempted suicide several times, but he was unsuccessful. Instead he was shot to death on a crowded subway platform last May. His killer was a man by the name of Jeremy Carthon. Jeremy was a recent parolee, who had served four years behind bars for armed robbery. According to eyewitness accounts, Harry Landers suddenly jumped on top of Jeremy, choked him with his hands, and shouted peculiar things at him. He appeared crazed, and was shouting that he could see the past and the future. He then accused Jeremy of raping a thirteen-year-old neighbor, and murdering the girl's father. Jeremy emphatically denied these allegations by blasting two bullets into Harry's skull. The police never found enough material evidence to link Jeremy Carthon to these crimes, but he was their prime suspect.

"Jack were you going to say something?" Sharon asked, noticing that Jack was lost in thought.

Jack's face turned flush and his heart skipped a few beats. He recalled the episode in the park several days ago. While he was running, a homeless man emerged from the brush and asked him, "Have you seen her yet?" Later that morning, he ran into Ellen McCormick in the subway. Jack wanted to gasp. He was really beginning to feel uneasy about this whole Perceptive thing, and he made a concerted effort to forget about it for now.

"No, no, not me. I wasn't going to say anything. Say, how about that lunatic writing that nasty editorial this week? Was that vicious or what?" Jack quickly changed the subject.

Ryan Forbes responded with a chuckle, "I know! That was unkind, huh? Casper Lolly, he's a piece of work."

"Hey Jack, don't worry about what he said to you in there." Sharon grabbed his arm affectionately. "We all know that he's a little crazy."

"I won't Sharon, but thanks."

Once all of the psychiatrists had entered the room, the pharmaceutical representative gave a brief sales pitch for a new antipsychotic medication named *Novolept*. She was attractive and sharply dressed. Casper was standing by her side, smugly whispering something to a friend as she spoke. He leaned backward and glanced at her rear. He grinned as he recalled something that was undoubtedly sexual.

Jack Benedict mentally reviewed the rest of his patients. There have been quite a few Perceptive patients in his lengthy career. Many of the established psychiatrists in the room were admitting the same. Jack thought that this was a fitting testimony to Casper Lolly's genius. Here was a room full of distinguished thinkers. All of them had experienced this strange phenomenon of Perception before, yet nobody recognized it as a clinical entity. Casper was undeniably brilliant, and Jack never contested this.

The pretty pharmaceutical representative inconspicuously placed her arm around Casper's waist and squeezed his ass. The move was subtle and quick. In fact, nobody even seemed to notice it except for Jack. Casper was becoming aroused by the confidence she displayed. He smiled and recalled how he thoroughly dominated her last night in her hotel room. She had invited Casper to a restaurant for a complimentary dinner the night prior to his lecture. After a few drinks, they were back in her room. Casper insisted that she keep her panties on, but ordered her to remove everything else. She did so obligingly. Casper then tied her up spread eagle on the bed. He used his necktie and her silk stockings to bind her wrists and ankles to the bedposts. Casper repeatedly took her until they were both exhausted.

Some of the psychiatrists had already began to gorge themselves when the pharmaceutical representative invited everyone to enjoy the food and drink. Jack took a glass of Merlot from a waiter's tray. The wine was warm and dry. He let the scarlet warmth slip down his throat and into his belly. Another waiter with hors d'oeuvres approached him, and Jack surveyed the puffy treats. His hands were full. The drink was in one hand, and the journal was folded in the other. In a mock gesture of defeat, he tossed the journal into a nearby trashcan, and grabbed a few of the puffs from the tray.

Casper swallowed his third drink in one gulp, and held up his glass. He signaled the waiter to bring him another gin and tonic. A substantial crowd had gathered around him by now, but he ignored most of their insipid questions. Frankly he had little respect for the majority of the psychiatrists in the room. Most were pretentious and self-serving, while the others were simply flaky. Casper just did not fit in with this lame crowd. The waiter finally arrived with his potent drink.

"Here you go, Doctor Lolly."

"Are you sure there's no beer?" Casper asked for the third time, putting his arm around the small but handsome waiter.

"Yep, I've asked my boss...but if you want I'll run out to a deli and get some for you, Doctor Lolly?" He was barely seventeen.

"No, that won't be necessary, but thanks for asking. What's your name anyway?"

"James."

"Well James, I think you are doing a fantastic job. Keep the drinks coming." Casper slipped the kid a one hundred-dollar bill.

"Sir...I mean Doctor Lolly, we don't take tips, and besides..."

Casper interrupted him and winked. "Shhh, just take it, it will stay between us friends. Just keep the drinks coming." Finishing his fourth drink, he pressed the empty glass into the waiter's hand, and the waiter hurried off.

Casper had a strange respect and admiration for all working people. Casper himself was typical working class, and he was much more comfortable with this segment of the population. They all shared a common heritage of pride, and principles. Although Casper proudly refused to abide by any defined principles, he deeply admired those who did. Perhaps this was part of the problem he had relating to his colleagues. Most of the psychiatrists in the room were white bred. Many came from generations upon generations of wealthy physicians. In fact, the first question on virtually every medical school application, after name and social security number, asked if any family member, or friend, had ever attended the particular institution. Being the son of an auto mechanic, Casper had no tenable connections, and he was by far the poorest medical student at Yale. The sad truth was that many medical school admissions were not rewards based upon merit, but rather legacies based upon privilege. Most of his contemporaries were products from this world of power and pretense, and Casper detested them for it.

Jack was slowly making his way toward the front of the room where Casper was standing. He ate creampuffs and drank wine as he walked, and he often stopped to chat with friends and colleagues. Jack had finished two glasses of Merlot, and was in the middle of drinking his third. He was getting dangerously close to Casper, and the crowd soon realized this. Conversations slowly became hushed, and people glanced furtively at the two famous adversaries. The tension in the room peaked when Jack stopped only a few feet from the younger speaker. Both psychiatrists looked up, and their eyes met.

"Doctor Lolly." Jack greeted him first, cordially raising his glass.

"Doctor Benedict." Casper returned with an ice-cold welcome.

The crowd stepped backwards in anticipation of verbal fireworks. They formed an uneven semicircle around the two psychiatrists, as if they were expecting to see a brawl in the schoolyard.

"Interesting lecture." Jack said, stalling and trying to think of something wise to say.

"Thanks." Casper nodded.

"I'm surprised Dionne Warwick couldn't make it. Miss Cleo wasn't available either, I take it?" This was all that Jack could think of, and someone behind him giggled stupidly at his remark. "Tell me, Doctor Lolly, do you get all of your patients from *The Psychic Friends Network?*"

Casper smirked, and shook his head. "That's a good one, Jack. But, I expected a lot more from the famous Doctor Jack Benedict."

"Well, I expected a lot less from the infamous Doctor Casper Lolly." Jack delivered a clever left-handed response. He was winning this one. The crowd studied Casper's face looking for the subtle signs of detonation.

Casper remained oddly in control. "I'm flattered that you enjoyed my talk Jack, I was beginning to doubt your capacity for high order thinking."

"It's possible that I'm growing dim witted in my old age."

"Oh, I don't know Jack, I think you've always been a little bit slow. "

"That really hurts coming from and immature clinician like yourself."

"Immature? Are you jealous of my youth, you old prune? I know a good psychoanalyst who can help you deal with that."

"Your concern for my mental welfare is deeply moving, Casper." Jack bowed his head, and pounded his heart with an open hand.

The crowd intently watched as the two psychiatrists continued to trade insults for several minutes. Then there was an awkward pause. Jack slowly lifted his head and smiled warmly at the volatile speaker.

"Casper..." Jack said, opening his arms. "You nasty son of a bitch! How's my favorite student doing?"

"JB, you old stupid, stupid fool. Where've you been?" The two men embraced, sending the crowd into utter confusion.

"I moved to the opposite side of the city, and I don't see you anymore?" Casper said, patting Jack on the back. "Seriously Jack, what have you been up to?"

"Gosh, I don't know. What's it been? Over a year?"

The two men broke from their embrace, but still held one another by the elbows. The crowd tried to make some sense of this senseless scene.

"Hey, I'm sorry about that dinosaur comment...but I knew it would flush you out of hiding." Casper laughed apologetically.

"That's okay Cass. Wait until next week, just wait until next week." Jack slapped him lightly on the cheek, and the two psychiatrists suddenly noticed the awestruck crowd surrounding them.

Casper sneered at the onlookers. "Hey, you guys got something against homosexuals? Never seen fabulous gay love before? Turn around, and go away...go away, shoo!"

The crowd reluctantly turned and dissipated at Casper's request. They softly gossiped to one another and spun off into little cliques. Few people were aware that Jack was Casper's preceptor during his undergraduate years at NYU. Casper spent two full semesters working closely with Jack in his clinical lab. In fact, Jack introduced Casper to the field of psychiatry, and even wrote him a glowing letter of recommendation for his application to medical school. This letter was partly the reason for his acceptance at Yale.

Despite their bitter public resentment, the two psychiatrists actually admired one another. Jack admired Casper for his fiery disdain of authority, and Casper admired Jack for his relentless honesty, and academic integrity. However, Jack truly hated the way Casper practiced psychiatry, and the converse was true as well. Their difference of opinion was the cornerstone of their relationship, and they both enjoyed insulting each other on the editorial pages of the psychiatric journals.

"Hey Jack, what do you say we get outta here? Leave the food to the vultures."

"Let the dead, bury the dead, Casper. Where to?" Jack shrugged, and thought for a moment.

Following a brief silence, both men suggested a bar called *The Sacred Cow* simultaneously. They frequently shared drinks here years ago, and they both had many fond memories of it. By now, the crowd had resorted to entertaining themselves, and Jack ducked through the exit. Casper grabbed the pharmaceutical representative by the wrist, and led her quietly out the door after Jack.

CHAPTER EIGHT
◆◆◆◆◆

On a typical Saturday night in the East Village, the sidewalks were littered with hippies, beatniks and derelicts. Resting near Alphabet City, this neighborhood was a vague transition zone between the drug scene, and the smug scene. Dilapidated six story walk-up apartments cluttered the skyline, and stray cats infested the murky alleyways. Most of the grungy residents went club hopping at night, and slept all day. Some of them had jobs at the local video stores, taverns, and pizzerias, but most did not. And although there was a smattering of business types in this unruly neighborhood, only a handful of them dared to dress that way.

Nearby, the face of the *Orpheum Theater* projected over the sidewalk. A noisy show entitled 'STOMP!' was playing there. Several homeless men swarmed around outside the doors, waiting for the theater-goers to exit. On the corner of First Avenue, a thin Chinese man stopped on his bicycle, and spoke to a man selling counterfeit baseball caps on the curbside. Two men in knit caps exchanged money on a small porch a few doors away, on Astor Place. One of the men kicked a used hypodermic needle off of the top step, and it landed in the trash beside the cement stoop.

The two hatted men stopped their seditious activity as a blue van with tinted windows squeaked slowly around the corner. The invisible driver softly tapped the break a few times, and the van wobbled to a crawl. This was a provocative stimulus for the two men, but it was probably just the police. They were the absentee landlords of this lawless town. They frequently combed this neighborhood in conspicuously unmarked vehicles. They were looking for squatters and dealers, the two most troublesome vermin in the area. The mysterious van never came to a complete stop, and it slowly crept in and out of potholes, waddling toward Avenue A.

Despite the seedy conditions, people from all over New York City congregated here on a Saturday night to take advantage of the temptations of the Village. This was a phenomenon known as 'Village-Spillage'. Residents from the Eastside, Westside, Midtown and Uptown all tried to blend in with the funkadelic native villagers. Anonymity was a refreshing way of life down here, and there was no better place in Manhattan to shed inhibitions and indulge bizarre fantasies.

Two petite models walked up First Avenue. Both of them were sporting black polyester pants, and tight white spandex tops. They walked quickly in the cool autumn air, folding their arms across their chests. In Manhattan, a coat was often cumbersome, and these women were not going far anyway. A yellow cab passed the two models as they entered a Mexican restaurant.

"Right up here on the left." Casper told the cabby.

The cabby pulled the car abruptly over to the side of the road, and it bumped solidly off the curb. He pressed the button on the meter, and a receipt popped out.

"Thanks Buddy..." Casper told the cabby as he poked nine dollars through the partition. "...Keep the change."

"Sank you berry much." The cabby slipped the folded bills into his shirt pocket.

"Okay this is the place." Casper told Susan, the pharmaceutical representative.

Jack helped Susan climb out of the cab, and Casper soon followed. He shut the door, and the taxi recklessly darted across the busy street to pick up another fare.

"It's between First and A." Jack pointed down St. Mark's Place.

"Is it far? I don't see any bars." Susan asked, she was a little tipsy.

"It's not really a bar Sue, it is more of a club." Casper told her.

"I'm not dressed for a club...Guys?...Hey c'mon."

"It's not that kind of club, Susan." Jack added.

The Sacred Cow was indeed unique. It was one of a few underground clubs that was fabled to exist in the Village and SoHo. They did not advertise, nor did they promote themselves. Admission was based solely upon facial recognition, and newcomers were expressly not welcome. This system kept the police, and other undesirables out of the illegal institution.

The three of them walked to the middle of the block, and across the street. They stopped in front of an unassuming entrance to a basement apartment. There was a simple black cow, with a small halo around its head, spray painted on the cement wall of the stairwell.

"This is it." Casper pointed down at the cow.

"This is it?" Susan asked.

Casper and Jack led the way down the steps, and rang the bell. After a few seconds, a slot on the door slid open. Two bushy brown eyes appeared, and they blinked several times adjusting to the darkness. Casper and Jack smiled at the man behind the door.

"Who's the chick?" the eyes motioned to the woman behind them.

"Sus..." Susan was interrupted by Casper.

"She's with us." Casper told the man.

The slot quickly shut, and there was no sound from the door. Susan turned to leave, but Casper motioned for her to stay. After several seconds of waiting, the slot slid open again.

"Let me see her legs." the eyes requested.

"Uh...sure." Casper motioned to Susan, and she hesitantly stepped forward.

"Pretty please?" Casper boyishly whispered with his hands clasped in prayer. Susan took a few more tentative steps forward, and quickly curtsied to the man behind the door.

"Her skirt is not short enough." the doorman bargained.

"We can fix that." Casper eagerly nodded towards Susan.

"What are you doing, Casper?" she asked.

"Don't worry." Casper ran behind her, and rolled her skirt up at the waist. "How's this?" he asked the doorman.

"More."

"Now?" The skirt was about mid thigh.

"More."

Casper rolled the skirt again and again, until the hemline fell just below Susan's crotch.

"Now?" He could not roll it any higher.

The slot shut abruptly again, and the eyes disappeared behind the door. Jack noticed Susan's spectacular legs. Her muscular inner thighs were becoming goosebumped in the chilly night air, and she slowly rubbed them together to keep the skin warm.

There was a noise from behind the door, and it loudly swung open. Muffled house music poured out from the club. Jack, Susan, and Casper entered, and the door slammed shut behind them.

"Doc, nice to see you again." The bearish doorman pawed at Casper's hand.

"How are you doin', Ditch?" Casper asked. "You remember Freud don't you?" Casper placed a hand on Jack's shoulder.

"Of course. It's been some time, Freud."

"Sorry about that. Nice to see you again, Ditch." Jack shook his meaty hand.

For the sake of privacy and the preservation of security, staff and patrons referred to one another exclusively by nicknames. None of the patrons could identify the staff, nor could the staff identify the patrons. Among themselves, the patrons usually referred to one another by their proper names. When mixing with the staff, this was strictly forbidden.

"Who's your lady friend?" Ditch asked the two psychiatrists.

Susan extended her hand, and was about to introduce herself when Casper warned her.

"Just remember, we all go by nicknames here. So make it a good one."

Susan placed a finger on her lips, and bit down softly on her fingernail. She looked at the dramatic statement her thighs were making. "Vixen."

"Okay, Vic it is." Ditch tailored each nickname to his own liking, nobody ever argued about it, and Susan reluctantly accepted her new handle.

"Why the hard time at the door, Ditch?" Jack asked the giant doorman.

"You almost didn't make it in, Freud. We really need a compelling reason to permit strangers." Ditch looked down at Susan's legs. "...And boy, are those legs compelling!"

"Thanks." Susan replied somewhat nervously, and curtsied one last time.

They turned to enter the main bar, and pushed through the swinging metal door. Music exploded outwards as they ventured into the tiny smoke filled room and multicolored lights swirled wildly across the smoky air. A girl with blue hair was working behind the bar, and she looked pissed off. Bad hair-do on a bad hair day. Jack surveyed the crowd a while longer. It was always interesting, and oddly comforting. He received a few familiar nods, so he nodded quietly back. Freakish women were gyrating on the dance floor with a few clodhopping men. The rest of the place was packed with hordes of sexually ambitious women, and sexually ambiguous men—The usual inhabitants of Greenwich Village.

Casper watched a girl in blue tube skirt. She left the dance floor, and stumbled into a booth in the corner. She placed a cigarette between her glossy red lips, and ignited it. The orange flame cast a curvy shadow over her ample breasts, and after inhaling, she noticed Casper looking at her. Her eyes lingered on him for a subtle moment, and then she turned coyly away.

Casper pointed towards her booth. "Let's sit over there." Jack and Susan followed him as he quickly pushed through the pulsating crowd.

○○○○○○○○

Jack, Susan, and Casper had been chatting with Isabella for about an hour. She was an exotic dancer at a midtown gentleman's club. She insisted that her profession was a legitimate form of artistic expression, and Casper was mockingly agreeable. Susan however, was truly enticed by this conversation, and she revealed that she had fantasized several times about being a stripper.

"It's very liberating. You should try it. I guarantee better pay than what you're doin' now, Honey."

"I could never!" Susan laughed, flirting with the Hispanic dancer.

Jack and Casper looked at one another as something carnal evolved between the two women.

"I'd give you some lessons. Free of charge. You've got a great body."

"Ha! Are you joking?"

"No, I'm being serious. One hundred percent." Isabella wrapped her shiny lips around the mouth of the beer bottle and took a slow swig from it. She looked seductively at Susan, then turned similarly to Jack. He smiled, leaned back into his seat, and signaled for another round of beers.

OOOOOOOO

"So many physicists think that 'space-time' is the fourth dimension..." Casper was drunk and feeling philosophical. He was trying to discuss physics with his new friends. Jack was drunk also, and he had heard Casper's theories before.

"I don't follow." Susan pushed a lock of hair behind her ear, and casually sipped from her beer.

Jack intervened. "Okay Susan, imagine yourself as a batter in a baseball game." He looked at Susan and Isabella for acknowledgement. They appeared to be following him.

"Now, suppose you wanted to hit a ball to the outfielder. Let's say, about one hundred yards away." Jack continued slowly.

"Okay." the women answered simultaneously.

"If you were to hit a fly ball to this outfielder...It would take, maybe six seconds, to reach him. If you were to hit a line drive...It would take much less. About one second to reach him. You could never hit a line drive that would take six seconds to reach the outfielder. Nor could you hit a fly ball that would take one second to reach him." Jack looked at them.

"Uh-huh." they both nodded.

"So you already knew that space, the distance between you and the outfielder, and time, are intimately related. You can't separate the two." Jack finished, and Susan looked curiously at Isabella.

"I never liked baseball." Isabella admitted, not realizing the humor in her remark.

Casper laughed. "Nice analogy JB. Way to go! You can't relate this to stripping, can you? Something a little more pertinent to our friends?"

Jack shrugged stupidly, and Casper reached across the table and removed a pen from his shirt pocket. Unfolding the napkin on the table, Casper drew a stick figure on it.

"We live in a three dimensional world." Casper started simply. "We all have a height, a depth, and a width." Casper demonstrated these dimensions on himself. "This is how we see the entire universe. We physically appreciate things in terms height, depth and width. Now..." Casper pointed to the man on the napkin. "Suppose there was another world...A two dimensional world, like this napkin. Imagine that there is no thickness to this napkin. It is infinitely thin. We call it 'Flatland'. In Flatland, our little man exists only in terms of left, right, up and down. There is only height, and width in his world...There is no depth."

The girls seemed to be following Casper's analogy and Jack tried to guess where he was taking this. Casper lifted the damp napkin slightly off the table, and continued.

"Now what would happen if there was an unexpected intrusion, from our three dimensional universe, into his two dimensional world?" Casper poked a hole through the napkin with the pen, leaving it partly through the napkin. "How would this appear to our two-dimensional Flatland man?"

They all shrugged their shoulders, and Casper fiddled with the pen. "Our two dimensional man would not appreciate this expensive ball point pen, ripping through his world. This is something that only we can appreciate from our three dimensional perspective." Casper removed the pen, leaving a soggy hole in the napkin. He turned it to face Jack and the women. "Our man would only appreciate this intrusion as a large, unexplainable hole in his two dimensional universe. A Flatland mathematical mystery." Casper looked queerly through the hole in the napkin at the others. "This is the best way to imagine alternative dimensions. There are probably four dimensions to our universe. Perhaps more. Just because we don't appreciate them, doesn't mean that they don't exist."

"Absence of proof, is not proof of absence." Jack said, and began to clap for Casper. The women soon joined him.

"Encore!" Susan screamed, "Bravo!" Isabella added.

Casper blushed a bit, and humbly took his applause.

OOOOOOOO

"Hey Isshabella..." Casper slurred, they have been drinking for over two hours.

"Yeah?"

"Can I ask you something?" he shouted above the thrashing music, while Jack drunkenly smirked at his friend.

Isabella nodded, expecting a clever comment.

"How come today, everybody with the name Jesus, either comes from South America, or Mexico?" He looked at Jack, and Jack started laughing. Susan nearly choked on her beer, and Isabella shrugged her shoulders playfully.

"That's an excellent question, Doctor. " She laughed.

"Here's another one...Okay?"

"Sure."

"It seems to me that everything in the known universe exists naturally in a round state. For instance, planets are round, atoms are probably round, stars and our Sun appear to be round, tree trunks are round...Hell, even human beings are somewhat round. Our eyes, our brains...You know, all the important stuff is round." Casper looked at Susan and Isabella, then continued. "So why do we find it easier to deal with squares? We build them everywhere! Our homes, our offices, our packaging...They're all squares! What is it about us humans? Why do we need to defy the natural order of the universe?"

"Yeah...Why is that?" Susan furrowed her brow.

"Good question, Cass. A real ground breaker." Jack said.

"That's a good point, I never thought of that." Isabella also sided with Casper.

"Come to think of it, I even have a few square friends." Casper joked, looking at Jack. The two girls laughed with Casper at Jack's expense, and Jack defensively straightened his shirt.

"What? Is it the way I dress? My wife makes me dress like this! She likes it."

OOOOOOOO

It was now approaching midnight, and Jack quickly called Caroline to tell her he will be leaving shortly. She was already in bed, and was just about to nod off when he called.

"Hurry home." she sleepily requested. "And be careful."

"I will, Babe."

Jack staggered back to the booth. There was a fresh round of beers on the cluttered table. Jack felt nauseous. It had been a long night and he was full of eggplant, hors d'oeuvres, and beer. Isabella slid down the bench and made room for him. Jack declined by holding up his hand.

"I'm finished. I can barely see, no more for me."

"Jack, don't leave us!" the sexy dancer begged, groping at his arm.

"Isabella, it's been a pleasure, but I have a wife to get home to."

Casper tried to get up, but his lap was trapped underneath the table. Falling back down onto the bench he called to Jack, "C'mon JB, just a little while longer?"

"Sorry Cass, I can't"

"I'll make it worth your while, Jack." Isabella rubbed his thigh, and Casper raised his eyebrows, coaxing Jack.

"That's quite tempting Isabella, quite tempting. But I really gotta go."

Isabella sadly released Jack, and after saying goodbye to Susan, he turned to leave. Casper struggled to get out from the booth, and finally resorted to climbing underneath it.

"Hey JB...Hold on!" Jack turned to see Casper crawling on his hands and knees. Jack helped him to his feet, and Casper hugged him.

"I'll see you later, Cass." Jack hugged him back. "It was great seeing you again."

"Jack?" Casper looked deep into the face of his friend.

"What?"

"Would you help me with something? I mean, would you do me a favor?"

"Sure Casper, anything you want." Jack humored Casper. He just wanted to get home to his wife.

"Anything?"

"Anything." Jack nodded.

"Would you help me with a project? An experiment?" Casper was drunk, but he was serious. Jack looked back at him strangely.

"You want me, to help you with a project? Casper, we're opposites...I can't see how I could help you." Jack shook his head, avoiding Casper's stare.

"Please, Jack...please." Casper held him more tightly in a bear hug.

Jack rolled his eyes. "Why me?"

"You're the only one I could trust JB! You're the only one...I...trust."

"Casper..." Jack reluctantly looked at him. "What kind of project? What sort of experiment do you have in mind?"

"I'll call you tomorrow." Casper looked at his watch, it was slightly past twelve o'clock. "I mean, I'll call you this morning. Okay? Will you do this for me? It'll be just like the old days, you and me. Ground breaking science, Jack. Do it for science...Do it for me."

Jack contemplated for several seconds, and Casper did not say a word.

"Okay Cass, you win. I'll play scientist with you. We'll talk about it."

"Thank you JB! Thank you, thank you, thank you!" Casper crushed Jack, then finally released him from the hug, and wiped away a phony tear.

"What experiment?" Jack asked again.

Casper walked backwards toward the booth. He pointed both hands at Jack, and mouthed "Thank you."

"What project?!" Jack screamed above the crowd, but Casper had already returned to the booth with the two women. They sandwiched him on the bench, and Casper put an arm around each of them. Jack put on his coat, looked again at his watch and grudgingly left the club.

CHAPTER NINE
◆◆◆◆◆

Jack stepped out of the cab in front of his brownstone, and into a puddle. Cool brown water seeped into his shoe and under his foot. He shook his leg disgustedly and stepped up to the curb with a squish. He was still buzzing, and he felt slightly unsteady on his feet. He grasped the handrail tightly as he climbed the concrete steps.

All of the lights in the brownstone were out. Caroline was upstairs sleeping already. Jack quietly entered and shut the door. He carefully pulled off his shoes by the door, and laid them on the floor. The wet sock left damp footprints on the parquet wood floor as he staggered over to the closet. He removed his coat, and accidentally dropped it on the floor. It made quite a racket, echoing through the brownstone. Jack listened for a moment. Caroline stirred upstairs, and clicked on a light.

"Jabes?" she asked from the bedroom.

"Yes Honey, I'll be right up." his voice was loud and slurred.

Jack hung his coat in the closet, and went to the kitchen. He drank a tall glass of water, and swallowed two aspirin for good measure. He went upstairs to the bedroom. The light on the night table was still on, but Caroline had already fallen back asleep.

"Hey Babe." he greeted her in a whisper, but she did not respond.

He quietly removed his pants, and then his shirt. He placed the pants on a wire hanger, and tossed his dirty shirt into the hamper. It smelled like smoke and alcohol, mixed with a trace of cheap perfume. He softly closed the closet door, and turned the light off. In the darkness he felt for the bedposts, and carefully climbed into bed next to his wife. Jack gave her a soft kiss on the back of her head, and sank himself into the pillow.

"Goodnight Sweetheart." he whispered, before falling into a deep sleep.

Several peaceful hours had passed when Jack was suddenly startled from his sleep by a strange noise downstairs. It was nearly four o'clock in the morning. After picking the crust out of his eyes, Jack turned the light on and turned towards his wife. She was gone.

"Caroline?" Jack said, and sat up in bed.

The strange noise stopped momentarily, but there was no response. Jack climbed out of bed, and walked in his boxers to the stairwell. The light was on in the kitchen.

"Caroline?" he called down the stairway. Again there was no response. Jack listened carefully. There was definitely someone down there. He heard footsteps. They were heavy footsteps, as if the person was wearing boots. They squeaked on the wooden floor as if they were wet. With his heart pounding in his chest, Jack descended a few steps and called again.

"Who's there?" Jack said. The footsteps stopped.

Jack descended the rest of the way down the stairway, and stepped into the hallway. The light from the kitchen dimly lit the hallway floor.

Footsteps again! Definitely footsteps. A dark shadow moved quickly across the kitchen wall. Jack stopped for a moment and held his breath. His heart relentlessly beating at his ribs and with sweat gathering in a small pool above his brow, he tried to calm his nerves. He quietly pushed himself against the wall and tightly closed his eyes. Somebody was in the kitchen. It was somebody big. He listened carefully as he inched himself along the wall toward the kitchen. Jack heard labored breathing. There was something familiar about this heavy breathing. He had heard it before. He couldn't recall where or when, but he definitely had heard that strained respiratory pattern before. Jack took another deep breath, held it for only a second and jumped into the kitchen.

"Good evening, Doctor Benedict." It was Harry Landers, the Perceptive Schizophrenic. He was wet, and wearing a long gray slicker.

"Whoa! Shit!" Jack was startled and he backed into the hallway, toward the door. "Mister Landers...What? What are you doing here? I heard you died!"

Harry Landers pursued him slowly, almost curiously. "I've been dead for a thousand years. I'm here to deliver something to you."

"Harry, what do you want? What are you doing in my house?" Jack was panicking.

"I told you, I'm on a delivery." the Perceptive calmly told him.

Jack backed himself into the front door, and he fumbled desperately for the doorknob. He then remembered that Caroline was missing.

"Caroline?!" he called into the kitchen, but there was no response. "Call the police, Honey!" Again there was no response. "Caroline?!...If you can hear me, call the police! And run out the back door...Okay? Go to the neighbors!"

Harry Landers dropped his head and laughed.

"What'd you do to Caroline?...Where's my wife, Harry?"

"I've delivered her unto the Lord." There was blood and bits of flesh on the sleeves of his trenchcoat. "Phew...What did she have for dinner anyway?...Eggplant? I hope these stains come out, Doc!" He laughed again.

"Harry, did you hurt my wife?!" There was an unbearable ache in his chest.

"No...I did not hurt your wife. You, Doctor Benedict, you hurt your wife. I just saved her...Covet thine own! Said the Lord...And covet not thy neighbor's wife. Infidel!..Infidel pig.""

Jack lunged at Harry, but the Perceptive easily evaded the drunken tackle. Jack crashed headfirst into the wall, and fell to his knees. He turned to Harry, the bloody trench coat was now open, and there were several sticks of dynamite strapped to Harry's chest. The wires were connected to a digital clock.

"There's not much time, Doctor Benedict...Salvation is at hand. Miss McCormick, and your wife have been saved...Now, it's time for me and you."

"Harry, don't! What are you doing, Harry?" Ten seconds remained on the clock.

"I am the lamb of God, who taketh away the sins of the world."

"Harry...Please, no!" Eight seconds.

"Have mercy on us!"

"Caroline!...Caroline!" Five seconds left, and Jack tried to scramble to his feet.

"Deliver unto me the sinners of the world! From dust thou art, to dust thou shall return." Harry outstretched his arms in mock crucifixion.

The clock stopped and blinked 00:00. Jack closed his eyes and dropped to the floor in fetal position. Harry started to sing.

"Allelujah...Allelujah...Allelujah!"

The clock began to ring and then stopped. *A digital alarm clock that rang?* Harry looked down at the clock on his chest and smacked it several times.

The ringing resumed, but then stopped again. Jack looked at Harry.

Another ring. *What a strange alarm clock...The phone!* The phone was ringing! Jack snapped his head from the pillow and violently shook his mind clear. It was just a dream. He flopped over in bed and groped at the night table for the phone. The alarm clock read 5:57 a.m. Jack quickly patted the cold sweat from his face with the bed sheets. He picked up the phone and lifted it off the receiver.

"Hello?" he asked, and turned toward his wife. She was sleeping quietly next to him.

"JB?...It's me. Hope I didn't wake you." Casper said.

"Casper, it's not even six." Jack looked at the clock again.

"I know JB, but I want to get this project thing going."

"What?" Jack tried to recall the vague events of the night before.

"You're not thinking of backing out on me JB, are you?"

Jack heard two women giggle in the background at Casper's apartment. It was Susan and Isabella. The night suddenly became more familiar to him. He recalled the lecture, the Perceptive Schizophrenics, and the drinks at *The Sacred Cow*.

"JB?"

"Yeah." he answered, slowly rubbing the crust out of his eyes. His mouth was dry, and sore.

"Can you meet me on the southwest corner of Tenth Street and Greenwich Avenue?"

"Today?"

"I was thinking more like, right now?"

"Now? Casper have you even slept yet?" Jack accidentally raised his voice, rousing Caroline from her sleep.

"A little bit." Casper admired Isabella, and Susan. They were both naked on his bed, and Susan was caressing Isabella's breasts. Isabella writhed on the bed with pleasure, and kissed Susan wetly on the mouth.

"How about in a few hours, Cass?"   •

"Um...Eight o'clock? Would that be enough beauty rest for you, JB?"

"Eight-thirty...No sooner."

"Ugh...Okay, you win. Eight-fifteen it is. On the corner of Tenth and Greenwich."

"Eight-thirty, Casper!" Jack insisted.

Casper did not hear him, and he dropped the phone to the floor. They were still connected when he crawled into bed with Susan and Isabella.

Jack heard the phone crash on the other end, and he listened for a few seconds. The bed started squeaking, and the girls giggled uncontrollably. Somewhat embarrassed he quickly placed the phone back on the receiver. He fell back onto the damp sheets and turned to Caroline, snuggling up next to her. Her eyes still closed but she was clearly awake.

"What'd he want?" she asked.

"Sorry Honey, he needs help with a project...I'm gonna meet him downtown in a few hours."

"How was the night?"

"Just as I expected. Very interesting." He pulled himself closer into her.

"You're all wet, Jabes." She arched her back away from his sweat soaked body. "What the hell happened?"

"Bad nightmare. It was just a nasty dream."

"Was it about that schizophrenic who got shot again?"

"Yeah, I don't know why. Can't seem to shake it." Jack propped himself up onto his elbow. Caroline pushed the wet hair off of his face. His cheek was rough and hairy.

"Are you okay, Jabes?"

"Fine. A little hung over, but fine." Jack kissed her hand lightly.

He was exhausted. He rolled onto his belly, but still faced Caroline. He told her about the lecture, the drinks at *The Sacred Cow*, and the two girls. Caroline hid her jealousy by nearly swallowing him in a passionate kiss when he finished. They then warmly made love for the next hour.

CHAPTER TEN
◆◆◆◆◆

The C-train roared below the street and shook the cement. Jack stretched and yawned as he emerged from the subway station. After taking a quick look at his *Rolex* watch, he headed toward Fourteenth Street, and turned down Greenwich Avenue. A few coffee drinkers straggled by, and Jack felt compelled to grab a cup for himself from a nearby *Starbucks*.

The wind blew bits of trash across the street. Jack stepped back out onto the sidewalk with the coffee. He closed his coat and hurried across the street. Once he was on the other side, he clasped both hands around the warm cardboard cup and removed the cap. He blew a cloud of steam from the surface of the coffee and took several sips. The warm nutty flavor warmed the core of his tired body with each gulp. He continued leisurely down Greenwich Avenue.

It was nearly eight-thirty when Jack reached the corner of Greenwich and Tenth. There was no sign of Casper. Jack decided to wait against a pole on the sunny side of the sidewalk. In the distance Jack heard an ambulance approaching Saint Vincent's Hospital. He hated that sound. It usually meant serious trouble.

Suddenly there was a loud noise from behind him. Jack turned quickly and accidentally dropped his coffee on the sidewalk. A disheveled homeless man had tripped over a garbage can in an alleyway just off Tenth Street. Jack was about to come to his aid when the man stumbled to his feet. He glanced at Jack for a moment, and then brushed off his soiled pants. Scowling harshly, he kicked the can and then staggered by Jack down Greenwich Avenue.

Jack watched the homeless man as he drunkenly zigzagged down the street. He would occasionally sift through the trash and look for aluminum cans. After several blocks the man disappeared around a corner.

A lit cigarette bounced down the street, and stopped near Jack's feet. Jack searched the block for its owner, but it was strangely alone. He followed it as it rolled to the curbside and then stepped on it. He mashed the flame firmly into the ground until there was no longer smoke. Suddenly a yellow taxi careened wildly around the corner, and swerved to the sidewalk. It screeched to a stop, splashing a small pile of sludge onto the curb just inches from Jack's feet. He jumped back slightly, and bent over. He peered into the back seat of the cab. Casper was inside and he was shoving some money at the cabby. The cabby took the money, and Casper scooted himself off the seat and out of the car. He was wearing a baseball cap backward and old blue jeans. He slammed the door, patted the roof of the cab, and it sped off.

"Good morning, JB." Casper was unshaven, but appeared remarkably refreshed.

Jack nodded, "Hey Cass. I don't know how you do it." He shook his head playfully. "Did you have a good night?"

"I don't think they get much better, JB. How 'bout you? Did you have a good time last night?" He punched Jack softly in the chest.

"Sure." Jack shrugged. He was somewhat envious of Casper's unfettered lifestyle.

"Thanks for meeting me, JB, it's over here." Casper walked past Jack, towards an abandoned auto repair shop.

"What do you have in mind, Cass?"

"Something you've never thought of before."

"Don't underestimate me, Cass." Jack warned him sarcastically, as he followed Casper.

"I'm not."

Casper led him behind the shop, and up the alleyway past the trash and piles of junk. He stopped at the side door of the auto shop. It was locked securely with a chain and several deadbolts.

"What are you doing, Casper? Isn't this your family's old garage?"

"Uh-huh." Casper dug around his coat pockets and pulled out a ring with several keys on it. He began to unlock the door first by removing the lock and chain, and then the he turned the deadbolts. He dropped the chain on the ground, and shoved the door open.

"I've been working on this steadily for about a year, JB."

"Working on what?" Jack squinted into the dark garage.

Casper motioned Jack to step inside. "Age before beauty."

Jack stepped into the auto shop. It was dark except for some flashing red and blue lights in the distance. Casper followed him, and pulled the door shut behind them. For a moment, the room was almost completely dark. Casper waited a few seconds and flipped on the light switch. The room instantly lit.

"Oh my God, Cass...What is this?"

Jack was awestruck. The interior had been completely gutted, and refurbished. There was no semblance of an auto shop anymore. The walls were painted in an immaculate white, which gave the old place a new cleanliness. It was so clean it appeared sterile. On one of the walls, a state of the art control panel faced a large darkened pane of glass. Next to the glass was a closed metallic door. Three television screens were suspended above the console, as well as several videocassette recorders. On the console, sat a desktop computer, a panel of about fifty buttons, and several dials and meters.

Against the far wall, there was a small library with the latest editions of standard psychiatric and neurological textbooks. *Sphelmann's* textbook on Electroencephalography was laid upon a small table by the console.

"What's all this about, Cass?" Jack was perplexed.

"How do you like it?" Casper pointed to a quaint lounge area near the library, and walked over to a small refrigerator. He opened it, and asked Jack if he would like a drink.

"No thanks, Cass...What have you done here?" Jack looked up at the ceiling girders, and then back at Casper.

"This is the experiment...The project. I've done a lot of work, don't you think?"

"Yeah Cass, but what experiment? What have you been doing down here?"

"Oh, I haven't done anything yet. That's why I need your help."

"Uh-huh, I'm listening." Jack was curious, and he brushed his hand across the shiny console.

Casper followed him over to the console and leaned against it. He kicked the chair at the desk, and it spun several times.

"Did you like my lecture last night, Jack?" Casper was stalling.

"Sure...Like I told you..."

Casper interrupted him. "No, I mean...Do you believe in Perceptive Schizophrenia?"

Jack sighed and looked down at the floor. "You know, Cass...I..."

"Forget it. You don't have to answer that."

"But...I..." Jack insisted.

"I know how you feel, JB."

"I don't think you do, Cass."

"What?"

"I do. I believe you. I really do."

"You do?!" Casper was genuinely surprised, and he jumped from the console.

"Yeah, I hate to say it, but I do." Jack shrugged.

"Well you sonofabitch! That's terrific! A guy like you, believes in this?"

"That's right. Call me crazy."

"You're a real fuckin' whacko, Jacko. So, I don't get it...Why have you been riding me for all these years?"

"Someone's got to control your ego, Cass."

"Wow. Seriously, I'm so surprised." Casper shook his head amusingly. "Why Jack? How did I convince you?"

Jack confessed everything to him. He told Casper about several patients from his own practice that were probably Perceptive Schizophrenics. He mentioned Harry Landers, and the recurrent nightmares he had been having. For the first time he told Casper the details about his affair with Ellen McCormick. He also told Casper how Harry Landers somehow knew about it. Casper was not surprised by any of this, and in fact he told Jack that he had suspected the affair all along.

"You just seemed too relaxed." he kidded with him.

"You know, Cass. All joking aside, I don't fully understand it, but there has to be something more to this Perception thing...There has to be." Jack finished and dropped his hands limply to his sides. "They can't all be coincidences."

"That's how I feel, JB! That's why I...I mean, we have to find out." Casper was excited. "That's why I've devised this experiment. Because there is certainly something else. Something more."

"What do you have in mind?"

Casper turned to the console, and flipped on a few switches. In front of the console the pane of glass ignited, revealing an austere room behind it. Jack walked to the pane of glass and looked inside. He pressed his hand onto its cool surface. Inside the room there was a steel table with two steel chairs, a small cot, and three video cameras bolted in the corners of the ceiling. The walls were made of concrete, and were unadorned except for a solitary stereo speaker implanted into each of them. A microphone and a swinging lamp dangled from the ceiling over the table.

"There's a small sink and toilet over in the corner, but you can't see them from the window." Casper told him from the console, but Jack was speechless.

"What do you think?" Casper asked, joining Jack at the glass partition.

"I think it's a prison cell." Jack looked strangely at Casper.

"I prefer the term Isolation Chamber."

"Huh?" Jack was feeling uneasy already. "What the hell do you plan to do with this Isolation Chamber?"

"JB..." Casper touched him. "I'm sure you know that there are certain clinical scenarios that mimic the psychotic state."

Jack did not respond, and looked again through the partition at the Isolation room.

"LSD and the other ergots, are well known to promote psychosis and hallucinosis."

"Yeah...so?"

"A state clinically indistinguishable from schizophrenia has also been induced by amphetamine abuse, sensory deprivation, and sleep deprivation."

"I don't understand, Cass." Jack turned to him, but he was beginning to piece things together.

"Jack..." Casper moved closer "...I want you to make me psychotic."

"Are you fuckin' nuts?" Jack pushed him away. He was completely shocked. "You're already psychotic, Casper. What? You're gonna take LSD, and go bonkers? What's my role? I'm gonna watch you throw your career away? Is that the plan, Cass?! That's some fucking experiment! Jesus Christ!" Jack hurried away from the glass and Casper followed him.

"C'mon Jack!" he pleaded, chasing after him. "I wouldn't be that stupid."

"I'm not sure of that, Cass!"

"I wouldn't." Casper insisted, grabbing Jack by the arm now. "Trust me, I wouldn't. We can do this."

"Casper listen, I went to college in the sixties, and I don't care to relive them."

Casper released Jack's arm, and continued. "Jack, I need your help. You're the only person whose judgement I trust. I have no one else."

"Well, my good judgement says 'no'."

"Jack, just listen. It's not what you think."

"What is it then, Casper?"

"I have worked very hard on this. I have established safeguards. The Isolation Chamber is a very controlled environment, and you can terminate the experiment at anytime. You are one of those safeguards. I need you to be there."

"Casper, this is crazy." Jack shook his head.

"No Jack, it really isn't. You, yourself, even said that you believe in Perception...You believe, I know you do."

"I'm not peddling LSD for the sake of psychiatry."

"I don't need LSD, JB...I need only your time and cooperation."

Jack felt queasy. "What do you want me to do, Cass?"

Casper slowly approached him. "Okay, first of all, I have this Isolation Chamber set up, and I've worked very hard on it. I have tested all of the equipment. I have a plan and I know what I'm doing."

"Keep going..." Jack reluctantly listened.

"I will enter this chamber, and live inside of it for a month." Casper spoke plainly so there would not be any misunderstanding. "Nobody will miss me. I have no close family. And besides, the university will be glad to get rid of me for a while." Casper returned to the console and Jack reluctantly followed him.

"The experiment starts once I'm inside. From that day on, I will be sleep deprived, sensory deprived, and my food will be laced with legal amphetamines for twenty days. I'll be allowed two hours of sleep each day...No more and no less. I can take these sleep-hours one at a time, or both together. I just have to hit a button on the wall. After the twenty days are over, we will begin detoxification and psychiatric rehab. This is where you're most important. Hopefully you can return me to my demented baseline." Casper chuckled hoping that Jack would soften to the idea.

"I'm not gonna do this, Cass." Jack confirmed by shaking his head.

"You don't have to do most of it, JB. It's all automated, except the food of course. You're gonna have to give me that...and feed my fish." Casper pointed to Pontious and Pilot who swam in a small bowl by the console.

"So what else do you need me to do, Cass?"

"Just watch me, JB. Document me. Document what happens to me. I will need you to make sure that everything is running all right. You know, make sure that I am still alive and little stuff like that. Plus, I need you to conduct a daily psychiatric interview with me...for one hour."

Jack listened quietly, avoiding eye contact, while Casper continued to make his pitch.

"This one hour of interview per day will be the only human contact I'm allowed. The rest of my time will be spent alone in that room. You would watch me through the glass, take notes, and review the videotape from the night before. You can watch TV, read, and even leave for a while." Casper studied Jack for a reaction, but there was none. "You can even bring work from the office. This computer has all of the latest software...I'm sure you'd get a lot of busy work accomplished."

Jack's face twisted in thought.

"I have wired standard EEG electrodes to the stereo system. Two of the electrodes will be placed on my superior orbital ridges, just above my eyes. Anytime I close my eyes for more than fifteen seconds the stereo will blast the song *New York, New York* into the chamber. If I don't wake-up, the computer will administer a small shock."

"New York, New York?"

"Yeah, by old blue-eyes himself. It was the most obnoxious music I could come up with. The song will play, and play, and play until I open my eyes. The other electrodes will continuously record my brainwave activity. The amphetamines will help me stay awake, and hopefully hasten the evolution of psychosis."

Jack pretended to be uninterested, but he was growing curious.

"JB, there is more to the psychotic state, and I truly believe that there is a Perceptive state. My patients have proved this to me. They've proved it to you also, Jack. I need to find out if there is more. I need to know, please. Please Jack, help me."

Jack finally looked at Casper and shook his head. "Cass, do you realize what you're doing? Do you realize what you're asking me to do?"

"I want to cross that line, JB. I need to cross that line. I need you to document this for me. Review the videotape, and the EEG data. I trust you like a brother...I trust you like a father. I need you here to make sure that I cross this line safely. I need you to make sure that I come back in one piece."

"You're asking me to document your descent into psychosis, a schizophrenic like state?"

"Yes, but it is much more than that. I need you to ensure that I get there, and most of all, I need you to bring me back safely." Casper implored him.

Jack stared blankly at the floor and nodded.

"I need to find out if there is more, Jack. I need to know. I am searching for Perception. I know it's there. I've just got to find it."

Jack exhaled. He rubbed his eyes, and then the back of his head. He walked around the control room and then again to the glass partition. He turned to Casper, who was watching him intently.

"You're gonna do this anyway, aren't you Cass?"

"Yes...If I have to find someone else, I will."

Jack was still reluctant. "All I have to do is interview, watch, and document this?"

"Yes. That's all, and feed me and the fish."

Jack chuckled and contemplated the proposal for several minutes. He again paced the perimeter of the garage. "You know Cass..." He spoke loudly from across the room. "I have to say, it's an interesting idea. Very stupid, very reckless, but interesting nonetheless. Two psychiatrists document the progression from normalcy to psychosis. I would document this from a clinician's point of view, and you from a psychotic's point of view. Both of us have considerable insight into the psychotic state, and that documentation would be nothing short of sensational. But even if you did become psychotic, and God knows you don't have far to go..." Jack quipped and continued, "What makes you think you'll become Perceptive?"

Casper shrugged his shoulders. "I have no guarantee, but I will be looking for it. That's for sure...I will be looking for it."

"What about your practice and your patients? I have a practice too, and academic responsibilities. How do you plan to get around this?"

"Vacation...Something came up...Sabbatical. Take your pick. You'd have to do the same, for an entire month Jack. I'll need you here, from eight o'clock in the morning to six p.m."

This hit Jack hard. "Whoa! That's gonna be tough, Cass."

"I know JB, I know. But I will make it worth your while. I'll pay you in advance."

"I don't want your money, Cass."

"This experiment will be a landmark, JB. I guarantee it. We will turn psychiatry on its ear."

Jack was relenting and he knew it. He also knew that Casper was probably right. This experiment had the potential to be something extraordinary. Even if Casper never became Perceptive, he would likely become acutely psychotic. A well-constructed chronicle of this alone would be enough to attract international attention. Such attention was not an important consideration for Jack however. He has traditionally shunned the professional limelight. He felt that it was counterproductive to his scientific objectivism. He would never enter a study unless he was convinced of its merit. Unfortunately, the merit of Casper's experiment was undeniably convincing. He believed in Perception, and he believed in Casper.

"Okay." Jack relented. "I'll do it."

"Okay?!" Casper leaped at Jack. "I knew I could count on you, JB!"

"I'm gonna need time, Cass. I need to arrange coverage." Jack pushed him away. "It'll take some sweet talking to Gladys."

"It shouldn't be too hard, you can still take call at night. I just need you from eight a.m. to six p.m. Normal business hours."

"Give me two weeks. Perhaps Doctor Janice Clifford will cover me. She owes me a favor, or two." Jack mentally planned his sabbatical.

Casper further discussed the particulars of the experiment with Jack. He instructed him on the use of the computer, the software and other machinery. He pointed out the operational manuals and the trouble shooting protocols in the library. After giving Jack a brief tour of the Isolation Chamber, Casper then reminded him that he could terminate the experiment at any time. Jack expressed some last minute reservations, but ultimately he again agreed to participate.

It was a bit past noon when Jack and Casper left the garage. Casper hailed a cab from the corner, and asked Jack if he was heading uptown.

"No, no thanks Cass. I'll take the subway, and I've got some things to do." This was an obvious lie, but Jack just wanted time to think this out.

"Okay JB...Thanks again." Casper kissed him on the cheek.

"Sure."

Casper climbed into the back seat and pulled the door shut. He told the driver to wait a minute, and he rolled down the window. "Hey Jack."

"Yeah?" Jack turned, wiping the slobber from his cheek.

"Let's keep this between us...Until it's over, okay?"

"Not even Caroline?"

"Please, not even Caroline."

CHAPTER ELEVEN
♦♦♦♦♦

Jack returned to the Upper Eastside by subway, and stopped in a nearby deli to pick up lunch for he and Caroline. While waiting on line, he wondered what he should tell Caroline about the experiment. He considered not telling her at all, but she was probably going to ask him about it. He decided to tell her very little, because if she knew the details of Casper's experiment, she would certainly try to talk him out of it.

A man wearing a greasy white apron shuffled to the counter and asked Jack for his order. He purchased a loaf of bread, some cold cuts and then left the store.

Bicyclists and rollerbladers whisked through the traffic and weaved their way down Third Avenue. It was turning out to be a beautiful day, and people were heading to Central Park to socialize and work out. Jack did not feel like joining them today. He was too tense. He tucked the groceries under his arm, and turned down his block. At the door to his brownstone, several journals and the newspaper were stuffed into the mailbox. Jack briefly leafed through the mail, and placed the stack in the grocery bag as he entered.

"Honey?" Jack called to Caroline. "I'm home." There was no response.

"Caroline?" Jack entered the kitchen. She was not there either. He placed the groceries on the kitchen table, and unloaded its contents. He opened the refrigerator, pulled out a bottle of *Coca-Cola*, and poured himself a glass. There was a notepad on the counter, but there was no message on it.

He walked casually into the living room. "Caroline?.." The windows were slightly open, and a cool breeze rattled the venetian blinds. He checked the answering machine by the phone. Again there was no message. Returning through the kitchen, Jack placed his glass on the table and nervously turned up the steps. He suddenly collided with something big, white and fuzzy.

"Jack!" Caroline screamed. She was standing above him on the steps. She was wet, and her hand clutched the lapels of her robe. "You scared me!"

Jack's heart was pounding also. "I'm sorry, Honey...I came in and you were not around." he gasped, "I guess I got a little spooked or something."

"I was in the shower, and I heard something." Caroline was spooked herself.

"Oh, phew...okay..." Jack said as he and Caroline both recaptured their breath. "You hungry? I brought lunch home."

Caroline raised her eyebrows and smiled. "Good, I'll be right down." She hurried back up the steps, and turned into the bedroom. Jack returned to the kitchen and began to fix lunch. He thought again about the experiment. He did not want to lie to Caroline, especially after all they had been through, but he felt obliged to do so. Smearing mayonnaise onto a slice of white bread he decided to act cool, and minimize his meeting with Casper.

Caroline bounded down the steps, and joined Jack in the kitchen.

"That's a cute outfit." Jack said, she was wearing mismatching plaids and stripes.

"I'm setting a trend. All the kids will be doing it soon."

Jack continued to make sandwiches, mindlessly slapping roast beef and mustard together on the bread.

"How'd it go?" Caroline asked, and Jack cringed with indecision.

"Huh?"

"Your thing with Casper?"

"Oh, it went okay. He is certifiable though." Jack carried the plate of sandwiches over to the table, and sat next to Caroline.

"What did he want?"

Jack chomped into his sandwich, and washed the food down with a swig of *Coke*. "He wanted my collaboration on a project."

"Yeah?" Caroline fished for more information.

"Yeah, nothing big. Just a new drug protocol."

"Hmm..." Caroline bit into her sandwich and swallowed. "And he called you at six in the morning for that?"

"Yep. You know Casper." Jack chewed and talked simultaneously.

96

"How rude..." Apparently Caroline was not going to let this one drop. "What's it about?...Something exciting?"

Jack shrugged. "Somewhat interesting. It's just another placebo controlled randomized trial. Sounded like a lot of work to me."

"How much of a commitment does he want from you?"

"Pretty significant. I'll have to rearrange some of my outpatients, but that's not too bad. But it's gonna take us about a month to finish."

"So...You've decided to help him?"

"Uh-huh." Jack nodded, as if the experiment was inconsequential. "Off and on, I'll meet with him throughout the month."

"Oh..." Caroline finally grew disinterested.

"How's the book coming?" Jack changed the subject.

"Blocked, completely blocked." Caroline had been stuck on writing the same novel for two years. Although she attained a modest amount of success in writing children's books, her true passion was to complete a novel. She had been floundering on chapter twelve of the book for several months now. It was a story about a troubled psychiatrist and his devoted wife. It was more than a little autobiographical, but it really didn't bother Jack. It truly helped Caroline cope with the emotional pain he had caused her. It was necessary therapy as far as he was concerned. It helped her make sense of things. But Caroline was happier now, and the writing was often difficult. As the marital troubles faded, so did her creativity. And now, the novel that began as her pride and joy, had become a bit of a ball and chain.

After eating lunch, the two of them flipped through the pages of the Sunday *Times* and the mail. They affectionately held hands underneath the table and chatted. Jack then kissed her on the forehead, and retired to the study with several journals under his arm. Caroline grudgingly opened her laptop computer at the kitchen table, and began to type about her uneventful life.

The following morning, Jack awoke early and went for his morning run. He did not sleep well last night, being partly anxious and partly eager. He still felt somewhat sleepy and his legs stiffened quickly in the cool morning air. He decided to cut his run short and he returned home. He hopped into the shower, and then quickly dressed. Today was going to be a stressful day, and he needed to hit it head-on. First he had to rearrange his schedule to accommodate the month-long experiment. This would take some real smooth talking to get by Gladys. Then he would speak with an associate to arrange coverage during his absence. He had to notify the medical school as well, and cancel his upcoming preceptor rounds.

Jack entered his office. It was calm as usual, and two of his patients were reading quietly in the waiting room. He paused for a moment before entering. Although he felt a little apprehensive about the experiment, he was strangely invigorated. Was it the danger? Was it the novelty? The mystique? Jack could not explain it, but somehow Casper's experiment had revitalized his intellectual core. He shrugged defeatedly and smiled. In the waiting room, he warmly greeted his two patients, and proceeded to his secretary.

"Good morning, Gladys..." he greeted her and offered her a cup of coffee, "How was your weekend?"

"Good, and yours?" She knew something was up, and she continued her work at the desk.

Jack sighed, "Yep, the same old, same old. Nothing new to report." He continued around beside her, "Hey Gladys, what's my schedule look like next week?"

Gladys placed her pen on the desk, and looked up at him from under her bifocals. She was expecting the unexpected. "Packed." she barked at him.

"Hmm..." Jack cringed. "How about the week after that?"

Gladys roughly flipped a few pages in the appointment book. "Packed solid."

"I see..." Jack softly kicked his feet against her chair. "Gladys?"

"Jack?..." She playfully stopped his foot.

"Something's come up...And I need to cancel some appointments." he grimaced as he spit this out.

"Ugh..." Gladys gasped and flipped back the pages in the appointment book. "Where do you need time?" She was clearly annoyed.

"Uh...This whole month?" Jack said quickly.

"What!?" Gladys jumped to her feet, drawing the attention of the patients in the waiting room. "Is everything all right?"

"Shhh, Gladys." Jack grabbed her softly by the elbows and drew her out of view from the patients in the waiting area. "Everything's fine. Never been better actually."

"Why do you need a month?"

"I just do, Gladys...I just do."

"For what?!"

"I'm collaborating on a project, and it needs to be started immediately."

Gladys did not say anything. She looked up at the ceiling in frustration, and clenched both fists. "God, give me strength."

"I'm gonna finish up this week, Gladys...preferably with my more serious cases. Then I'll be pursuing this project for four weeks...and then I'll be back before you know it." Jack attempted to look her in the face.

"You're gonna help me on this, right?" Gladys asked politely, but this was really not negotiable.

"Sure, whatever it takes."

"Make a few phone calls?"

"Uh-huh."

"Okay..." She stomped over to her desk, and uncapped a yellow highlighter. She tore through the pages in the schedule book and began to highlight all of the upcoming appointments in yellow. The marker made a horrible squeaking noise, and Jack winced with each stroke of the pen. After she finished, she recapped the marker and tossed it onto the blotter.

"Start calling, Project Boy...I'll triage your first patients."

Jack smirked, and obediently picked up the phone. "Thanks Gladys, I really appreciate this."

"You're the boss."

Jack quickly made several phone calls. He started with his less dependent patients, and gingerly informed them of the cancellations. Most of them were content to follow up in one month's time. A few of them preferred to have an appointment with a covering psychiatrist. Jack then rescheduled his more acute patients for appointments this week, and finally arranged coverage with Doctor Clifford. He phoned in prescriptions to several pharmacies, and reviewed the day's charts.

Jack did not discuss the details of the experiment with Gladys, despite her incessant nagging. He reassured her that he would always be available by pager, and he would except emergency consultations after six p.m. only. He instructed her to forward all personal phone calls to his voice-mail service, which in-turn would activate his pager. After profusely thanking her again, he called in his first patient.

ooooooooo

Casper slugged back a cup of coffee, finishing it in big gulps. He wiped his mouth on his sleeve, and tossed the cup into a metal wastebasket on the street. He surveyed the parade of pretty nurses and social workers across the street. They turned and entered New York Hospital. He knew several of them quite intimately. He impatiently waited for the signal to change, and finally darted across First Avenue and up to the hospital's entrance. He barreled through the revolving doors, sending them swirling crazily for several seconds.

"Good morning!" Casper smiled, and slapped an unsuspecting security guard on the back. "Look alert everyone!"

"What's up, Doc?" the officer responded only after looking at Casper's identification tag.

Casper walked through the lobby and turned toward the elevator bank. He took the elevator up to the psychiatry floor and stepped off. Monday mornings were particularly chaotic in Casper's office, and today was no exception. Sara, his secretary, was already frazzled, and the patients were whipped into a psychotic frenzy.

"Smiles everyone...Smiles!" he shouted as he entered, and this simmered the patients somewhat.

"Help!" Sara smiled playfully, but pathetically.

After hushing the crowd, Casper spoke. "Sara...I'm so excited to be here today. I'm here to present the award for the Most Frightening

Lunatic, Not-*Presently-* Institutionalized category." He reached back to Sara, grinning like an anchorman on ecstasy, and she knowingly reached for a blank envelope. "And the nominees are..." Sara handed Casper the envelope. "Nominated for his excessive masturbation in public places, and intensely fierce mania...Tom Ferguson!" Tom blushed, and slowly unzipped his fly. Casper went on, "Nominated for performing a gruesome surgical procedure on her husband's genitals with a butter knife...Amanda 'the ball-butcher' Kutcher!" The ball-butcher clapped wildly and bounced in her seat, while Tom Ferguson quietly zipped himself back up. "For her work as Napoleon, Joan of Arc, Gerard Depardieu, and everyone that's French and annoying, we have the split personalities of...Christine Korbel! And lastly, nominated for his tireless work in the field of Coprophagia, a man who both *loves* and *knows* his shit...He's the lean, mean, poop-eating machine...Dean Michaels!" Casper gave them all a small round of applause. "Congratulations to all of our nominees, and in my book you're all winners! But as you know, there can be only one *true* winner..." Casper started to nervously fumble with the empty envelope. "God, I'm so nervous." After opening the flap, and taking a big, startled breath, he went on. "And the Most Frightening Lunatic Not-Presently-Institutionalized award goes to...Amanda Kutcher! Come on down!"

Applause was shared around the room, as Amanda Kutcher, a disorganized schizophrenic by diagnosis, jumped from her seat waving her arms over her head.

"Come on down, girl!" Casper said again, pushing and pointing her toward the office. He followed her at first, but then turned and called to Sara from the hallway.

"Yeah?" she answered.

"About next month?..." Casper poked his head around the corner.

"Yeah?"

"Cancel all my appointments."

"Huh?"

"No appointments after this week...okay? I won't be here for a month."

"What?...Where are you goin'?" Sara dumbly smacked her bubblegum.

"I hope, I'll be goin' crazy!..." He approached her, slobbering like a rabid dog. "With a little luck, I'll be going *crazy!*"

CHAPTER TWELVE
♦♦♦♦♦

The heavy rain had just about stopped, and now only drizzle wet the Village air. The alley next to Casper's garage was muddy and flooded with rainwater. Several puddles coalesced to form a murky lake, and a soggy cardboard home had collapsed upon itself by the back fence. Jack wiped the drizzle from his forehead, and reangled his umbrella. There was a set of footprints in the mud, and they led to the side door of the garage. Jack rolled up his pant leg, and carefully placed a loafer into the mud. It sank quickly, so he decided to just dart for the door.

Casper was in the Isolation Chamber, checking the equipment when Jack entered. It was seven-thirty in the morning. He had been tinkering for at least an hour already, going over some last minute details. Jack stomped his feet dry and closed his umbrella.

"Good morning, JB." Casper loudly greeted him through the microphone, as he tested the sound system. "Check, check...two, three, four...Check, check...Welcome to *McDonald's*, would you like to supersize your order?"

Jack laughed, and Casper clicked off the microphone. "Can you Karaoke with that thing, Cass?"

"Sure, we'll turn this place into a helluva niteclub when we're done, JB...How'd that sound?" Casper emerged from the chamber.

"Sounds all right to me."

Casper briefly refreshed Jack on the protocols and operations of the equipment. He turned the computer on, and made Jack demonstrate his proficiency in several technical situations.

"Hey did you bring any work with you?" Casper asked him.

"Yeah..." Jack removed a diskette from his jacket pocket. "I downloaded the information on all of my Depressives. I've been looking forward to stratifying their response to treatment for some time now. This experiment may give me a chance to do that."

"Sounds like real fun, JB." Casper was being sarcastic. "Let's give this baby a whirl. What do you say?"

Jack shrugged, and sat at the console. Casper entered the Isolation Chamber for a one-hour practice run. Jack watched the videotape, the EEG, and took occasional notes. Casper sat at the table in the chamber, and fixed the remote electrodes on his head. He intentionally closed his eyes. Fifteen seconds later the obnoxious music was triggered inside the chamber. Casper held his eyes tightly shut until he received a small shock.

"Whoa!" he shouted as his face spasmed. The music promptly stopped when he opened his eyes. "That's the perfect amount of juice for me."

"You are fucking crazy." Jack whispered to himself.

"Now Jack..." Casper yelled into the mirrored window. He could not see out, but Jack could see in. "When I press this red button by the door, it will deactivate the music so I can sleep. One push and the music is deactivated for one hour...Two pushes, and it is deactivated for two hours. But that's it. It can only be deactivated for two hours per day." Casper first turned away and surveyed the room one last time. Everything appeared to be in order. He returned to the wall, and knocked three times on the mirror.

"Okay Jack...Let me out."

Jack unlocked the chamber door, and Casper stepped out.

"Looks like all systems are go!" Casper clapped his hands together.

"Yeah, just a few more things, Cass."

"What?"

"I can't speak to you through this microphone?" Jack tapped a chrome grill on the console. "I tried several times, but you apparently couldn't hear me."

"That's not a microphone, JB. That's a speaker. You can hear what is going on in the chamber at any time."

"Oh?..." Jack was puzzled for a moment. "So how do I speak with you?"

"You don't, JB. I don't want you to...Only during our daily interview."

"What if there is an emergency?"

"There won't be."

"But, what if there is?"

"Well then, I guess you would have to stop the experiment."

"Uh-huh, I see." Jack nodded, and pushed several buttons on the console. The three monitors on the console turned on. Two of the screens showed the inside of the Isolation Chamber from different angles, and the third was tuned to *CNN*.

"That one has cable, but it can also be used as a third monitor." Casper pointed at the television like a proud father.

"Wow Cass...Pretty impressive, any premium channels?" he quipped, slapping Casper on the back.

"Hey, I'm not running a hotel here, Jack."

Jack smirked, but then recalled an important question. "Oh, Cass!...What about the food?" ·

Casper raised his hand, pointing a finger into the air. "Good thing you asked. The fish food is in the drawer. Feed my boys once a day. As far as I'm concerned, you can get me anything you want. But I prefer Italian and Mexican. Junk food's okay. Treat yourself to anything, but mix it up a little for me, would you? And caffienated beverages only, please. The money for all of our meals is also in the top drawer of the desk...and..." Casper walked over to a large closet, and opened it. Boxes of new videotapes, and supplies were stacked on the shelves. Casper walked inside, and Jack followed him.

"Over here are the videotapes, and the labels...Over here are the amphetamines." Casper pointed to a caseload of *Primatene* tablets.

"What is this Casper?...A case of *Primatene*? Isn't that an asthma medication?" Jack picked up one of the small boxes.

"Yeah...It's also an amphetamine. The active ingredient is Ephedrine Hydrochloride, a stimulant." Jack nodded, and Casper continued. "There is twelve-point-five milligrams in each tablet. Grind up three tablets and mix the powder into each meal...Breakfast, lunch and dinner...That's thirty-seven point-five milligrams with each meal, and nine tablets a day. I have more than enough here to last the entire month. They thought I was nuts at the pharmacy."

Jack flipped to the back of the medication box, and read the precautions. "I don't blame them." He casually tossed the box back into the case.

Casper picked up a smaller case from the shelf and opened it. Inside there was an empty syringe, a sterile needle, and two bottles of injectable

Haldol, the powerful sedative and antipsychotic. There were ten milligrams in each vial, and Jack had little doubt what this was for.

"Just in case things get out of hand, JB. Just in case." Casper shut the box and placed it back on the shelf.

Jack left the closet, and Casper shut the door behind them. "I believe that's all, JB. Any questions?" Casper dropped his hands to his sides.

Jack shrugged and shook his head. "Nope."

Casper dropped the keys into Jack's palm.

"Okay then...Let's get started!" Casper entered the chamber, and sat in one of the chairs by the table. He began to re-fix the EEG electrodes onto his scalp, and Jack came in to help him. They talked about some last minute details, until all of the electrodes were in place. When they were finished, Casper stood up, fixed the wires attached to his head, and looked at himself in the mirror.

"Cute." His voice softened.

"Are you okay with this, Casper?"

"Yep."

"Positive?"

"Absolutely."

Jack turned to leave the Isolation Chamber, when Casper called to him. "Hey Jack..."

"Yeah."

"Thanks."

"You got it."

"I'll see you tomorrow."

Jack nodded, and left the Isolation Chamber. He locked Casper inside. He sat at the console, and started the videotape. He watched Casper through the window. He was pacing the floor, like a caged animal. He walked the entire perimeter of the chamber several times, and then sat at the table. Mindlessly drumming his fingers, and smacking his lips, Casper finally relaxed. Jack flipped the switch on the computer, and began to type.

Day One: 10:57
Subject entered the chamber at 10:57hrs. He was mildly anxious, but he was psychologically within normal limits.

EEG: Normal background activity, at 9 megahertz per second, and occipital predominance of the alpha rhythm.
　　　　　　　　　　　　　　　　　-JB

○○○○○○○○

Jack stepped out briefly around one o'clock in the afternoon for lunch. He stopped at a nearby pizzeria, and ordered two dishes of baked ziti. When he returned to the garage, he noticed that the continuous EEG tracing was jagged and jumping. He dropped the food on a small table in the lounge, and he ran to the window. Casper was on the floor doing push-ups. Jack heaved a sigh of relief, and then turned to the console. He typed on the keyboard.

Day One: 13:28
EEG recognized as wildly abnormal. This abnormality is an artifact. Subject was exercising.　　　-JB

Jack mixed three tablets of the *Primatene* into the ziti, and he watched the white chunks disappear into the ricotta cheese. He grabbed two cans of *Coca-Cola*, and slid the food through a slot in the door. He heard Casper shuffle over to the door, so he quickly shut the slot.

Several hours after lunch, Casper was again wandering aimlessly around the chamber. He was only hours into the experiment, and he was bored to death already. He turned to the mirrored window, and raised his eyebrows. He looked at his own reflection and wondered if Jack was watching him. "I can't wait to go crazy, JB...Maybe it'll bring a little excitement into this place."

Backing up, Casper glanced for a moment at his physique. His chest was pumped up with lactic acid from the push-ups. He suddenly felt the ziti snaking through the loops of his bowels.

"Jack?..." Casper asked through the glass. "I'm gonna take a dump now." The toilet was cornered in such a way that it was not seen on camera, nor could it be seen from the window. It was a functional blind spot. There were some things that good friends should not share. Near the toilet, there was a small sink, but otherwise the chamber was without personal amenities.

OOOOOOOO

Jack had a strange feeling when he awoke the following morning. He did not recall having a nightmare, yet he had a sense of impending doom. Casper was alone in the garage for the first time last night, and Jack felt very insecure about this. He quickly showered and left the brownstone early. He did not take the subway, and instead opted for a cab.

He arrived at the garage a little past seven a.m., and he immediately looked through the mirrored window. Casper was alive and well. He paced the floor tiredly as Jack let out a sigh of relief.

Before preparing breakfast, he rewound the two eight-hour videotapes from overnight. He played them simultaneously, on fast forward. While scanning the events from the night before on the two monitors, he mixed the crushed *Primatene* into a styrofoam container of scrambled eggs and bacon. He opened the slot, removed the dinner tray from last night, and left the breakfast tray with a warm cup of coffee. He shut the slot securely, and returned to the console. After lunch he planned to conduct a brief psychiatric interview with Casper.

Jack tuned the television to *CNN*, and absorbed the morning news. There was nothing but bad news to report. Between sips of coffee, he reviewed the EEG data collected by the computer, and then began to write.

Day Two: 08:00
The subject appears to be tired, but in good spirits. He has not yet manifested any overt psychiatric disturbance.

Videotape reviewed from overnight: No abnormal events. There was only one episode of music triggering last night, at approximately 04:00 hours.

EEG reviewed: Again, no focal disturbance. Mostly fast, alpha activity with occasional slower theta activity. No sleep, or K-complexes on the record.

-JB

Casper devoured his breakfast, and he wiped his mouth with a napkin. He still felt tired, but was somewhat rejuvenated. Becoming a little nostalgic, he recalled his year as an intern at Yale. During this first year of residency training, it was still commonplace to work thirty-five hours straight. At times they worked one hundred-twenty hours per week. He stretched and walked to the mirrored window, flexing his tired muscles defiantly. Jack was probably watching him, and Casper felt like grandstanding. He cupped both hands around his mouth and breathed into them. Sniffing the stale air in his palms, he crinkled his face.

"I'll brush before our interview."

○○○○○○○○

Shortly after lunch, Jack removed a yellow legal pad from the drawer in the console and unlocked the door to the chamber. Casper smiled when he heard the bolts turning. It had been over twenty-four hours since he had seen anyone, and he was looking forward to the interview with Jack.

Jack stepped into the Isolation Chamber, and shut the door. He was clean-shaven, and well dressed as usual. "Good morning, Cass...How ya doin'?"

"Hey, JB! It's been a long twenty-four hours...I feel like an intern again!" Casper laughed, and Jack sat with him at the table. He pushed the lunch tray aside. Casper looked well, except for his unkempt hair, which was studded with electrodes. Casper's habit of partying all night had probably helped him, or perhaps it was just the amphetamines. The two men then talked briefly about their first day experiences.

"Let's get started..." Jack stopped the small talk abruptly.

"Okay." Casper responded, but he silently cursed Jack. He was always so rigid, always sticking to protocol. He was so perfect for this experiment, and Casper realized the importance of this. "You're the shrink."

Jack led Casper through a small series of mental tasks, and then conducted a modified mental status exam. There were no definite abnormalities. Casper's mathematical, and linguistic abilities remained above normal, and there was no demonstrable lack of insight or judgement. Jack then asked Casper to describe his feelings during the first day of the experiment.

"It fucking sucked...I was bored, JB...Bored to death."

"At any time did you hear voices?"

"No."

"See anything out of the ordinary."

"No."

"Well, what types of things did you do to amuse yourself?"

"I tried to do nothing, JB. That's the point! I can't tell you how many freakin' times I picked up that tube of toothpaste and was tempted to read the back, the ingredients, the manufacturer...anything!" Casper pointed to the sink, and then frustratedly ran his fingers over some of the electrodes on his head. "But that would be counterproductive to the experiment...I need as much sensory deprivation as possible, and even though the back of the toothpaste is not all that exciting...It was the best thing I had last night. But I resisted the temptation."

"The tube of toothpaste?...You wanted to read that?"

"Yep. Anything...The back of the soda cans, the coffee cup...I had to resist that all." Casper shook his head at the sudden ridiculousness of this.

"Quite a conflict, huh?"

"You could not believe, JB, like you could not believe."

After several more questions, Jack and Casper exchanged good-byes, and Jack left the chamber. Casper was again alone, and he pushed the two chairs neatly under the table. There was no more housekeeping to do, so he simply folded his arms across his chest, leaned against a wall, and thought. He thought mostly about the length of the experiment, and wondered if he would be able to make it. He doubted it actually. It was too long, and secretly he wished he had made it shorter. Even tonight was going to be difficult for him. He was already feeling tired and frequently yawning. After only twenty-four hours, he was sure of only one thing...This long, and painful wait for madness was going to kill him.

Jack added some notes to the computer diary. He included a brief discussion of the psychiatric interview with Casper.

Day Two: 15:30
...and there was a subtle hint of submission in the subject's voice. While I know him to be self-secure, confident, and frankly arrogant, his persona is much attenuated today. He apparently has relinquished some control of the experiment, both to the automation and me. There was no lack of judgement or insight, and despite fatigue, the subject performed in the superior range on subjective mental tasks.
-JB

Jack's beeper was going off. There were several messages on his voice-mail, and a page from his office. Caroline called about picking up something for dinner, and Doctor Clifford called regarding one of his patients. Jack responded to Doctor Clifford first, and then called his wife. Caroline did not ask any particulars about his day, and instead they chatted about dinner plans. Jack watched Casper through the mirror as Caroline talked about something, and then he briefly looked at the EEG monitor. Still there were no abnormalities. Jack was expecting mild abnormalities to start appearing in the next twelve hours, as Casper grew progressively more tired. But as of right now, he was doing fine.

"...so I said, I'll ask Jack how he feels..." Caroline was still talking, and Jack had missed a large portion of what was said. "...What do you think, Jabes?"

"Huh?" Jack forgot to conceal his preoccupation.

"You weren't even listening, Jabes." Caroline was used to this.

"God, I'm sorry Honey...I'm just preoccupied. What was that again?"

"The publisher. They won't officially accept the manuscript without an agent, but they will send it to a first reader when it's finished...No money of course."

"Well that's terrific, I'd send it." Jack changed the montages on the computerized EEG machine. This allowed him to analyze Casper's brainwaves from different electrical standpoints. "We don't need the money. Getting it to the editor is the hard part, right?"

"That's what I think...So this is good?"

"Excellent, Babe, excellent. How's it coming?"

"Chapter twelve is...done."

"Done!...Great babe, so there's reason to celebrate." Jack was truly happy for his wife, and after saying goodbye to her, he turned his attention back to Casper, and the EEG. He counted the number of cycles per second on the screen--Still normal.

OOOOOOOOO

Day Three: 09:15
Upon arrival this morning, the subject was barely awake. In fact, he shut his eyes shortly after my arrival, only to be awakened by the triggering of the music. This cycle was repeated several times.

The patient was given his breakfast, which he did not completely finish. The patient appears exhausted, and his behavior is slowly becoming repetitive, and predictable (i.e. Washes face, scratches head and paces). There is an occasional myoclonic jerk when the subject nearly falls asleep, and this is seen on the EEG as well.

Videotape reviewed: Subject frequently triggered the music last night. At one point, approximately 20:00 hours he required a small electric shock to be aroused. There were no overt signs of psychosis, or hallucinosis on the screen, but the subject has now resorted to talking to himself quite frequently.

EEG reviewed: Patient is sleepy on this record, with intermixed brainwave activity suggestive of both stage-one sleep (drowsiness), and stage-four sleep (deep sleep). Periods of REM sleep, the stage in which dreaming takes place, was also present on this record. These are confounding findings.

There is some electrical evidence of sleep, but at no time during the video record was the subject sleeping.
-JB

Jack could not believe what he was seeing. He reviewed the EEG data and the videotape several times. He had never seen this before, and he searched through the many textbooks in the library. Apparently no one else had seen this phenomenon before either. Casper's EEG clearly demonstrated periods of sleep, and dream stages, but strangely during the entire sixteen hours of videotape, Casper was awake.

CHAPTER THIRTEEN
◆◆◆◆◆

"Casper?"

It was day five of the experiment, and Casper had now progressed to the point of extreme lethargy. When questioned, he answered slowly and deliberately. Dark circles had formed under both eyes, and his head swiveled weakly on his neck.

"What?" he mumbled in return. His eyelids were drooping, and finally they closed completely. A few seconds later, Frank Sinatra's *New York, New York*, trumpeted off the walls of the Isolation Chamber. Jack covered his ears. The music inside the cement room was frankly deafening. A small shock followed. Casper's face convulsed and his eyes popped open.

"What?"

"Do you remember your name?"

"Uh-huh...I do."

"What's your name?"

"Cass...Casper." His eyelids sagged again and his eyeballs rolled backwards in the sockets. He was so tired now. He tried to concentrate on staying awake, but his ability to concentrate was failing him. Although he was profoundly fatigued, there was a new and strange sensation in his head. This was not ordinary exhaustion. The sensation was almost indescribable. There was a definite mental malfunction. It was a subtle, but definite, disruption among the neurons in his head. His brain was short-circuiting. He could not stop the dysfunction, and he was painfully aware of this.

"Do you remember what we're here for?" Jack carefully watched him and took notes. After a steady deterioration, Casper had been relatively stable for the last twenty-four hours. His fatigue progressed to the point of frank exhaustion sometime during day four. Currently Casper had stopped progressing, and had reached some sort of weary equilibrium.

Casper nodded and mumbled, "Perception...perception...perception..."

"What is the year, Casper? What is the year?"

"Perception...perception...perception."

Casper closed his eyes again, and Jack braced himself for the loud music. No anticipation was enough however, and Jack was startled by the big-band theme song anyway. Casper did not wake, and several seconds later he was jolted back to reality again by a small electric shock.

"Whoa!" Casper opened his eyes. "Hey, JB." he said with a faint smile.

"Casper? What is forty-two times eight?"

"Huh?..."

"Multiply forty-two by eight." Jack pushed the pad in front of Casper. "You can use the paper."

"Forty-two by two?" Casper could not retain the simple equation that was posed to him. Recurrent bursts of negative activity stunned his brain. The very purpose of thought was eluding him.

"No...Forty-two by eight...Can you do that?"

"I can't, JB...Multiply what?"

"That's okay, Cass. Forget about it. That's all for today."

Jack stood, and took the pad and pen away from Casper. His ability to concentrate had really deteriorated. He was equally impaired linguistically, and mathematically. His thinking had also assumed a more concrete pattern, and his ability for abstraction was almost non existent.

Jack left Casper listlessly sitting at the table when he exited. No sooner than the deadbolt was locked, the young psychiatrist fell asleep once again. He slept peacefully, immersed in resounding Frank Sinatra, for a few blissful seconds...Then there was the shock.

Once outside, Jack sat at the console and watched Casper through the mirror. He was trapped in an endless cycle of sleep, music and electricity. Jack pressed the button on the console, and he could hear inside the chamber.

"...I wanna wake up, in a city...that doesn't sleep."---SHOCK!

"How appropriate." Jack mumbled to himself and depressed the speaker button. The room was silent again. He turned to the computer, and entered the day's events.

Day Five: 12:30
The subject is progressing to apathy. He is languid most of the day, and only occasionally shuffles across the room to urinate, and defecate. He is responsive, however, and despite the concentration difficulties, and concrete thinking, I am hesitant to call this state psychosis. The patient has neither delusions, nor hallucinations.

The videotape shows little difference from hour to hour. Mostly inaudible utterances, and inactivity.

The EEG was reviewed. There is still this strange intermixed pattern. The alpha rhythm, the rhythm that is associated with conscious thought, has just about disappeared. BUT the patient is still minimally conscious. Furthermore, diffuse slow REM activity, in the delta range now dominates his brain wave activity...But he is not actively dreaming--Or is he?

-JB

OOOOOOOO

Day Seven: 13:45
The subject has now progressed to total catatonia. He no longer mumbles to himself. Nor does he respond to my questioning. He rocks in the corner most of the day, and he has not finished a meal in several days. I have resorted to feeding him the *Primatene* directly during our interview time. He has been urinating on himself, and defecating on himself. I cleaned it as best I could.

He also exhibits waxy flexibility (When I position his limbs, he holds that position like a statue)-- Complete Catatonia.

His current condition is concerning to me from a medical standpoint. I have taken his vital signs, and these remain stable. However, his current status is still worrisome, and I may terminate the experiment in another day.

Unlike previous days, his eyes are open today. In fact, they blink only rarely. His EEG has slowed to a burst suppression pattern. This is usually seen with near death, or severe brain injury. This is clearly not the case in this subject, and the clinical significance of his EEG record remains to be established.

-JB

Casper rocked rhythmically in the corner. He was buried in a chaotic blackness. He could no longer distinguish between taste, touch, sound, sight or smell. His brain was a disorganized mass of misfiring neurons. Opposing neuronal forces fired at the same time, inhibiting one another, and the result was a static state of confusion. Worse yet, his ability to appreciate his current condition was lost with his other faculties. His brain was stunned and paralyzed. He was more than catatonic, he was completely unaware of himself.

OOOOOOOO

Jack washed the sweat off of his body, and the salty water swirled around the drain in his shower. He had tossed and turned all night, and just about saturated the bedsheets. Rubbing a soapy lather into his head, he cursed himself. He should end the experiment. He had no doubt about this now. Casper had been disintegrating before his eyes, and Jack had done nothing to help him. In fact, Jack had probably hurt him by not ending the experiment earlier. But Casper worked so hard, and was so adamant about completing the project, that Jack was reluctant to dismiss it as a failure.

After eight long days of sleep deprivation, sensory deprivation, and amphetamine abuse, Casper was nothing more than a zombie. No definitive evidence of psychosis had developed, and Jack doubted that it ever would. Now on the ninth day of the project, Jack arrived at the garage discouraged and completely depressed. The experiment must end today.

The alleyway was carpeted with dry mud, and Jack quietly shuffled over to the side door of the garage. The morning sun felt warm on the back of his neck, and he briefly stretched his soar muscles. He removed the chain and lock, jiggled his key chain and searched for the key to the deadbolt. Suddenly, he heard someone singing in the alleyway.

"I'm king of the hill...Top of the heap..."

"Excuse me?" Jack asked while scanning the alleyway, but there was no response. He stepped halfway into the alley. "Hello?" he whispered, "Is somebody there?" Again there was no response, and Jack ventured further down the alley. He accidentally stepped on a styrofoam cup, and it made a loud crunching noise. This startled him momentarily.

"Is everything alright?" he asked, looking through the piles of trash.

There was a small amount of movement in front of him, and Jack cautiously approached. A homeless couple was quietly sleeping underneath an old box spring, but the rest of the alley appeared to be uninhabited. Jack was puzzled. He shrugged this off to stress, and then quietly tiptoed back to the door, careful not to rouse the sleeping indigents. After wriggling a key through the lock, he turned it and pushed the door open.

Jack hung his coat on the back of the door, and placed the breakfast on the console. He proceeded immediately to the mirrored window. At first he did not see Casper, and Jack stretched his neck to visually inspect all four corners of the Isolation Chamber. Casper finally appeared by the sink. He was walking again, slowly shuffling across the room. His eyes were open, and he was mouthing something. Jack returned quickly to the console, pressed the speaker button and listened into the chamber.

"Person...person....person..." Casper's voice was audible, but barely intelligible.

Jack watched him as he pulled a chair out from under the table and sat on it. The EEG pattern was somewhat improved, but it was still wildly abnormal. Dream stages still dominated the rhythm, but it was now intermixed with some faster activity. Jack walked back to the cold glass, and pressed his forehead against it.

"I'll be damned." he said.

Day Nine: 15:25
Thankfully the subject has started to improve. In fact, it was my intention to end the experiment when I arrived this morning. But during our daily interview, he was able to communicate that this was not his wish. When told about my intention to terminate the experiment, he responded simply..."No."

The subject is still extremely lethargic, with disorganized thoughts. This leads me to believe that the subject may have lost the capacity to make such decisions for himself. I will carefully observe him for now, and if subject does not continue to improve, I will have a low threshold for stopping the experiment.

-JB

OOOOOOOO

"Good afternoon, Casper."

It was day ten of the experiment, and Casper was at the sink when Jack entered the chamber. He picked up the tube of toothpaste, and then forcefully placed it back down on the sink.

"Are you going to come sit, Cass?" Jack offered him a chair.

"Humph..." Casper mumbled something, and reluctantly picked up the tube of toothpaste again, only to place it firmly back on the sink. This action was repeated several times. Finally Casper tossed the toothpaste into the sink, and ran the water for a few seconds. The compulsion to read the back of the toothpaste was broken. Casper then turned awkwardly and shuffled over to the table. His ability to ambulate had significantly improved, but his gait was still deliberate and unsteady. His mouth was cracked and dry, but he managed a faint smile.

"Hey, JB." he said, as he sat at the table across from Jack. Jack noted a few observations on his pad. Casper had been at the sink for several hours, battling with the toothpaste. This was truly a showdown between impulse control and compulsion. So far, Casper had managed to remain in control. Jack conducted the interview and found that Casper had improved in a variety of cognitive abilities. He still had marked impairment of judgement and insight.

"What does the saying, *One swallow does not make a summer,* mean?"

Casper looked up into his forehead. He was either searching for an answer, or an effective means of processing the question. He was stumped regardless.

"What does that mean, Cass?"

"In the summer...you can eat a hamburger...You sometimes swallow it."

Concrete thinking! Jack scribbled on the bottom of his notes, and underlined it several times.

○○○○○○○○

Casper appeared euphoric this morning, inappropriately so. At times he would laugh to himself for no apparent reason. Unlike the previous two mornings he did not confine himself to the small area by the sink and toilet. Apparently, he had overcome his strange obsession with the toothpaste. This morning, he was pacing the floor vigorously, almost eagerly, and yammering in a low voice to himself.

Jack pressed the speaker button on the console, and listened into the chamber. He was repeating something, but Jack could not distinguish exactly what Casper was saying. The words were long, garbled, and possibly mispronounced. Jack could not tell. He rewound the videotapes from overnight, and examined the EEG record.

Day Ten: 10:30
Casper spent most of the night pacing the floor, and talking to himself. He did occasionally wander off camera, presumably to use the bathroom, and possibly to play with the toothpaste. But only a few of these 'visits' were seen overnight.

Videotape reviewed: Again, most of the night was comprised of walking and nonsensical speech. No abnormal events witnessed. His stereotypic behaviors persist, but to a lesser degree, and he has not developed any new automatisms.

No music triggering last night. No definite hallucinations.

It is becoming apparent to me that the subject has grown stronger over the last several days, both mentally, and physically. This is despite the fact that he has not slept in nine nights. Furthermore, I get the vague sense that he may be enjoying himself.

EEG reviewed: Unlike his clinical picture, the EEG record becomes more bizarre with each passing day. There is still a predominance of variable slow, dream like activity, but now there are frequent bursts of faster activity. Some of these are quite long. I have never seen a record like this, nor have I found a similar example in the psychiatric or neurological literature.

-JB

OOOOOOOO

Casper's head was tilted downward, almost shamefully. There was something wrong with him. There was a distinctive malice in his eyes today. They were unblinking and fixated, lurking suspiciously in the thickets of his wild hair.

"Sodium Fluoride." he said, barely opening his mouth.

Jack was a little unsettled by this but he dispassionately stared back at him. "What are you talking about?"

"Sodium fluoride, 0.15 percent fluoride ion, in a dentifrice base of Sorbitol, Water, Sodium Bicarbonate, Hydrated Silica, Glycerin, Sodium Lauryl Sulfate, Sodium Carbonate, Flavor...Cellulose Gum, Sodium Saccharin, and FD&C Blue number one...That's all." Casper cleared his throat, giggled, then his eyes locked on Jack.

He had read the back of the toothpaste. Impulse control had surrendered to irresistible compulsion. Jack was not surprised, and he quietly placed the pad on the table. He recapped his pen and placed it back in his pocket. After several seconds of intentional silence, Jack attempted to probe Casper's mind further.

"What have you learned from reading that tube of toothpaste, Cass? What did you gain?" Both psychiatrists were unflinching.

"If you have any questions or comments about the product, you can call the hotline at 1-800-492-7378."

Day Eleven: 13:00
...The subject has grown mildly antagonistic. He no longer answers many of the interview questions, or complies with the tasks set before him. However, I believe that the patient continues to improve in many realms--As evidenced by his remarkable memory, and mathematical skills.

Judgement and insight remain impaired as far as I can tell.

EEG remains intermixed, slow activity (dream), with occasional bursts of apparent consciousness.

Videotape reveals a lot of physical activity. (i.e. examining walls, furniture, cameras, the sink, toilet, and the mirror.) Furthermore, the subject has not triggered the music in two nights with the exception of last night...Where it appeared to be...intentional?

-JB

OOOOOOO

Eight o'clock, and Casper was alone in the chamber. After devouring dinner, he felt reborn. His youthful exuberance had finally returned, and he felt great for the first time in nearly two weeks. He looked into the mirror and admired himself.

"Cass, you are so damn handsome! Yeah baby." He removed his shirt and danced seductively for the three cameras.

"And what a bod! Like a porn star." He flexed, and posed in front of the mirrored wall.

Casper raved about himself a little longer, and then exercised for about an hour and a half. The air was stale and warm in the chamber, and he was quickly soaked. Sweat droplets ran down his gruff jaw and plopped onto his chest. His body was much more defined now. After ten sleepless nights, and eleven amphetamine-powered days, his body was leaner, and meaner than it ever had been before.

"Grrrr....Jack....Grrr." he growled.

You look good Cass! A voice complimented him.

"I sure do."

I think so too! Silky smooth. Another voice from the mirror.

Damn straight!

"Mirror, mirror on the wall, who's the fairest shrink of all?" Casper spun in front of the mirror.

Can't keep you down man! Step aside and let the man go through.

"Let the man go through, let me go through! Let me go through!"

Cass, you can have it all.

Come join us.

"Perception will be mine!"

Yours and only yours!

"Mine! All mine!" Casper grabbed his crotch, and rudely gestured to the mirror.

We've got to take care of JB first though.

"Fucking old parasitic bastard!"

We'll deal with him later! But for now let's enjoy one another.

"How does a little Frank Sinatra sound?"

Perfect! Let's do it...his way.

Casper shut his eyes tightly and the big band began. He continued to hold his eyes closed and he ultimately received a shock. He convulsed wildly, but did not open them.

"Woooo, wooo..." He jumped around the room as the music continued. Casper clenched his eyes even tighter, and sang along with the music.

"Start spreading the news...I'm leaving today." SHOCK, twitch, and Casper was on his toes again. "I want to be a part of it...New York, New York." SHOCK, SHOCK! He still held his eyes closed. "These vagabond shoes...Are longing to stray...." SHOCK, and a tear squeezed out from under Casper's eyelid.

"Right through the very heart of it...New York..." SHOCK. "New York!" SHOCK, SHOCK.

○○○○○○○○

The following morning when Jack arrived, Casper was sitting still at the table. His face was expressionless, and his arms dangled loosely at his sides. The skin under the electrodes was hot and almost charred. Some of the leads had popped completely off of his scalp. The unmistakable odor of singed flesh filled the Isolation Chamber, and a thin layer of moisture coated the mirror.

There was a flashing red light on the console signaling epileptic events, or convulsions. Jack was alarmed and he glanced at the video monitors. Casper was clearly not seizing. Then Jack reviewed the computer's EEG record. The computer had recorded multiple short bursts of electrical activity across Casper's brain. He rewound the videotapes.

There were hundreds of these electric events in the computer's EEG record, and Jack stopped one of the videotapes somewhere in the middle. He watched the monitor. On the video, Casper was singing and dancing with his eyes closed tightly. Then there was a shock, and a convulsion. Jack rubbed his eyes. "My Lord..."

CHAPTER FOURTEEN
◆◆◆◆◆

Day Twelve: 11:00
This has truly been a bizarre night. The subject spent most of the night, singing and intentionally shocking himself. This was accomplished by closing his eyes, and holding them closed despite the loud music, and application of electrical stimuli. The subject appeared to be in discomfort each time he was shocked, yet he still held his eyes closed. Masochism would be the best description of his behavior last night...He seemed to be enjoying the pain he was inflicting upon himself.

The masochistic behavior ceased in the early morning hours, just prior to my arrival (About 07:45). Since that time the subject has been lethargic, and sitting at the table.

There were also periods where he was apparently talking to himself, but now in a conversational manner. From the video record, I cannot tell if he is experiencing any true auditory hallucinations.

EEG reviewed: External electrical discharges in fifteen-second intervals, throughout the night. According to the computer record, the subject received 716 electrical shocks across his temples last night.

-JB

OOOOOOO

After lunch Casper had almost fully recovered from his fitful night. He rubbed a patch of dried saliva from his hairy chin, and gulped a mouthful of *Coca-Cola*. The caramel flavor coated the back of his mouth and he swallowed the painful little bubbles. His eyes were bloodshot and outlined by dark rings. He massaged them with his palms and then looked around the chamber.

There was a tremendous cockroach crawling across the wall, and Casper shuddered in disgust. He could not believe his eyes. The garage was immaculate. There was nothing in the Isolation Chamber that would attract such a vermin. He rubbed his eyes again and this blurred his vision for a few seconds. Gradually the fuzzy brown image on the wall resolved back into a giant cockroach. Casper jumped to his feet and followed the unwanted pest. It was huge and ugly, perhaps an entirely new species. The six-legged monster crawled rapidly across the wall toward the sink and toilet. Once on the porcelain ledge of the sink, it crawled across Casper's toothbrush and stopped for a moment as the crazed psychiatrist approached. The bug was in big trouble. They both knew it. It suddenly tried to flee but awkwardly slipped into the basin of the sink. Its six spindly legs kicked violently in the air, a survival reflex that would not work this time.

Turn on the hot water Cass!
Burn it to hell.

Casper turned on the faucet, and the roach was tossed again onto its belly by a wave of steamy tap water. The huge bug scampered around the drain, but finally managed to climb out of the sink. It crawled along the ledge, sampling the unfriendly air in the chamber with its long antennae. It stopped again, paralyzed by its own hesitation. Casper's menacing figure was towering over the frozen insect. He acted quickly and decisively. He cupped his hands over the bug and trapped it on the sink. The roach scampered desperately underneath his hands, running from palm to palm. Casper slowly brought his hands together, and pinched the insect between his fingers. He held it up, and looked into its dark eyes.

Millions of years of evolution!
Still no match for us!

"How does it feel to look into the eyes of your executioner?" Casper asked the bug, as its legs thrashed uselessly in the air.

There's not enough respect for our power, Cass!

"Do you realize the power I have?" Casper shook the insect violently. "Do you fear nothing you disgusting piece of shit?"

Show it what fear is, Cass!

Show it the power we possess!

Casper pulled the roach closer to his face, and slowly yanked an antenna from the insect's head. The bug wriggled in painful confusion, and Casper laughed. "A little unpleasant, isn't it?" Casper tugged lightly on the remaining antenna, before pulling it out as well. He dropped the wounded bug to the floor, and it circled aimlessly at his feet.

Act with no mercy!

Deliberate!

Casper removed one of his shoes, and held it high over his head. "May all who witness this fear me." He crashed the shoe onto the roach, splattering its guts on the floor. The insect's hard protective shell cracked completely in half, making an obscene crunching noise.

"Die parasite!" Casper struck the carcass again and again.

Die parasite!

Jack was watching all of this transpire from the console. Casper was behaving very strangely, repeatedly smashing his shoe into the ground. Jack pushed the speaker button, turned up the volume, and walked to the window. He looked into the chamber, but was still perplexed. Casper was killing something, but there was nothing there.

"Die parasite! Die...Die...Die!" Casper swatted, and swatted.

I think it's dead, Cass!

Way to kill, Cass...Beautiful work...

Casper was breathing heavy, and his arm had grown heavy. Yellow insect guts bubbled on the concrete floor, and pieces of its shell were stuck to the bottom of his shoe. He wiped it on the ground several times, but finally resorted to rinsing the shoe in the sink. As the insect's entrails spiraled down the drain, Casper continued to talk to himself.

"Fucking disgusting bastard." He scrubbed the gluey guts from his shoe.

Good swatting, Cass.

"Worthless piece of shit! I hate those things!" Casper placed his wet shoe back on the ground, and stepped into it.

Watch your mouth Casper...The walls have ears.

Casper looked suspiciously at the speakers on the walls, then the video cameras, and then finally the mirror. He nodded his head without a word.

Sshhh...Jack's watching us. He's watching us right now.

"Where?" Casper squinted into the mirror, and saw nothing but his own reflection. He was greasy, unshowered, and several electrodes dangled loosely from his head.

Right there!

"I can't see him." Casper tried to look through his own image.

Jack was just a few inches from the mirror when Casper approached the glass. "What are you doing Casper?" he said softly to himself. Casper pressed his face into the glass, cupping his hands around his eyes. He peered out of the chamber.

He's right in front of us.

"How do you know?" Casper still could not see anything but himself.

He's afraid of us, Cass. He's afraid of the power we have...He's afraid of the power you have. Can't you feel that fear?

"Yeah..." Casper smiled. "I can."

He sent that roach in here.

He's trying to sabotage the work we've done!

Casper stepped a few feet back from the mirror. On the other side Jack also took a few steps backward. He was astonished by Casper's behavior.

"Jack?...Oh Jaaaack?...Are you there?" Casper taunted him. "I can take anything you give me!"

He's there all right!

You can be sure of that!

Casper snorted deeply, accumulating phlegm in the back of his mouth. "I can take anything you can give me!" he shouted at the mirror, and spit a glob of sputum onto it. Jack flinched needlessly, and watched the wad of phlegm slide down the glass surface. It left a thin trail of mucous as it oozed downwards, and finally collected at the bottom of the mirror in a green clump.

ooooooo

It was day thirteen, and Casper was obviously exasperated with Jack's questioning. Today's interview was now an hour old, and the questions were becoming a little repetitive.

"Tell me about the visions again." Jack was jotting many notes in his yellow pad.

Again with the visions, Cass...He doesn't see what we see.

"I know." Casper answered. He was clearly frustrated.

"You know what?" Jack asked him. Casper seemed distracted, as if there was someone else in the Isolation Chamber.

Watch what you say Casper...He'll ruin us.

"I know a lot of things, JB." Casper smirked. "What do *you* want to know?"

Jack was frustrated also. Interviewing someone who was actively hallucinating was probably the most challenging aspect of psychiatry. "Tell me about the visions."

"Visions!" Casper laughed. "Funny that you call them that. You know what they are. They're a part of me, JB. They're real, as real as I am! The visions are reality...only now I can see that."

You're telling him too much Casper!

"Shut up! I know what I'm doing. " Casper responded, and then turned back to Jack. "I see things, Jack...I see all types of things." Casper surveyed the room, obviously seeing things that were not physically there. "I see all types of things now."

Cass! You shut up! Listen to us.

Casper jumped from his seat, startling Jack. "That's it! You're not the boss!" he screamed at the voices in his head, his face turning purple with rage. "I'm the boss here! I tell you what to do! You don't control me! You're not the boss! I control you! You don't control me! I'm the boss! I'm the boss!..Is that clear?!"

Only silence. "Is that clear?"

Crystal clear.

"Good." Casper straightened his clothing, and sat calmly back at the table. He turned to Jack again, "Now where were we?"

○○○○○○○

Day Thirteen: 12:30
The subject has progressed from hypomania, to mania, and now finally, I believe psychosis. He is actively hallucinating. I believe he is experiencing both auditory, and visual hallucinations. He holds conversations with these auditory phenomena, and interacts physically with the visual phenomena.

The patient still occasionally self stimulates (Electric shock), and he continually asserts his control over the situation. He has grown suspicious, and paranoid, with a profound distrust of me.

EEG reviewed: The record has not normalized. There are cyclic intervals of unconsciousness, but these are brief, and strangely the subject is conscious! Furthermore, there is a tremendous amount of variable slow activity, particularly in the frontal region. This is consistent with the hypofrontality that is often described in schizophrenics, but again, I have never seen this on an EEG before.

-JB

○○○○○○○

Looking into the mirror, Casper tried to affix the dangling electrodes to his scalp but they were not sticking any longer. After several frustrating attempts, he ripped all of the electrodes off of his head. Taking clumps of hair along with them. He was a lot more comfortable now, and he scratched his head vigorously, knocking flakes of glue and skin onto the floor. At the sink he washed his face and rinsed his hair for the first time in two weeks. His face was hairy and thin. He had been neglecting himself over the last several days as his psychosis progressed.

"Pretty again! That feels so much better!"

Casper pushed the wet hair from his face, and began to shave his face with the electric razor. The razor gently massaged his face in soothing semicircles, and it left his skin warm and smooth. He removed the top of the razor, and emptied the tiny hairs into the sink. The small black shards of hair began to crawl in the basin. Each piece of hair had transformed into a tiny black ant, and they huddled together in a swarm around the drain. Casper looked at the razor, the severed bodies and heads of ants were tangled in the rotating blades. He dropped the razor into the sink and ran to the mirror to examine his face. Little ant heads were wiggling through the pores in his face. After squeezing totally out of his skin, they teemed into his hair. Casper brushed them off wildly.

"Get them off! Get them off!" He knocked sheets of ants from his face with his hands, and ran around the room.

Casper, calm down!

Look...they're gone...We took care of them.

"What the hell?" Casper looked in the mirror. Indeed all of the ants were gone. His face was clean and so was his hair.

See what we can show you?

"But there was, there were bugs...ants?" Casper parted his hair close to the mirror, and pinched several of the pores in his face...Nothing.

There was never anything, Casper...We just created them to show you our power.

Casper examined the sink again, nothing but hairs. "Wow...cool."

We couldn't do it without you, Casper.

But together we can do anything.

We'll show it all to you Casper. But no one must know.

Especially Jack.

"Okay." Casper nodded in disbelief.

That bastard will put an end to this. Perception will be lost forever.

"Show me more! Please, show me more!"

Step back from the mirror, and look.

Casper took several steps back from the mirror, and watched the glass. His own reflection stared back at him into the chamber.

See that?

"See what?" Casper squinted.

Look harder.

Casper squinted again into the mirror. Suddenly a shadow moved on the other side. "Who's that?" he asked, struggling to keep the image in focus.

The great Jack Benedict...Doctor Morality!

Casper laughed, the shadowy figure was more discernable now. Jack's husky body was lumbering behind the console. He was removing things from the top of the desk. Suddenly another shadow appeared. It was the silhouette of a young woman.

"Who's that?" Casper was mildly aroused by her seductive figure.

It's not his wife...

"Jack's favorite graduate student?"

Doctor Ellen McCormick at your service.

The two shadows blended together in an apparent kiss, and then Jack started to remove her clothing. After taking off his own shirt and unzipping his pants, Jack sat the woman on the console and hiked up her skirt. He caressed her breasts and wrapped her legs around his pelvis, before he plunged deeply into her.

Fucking pig.

"Unbelievable hypocrite."

○○○○○○○

Day Fourteen: 09:20

...The subject continues to experience auditory hallucinations, and visual hallucinations. He is easily distracted by these images and voices, but he has somehow learned how to exercise a considerable amount of control over them. Unlike many schizophrenics, this subject is able to continue normal daily activities while actively hallucinating. Perhaps this is due to his superior intellect, but the subject may also think he has reached "Perception."

I have no evidence that this subject is experiencing prophetic imagery or voices (like the Perceptives I have seen in my clinical experience). Furthermore, his hallucinations have been largely nonsensical as far as I can tell.

EEG reviewed: Patient removed all electrodes, No record.

-JB

○○○○○○○

"I know what you did last night, JB."

"What are you talking about, Casper?" Jack shrugged, uncertain what Casper was talking about.

"Did you enjoy the fuck?"

"Huh?" Jack shook his head. "I don't know what you're talking about." He felt strangely defensive.

Casper leaned toward him and lowered his voice to a malevolent pitch. "I saw you bang that girl last night on the console, JB...I saw it all!" Casper pointed to his temple. "I saw it all, Jack."

"You saw me here? In the chamber?" Jack was confused. He and Caroline spent a relaxing night alone in their brownstone. There was no sex.

"No, out there." Casper pointed to the mirror.

"Casper, I was with my wife last night." Jack stared into the mirror, and then turned back to Casper. "I wasn't here."

"I know Jack...I know." Casper whispered, nodding his head. "You've been a bad boy!"

After reasserting that he was at home with his wife last night, Jack continued the questioning. "Casper, what is sixty-eight times four?" He was testing Casper's cognitive abilities to see if they had changed from his baseline. He slid a piece of yellow paper and a pen toward him.

Don't tell him anymore than you've told him already.

Casper just looked at the paper and sneered at Jack in return. "You were always jealous of my work, JB, weren't you?" He leaned across the table and studied Jack's face. It was changing, twisting like a rubber mask, as if it was suddenly disconnected from his facial bones.

"You're face twists with lies, JB. You can no longer fool me." Casper grimaced, as the hallucination continued.

Ewww, that's gross!

Jack made a note. Casper was delusional, paranoid, and in all likelihood, actively hallucinating during this interview. He ignored Casper's absurd comments and continued the questioning. "Who invented the cotton gin?"

Look what that sicko is doing now!

Casper was disturbed by another vision. Jack was slicing his thumb, back and forth, on the edge of the notepad. His blood dripped slowly onto the table, making a small crimson puddle. He continued to slice, making the wound deeper and deeper until the bone finally appeared.

"You're a sick man, JB."

Jack groaned in frustration, and probed with more difficult questions. Casper loved to be challenged, and if given the chance to flaunt his superior intelligence, he would probably do so. Even if he was psychotic. "Who became president when William McKinley was assassinated in the year nineteen hundred?"

This guy can't be trusted Cass!

You see? What did I tell you?

The yellow pad was now saturated with blood, and Jack's plastic face wiggled loosely on his head. Casper hissed at him. "You are not here to help me, JB. All along you've been plotting against me. I know that now...I was so naive before...So naive."

Jack was concerned with Casper's progressing paranoia. So far it was manageable, and benign. But he wondered how long that would last. He decided to address it later, perhaps in the next interview. But today he needed to evaluate Casper's cognitive skills. It was an important parameter that could provide new insight into the evolution of the psychotic state. He continued with the provocative questioning, daring Casper's large ego to respond.

"What is the capital of Wyoming?" Casper again offered no response, but was clearly growing eager to respond.

He's testing us, Casper! You know this crap. He knows you know this stuff.

Jack wrote several notes in his pad. "What is the area of the brain responsible for the production of Dopamine?" Again he gave no answer. Jack was now tired of Casper's refusal to participate, and he decided to give up for the day.

Casper wrestled with the urge to answer him, and he was on the verge of responding when Jack stood up, and quickly left the Isolation Chamber. Casper was upset by Jack's sudden departure, and he ran to the mirror, pressing his face into it.

Casper don't!

"Two hundred-seventy two, Eli Whitney, Theodore Roosevelt, Cheyenne, and the *Substantia nigra!*"

○○○○○○○

Day Fourteen: 14:30
The subject has grown extremely distrustful, and his delusions are becoming more disorganized. His impulse control is poor, and many of the subject's ego defenses have disintegrated. Action is now on a more instinctual level. Insight about his psychotic condition is completely absent, and judgement remains impaired. The subject is frequently hallucinating, and although he is overtly bothered by these hallucinations, the subject is still remarkably autonomous. He is capable of ignoring the visions, and challenging the voices. A functional coexistence has been established between the subject and his hallucinations...This is very unusual for an untreated psychosis.   -JB

ooooooo

"Casper...What is it you think I've done?" Jack confronted his paranoia.

"You know damn well what you're doing here, JB. Don't play stupid with me!"

"What do you think I'm doing?"

He knows, Cass. He's giving us no respect.

"For years, ever since college in fact, you've been jealous of me and my abilities. And now you are trying to undermine the biggest neurological and psychiatric breakthrough of the century!"

Perhaps of all time!

Casper briefly acknowledged the voice in his head. "Yeah! That's right, the biggest discovery of all time! And this is killing you, Jack...It's fucking killing you!" Casper screamed, drooling onto his clenched fists. The absurd visions now continuously colored his reality, and the voices had become incessant. Jack sat calmly at the table, with his legs crossed.

Get rid of him Cass.

You're right Cass...He's scared...Once and for all.

Look at that pathetic has-been.

Jack uncrossed his legs, and assumed a more offensive position at the table. "Casper, what discovery are you talking about?"

He knows! Manipulative bastard.

"Perception Jack!...Perception! I'm there! You know it, I know it, the world will know it." Casper's fantastic delusion continued, as another vision appeared. Jack's lips were dry and cracked. His tongue was forked and it obscenely licked the flaking corners of his mouth. "Nothing but a wretch, Jack...You're nothing but an envious wretch."

"So, you believe you're Perceptive, Cass?"

"I know I'm Perceptive, Jack! Now get the hell out of here before you get hurt." Casper closed his eyes, and turned away from Jack.

Jack was somewhat surprised by Casper's last statement, and he took it as a meaningful threat. He didn't want to further antagonize Casper. Without a word or goodbye, he quickly left the room and shut the door tightly behind himself. Once outside the chamber, he breathed a small sigh of relief and securely locked the chamber door.

ОООООOO

Day Fifteen: 14:10
The subject has grown combative, and aggressive. Again, he has a severe impairment of judgement, and insight. He believes that he has actually attained Perception. This is speculative at best, and he has shown me no hard evidence of this. I believe the subject is experiencing a simple agitated psychosis. He remains distrusting and overtly paranoid, and his days are spent in an endless cycle of mania, and hallucinosis.

Of particular concern is his growing hostility. While he has managed to control it up to this point, his animosity is swelling. He no longer complies with my daily examinations, and I have again begun to question the value of continuing this experiment.

-JB

CHAPTER FIFTEEN
♦♦♦♦♦

The air was oppressively cold the next morning, and the sky was painted in a doleful gray. Although not unusual for this time of the year, this sudden coldness was an unwelcome change in the weather for Jack. Curling his stiff hands around his coffee cup, he hurried across the street when the signal changed.

He closed his coat snugly around his neck, and turned down Greenwich Avenue, heading toward the garage. The experiment was in trouble and Jack was very concerned. Casper's aggressiveness had now escalated to such a point, that the entire project was in jeopardy. Their interview sessions were virtually useless, and Casper flatly refused to partake in mental status examinations. Somewhat depressed, Jack blew a cloud of milky steam off his coffee, and wished that Casper would make another turn-around.

Jack unlocked the chain around the door, and released the deadbolt with a key. After pushing the door open, he was struck with a faint but distinctly foul odor. Sniffing the air, he cautiously entered the lounge. As usual, he glanced into the chamber first. Something was very different today, and Jack's jaw dropped open in disbelief. He placed the coffee on top of the console, and hurried closer to the mirror for a better look.

Casper was standing in his underwear, and he had written something on the walls. He paused for a moment as if he was aware of Jack's arrival, but then continued writing. The walls were covered with words and sentences. The bulk of the text was written in feces, smeared on the concrete, and the remainder was written in blood. Jack wiped the condensation from his breath off the mirror, and began to read some of what Casper had written.

"Oh my God." Jack said to himself. He was truly afraid for the first time, and he ran to the closet to retrieve the *Haldol.*

Casper continued to write on the wall, using his knuckle against the concrete as a pen. He squeezed a few more drops of blood from his skin. The four other knuckles on his right hand, had long been whittled dry, and he was down to his last digit. This composition had taken him nearly all night, but he finally finished it and signed, *'Lolly MD'*, underneath the blood red text.

Jack drew five milligrams of *Haldol* into the syringe, and flicked the bubbles out with his finger. He depressed the plunger and a small amount of *Haldol* shot out of the top of the needle, and landed on the floor. The syringe was full, and after recapping the needle, Jack hid the syringe in his shirt pocket. He dropped the vial with the remaining five milligrams of the sedative into his pocket also...Just in case he needed more.

Casper placed his scarred hands on his hips and smugly admired his masterpiece. The filthy text spanned all four walls of the chamber, and a small area underneath the mirror.

Brilliant work, Casper.

Jack shut the closet door, and began to unlock the door to the Isolation Chamber. Casper listened expectantly for Jack, and he turned to face the door. The doorknob did not turn, however. At the last moment, Jack decided not to enter the chamber. If he was to enter right now, it would be a break in the routine he had established over the last sixteen days, and a certain sign of his intention to terminate the experiment. To avoid a potential conflict, he decided to wait until after lunch. The usual interview time.

○○○○○○○○

Sitting at the table, Casper had fully dressed and washed himself again. The scribble on the wall had just about dried into the concrete when Casper shoved the last bite of a sandwich into his mouth. A few crumbs fell on the table, and Casper ate some of them off his fingertip. He swept most of them onto the floor.

There was a scratching noise at the door, and Casper had never heard this sound before. It was a strange raspiness, and he rose from the table to investigate. The door was still shut. He checked the knob. It was firmly locked. Casper placed his ear carefully to the door's surface and listened.

"Jack?" There was no response, but the scratching continued.

It's coming from underneath, Casper.

Casper slowly lowered himself onto his knees, then lied himself completely prone on the ground. Something purple, wet and disgusting was flickering underneath the door. It was a thick meaty tongue, and it hungrily licked the door, the floor, and the air in between.

Jack's taunting you, Casper!

"Jack are you trying to french me?!" Casper shouted underneath the door. He stuck his own tongue underneath it, and attempted to meet the purple invader.

A little tongue action never hurt anyone.

Jack looked at his watch, and shook his head remorsefully. He had been watching all of this transpire from the window. Casper's hallucinosis had really progressed, and his current behavior at the door was simply bizarre. Rehabilitation was going to be difficult, and Jack hoped that it was not too late.

"How's that, Jack?! Deep enough for you?!" Casper shouted, and resumed licking, probing further underneath the chamber door.

It's time. Jack thought to himself, and devised a plan. Casper would probably resist the injection of *Haldol,* so Jack would have to surprise him with this.

At the chamber door, Casper was still licking and shouting profanities. Jack jostled the doorknob intentionally, to alert Casper that it was time for their interview. Casper climbed from the floor and returned calmly to the table. Jack unlocked the chamber door and pulled it open. He grimaced at the putrid smell that greeted him, but he entered and reluctantly shut the door behind himself. He stopped momentarily to examine Casper's handiwork. All four walls of the chamber were indeed covered in his vile graffiti.

"Nice work." Jack said.

Casper smiled perversely, and waved when Jack entered. "Did you get a chance to read any of it?"

"Not yet." Jack responded, shaking his head.

Casper waved his hand at the wall. "Please."

Prior to sitting down, Jack read the passage in its entirety. On the first wall, the title *'My Manifesto'* was written in thick fecal letters. Three walls later, *'Lolly MD'* was thinly autographed in blood.

My Manifesto-
There are those who would have you believe that there is nothing more to Earthly existence. This is a travesty, and a lie. A lie perpetuated by the pseudo-intelligencia of the world. I have seen this fallacy fall in my lifetime. I have been privy to the evidence. The truth has been revealed to me. I am the chosen one. But still, those who choose to perpetuate this ignorance persecute me.

Jack turned to the next wall and the writing continued.

...There are a certain few who know what I know. Fellow witnesses to my power. But these few are the most despicable of all. They are afraid of what I have uncovered, they are afraid of me. They are envious of my ability to harness, and control this unbelievable power. My profound existence is beyond the scope of their limited imagination...

Feces had now turned to blood, as Jack read the final wall.

...Perception is both my salvation, and my damnation. I am damned by those around me who will try to corrupt my efforts. My destiny is greatness, and my fate is sealed. The truth has been revealed to me, and I will destroy all those who try to extinguish it.
Lolly MD

Paranoia, persecution, delusions of grandeur—were all depicted in feces and blood. This was a fitting testimony to the depth of Casper's psychosis. Jack was shocked and disturbed by Casper's manifesto, but he did not reveal this to him. Instead, he shrugged nonchalantly, and sat at the table with him.

"How are you, Cass?" He smiled warmly at Casper. He was anxious to end this whole thing.

"I feel better. Especially now that you're here."

"What does all this mean?" Jack asked, pointing at the writing on the wall.

There he goes again! He wants you to believe he's naive.

"We both know what you're doing, Jack."

"What do you mean?"

"Don't play dumb with me, Jacko."

"I don't understand, Casper. What am I doing?" Jack softly patted his chest, accidentally tapping the syringe that was concealed in his breast pocket. Casper noticed.

Take him now Casper!...He's trying to destroy us!

"You undermine me, you undermine my work. Your envy is my enemy." Casper showed his teeth like a wild animal.

Do it!

"Casper, I'm your friend. I'm here to help you!" Jack insisted, and attempted to calm his friend.

He's a filthy liar!

"You were never my friend...I see that so clearly now." Casper looked around the room, the images and voices continued.

He's destroying the effort.

"You're undermining my power...My gift."

"What gift, Casper? Do you think you're Perceptive?"

Casper did not answer him, and Jack posed the question again. This time more forcefully. "Casper?...Do you think you're Perceptive?"

He resents you for your insight...and your ability.

He always has, and he always will.

Casper nodded slowly. "Oh, I am Perceptive all right." Lost in fantasy.

Jack leaned forward and confronted Casper. "You're not Perceptive, Casper."

It's the envy...so much envy.

"You're drowning in jealousy, Jack. I see everything so clearly now."

"If you're Perceptive, Casper, what have you perceived? What have you prophesized?" Jack tried to reason with him, hoping to add a dose of organization to his hopelessly disorganized mind.

I see us beating you senseless, if you don't shut up.

"I know why you find my power so threatening, Jack." Casper was smug, and certain in his response. "Cause I know things about you. Things you try to hide. Things you hate about yourself. I see it all, Jack...The hate, the lust, the anger, the envy..." Casper stopped for a moment, lost in revelation. "Ah! You're having trouble getting it up for your wife. That's it! I bet she could use a good fucking, huh JB? That's what you're afraid of...Your wife wants a man. See? I know this about you, Jack...I know everything about you."

"You are not Perceptive Casper!" Jack's patience had been exceeded, and he slammed his fist onto the table. "Listen to me! You are not Perceptive!"

A long silence, as Casper contorted and twisted at the table. He was breaking. "Am too," he childishly responded, avoiding eye contact with Jack.

"You're delusional Casper." Jack said, and Casper rolled his eyes. "Remember the experiment, Cass? We tried, we tried real hard. But we did not find Perception. We found only psychosis, Cass. You are simply that...psychotic."

Casper looked at the fecal matter on the wall, and then stared at himself in the mirror for a while. His lower lip began to quiver, and a gloomy expression suddenly overcame his face. He turned to Jack, on the verge of tears.

Jack believed he was gaining a psychological advantage. "You're suffering from an acute psychosis, induced by amphetamines, sleep deprivation, and sensory deprivation. I know this is difficult for you to understand, but that's because you've worked so hard on this. We've both worked so hard, and have come a long way. But it's over, Cass. There's no Perception here. It's over."

Casper hung his head, and sniffled.

"I'm here to help you, Cass. I'm here to help." Jack sympathetically told him.

"I know..." Casper sniffled again and the first tear splattered onto the table. "...I'm just so confused," he was fully crying now. "I don't know what's going on anymore!"

"I know, Cass. I'll help...It's over, it's over."

"Please Jack, help me! I don't know what's happening to me." Casper pleaded with him.

"I will, Cass...I will."

"I see things. I hear voices, JB. They're so real to me. I can't understand it."

"I know, Cass. But they're not real."

"Help me, Jack." Casper pleaded again. "I can't take much more."

"That's why I'm here, Cass." Jack reached his hands sympathetically across the table, and reached for Casper's.

Get 'em, Cass!

Casper sprang out of his seat and violently slammed his hands on top of Jack's. Jack's wrists were trapped underneath Casper's powerful grip, and he struggled to pull them free. "What are you doing, Cass?" Jack asked as Casper tightened his grip.

"Whatcha got in the pocket, Jack?!"

The voices in Casper's head were laughing and cackling.

"Could it be *Haldol?* A small dose of vitamin H for me? The psycho? Is that whatcha got, Jacko?" Casper drooled onto the table, his eyes were wild and furious.

"Casper let me go!" Jack wrestled and twisted, but Casper was just too damn strong. "Let me go!" he insisted.

If he wants to go...Let him go!

Casper released Jack's hands and they recoiled instantly to his chest. Casper grabbed the table from underneath and flipped it high into the air. Jack was tossed backwards from his chair and onto the floor. He landed flat on his back and his head bounced off the concrete. The table crashed to the ground by the chamber door and Jack frantically started to crawl toward it.

Casper yanked the microphone from the center of the ceiling and shouted into it, like an announcer at a championship fight.

"Ladies and Gentlemen! Let's get ready to Rrruuuuumble! "

Jack scurried for the door, but Casper pursued him. He grabbed Jack by the ankles, and dragged him back to the center of the chamber. Jack clawed at the table and floor as he was being dragged under the swinging microphone.

Casper spoke into the microphone again. "This will be a regulation bout, with no three knock down rule." Jack attempted to get to his feet, and Casper continued.

"There will be no kicking." Casper kicked Jack squarely in the groin. Jack dropped to his knees, blinded by the pain. Casper simulated a cheering crowd. "There will be no stomping." And he stomped Jack fiercely to the floor. "No biting." He bent down and bit Jack on the shoulder. "No punching, or pinching." Casper delivered both, splitting Jack's lip and leaving his nipple purple.

"...And most of all, ladies and gentleman, no wagering." Casper viciously kicked Jack a few more times, leaving him curled into a ball on the floor. Jack spat blood from his mouth, and held his testicles tightly in his hands.

Way to go, Cass!

Casper raised his hands over his head victoriously. "I'm the king of the world!"

You're the king...You're the king.

Casper bent down close to Jack, and grabbed his head by the ears. Jack's neck was stiff with pain, and a thick film of blood coated his chin.

"Thanks for nothing, JB." Casper released his head, and it landed with a thud on the concrete floor. He removed the syringe of *Haldol* from Jack's pocket. He theatrically uncapped it, and danced for several seconds around the Isolation Chamber. Jack was physically unable to mount a resistance as Casper approached him with the needle.

"Pleasant dreams, Jacko." Casper hissed. "I'll see you on the other side." He plunged the syringe through Jack's shirtsleeve and deep into his arm.

CHAPTER SIXTEEN
◆◆◆◆◆

A violent twitch and Jack was blindly thrashing on the chamber floor. He was completely disoriented, and his head was throbbing. His eyelids were heavy, and he struggled to lift them. Slowly his lids parted and the intense light burned the back of his eyeballs. The room violently swirled around him several times and Jack quickly closed his eyes again. His entire body was drenched in a profound fatigue, and it was an exhaustive effort just to overcome this limpness. Rolling onto his belly, he attempted to lift his head off the floor, but his neck was too weak. His skull fell solidly back to the concrete...Then there was blackness again.

Hours later, Jack reawakened. This time he felt somewhat stronger. The fatigue in his muscles was slow to dissipate, but he managed to push himself from the floor and stagger to one of the aluminum chairs. Bracing himself between the arms of the chair, he looked confusingly around the chamber. The room still listed around him, and he tried to steady his head. The table was overturned by the open door. The microphone dangled loosely from the ceiling, and feces and blood were smeared on the wall. The Isolation Chamber had been trashed, and Casper was gone.

Jack scratched his head, and tried to recall what had happened. He clearly remembered the previous night with Caroline, and most of the events of the morning. Casper's manifesto, which was still on the wall, seemed vaguely familiar to him, but the rest of the day was foggy. Jack shook his head, and his brain rattled painfully against the walls of his skull. He took a deep breath, and pushed himself to his feet. There was a knotting sensation in his groin, a dull pain that prevented him from standing completely erect. His face and his ribs also hurt.

He stumbled over to the mirror, and looked at his face. His lower lip was scabbed and swollen, and a layer of dried blood coated his chin. He touched his lip, and it was exquisitely tender. He grimaced sharply, and suddenly recalled the punch that Casper laid upon him. Jack turned to look back at the chamber. There was a maroon bloodstain on the floor, next to an empty syringe. Jack rubbed his shoulder. It was sore. Everything suddenly came back to him. He recalled the paranoia, the accusations, the beating, and then...the *Haldol*.

Jack leaned his body against the wall, and then tottered his way out of the Isolation Chamber. In the observation room, he awkwardly lunged for a seat at the console, and sat for several minutes. Once his head had steadied, Jack rewound the videotape to the point of the interview, and watched. He turned the volume up. On the tape, Casper began to feign desperation, and Jack stupidly fell for it. Then the violence started.

After watching himself get kicked in the groin, then bitten, punched, and pinched, Jack closed his eyes remorsefully. The tape continued to roll as Casper removed the *Haldol* from Jack's pocket, and jammed it deeply into his arm. Casper discarded the used needle next to Jack's beaten body, and after a brief wave to all three cameras, Casper disappeared from the video.

Jack forwarded the tape. Throughout the remainder he was alone on the floor, soundly sleeping for several hours. The monitor finally turned to electrical snow as the tape finished, and Jack turned off the VCR. He looked around the observation room. The storage closet was wide open, and empty boxes of *Primatene* were scattered on the floor. He opened the drawer to the console, the food money was gone as well. Everything else outside the chamber appeared to be in order.

Jack picked up the phone at the console and dialed 911. He searched the remaining drawers of the desk, while he waited for the emergency operator to answer the phone. One of the drawers contained an old picture of Jack with Casper as a student. A thin layer of dust covered the frame, and Jack brushed this off with his free hand.

"Hello...Emergency?" a voice cracked on the phone.

Jack was startled, as if he was suddenly removed from a pleasant daydream. "Uh...yeah..."

"Is there an emergency, Sir?" In the typical New York fashion, her voice was impatient and testy.

Jack lingered on the picture, recalling all the good times he had spent with Casper. He opened his mouth to speak, but could not utter a word. He was stunned by indecision for the first time in his life.

The emergency operator became even testier. "Sir, this is an emergency line, if there is no emergency, I will disconnect you." Jack stuttered, "I...I'm sorry...There's no emergency." He quickly hung up the phone. "I'm very sorry." He removed the photo from its frame, and shoved it into his pants pocket. He stood to leave, but his legs were still rubbery underneath him. Supporting himself like a toddler on the furniture, he managed to stumble out of the garage and into the alley.

○○○○○○○

A full moon hovered lazily above the jagged apartment buildings, creating a peculiar, almost daylight urban landscape. The warm aroma of roasted nuts tempered the cold air, and couples of all persuasions salted the chilly sidewalks. It was seven thirty in the evening, and Jack clutched his coat around his neck as he staggered around the corner. He leaned against the brick facade of an apartment building, and searched the streets. There was no sign of Casper.

Jack swallowed a mouthful of bloody saliva, and pushed himself off the wall. He teetered down Greenwich Avenue, tripping over his own feet several times. The block was dark and murky, and Jack was growing weak. He could not make it the whole distance, and after inadvertently bouncing against a chain link fence, he decided to rest a moment. An obviously gay couple had been watching him, and after a few whispers they approached him.

"Excuse me?" one of the tall good looking men asked him. "Do you need any help?"

"Something's wrong with his lip, Andy." the other man said.

"I'm fine..." Jack's voice cracked. "Can you help me?" He slouched limply against the fence, he felt suddenly nauseated and dizzy. Both of the men came to his aid, and supported him from under the arms.

"Call 911 Jordan." Andy pointed his lover toward a pay phone on the corner.

"No!" Jack howled, grabbing Jordan by the shirt.

"Let me go! I think he's drunk, Andy."

"I'm not drunk." Jack said, as the two men wrestled free from him. Jack bounced back into the fence. "I'm a doctor. I was jumped by someone I know."

Andy approached him again. "Are you hurt?"

"I'll be fine...just fine." Jack started to dig around his pockets. "But can you tell me if you've seen this man tonight? In this neighborhood?" Jack removed the picture of Casper and himself, and handed it to the two men.

Jordan whistled as he looked at the picture from over Andy's shoulder. "He's a sweetie all right!"

Andy gave the picture back to Jack. "Had a lover's brawl, huh?"

Jack took a moment to process the question. He then reexamined the photo. His arm was tucked snugly around Casper's waist, like a sugar daddy and his young gigolo. "Yeah, something like that." Jack smirked, and was painfully reminded of the cut on his lip. "Have you seen him?"

"No, we haven't seen 'em." Andy turned to Jordan, and they both shook their heads.

"He may have been acting peculiar?"

"Boyfriend..." Jordan scoffed, "Where do you think you are? This is Greenwich Village! We're all a little peculiar down here." Andy laughed along with him.

"Uh-huh, I see." Jack frowned and shrugged his shoulders. "Thanks for the help. I appreciate it." And he began to stagger down the avenue again.

"If *I* see him *daddio*, you may not get him back!" Jordan said, as Andy forcefully yanked him down the street in the opposite direction.

Jack waddled clumsily uptown to Fourteenth Street. Occasionally he asked small groups of people if they had seen Casper, showing them the picture. Most of the time, he was met with intense derision or simple indifference. Nobody had seen Casper, and nobody seemed to care. Standing on the corner of Fourteenth Street and Seventh Avenue, Jack gently swayed bracing himself against a mailbox. The traffic was making him dizzy again, and without further warning he hit the concrete. His body crashed into a nearby trashcan and its contents spilled into the street. Pebbles from the sidewalk dented his chin and cheek, and he quickly brushed them off as he attempted to rise to his feet.

His fall to the ground attracted the attention of police officer across the street. The detective was out of uniform, but was wearing a blue NYPD windbreaker. The officer shut the door to his *Crown Victoria*, and watched Jack through the traffic. The traffic signal changed, and the officer made his way toward him. Jack rose quickly to his feet, stumbling away from the approaching policeman, and signaled a passing taxicab.

"Hey you...hold on!" the policeman shouted to Jack from the street.

Jack ignored him. He was unsure if he wanted to involve the authorities. The cab stopped on the side of the road, and Jack opened the door.

"Buddy!" the cop shouted again, "Hold up!"

Jack pretended not to hear the policeman as he jumped into the back seat of the cab. He slammed the door just as the cop made it to the corner.

"Eighty-fifth Street, between Lex and Third, please."

After a brief glance in the rear view mirror, the cabby tore off. The policeman waved uselessly at Jack, as the cab sped away uptown. Shaking his head, the cop bent down and picked up a wallet from the sidewalk. He flipped it open, and looked through the pockets to find identification. Placing the driver's license between his fingers, he held it up to the street light and read it. Jack Benedict, MD. 1127 Eighty-fifth Street, New York, New York.

○○○○○○○

"Listen..." Jack was trying to calm the cab driver, who was completely agitated on the other side of the *Plexiglas*. "I was jumped. I must have...I must have lost my wallet."

"I call police! You will pay!" the Iranian cabby spat.

The fare was only six dollars and fifty cents. Jack had been through all of his pockets several times, and he still could not find his wallet. *Why would Casper take my wallet?* He wondered.

"Listen..." Jack looked at the name on the taxi license. It was a wild mix of many consonants, and very few vowels. He made no attempt to pronounce the foreign cabby's name. "Listen Buddy, I'll go inside my house, and get you the money from my wife."

"No." The cabby turned to him. "No, you pay me now or I call police!"

Jack sat back in the seat, and frustratedly rubbed his hair. "I haven't got any money."

"Police!" the cabby shouted, rolling down his window. "Police! Police!"

Jack was confused by the cabby's unexpected actions, and he tried to calm him at the *Plexiglas* partition. Suddenly there was a knock at the passenger window. A police officer was standing outside the cab on the sidewalk, and Jack rolled down the car's rear window.

"Doctor Benedict, I presume?" the officer smirked. Jack's heart dropped into his stomach. Something was terribly wrong.

"Yeah?"

"Are you having a little trouble paying for your ride?"

"Huh?"

"You dropped your wallet downtown."

"I did?"

"Yep. A doctor's wallet goes a long way in this town, so I thought I'd bring it to you before I went home for the night. I take the bridge to Long Island, so it wasn't out of my way." The officer handed a wallet through the window.

Jack recognized it immediately and then recognized the cop. It was the same officer he avoided moments ago from downtown.

"I shouted at you, but you didn't hear me, I guess." The cop shrugged.

"Thanks officer. Thanks a lot." Jack hurriedly ripped a ten-dollar bill out of his wallet, and handed it through the *Plexiglas* to the irate cabby. "I'm sorry about the inconvenience. Please keep the change." The cabby did not respond. Jack popped the door open, and stumbled out of the cab.

The policeman was still standing there, and he helped Jack to his feet.

"You okay, Doc?" The policeman noticed the bloody lower lip. "Looks like you been roughed up a bit."

"I'm fine officer. It happened a while ago."

The officer did not believe him, and Jack almost fell on him again. "Whoa! You had a little too much to drink tonight, huh Doc?"

Jack nodded. "It's been a bad day...A real bad day."

The officer smiled. "I know the type. I know the type. Is this your house?" he asked pointing to Jack's brownstone.

"Yeah, thank you, Officer?..." Jack asked his name.

"Detective...Detective Cavanagh, John Cavanagh." He helped Jack through the gate to the steps.

"Well thanks again, Detective Cavanagh, I owe you one."

"You got it. Get to bed, tomorrow's another day."

"Thanks again." Jack stumbled slowly up the steps and finally into his brownstone. He rested against the door, and breathed a sigh of relief.

Detective Cavanagh watched Jack stagger inside, and shook his head with a smile. Once a light turned on in the foyer, he turned to leave. While returning to his cruiser, he stopped suddenly. Someone had been watching from across the street. It was a shadowy figure that initially startled the detective.

"Everything all right, Officer?" Casper asked.

"Just fine." he said, entering the unmarked cruiser. "He'll be just fine. Have a good night." He pulled the door shut, and drove down the street.

"You too, Officer." Casper waved and watched the police car turn the corner.

○○○○○○○

Caroline was upstairs in the bedroom, and Jack kicked off his shoes in the foyer. He removed his coat and sloppily threw it in the closet.

"Caroline?" he shouted up the steps.

"Up here, Honey."

Jack walked toward the kitchen without acknowledging Caroline. He desperately needed coffee, and he fumbled with the automatic coffee maker, spilling coffee grinds onto the counter top.

"Jabes?" Caroline was at the top of the steps.

Jack swept the grinds from the counter top into a cone filter with his hand. Caroline descended the steps, and entered the kitchen, turning on the light.

"Oh my god, Jack!" she shouted, scaring him.

"What?" Jack was bloody, and hunched over the kitchen counter.

"What happened to you?" She rushed over to him, and looked at the cut on his lip.

"I'm fine, Caroline." Jack pulled away from her, and staggered to a seat at the table. Caroline followed him closely, and squatted by his chair.

"Are you all right?"

He pulled away again. "Yes, Caroline. I'm fine. I just need coffee."

"What happened, Jack? Tell me!" She was becoming upset.

"I don't want to talk about it! I just don't want to talk about it."

Caroline backed away from him. "Jack, have you been drinking?"

"No, Caroline, I haven't. Now please...Can you make me some coffee?"

Tears broke out on Caroline's face. "Make your own damn coffee!" She ran back up the steps to the bedroom, and slammed the door.

Jack hung his head into his hands, and slowly lowered it onto the table. "Fucking terrific." he complained to himself. "Just fucking swell." He was unusually comfortable in this position tonight, and he quietly fell asleep in the kitchen chair.

○○○○○○○

The sink water took several minutes to heat up, and Jack looked at himself in the mirror while he waited. He removed his shirt. His ribs were bruised and tender. He carefully pressed on them, feeling for crepitance, a bubbly sensation often felt through the skin when ribs were broken. Thankfully, there wasn't any. He took a deep breath, but a sharp pain restricted him from taking a full inspiration. He shrugged, and resolved to breathe shallow for a while.

Steam was now coming from the sink water, and Jack adjusted the temperature until it was warm. He wet a towel underneath the faucet, and applied it to his lip. He cringed and tears came to his eyes. He slowly massaged the dried blood off his mouth, and the purple clots fell into the sink and swirled down the drain. The laceration on his lip was small, but it sure did bleed a lot. It was still oozing a bloody fluid, and Jack applied pressure to it with the washcloth. He dried his face once the bleeding had slowed sufficiently, and left the bathroom.

Most of the *Haldol* had worn off, and he felt coordinated again. It was nearly midnight, and after sleeping for over two hours at the kitchen table Jack joined his wife in the bedroom. The lights were still on, and Jack quietly changed into his pajamas. Caroline was still awake, and pouting. She completely ignored Jack as he climbed into bed next to her. The mattress bounced as Jack climbed under the sheets, and Caroline turned away from him. Jack snuggled next to her from behind, and she pushed him away.

"I'm sorry, Honey. I just..." Jack tried to apologize, but was interrupted.

"You just what Jack? Got drunk? Got beat up?" She turned to him. "For Christ's sake, Jack, how old are you?"

"I wasn't drunk, Caroline."

"You sure looked it, Jack...Remember, no more lies."

"That's not what happened, Caroline. I could explain everything." Jack had decided to tell Caroline about the experiment while he was washing his face.

"You better." she demanded, turning away from him again.

"Okay..." Jack nervously took a deep breath. "It all started about a month ago, when I went to Casper's lecture..." Jack proceeded to tell Caroline everything. He told her about Perceptive Schizophrenia, Casper's experiment, his subsequent psychosis, the manifesto, the beating, and the escape. After an hour of details, Jack finished and waited for her response.

"How could you be so irresponsible, Jabes?" She looked at him incredulously.

"I don't know...He told me he needed me, and that he'd do it without me if I didn't help him."

"That's all?"

"Uh-huh...And part of me was excited about the experiment. I guess I just got caught up in Casper's enthusiasm."

Caroline shook her head again, and did not speak for several seconds. "Why don't you go to the police?"

Jack sat up in bed. "I almost did. I almost did. I had the phone in my hand, and I dialed 911 but..."

"But what?" She was still quite upset.

"I looked at the pictures of him and I in the garage. Then I came across this one picture of Casper and I...and I got to thinking."

Caroline silently looked up at him, and he continued. "Caroline, I would ruin my career. I would ruin his career. Think about it. Two of the country's leading psychiatrists pull a stunt like this..." Jack rubbed his eyes. "Jeez, the press would be all over it. It would be a professional catastrophe for both of us."

"I don't think being a psychopath is gonna help Casper's career either." Caroline smartly reminded him.

"You're right, Caroline." Jack nodded. It was a very good point. "You're right. But if I can find him, I can help him. I can bring him back. That's what he wanted me to do. That's what I promised him, so that's what I have to do."

"How, Jack?"

"I don't know. I don't know. But I've got to find him first."

CHAPTER SEVENTEEN
◆◆◆◆◆

The phone had already been ringing for several minutes before Caroline awoke from her deep sleep. Jack was still heavily snoring next to her, and she shoved him a few times. "Jabes, Jabes, wake up! The phone!" She shoved him more vigorously, until he began to stir.

Jack rustled himself from under the sheets, and lifted his head from the pillow leaving a blood-tinged puddle of drool on the pillowcase. His eyes had been cemented shut overnight by a yellow crust, and after prying them open he squinted at the alarm clock. It was five fifty-five in the morning. The phone rang again.

"Hello?" Jack answered, picking up the phone. His voice cracked and was barely audible. He cleared his throat, and started again. "Hello?"

A brief silence elapsed, and then a voice came from the other end. "How're your nuts doin' JB?" It was Casper, calling from a dingy hotel room on the Lower Westside.

"Casper!" Jack sat up in bed. "Where are you? Where are you right now? Are you all right?" he asked, throwing the bedsheets off his lap, and placing his feet into the slippers at the bedside.

"Those are difficult questions, JB ol' boy." Casper looked around the grimy hotel room. He was truly uncertain of where, and how he was. There was an exhausted whore sleeping on the bed, and Casper walked quietly over to her. She was wearing only shiny black latex panties. He was wearing nothing at all.

"I know this much, JB..." Casper whispered, as he began to massage his own genitals, "I'm where I'm supposed to be."

"Cass! You need help!" Jack paced around his bedroom, and Caroline watched him intently. "Let me help you Cass, that was the deal. I'll meet you anywhere."

Don't listen to him Cass!
He'll destroy us all...That's been his goal all along.
He's no friend of ours.

"Jack!" Casper impatiently responded. "There is no deal! How fucking stupid do you think I am?!" A trail of spit fell from Casper's mouth and onto the urine stained carpet.

The whore on the bed was awakened by Casper's outburst, and she rolled lazily onto her back. "You're an envious little man, JB." Casper continued, lowering his voice to a whisper. "You're the only one who realizes the power I have discovered. That's what makes you so dangerous to me. That's what makes you *so fuckin' dangerous!*" Casper raised his voice again.

The whore stretched and yawned, spreading herself across the bed. "What power is that?" she asked and sat up, covering her large breasts with a flat yellow pillow.

Casper calmed the fury he was feeling. "Don't worry about it, Toots." he told her with a wink and a forced smile.

"Casper, who's with you?" Jack asked.

"Don't worry about it, Toots." Casper repeated into the phone, and turned his face upwards to the mirror on the ceiling.

He was hallucinating wildly. Bizarre images and voices were now his reality, and he loved it. He could now appreciate the pink fragrance of sex wafting off the walls of the hotel room, and feel the reckless lust of those men who visited this room before him. He believed that he could read the thoughts of the whore he was with, and he suspected that she could read his thoughts too. He contemplated killing her for this, but ultimately he decided that her Perceptive abilities were too primitive to do him any harm.

"Casper, I need to talk with you, please." Jack looked up at his bedroom ceiling, feeling frustrated and lost.

That's it Cass, no more.

"Wish you were here." Casper joked.

"Casper let me help you. You're experiencing an acute psychosis. You're a danger to yourself right now. Trust me. I can help you. Tell me where you are so we can talk. Please Cass...please." Jack pleaded into the phone.

"Oh, I don't think so, Jacko. But I'll tell you this much..." There was a long pause as Casper stroked the tangled hair of his whore. "We will meet again. I assure you, we will meet again." He hung up the phone, and pulled the whore to her feet. He was fully aroused again, for the fifth time, and she could feel him pulsate against her weary pelvis.

"This is really gonna cost you." she said, trying to discourage his sexual advance.

"Don't worry about it, Toots." and he pushed her to her knees.

OOOOOOO

Jack placed the phone back on the nightstand, and sat in bed with Caroline. He fluffed his pillow, and noticed the blood stain on the pillowcase. He turned it over, plopped onto his back, and kicked the sheets over his beaten body. He had only been asleep for a few hours, and he was still exhausted. He softly massaged his temples, but this offered little release of the tension he was experiencing inside. Caroline sat up to face him, her auburn hair cascading gently over her bare shoulders.

"That was Casper?" She asked.

"Uh-huh."

"Where is he?"

"He didn't say." Jack dropped his arms limply to his side.

"What *did* he say?"

"He was very vague, Caroline...I mean, he's psychotic. He's paranoid and delusional. I think he's hallucinating. Like I told you last night, he believes that he's Perceptive. He doesn't realize how sick he is. In fact, he doesn't feel he's sick at all."

Caroline crossed her legs like a child, and fiddled thoughtfully with her hair. "Jabes, you should tell the police." She reminded him.

"I know, I know." Jack didn't want to hear this. "But I can't. Not yet, anyhow." He laced his hands tightly behind his head. "I'm gonna go find him, Caroline. I owe him that much. I've got to find him."

"Where are you gonna start?" She asked.

"At the garage. I'll start at the garage." Jack said, dragging himself out of bed. "First, I need a shower."

ooooooo

After a warm shower and shave, Jack hailed a taxi and headed downtown in a dented yellow cab. It was late morning and many business types, delivery personnel, and couriers hurried through the city streets. Jack deeply massaged his face, dislodging the residual crust that rested in the corner of his eyes. If he could not locate, and detoxify Casper by the end of the week, he would have to involve the police. There was no other option. He was frustrated and tired. The office was falling apart, and he had promised Gladys a week ago that he would return early. For the first time in his career, he was not looking forward to resuming work. Especially, if he could not find his friend.

"Pull over right here." he told the taxi driver as they neared the garage. The cabby swerved to the side of the road and stopped violently.

Jack winced as he stepped out of the car. His ribs still hurt badly, particularly when he changed positions. He passed the cabby six dollars through the passenger side window, and the cab sped off down the block. This was an emotional moment for Jack. It was an odd mixture of cautious fear and profound remorse.

After crossing the alleyway, he noticed that the door was unlocked. He must have forgotten to lock it when he staggered out last night. Carefully, he stepped inside the garage, and onto the dark concrete floor. He flipped on the light switch, and was surprised to find that nothing was taken or disturbed. The garage was exactly as he left it last night. Casper's rancid manifesto was beginning to fade on the wall, the table was overturned, and several *Primatene* tablet boxes were scattered on the ground. The fish, Pontious and Pilot, swam aimlessly in their fishbowl. Jack walked over to them, and tapped lightly on the bowl with his finger.

"You guys seen your Daddy today?"

The fish did not answer.

Jack salted some fish food onto the top of the water, and turned back to the closet. All of the *Primatene* tablets were gone, only the boxes were left. Jack counted them slowly, kicking them to the side as he did so. There were twelve boxes, each of which contained twenty tablets.

Altogether, two hundred and forty tablets were missing. This was enough juice to keep Casper going for several weeks, or maybe even a month. Jack sat dejectedly at the console, and waited for Casper to return. He reviewed the videotapes, and the computer log, looking for the actual point where he lost control of the experiment. As usual, Jack was meticulous, and his documentation of the daily events was no exception. He could not have predicted, nor could he have prevented this horrible outcome. That is why it was so difficult to study schizophrenia and the related psychotic disorders. There was simply no recurrent or predictable pattern to their behavior.

After several hours, there was still no sign of Casper. When Jack decided to leave the garage, it was already mid-afternoon. He rubbed his stomach. Despite the fact that he felt queasy, he figured that it would be best for him to eat something. He was probably going to need the energy. He carefully locked the garage door, wrapping a chain around the door handle. He decided to search the neighborhood for his friend and a good place to eat.

○○○○○○○

Casper heaved the door open and entered the lobby of his apartment building on the Upper Westside of the city. Sam, the chubby doorman, was startled at first, but after a brief gasp of surprise, he greeted Casper warmly.

"Hey Doctor Lolly...Long time, no see."

Although Sam had not seen Casper for several weeks, he did not think it was peculiar until now. Casper often kept strange hours, and was known to take lengthy vacations. But there was something very different about Doctor Lolly today. He seemed strangely out of place in this luxury apartment building. He was wearing a ratty overcoat, filthy blue jeans, and a plain white tee shirt. He held a duffel bag in one hand, and snickered incoherently as he walked. He seemed preoccupied and distracted, and did not acknowledge the doorman's friendly greeting.

"Doc?" Sam called out again, but Casper hurried by the front desk and disappeared into the elevator.

The sliding doors sealed Casper inside the elevator, and he pressed the button to the eleventh floor. The elevator began to ascend, and Casper suddenly heard voices calling out to him from the elevator shaft.

"Who's that?!" Casper asked up toward the ceiling, then down toward the floor.

Casper, help me! A tortured voice called from outside the elevator. More voices then joined in, and soon there was a chorus of hideous screams echoing through the darkened elevator shaft.

"What's the matter? Who are you?" Casper spun several times in the elevator.

They are the voices of the damned, Casper. Those from the underworld.

Help us! I'm burning...Help me!

"What do you want from me?"

Everyone wants what you have.

We want it all, Cass.

"Leave me alone! I've got a job to do!" Casper screamed and covered his ears, but this did not stop the awful voices in his head. Contorted flames and thick black smoke slithered underneath the doors and snaked their way across the floor to his feet. Casper jumped back from the imaginary flames, and leaned against the wall.

Don't forget the plan, Cass.

"Plan? I am the fucking plan. There is no *plan* without me!" he hissed. "You remember that! There is no *fucking plan*. I'm the plan, there is no other. I'm the boss! Not you! Not the others...Me! I'm the boss!" Casper raised his finger, punctuating his dominance over the visions and voices that cluttered his mind.

The elevator stopped abruptly at the eleventh floor, and the hallucinations disappeared as the elevator doors parted. Casper walked quickly to his apartment, unlocked the door, and ducked inside.

'No more fuckin' elevators for me.' he thought to himself.

CHAPTER EIGHTEEN
◆◆◆◆◆

Jack covered his mouth and belched softly into his fist. The two hot dogs he ate for lunch were beginning to repeat on him, and he hoped the other passengers could not smell his spicy breath. He was headed uptown on the Number One subway to Casper's apartment, and the trip seemed endless. The ride was bumpy and slow, and there were multiple unexplained delays between stations. Jack briefly closed his eyes and tried to calm himself.

The subway car was noisy and crowded, but Jack felt unbelievably alone. He was lost in deep thought. He should have listened to his gut. He should have known better. He should have taken a cab! Jack looked down at his watch. It was almost three-thirty in the afternoon, only three hours until sunset.

The train chugged slowly into Time Square, and crawled to a stop. The doors opened and a wave of passengers poured off the train. New passengers boarded the subway car and wrestled one another for the remaining seats. The conductor tried to close the small sliding doors several times, but was successful only on the fifth attempt.

"Come on!" Jack complained to himself, impatiently. *"Let's move!"*

The train pulled out of Time Square, and after three more grueling stops, it finally arrived at Sixty-eighth Street. Jack darted up the gummy steps, and walked briskly to Casper's Upper Westside apartment. He pushed through the revolving doors, and quickly crossed the lobby, giving the doorman a brief nod as he headed toward the elevator.

Sam, the fat doorman, quickly tried to swallow the last piece of a *Snickers* candy bar. He stood up and followed Jack. "Uh...Excuse me, Sir?" he mumbled through the nuts and chocolate. "Can I help you?"

Jack stopped just a few feet short of the elevator, and turned to face the doorman. Sam was too fat for his uniform, and he was sweating profusely underneath the polyester jacket. A small red hat sat loosely on top of his plump head, and there was chocolate crud in the corners of his mouth. Although his appearance was laughable, Sam felt omnipotent. He was the front line between this posh apartment building, and the rest of the big bad city. He defended this place with unbridled zeal, despite the fact that he would never be allowed to live here. He slowly wiped the brown crud away from his mouth with a handkerchief, and looked suspiciously at Jack.

"Can I help you, Sir?" he repeated, and placed the folded kerchief back in his pocket.

"Yes," Jack stalled. "I'm here for Doctor Lolly."

"Is he expecting you?" Sam asked and headed back to the front desk to check his ledger.

Jack followed him. "Well, no...But have you seen him lately?"

The doorman nodded twice "Uh-huh". He flipped through the pages of the visitor ledger. "I don't see that he's expecting anyone." Sam picked up the intercom phone. "I'll ring him for you...What did you say your name was?"

Jack stepped up to the desk. "Uh, I'd like to surprise him." Jack knew that Casper would run if he knew that he was here.

The doorman shook his head defiantly. "Sorry, against procedure."

Sam always spoke about protocol, procedure and regulations. He enjoyed throwing these terms around, especially at the pretentious residents and their guests. Those three words gave him power over these people, and he frequently abused this authority. Sam often dreamed of being a New York City police officer. They possessed the power he so desperately desired. A gun, a badge, and a bad attitude--these were the three things Sam admired most in men. But there was that test, that awful test which he could never pass. Beaten by 'the system', he was left a small man in a small job, in an awfully big city. Jack knew this at a glance.

The intercom was ringing in Casper's apartment, but there was no answer. After ten rings, Sam hung up the phone. "He's not in."

"I thought you said you saw him?"

"I did, about four...maybe five hours ago." Sam responded defensively.

"Did you see him leave?" Jack's speech was pressured and testy.

"No. And I've been here all day."

"You're sure."

The doorman gave Jack a nasty look, and scowled. "Who are you anyway?"

Jack's patience was thin. "Listen, I'm Doctor Jack Benedict...Doctor Lolly's psychiatrist." He showed the doorman his business card. "I think he may be in trouble. When did you last see him?"

Sam studied the card, and handed it back to Jack. "Doctors have Doctors?"

"Some of us need them."

"Like I told you, I saw him about four or five hours ago."

"Did you notice anything unusual?"

Sam thought for a moment, and then made a face. "Uh, yeah...He seemed out of sorts today."

"What do you mean?"

"Well, we're good friends. He's the only resident that invites me up for a drink every once and a while. Today, he completely ignored me. Like I wasn't even here. Usually we chat and stuff like that."

"That's all?"

"No." the doorman continued. "I haven't seen him in nearly a month, but he looked different, disheveled and dirty today. He was talking to himself, and giggling too. I don't know what his problem was, but he wasn't himself."

"Listen..." Jack interrupted. "I think Doctor Lolly needs my help." He slipped forty dollars across the desk. "Can you get me into his apartment?"

Sam swiped the forty dollars from the top of the desk, and looked up at the video camera in the corner of the lobby. "This is against procedure..." he whispered. "And probably illegal. I could lose my job."

Jack pulled another twenty out of his wallet, and handed it to the tubby doorman. Sam palmed the crisp new bill, and tucked it away in his pants pocket.

"But since you're his doctor, I think I can justify it."

OOOOOOO

165

The two men did not speak as they rode the elevator to the eleventh floor. Jack was not in the mood for idle chitchat, and Sam was too busy thinking of ways to spend his sixty dollars. When the doors opened, the two silently stepped out and looked for Casper's apartment.

The hallway was cold and drafty, and the autumn wind rattled through a half-opened window near the stairwell. Sam knocked several times on Casper's door, but there was no answer. He waited until he was certain that nobody was watching, and then wriggled the spare key into the lock. Surprisingly, the door had been left unlocked and it pushed open easily. Sam shrugged at Jack, and waved the psychiatrist inside.

The apartment was huge, and the décor was bold and expensive. House music was softly playing on the stereo, and several of the lights were left on. Jack walked to the stereo, and turned it off. "Cass?" he called out but there was no response.

"Doctor Lolly?" the doorman said.

Jack walked to the bedroom, and the doorman quietly followed. The bed was not made, and the pillows were thrown on the floor. The bedroom closet and several dresser drawers were left open. Most of the socks and underwear were taken, but the clothes in the closet were not. Jack turned to the doorman. "He's been here. He took some socks, and underwear, and maybe a few other things." The doorman nodded in return.

Together they searched the living room, and the study. The balcony was located just off the study, and the two men stepped outside. The view was simply breathtaking.

The doorman whistled. "Wow, this is some view." he said, as he admired Central Park from above.

"Yep." Jack agreed. He wondered if Casper was hiding among the shady trees, and even shadier characters that populate the great park. Jack knew from his experience that psychopaths loved public parks, especially this one. It was a phenomenon he could not explain, but everyone seemed to act a little crazier in Central Park. Jack went back inside to search the rest of the apartment. The doorman lingered for a while on the balcony, admiring the view.

Nothing was disturbed in the kitchen, the study, or the living room. Jack figured that Casper must have spent very little time in the apartment. The bathroom was located off the living room, and the door was conspicuously closed. Jack walked to the door, and knocked lightly with his knuckle.

"Cass?" There was no answer, but the faint sound of running water could be heard through the door. The doorknob was warm, and Jack opened the door carefully. A thick wet wall of steam poured out.

"Cass?" he shouted, guarding his face against the heat. Again, there was no response.

The water was running in the shower, and Jack swatted his way through the steam to the shower curtain, and tore it open. The tub was empty. Jack angrily reached in and turned the faucet off, briefly burning himself. The murky bathroom fell silent, and Jack waited several minutes for the steam to dissipate. He walked over to the sink, and noticed that the basin was still wet, and some gooey toothpaste was dripped on the drain. The toilet was unflushed, and a few pills of *Primatene* were in the soap dish.

The doorman appeared in the doorway. "What's goin' on in here?" he asked, waving at the steam.

Jack did not answer him, and he wiped the condensation from the mirror on the medicine cabinet. He looked at his lip in the blurry mirror. It was still swollen, and the scab was softening in the steam. He picked at it briefly.

"Well, I'd say he's been here. You're sure he didn't leave." Jack asked the doorman again.

"I'm positive." Sam did not appreciate being treated like a fool.

Jack reached for the medicine cabinet, and Sam interrupted. "You know Doc. This ain't such a good idea. Maybe we should leave...I'm getting' a bad feeling about this."

Jack shot him a look, and pulled open the door to the medicine cabinet. Hundreds of marbles suddenly poured out. The sound was deafening. They bounced all over the sink, into the toilet, across the floor, and even into the tub. Jack was startled, and he jumped back clutching his chest. Slipping on the marbles, he braced himself against the shower wall. On the inside of the cabinet door, Casper left a message for Jack.

'Dear JB—Do you think I've lost my marbles?' Was written in thick black marker.

The doorman found the scene very amusing, and he let out a satisfied giggle. "You shouldn't have done that." he said.

"Thanks for the news flash, Detective." Jack returned. He crossed the floor, stumbling several times on the marbles, and squeezed by the portly doorman.

The two men left the apartment, and Sam locked the door while Jack waited by the elevator. The hallway was unbelievably drafty, and Jack again closed his jacket snugly around himself. The window rattled loudly at the end of the corridor. Something was very strange. It was late fall, and the weather had not been really warm in nearly a month.

"Why would that be open?"

"What? Hey where are you going?" Sam asked, as Jack walked passed him towards the partially opened window.

"Why is this window open?" Jack asked again, and pulled the window completely open. He stuck his head outside the building, and into the cold air. He was looking onto the fire escape, which led eleven floors down to a patio in the back. Jack visually scouted the area from above. The patio was enclosed in barbed wire fence, which was an unfortunate necessity in New York City. Jack pulled his head back inside, and Sam was standing directly behind him.

"Could someone get out from here?" he asked.

The doorman shrugged in response. "I guess. But it would be awfully hard to get over that fence."

Jack thought for a moment, then climbed through the window, and stood on the cast iron platform.

"Whoa Doc!" Sam tried to stop him. "I can't let you do that."

"Why?"

"It's against procedure."

Jack placed both hands on the window, and pushed it snuggly down between them. "Fuck procedure." he told the doorman through the glass, and began to descend the metal staircase.

After spiraling down eleven flights, Jack hung from the last level and lightly dropped himself onto the patio floor. He dusted his hands off, and walked to the fence. It was tall, about fifteen feet high, and topped with jagged loops of razor wire. He doubted Casper would have gone over the top. Nobody was that psychotic. He must have gotten out some other way.

Jack carefully explored the perimeter, and at first glance the fence appeared to be intact. Then he noticed a small defect in one of the corners. He wrapped his hands in the chain link, and tugged on it. There was actually a large gap in the fence, and a grown man could easily fit through it. Jack carefully bent the fence over his head, and ducked underneath. He stepped over rocks and garbage, and entered a short dark tunnel. After feeling his way through the dark, he emerged on Sixty-eighth Street again. Jack scratched his head as he stood on the sidewalk, feeling somewhat humiliated and beaten. Casper was playing games with him, and he was feeling like a sore loser...A very sore loser.

It was a little after four p.m., and the temperature was dropping. The shadows cast by the buildings were fading, and it would soon be dark. Jack took out his cellular phone, and called Caroline. She was preparing dinner for herself again, and Jack apologized for his absence profusely. He promised that he would hurry home, and he meant it this time. He had been pounding the pavement all day, and he was getting tired. He hung up the phone, and dropped it into his jacket. After the traffic signal changed, he crossed the street and disappeared into Central Park.

OOOOOOO

Casper was clean and refreshed, but a thick lawn of stubble was again sprouting on his handsome face. He did not have enough time to shave when he was at the apartment, because he knew that Jack would soon come looking for him there. Instead he quickly showered, threw some essentials into a duffel bag, and left. He was now on a crowded express subway car, headed downtown towards the garage.

We've got to do something about the garage.

Casper, get rid everything.

Casper was sick, very sick, but he could not appreciate this. He was a prisoner to these mental distortions and distractions, yet he felt limitless.

In fact, he felt free beyond human comprehension, and he would die to protect this new psychic liberty. He closed his wild eyes and swallowed two more tablets of *Primatene.*

Everybody is after what we've got Cass.

Nobody can be trusted.

"That's for sure." Casper accidentally answered the voices aloud, drawing the attention of several subway passengers.

Cass, Don't be so stupid! They cannot know.

They must never find out what is going on here!

Casper nodded at the other passengers. "I've been under a lot of stress lately." He politely excused himself, and washed the pills down with a cup of warm coffee.

Stupid, stupid, stupid!

You're so fuckin' stupid sometimes, Cass.

Casper, angered by the indignant voices in his head, was about to lash out at them when he was interrupted by a sad, sultry voice from behind.

"Me too. There's too much stress in this life." she said.

Casper turned in his seat to face Jessica Johnston. She was twenty-eight years old, and looked a decade younger. She was sharply dressed with fabulous blonde hair, wide blue eyes, and innocently pouting lips. She was wearing a short skirt under her jacket, and her legs were firm and long. Casper swallowed deeply, and made room for her next to him on the subway seat.

Now you're thinking, Cass.

The two chatted as they headed downtown. She told him that she was an advertising account manager at one of the large firms in the city. She was engaged to be married, and was wearing a large diamond engagement ring. Her fiancé was a wealthy art dealer, and she seemed less than excited about being married to him. Casper told her that he was a psychiatrist, with a special interest in schizophrenia. Jessica laughed at first, but was immediately intrigued.

"Is it true about what they say about psychiatrists?" Jessica flirtatiously asked him.

"Well, what do '*They*' say?" Casper played along.

"All of them are freaking nut-jobs." She looked into his eyes. She found him mysterious, and unbearably attractive. Her palms were sweaty, and she slowly rubbed them dry on her black nylons.

"Craziness is in the eye of the beholder. It all depends on your particular perspective"

"What do you mean?"

Casper paused, and placed a finger to his lip. He was imagining all of the wild things he would like to do to her. "Take yourself for example. I think you're crazy for marrying this meatball. In fact, I bet you even think you're crazy for marrying this guy."

"You mean my fiancé?" she said in a hoity-toity way, and coyly touched his arm.

"Oh yes, your fiancé...That's what I meant." Casper rolled his eyes sarcastically.

"I didn't marry him...*yet*." She softened her voice, clearly inviting him.

The two talked and flirted as the downtown Number Two train barreled through several stations, and finally slowed to a stop. The doors opened at Fourteenth Street, and Casper stood to leave. He affectionately grabbed her hand, and spoke seductively.

"Okay then, Jessica. Tonight we start our stress free lives." He handed her a piece of paper, with a name and telephone number on it. "Here's my number, but I'll see you later, okay?"

"Yep." She hesitated only for a second, then shoved the piece of paper into her pocket. "I'll be at *Trilogy* at eight o'clock sharp."

"Don't stand me up." he warned her.

"Do I look like that type of girl?"

"Okay, eight o'clock it is. Don't be late." Casper winked at her, and stepped onto the platform.

Jessica's cheeks felt flush, and she fanned the heat away with her hands. She had not been so attracted to a man in a long time, and she felt giddy about this chance encounter. Perhaps things were changing for her.

The doors closed, and the train pulled out of the station. Casper watched from the platform as the subway disappeared into the tunnel.

Give it to her good, Cass.

"Jessica, Jessica, Jessica." Casper whispered, and took a deep breath of the stale underground air.

Jessica, Jessica, Jessica

"Oh, I'm gonna give it good to her all right." Casper thrusted his pelvis several times on the platform, and then headed towards the garage. "I feel like I haven't been laid in a month."

CHAPTER NINETEEN
♦♦♦♦♦

Jack searched Central Park for over two hours, and there was still no sign of Casper. His feet were throbbing and his calves ached, so he sat on a wooden bench and rested in the dark. The park was still crowded, but now most of the runners, skaters, and bicyclists were heading home, and the freaks were just beginning to show up. It was mid-November and the trees had shed most of their leaves, covering the ground in a carpet of orange and brown death. Against the moonlit sky the naked tree branches seemed vein-like and skeletal, giving the robust park an oddly diseased appearance.

Jack watched a group of gothic teens as they walked toward the Sheep's Meadow. They appeared to be looking for something. Uniformly dressed in black clothing, their anemic faces floated like balloons into the murky shadows. Jack knew from his experience that these were not normal kids, and this was no passing phase. They didn't laugh or sing as they walked. They didn't gossip about boys and girls, or school. They were clearly lost in problems larger than themselves, and this was how they coped. They escaped the horrors of daily life, by hiding themselves in costumes of death and gore. Perhaps this made them feel accepted, not only by each other, but also by the rest of the world. Death, even if manufactured, commanded sympathy and attention. This was probably what they were really looking for in the dark corners of the park.

The group slowly disappeared into the darkness, and Jack briefly closed his eyes. He thought about his psychotic friend, the botched experiment, and his devoted wife. His sterling career was now in jeopardy, as was one of his dearest friendships. The relationship he rebuilt with Caroline was beginning to crumble again, and Jack no longer had all the answers. He desperately wanted to return to his life before the experiment, but he was uncertain how to get there.

○○○○○○○

After Casper finished hosing off the wall in the Isolation Chamber, he turned the water off. He dropped the hose onto the chamber floor, and stepped into the observation area. He picked up the fish bowl and held it close to his face. Pontious and Pilot swam innocently above the blue gravel, completely unaware of the catastrophe that awaited them.

"Well guys, this is the end of the road for us." Casper told the two fish. "I'm onto bigger and better things now."

Casper listened to the fish as they pleaded for their aquatic lives.

They don't realize that there is more Cass.

"I know, I know guys." Casper told the fish. "But there is nothing to be afraid of. Believe me, I'm doing you a favor. There is life beyond this fish bowl, a life that you can only appreciate through your death. Sure it's gonna suck for a while, but you'll get over it. Trust me."

The fish pleaded to him again, but Casper would not listen to them.

"I'll see you on the other side, boys." he said, and turned the fish bowl upside down. "Welcome to my world."

The two fish crashed to the cement in a ball of water and gravel. They flipped and flopped wildly on the floor, slowly suffocating in the stale garage air. Pilot outlived Pontious by about a minute, and Casper patiently waited for the stronger fish to die. Once both of the fish were dead, he left the garage whistling *New York, New York,* and swinging the empty fishbowl in his hand.

It took only two hours for him to remove everything from the garage, and pile all the electronic equipment and furniture into a small hill on the sidewalk. After placing a new padlock on the chain, he locked it securely and tossed the fishbowl onto the top of the pile. He placed a cardboard sign in front of it. 'FREE STUFF' it read.

Casper had rented a West Village hotel room for five days, and he needed to quickly get back there. He looked at his watch...He was running late. He needed to wash up before his date with Jessica Johnston on the Upper Eastside. Leaving the pile on the sidewalk, he jogged to the corner, hailed a cab and climbed inside.

○○○○○○○

It was nearly seven thirty, and Jack had promised Caroline that he would be home early. He had rested on the bench for twenty minutes and although he now felt physically rested, he was mentally exhausted. He sighed as he rose from the bench. His muscles were tight, and he stretched his sore body before slowly walking out of the park. He wanted to check the garage one last time before heading home.

"Taxi!" he yelled, waving his arms at a passing yellow cab. The driver pulled abruptly to the side of the road, and punched the meter. Jack opened the door, and grunted woefully as he climbed into the back seat.

"Where to?" the cabby asked, looking at Jack's tired face in the rear view mirror.

"Tenth Street and Greenwich Avenue." Jack said, and the cab sped off downtown.

The ride was short and ferocious. They stopped only briefly for a red traffic signal, and arrived at Tenth Street in a matter of minutes. Strangely several cars and trucks clogged the narrow street, and the cab became stuck in this small traffic jam. Jack poked his face through the window. His frustration continued to grow. They were only about one hundred yards from the garage.

"I'll get out here." he told the cabby. "I'll walk the rest of the way."

He paid the taxi driver and stepped out of the car. He began to walk down Tenth Street when he noticed that something strange was happening down the block. There was a small but enthusiastic mob gathered on the sidewalk just outside of the garage. The crowd was noisy, and collected more people as Jack approached. Some of the people were placing heavy items into cars and trucks. Others were carrying computers, furniture, and fixtures on foot. Another man slowly walked up the block towards Jack. He was carrying a large piece of glass on his back, being careful not to break it. Jack looked inquisitively at the man and the glass as they passed. It was a mirror on one side, glass on the other, and Jack recognized it immediately. It was the mirror from the isolation chamber.

"Hey!" Jack shouted at the crowd, as he sprinted toward them. "Stop!"

The frenzied pack was indifferent to Jack's presence. He shouted again but they still ignored him. He tried to push his way to the center of the crowd but the mob was too thick, and he nearly got trampled. He looked back up the block. The man carrying the mirror slowly lumbered around the corner and out of sight. Jack cursed aloud, and then ran through the alley to the garage door.

"Cass!" he shouted, as he pounded on the side door.

He dug into his pocket, and fumbled for his keys. He tried several different keys in the padlock, but he could not get it open. None of the keys seemed to fit. He pulled on the lock with all his strength, but it would not budge. He looked around the alley for something heavy, and he found a brick against the fence. It was old and muddy, but was of considerable weight. He picked it up and ran back to the door. He used the brick as a hammer, and repeatedly smashed the lock until it came loose from the chain. He unraveled the chain, kicked the door open and stepped inside the empty garage. Everything was gone.

Jack could not believe what he was seeing. All of the computers, VCRs, televisions, and equipment were gone. The console and all the furniture were gone, and there was a large rectangular hole in the wall where the two-way mirror used to be. The isolation chamber had been cleanly hosed down, and the walls were now bare. Most of the electrical wires had been yanked from their sockets, and the closet was empty. Jack shook his head in disbelief. It was as if the experiment never happened.

Jack noticed the pile of gravel and the two dead goldfish. He walked over and squatted beside their tiny dead bodies. He touched them. They were dead, but still moist. Casper could not have left long ago, Jack thought to himself. He stood, and walked back outside. By now the majority of the crowd had dispersed, and most of the equipment was gone. Jack walked to the remainder of the pile on the sidewalk. Only a broken desk chair and a framed picture were left. The picture was face down on the seat, and Jack turned it over and picked it up. It was a picture of Casper and Jack on a fishing trip in June of nineteen eighty-seven. Jack dusted the glass off with his sleeve, and held it up to the street light. They both looked much younger then...Jack was newly married, and beginning his academic post at New York University. Casper just graduated college. Jack smirked and sighed deeply as he recalled the relaxing trip. He and Casper had gone fishing off Long Island to escape the hot city, and celebrate Casper's admission to Yale's medical school. Jack was almost overcome with emotion when suddenly someone nudged him from behind. He turned quickly, barely moving his feet, to see a burly man standing behind him.

"Uh...Excuse me." the man said, as he gave Jack another friendly New York push.

Jack stepped out of his way. "Can I help you?"

"Mind if I take this chair." Before Jack could answer, the man bent down, and heaved the broken chair to his barreled chest. "Thanks." he said, and tossed it carelessly into the back of his pick-up. Moments later he sped off.

Jack dropped his hands to his side, and hung his head. Everything was gone now. The whole experiment had been erased. He looked again at the picture in his hand.

"What are you up to, Cass?" he whispered at the picture. "What have we done?" Jack boiled for a moment, until he felt the arteries throbbing in his forehead. The city suddenly seemed cold and overwhelming. He closed his fist around the frame, gnarled his teeth, and threw the picture deep into the alley. It crashed against the back fence, shattering the glass and cracking its cheap wooden frame. He grunted forcefully after the picture broke, closed his jacket around his chest and headed home.

○○○○○○○

Caroline was already asleep when Jack returned to the brownstone so he quietly closed himself in the bathroom, and cleaned his face in the sink. His skin felt swollen and coarse, and after thoroughly washing, he carefully patted the warm water off his face with a dry towel. He tiptoed across the carpet to the side of the bed, and slipped under the covers. Caroline stirred a bit, but did not fully wake. Jack sighed and plopped his head deeply into the pillow.

It was nearly impossible to fall asleep. He felt hot and irritable. He tried to reposition himself many times, and even let his legs droop out from underneath the sheets. Nothing helped him. The sweat still oozed from between his thighs, and a pool of the salty fluid collected in the small of his back. Jack knew that this insomnia was simple mental hyperactivity, but the tension in his head would not abate. Finding Casper had become an obsession for Jack, and he was physically incapable of letting it go. Not even for a few hours. He was desperate for sleep, and the frustration grew over the next several hours, as he lay awake waiting for a respite that never arrived.

○○○○○○○○

The crowd at *Trilogy* was pretentious and distracting, so after a few drinks at the bar, Jessica invited Casper back to her apartment. They were having a great time with meaningful conversation. She thought she had finally connected with someone. They had just met, but it seemed like she had known him for years. They discussed their fears, passions, and desires. God, he was so damn charming, and she didn't want the night to ever end.

She lived in a one-bedroom Upper Eastside apartment, and was planning to move in with her fiancé in the next few months. He lived in a penthouse apartment on the Lower Westside, and there was ample room for the both of them. She hated that place.

Casper admired the enticingly feminine décor, while Jessica went into the kitchen to pour them wine. She had a few drinks to calm her nerves prior to meeting with Casper, and then three margaritas at the bar. She was a bit tipsy, but she felt great. She had not been this happy and carefree in over a year.

"Do you like red or white?" she called to him from the small kitchen.

"Uh…" Casper was vividly hallucinating. "Do you have a Merlot?"

"Yep." Jessica responded, and plucked the cork out of a bottle of *Glen Ellen*. She concentrated on the two glasses on the counter, and began to pour. She didn't want to make a fool out of herself tonight, so she was being careful not to spill. After the glasses were filled, she picked them up, inadvertently splashing some of the crimson liquid onto the counter-top.

Damn it! She thought to herself, and placed the wine glasses back down on the counter. She swept the small red puddle with her finger, and placed it in her mouth. "Mmmm" she moaned, and brought the two goblets into the living room.

Casper was trying desperately to ignore the voices and visions in his head. There was an unquestionable femininity here, and it was almost overwhelming for him. The provocative scent of silk panties and body perfume filled the air and seductive music was playing on the stereo. Casper closed his eyes and took a deep velvety breath through his nose.

"One Merlot for you," Jessica said, handing the glass to Casper, "and one for me."

She was wearing a very short skirt and a tight cotton blouse. Underneath her black stockings, her thighs were already moist and slippery. She felt flushed, and her heart was racing. There was something untamed about this man, something wild. She was unbelievably attracted to Casper, and she did not attempt to conceal the sexual urgency that she was feeling. She sat on the couch, crossed her legs, and invited Casper to sit next to her.

Casper took a large gulp of his wine, nearly finishing the glass. Some of the blood-red liquid trickled onto his chin, and he wiped it away with his sleeve.

I want a piece of that, Cass.

Go teach her, Cass. Show her what we can do.

Casper sat next to her, perhaps a little too close. Soon the two were kissing hungrily, and groping at each other's clothing. He slid her to the floor, and tore her shirt open. The buttons flew off in different directions, and he kept kissing her, smothering her. She was having difficulty breathing. Things were going too fast, and too furious, yet she didn't want him to stop. He hiked up her skirt, and pulled her panties aside. In one vicious thrust, he entered her and she screamed in pain. He was large and thick, almost inhuman. With each thrust he gave her, the pleasure subsided and the pain increased. After a short while, he flipped her over onto her belly, and lifted her rear into the air. Suddenly the kissing turned to biting, and the sex turned to sodomy. Tears rolled off her face and splattered onto the parquet floor as she protested in agony. An hour later, Casper finished with her and abruptly left the apartment. Humiliated and sore, Jessica pulled her knees to her chest and wept quietly on the floor for a while.

This was the latest in a string of misfortunes for Jessica. She was profoundly unhappy in her life, and had been spiraling out of control for several months. She was engaged to a man whom she did not love, and she frequently drank her sorrows away in the local bars. Casper was not the first stranger she had taken home. In fact, there were several others. But this was different. This encounter was violent. This was a violation. This was rape...but she hesitated to call it that. Like most victims, she placed blame firstly on herself. She was drunk, she invited him in, and she consented to sex. How would she explain all of this to her family and fiancé? Nobody would ever believe her. She didn't even know this guy! She only knew his name and profession, yet she was willing to sleep with him. She crawled to the bedroom disgusted with herself.

She decided to never tell anyone about what happened. It would simply be too painful, both for her and her family. She stood at the mirror by the dresser. Her eyes were swollen and reddened with tears. Her back was covered in bite marks, and her legs trembled from the pain in her backside.

"You're so fucking stupid!" she cried at her mirror image, and opened one of the dresser drawers. "No one can ever know about this." She shook her head shamefully. "No one can ever know!"

She pulled out a bottle of *Tylenol* and an old nightgown she had not worn since high school. She slipped the cotton nightgown over her head, and she felt safe again. In the drawer, hidden underneath the nightgown, was a bottle of vodka. She uncapped it, and waved it briefly in front of her nose. She unfolded the piece of paper that Casper had given her earlier on the subway, and placed it on the dresser. She scoffed at the scribbled name and telephone number.

"See you in hell, Doctor Jack Benedict...I'll see you in hell." she whispered.

She swallowed one hundred and fifty tablets of *Tylenol*, and washed them down with a quart of vodka. Looking one last time in the mirror, she vowed again to die with this secret...and on this night she did.

CHAPTER TWENTY
◆◆◆◆◆

Jack sat up quickly in bed, startling Caroline from a sound sleep. There was something on the balcony, a shadowy figure that moved silently in the moonlight behind the white curtain. Then there was a wriggle of the brass doorknob. Jack sprang to his feet and pressed himself into the corner by the door. He crouched by the nightstand, and picked up the lamp. He yanked the plug from the wall, and slowly pulled the curtain away from the French doors.

"What is it, Jack?" Caroline asked, clutching the bedsheets to her chest.

"Ssshhh." Jack silenced her with his finger. "Did you hear that?"

"Hear what?" She pulled the sheets even tighter.

"Someone was trying to get in." Jack whispered quickly, and peered out into the night. "I saw someone, and then the doorknob moved." Jack drew the curtain wide open and jumped in front of the doors...No one was there.

Caroline let out a relieved sigh, and Jack looked in all four corners of the balcony. "I don't understand..." he said, as he swiveled his head from one corner to the next. "There was someone there." He opened the doors and stepped onto the balcony.

"Jabes, come back to bed." Caroline pleaded. "You're making me nervous."

"One minute." Jack leaned against the railing, and searched the vacant streets. It was very early in the morning, and the streets were still dark. The cement floor chilled his bare feet, and he shuddered for a second. Strangely his body found the cold autumn night refreshing. He took a deep breath of the night air, and headed back inside.

"I don't understand..." He closed the door securely behind himself, scratching his head. "I could've sworn there was..."

"Jabes, have you even slept yet?" Caroline interrupted him.

Jack placed the lamp back on the nightstand and looked at the alarm clock. It was four-thirty in the morning. Jack recalled being awake at three forty-five, but could not recall anything else after that. "It's been a while. I'm not sure...I certainly don't feel like it."

"Come lay down. You need some sleep." Caroline urged him again, patting the damp bedsheets. "Jabes these sheets are soaked!" she complained.

"I know." Jack sat beside her, and pulled some of the sheets over his lap. "I can't sleep. I've been tossing and turning all night. All week."

"Aren't you going to the office in the morning?"

"Yeah." Jack rubbed his eyes. "I plan to stop by. See a few patients. But I'll start officially next week. Tomorrow will be a light day though."

"Why don't you call in sick?"

"I can't. It's my first day back."

"Jack." She pulled him firmly by the arm. "When was the last time you slept through the night?"

Jack thought about this for a while and realized that it had indeed been some time. He had lost a lot of sleep throughout the course of the experiment, and ever since Casper escaped, he had not really slept a wink. "I want to go to sleep, but I can't. I keep thinking about the experiment...I keep thinking about Casper. Shit, I hope he's okay."

"Please, Jabes...Please, try to get some sleep. You're starting to imagine things."

Jack chuckled softly, and looked back out at the moonlit balcony. "You're probably right, you're probably right." he relented...*But it seemed so real.*

○○○○○○○

Caroline had just begun to snore softly when the phone rang. Jack was still wide-awake, and he picked up the phone on the first ring.

"Cass?" he answered.

There was a short silence on the other end of the phone, and then a vaguely familiar voice. "Uh...Is this Doctor Benedict?"

"Yes, who's calling?" Jack asked, and sat up in bed.

"Doc, I hope you remember me…and I'd like to apologize for waking you up so early, but I'm Detective John Cavanagh from the NYPD."

"Who?"

"I brought you your wallet the other day, you were having trouble paying for your ride? Well, you looked loaded, so you may not recall…"

"Oh…Yes, yes, yes, I remember you Detective." Jack interrupted. "What can I do for you?" He became queasy, realizing that this may be bad news about Casper.

"Well, um…This is really horrible news, but it seems that someone you may know has committed suicide…Looks like an intentional overdose."

"Shit!" Jack swung his feet over the side of the bed, and was silent for a while. Finally he mustered enough strength to continue. "Who was it?" he asked with his eyes closed.

"I think her name is Jessica Johnston…That's what it says on her license." Detective Cavanagh was one of the best detectives in the city. He had an uncanny ability to find clues and leads where others had run dry. He was extremely observant. That was his gift, and he used it wisely. It was instinctual, and in this city, instinct went a long way. He had inspected her apartment from top to bottom. This was his routine because not every suicide was truly a suicide. This case was not so simple either. There were many loose ends, and he wanted to be thorough. He tossed the dead woman's purse onto the dresser, and picked up the empty bottle of *Tylenol*.

"Who?!" Jack was almost overcome with relief. "What name was that?"

"Jessica Johnston…Good looking girl, mid twenties, long blonde hair." He squinted into the mouth of the empty pill bottle.

"I'm sorry officer, but that name doesn't sound familiar to me."

"Really?"

"Not at all." Jack responded. "How did you get my number?"

"Your name and number were written on a small piece of paper by the vodka and *Tylenol*." He rummaged through her drawers and personal items. He was looking for photographs, momentos, and other personal items.

"Really?!" Jack was honestly surprised.

"Yeah, that's why I called. I figured she may have been a patient of yours, or something...I figured you would want to know about something like that."

"Of course, of course I would. But I really don't recall the name." Jack closed his eyes and searched his memory. He had been on leave, and did not receive any new consultations. "I'm sorry Detective, I wish I could help."

"Hey, don't be sorry. I'm sorry for waking you up at this hour, Doc. Someone probably gave her your phone number, and she never got around to calling. Someone probably tried to help her." Something didn't make sense to him.

"The poor thing." Jack sighed. "I wish I knew..."

"Yeah, well Doc, again...I'm sorry for bothering you. Get back to sleep." Cavanagh hung up the phone. He looked uncomfortable. There was definitely something wrong here.

"What'd you get, John?" asked Officer Bellows, a policeman who was standing next to Cavanagh.

"Something isn't right. The buttons on the floor, her blouse and skirt were tossed, ripped. The two wine glasses in the living room. I think there must have been someone with her shortly before her suicide. Something else transpired here. This young woman may have committed suicide, but who or what brought her to that point? There's something, or someone, missing from this picture. I'm certain of it. And besides, this Doctor guy seemed kinda peculiar. Follow up the post-mortem on her, make sure they do toxicology and a Sexual Assault Survey. And do a full sweep of the place."

He handed the paper with Jack's name and number to Bellows, and then turned back to survey the scene.

OOOOOOO

Jack was relieved that nothing had happened to Casper, but still uneasy. He placed the phone back on the nightstand. It was almost six in the morning.

"Who was that?" an exhausted Caroline asked.

"A Detective from downtown." He turned towards her. "It seems that some young woman down there took her life tonight, and they thought she might have been a patient of mine. But she wasn't."

"Why would they think that?"

"Well, my name and number were on her dresser."

"Humph...Someone probably gave it to her...Too little, too late." She rolled onto her belly, and buried her face in the pillow.

"Yeah, I guess that's possible, but...." Jack stood and headed toward the shower. His body creaked in protest as he crossed the floor.

"But, what?" Caroline muffled.

"It was our home phone number...How could she have gotten our home phone number?" He shut the bathroom door behind himself, and turned the water on in the shower.

The cold water was rejuvenating, and Jack reflexively hyperventilated when he stepped into the frosty stream. For a brief moment he felt alive again. He stretched and yawned, placing his face squarely in the stream. His joints creaked and cracked as he lathered himself up. He scrubbed the salty residue from his skin, and then used the shower massager to loosen the knots in his neck and lower back. As the suds swirled effortlessly down the drain, Jack closed his eyes and rested his head for a few seconds against the bathroom tile. He almost fell asleep, but not quite.

Jack turned off the faucet, and let the remainder of the grimy water gurgle down the drain. He dried himself off, and combed the hair back from his face. He spread some shaving cream across his stubble, and was about to shave. He decided not to. Shaving didn't seem like such a priority anymore. Besides, his face had changed so much in the last few weeks. He looked like a different man. His eyelids were puffy, and they sagged halfway over his eye sockets. His face appeared drawn and gaunt despite the fact that he had gained a considerable amount of weight. The wrinkles that had previously been a distinguishing feature on his face were now deep furrows that gave his skin a weather-beaten appearance. He felt gruesome and vowed to take better care of himself once he found Casper.

Since he was in the shower longer than he had anticipated, he dressed himself quickly in the dusky morning light. He went down to the kitchen and made himself a pot of coffee. He casually flipped through the morning newspaper as he sipped his coffee, and looked for any stories that seemed unusual. There weren't any.

After he finished his coffee, he picked up his briefcase and threw several journals and mail inside of it. He stepped outside and then headed off to the hospital. The streets were typically busy for a weekday. Yellow taxis clogged the streets, and swarms of business types hurried off to the subway and bus stations. Jack walked to the corner, looked at his watch and yawned deeply. Tears came and temporarily blurred his vision. He rubbed the clear fluid from the corners of his eyes, and complained to himself. He had just finished his coffee moments ago, but it only lifted his fatigue for a short while. He desperately needed to grab a more potent coffee from the café down the street. He turned the corner and entered the small shop.

"Hey! Good morning, Doc!..Long time, no see." Kylie happily greeted him from behind the glass counter.

"How are you, Kay." Jack wearily returned.

"Where've you been?"

"Around...around." Jack was terse as he spied the muffins and cakes underneath the glass.

She was blunt, "You look like hell." she said. His face was still scarred, and his lip was somewhat swollen.

This surprised Jack, and he glared at her. "It's been a rough month, Kay. I've got a lot on my mind."

Kylie tried to retract her statement "I didn't mean it like..."

"I know Kay, I know." Jack rudely interrupted her, and created an awkward silence.

"What'll you have?" Kylie reacted to this tension with formality.

"I'll have a large hazelnut...Light and sweet." Jack searched the glass countertop and then finally found what he had been looking for. "...And I'll take one of these Mini-Bundt cakes, the one with the chocolate on it."

Kylie pulled the cake from underneath the glass, and dropped it into a white paper bag. She slid the coffee to him, and Jack instantly opened it and began to drink. There was something very different about Jack today.

"Aaahh...That's more like it." He smiled, and swallowed the warm liquid.

He paid Kylie, and turned to leave. He was almost at the door, when Kylie called to him.

"Doc?"

Jack did not turn around when he stopped in the doorway. "Yeah?"

"Have a good day."

"Thank you, Kay." he mumbled, slurped from his coffee and left. "I'll see you."

Jack crossed the street, and sat on a park bench. He placed his briefcase on the ground, and crossed his legs. He intently watched the crowd, when suddenly he saw Casper in a small group of people headed toward the subway station. He stood and called out to him.

"Cass?!"

The man turned around, as did the rest of the crowd. It was not Casper. In fact, the man looked nothing like him. "That's strange." Jack said to himself and sat back down.

A courier on a bicycle approached Jack, swerving in and out of the morning traffic. For a brief moment, this man resembled Casper as well. "What the hell is going on?" Jack asked himself and rubbed his eyes.

A transit bus pulled to the sidewalk just in front of the park bench. Through the tinted glass, the driver appeared familiar. Jack stood and waited while several passengers stepped off, and then he approached the door.

"Are you coming on?" Casper asked him. He was driving the bus, and wearing a New York City Transit uniform. Jack gasped, and dropped his coffee onto the sidewalk. Some of the hot liquid splashed onto his pants.

"Buddy, are you getting on or not?" the driver asked him again. Casper was gone.

Jack was confused. He ascended the first two steps of the bus, and peered into the cabin. The passengers looked at him inquisitively, but there was no sign of Casper.

"Step all the way in, please." the driver demanded. "I've got a schedule to keep."

Jack turned and looked at him. The driver returned a sneer. "Get in, or get off, Bud. It's that simple."

Jack shook his head, and laughed lightly. He stepped off the bus and onto the sidewalk. The bus driver shut the doors behind him, and pulled away from the curb.

"Am I going crazy?" Jack asked himself, and turned several times on the sidewalk. "What the hell is going on?" He rubbed his face and slapped his cheeks, as if to awaken himself. He clicked on his cellular phone, and tried to call the office. There was too much static on the line, so after several attempts he headed for a pay phone and called Gladys at the office. It was nearly eight-thirty when she picked up the phone.

"Doctor Benedict's office." she answered.

"Gladys, it's me."

"Good morning, Jack. Where are you? Your first patient will be here in a few minutes." She shuffled papers on her desk.

"Yeah, about that Gladys...I don't think I can make it today."

"What?" Gladys was irate.

"Something is wrong with me." Jack looked suspiciously at the people around the pay phone. "I haven't been able to sleep in days." Everyone was starting to look like Casper. "Something just isn't right with me."

"You want me to cancel? This is very frustrating, Jack." Her demeanor was frank and impolite.

"I know, Gladys...I know. But I've got some things I need to clear up. Things haven't gone as planned. Something went very wrong." Jack buried himself in the phone booth like a frightened child.

"How 'bout tomorrow."

"Better cancel, Gladys." He closed his eyes.

"Wednesday?"

"Tentative...Very tentative."

There was a long frustrated silence as Gladys examined the appointment book. "Do you need anything, Jack? Can I help?"

"No Gladys. I'm sorry, but thanks." He wanted to cry, but struggled to maintain his composure.

"Okay, I hope to see you Wednesday."

"Yeah Gladys, thanks a lot. Listen page me if there is a problem, I have my pager on me."

"Sure." Gladys abruptly hung up the phone, and began to cancel the day's appointments. Jack's behavior was disturbing her, and she made a mental note to call his wife after she has handled the business for the day.

CHAPTER TWENTY ONE
◆◆◆◆◆

The subway roared to a stop at Fourteenth Street, Union Square Park. Casper pushed his way through the crowd, and stepped onto the platform. He had been riding the train all night, and was hallucinating wildly. He popped four tablets of *Primatene* in his mouth, and swallowed them without water.

Cass, Entropy is the structure here.

Order from entropy.

"I see everything so clearly now." he answered the voices in his head. There was an obese woman directly in front of him as the crowd ascended the steps.

I can see the cellulite from here.

She's taunting us, she knows we are here.

She knows we're watching.

At the top of the steps, Casper tapped the woman on the shoulder. She stopped and turned to face him with a cherubic smile.

She's one of them, Casper.

Tell her nothing! She'll figure it out.

Trust no one. Look at her...She's so phony.

"You know who I am?" Casper asked her.

"Excuse me?" the woman responded politely. She was on route to her job as a office manager, but was in no obvious rush.

Casper, you're losing it!

"Don't play stupid you fat bitch! You know who I am!"

The woman was speechless, and frightened. "I...I...I..." she stuttered.

"Who sent you? Was it Jack?" He grabbed her forcefully by the elbow, and shook her violently.

"I...I...I...don't know what..." She was in a state of panic. "Help, Help!" she called out to those around her. "Leave me alone! What do you want from me?" She started swinging at him.

Get the hell out of here, Cass!

You're gonna ruin everything!

"Shut up! Shut up!" Casper answered the voices, and then turned his attention back to the fat woman. She struck him several times in the head, and he slapped her once across the cheek. "Don't think that you can fuck with me, Pork Chop! Don't fuck with me or I'll destroy you." He pointed his finger at her, warning her.

Casper let the woman go and hurried down the sidewalk. A few people rushed to her aid, and the woman began to sob.

"I don't know what happened..." she began to explain. "He just grabbed me. I don't even know him." Several young men gave chase, but Casper hurried through the station, and disappeared into the crowd.

That was stupid, Casper.

You're gonna ruin it for all of us.

"Who? Who am I ruining it for. You're nothing without me!" he scoffed. "I am Perceptive. I'm running the show." He was talking to himself, but nobody seemed to care. People in New York City routinely ignored this type of behavior. It was simply to common to warrant attention.

He headed downtown, arguing with himself. This internal discussion became quite heated at some points, but still nobody seemed to care. After walking several blocks, he arrived at the hotel in the West Village. He entered the lobby of the sleazy establishment, and crossed the ratty red carpet. He had rented a room here for only five days. He figured that this would be enough time for him to complete his 'work'. He needed a retreat, a safe place to hide his new power. This sleazy area of the West Village was perfect for this. He would not be so conspicuous in such a freaky environment. He paid for his room in advance, all cash, and used a false name. Everyone did this down here. It was the convention. Nobody was real. In fact, the laws of relativity broke down in places like this, and Casper needed the camouflage this provided.

Whores and pimps cluttered the lobby, while a bunch of transvestites boarded the elevator. Casper approached the front desk. A wall of spit-stained *Plexiglas* enclosed the dilapidated desk, and the greasy man who sat behind it.

"What was that?" Casper asked him.

192

The grimy man turned to Casper, and answered him. "I didn't say anything." He failed to make eye contact with Casper.

The man removed a black plastic comb from his pocket, and pulled it through his slick hair. Insects collected in the teeth of the comb. Some were big and some were small. Some dead, some alive. Casper rubbed his eyes, and instantly they were gone.

He's playing tricks with us too, Cass.

"Uh-huh…" Casper laughed at the man. "Uh-huh. I see what you're up to. You're very clever, you're all very fucking clever!" Casper punched the *Plexiglas* lightly. "Fucking clever!" He punched it harder.

"Go about your business." the man warned. He was accustomed to assaulting behavior. "Go about your business." he repeated, and placed a pistol on top of the desk.

We'll deal with him later, Casper.

We've got other business to do. Keep your eye on the prize

"I'll be back." Casper said to the man, as he backed away from the glass. "I will be back." He crossed the lobby again and pushed the button for the elevator. He waited a few seconds for it to arrive, but it was moving very slowly. He began to hear haunting voices coming from the elevator shaft, so he decided to take the steps.

He had climbed to the third floor when he came across a transvestite prostitute in the stairwell. He was wearing a soiled black dress and a cheap wig. A cloud of cheap perfume surrounded him, and the pancake makeup failed to hide his undeniable masculinity.

Look at this poor freak.

That's disgusting.

Casper's stomach turned, and he tried to squeeze by the taller and significantly larger prostitute.

"Looking for a little company?" the transvestite asked Casper, grabbing him by the waist. His hands were strong and thick, and he pressed his silicone breasts against Casper's chest. "I'm quite a bargain." He began to untuck Casper's shirt. "I'm still partly preoperative…If you're into that."

I think I'm gonna be sick.

Casper pulled the prostitute closer, and whispered seductively. "You wanna know what I'm into?"

The transvestite's eyes were glossy and dark. Lost. "What?" he asked.

Casper opened his mouth as if to kiss him. The transvestite opened his mouth and waited for Casper's lips and tongue. Then there was blinding pain. Casper grabbed the prostitute by the groin, and squeezed tightly. He doubled over in pain, and was unable to speak. Casper grabbed his painted face by the chin, and lifted the man's genitals until he was standing on his toes.

Casper spoke softly, but sternly into the prostitute's ear. "I don't care what kind of fruit truck you rolled off of. Perhaps you had a horrible childhood, or perhaps you're simply confused about your sexuality?" The prostitute gasped for air, and Casper continued. "But let me introduce some reality into your little fantasy world. If you ever touch me again, if you ever proposition me again, I'll personally rip off your cock and make you swallow it. Do we have an understanding?" Casper waited for a response, but received none. He tightened his grip, and repeated himself. "Do we have an understanding?"

"Yes." the prostitute nodded.

"That's what I'm into. Got me, Queenie?" Casper let go, and the transvestite fell to the floor. "Now get the hell out of here." The man in the cheap dress could not move. "I don't want to see you on the way down. I'm feeling a little tense today."

The transvestite slowly rose to his feet, and Casper continued up the steps until he reached the sixth floor. The corridor was resounding in moans, groans, and an occasional cry for help. Casper ignored them all, opened the door to his room, and shut himself inside.

ＯＯＯＯＯＯＯ

The room was dark and dingy. Casper fiddled with a cheap clock radio by the bed, and finally found a suitable station. He turned the volume all the way up, and sang along. The music was heavy and fast, with the recurrent lyric *'Trip like I do.'* It was head-banging music by the band *Filter and the Crystal Method,* and Casper simply loved this song. He walked to the bathroom and yanked the chain that hung from the ceiling. A single lightbulb went on. Three or four cockroaches scattered in the light, and hid themselves in the crevices underneath the water stained walls. The bathroom was old and filthy, fitted with an old porcelain bathtub and a shower that had no curtain. The formerly white tub was stained in a brown film, and a paste of dust and pubic hair had cemented the drain long ago.

Casper was naked, and he admired his physique in the broken mirror above the sink. He turned on the faucet, and let the water trickle out. His stubble was thick and black, almost qualifying as a beard. He opened the medicine cabinet, and removed his razor. He splashed some of the tepid water on his face, and then wet his hair. He began to apply shaving cream to his face.

Trip like I do, Cass.

Why shave your face, Cass? You need a new look.

"A change in our appearance may actually help the situation." Casper spoke to his own jagged image in the mirror. "A new look...A disguise."

He pointed the can of shaving cream to his head, and massaged the white cream into his scalp. He slowly dragged the razor over his skull. Row by row, he removed the hair from the top of his head. Starting at the center, he then proceeded down the sides. He left only a small horseshoe of hair around his head, suggesting male pattern baldness. He rinsed the remainder of the shaving cream from his head, and admired his new look in the mirror. "Hi, I'm Sy Sperling, and I'm not only the *Hair Club* President, but I'm also a client." he said to his bald image.

The look was radical for him. His appearance was dramatically altered, and he looked fifteen years older. He rubbed his hand over his enlarged forehead, and smiled.

An excellent disguise.

Now you look like every other poor slob on Earth.

"Let's not dilly-dally, boys...We've got a lot of work to do." Casper pulled the chain as he exited, and the bathroom fell dark again. "This will be real nice in the summertime."

OOOOOOOO

Casper closed his eyes as he stepped into the elevator, but the voices started immediately. He pushed the button for the hotel lobby, pulled his trench coat tightly around himself, and tried to remain calm.

I can't believe you let that guy behind the glass bully us.

I would teach that slime-ball a lesson.

How dare he...Doesn't he realize the power we have?

"I'll take care of it." Casper told them.

I don't know if you're man enough to protect us.

"I think you're wrong."

Casper, are you afraid of a little gun like that?

Fucking pussy.

"I said I'd fucking take care of it!" Casper shouted as the elevator continued to descend.

Do it now!

There's no time to waste you worthless piece of flesh!

"Fuck-off."

Casper was fuming by the time the elevator doors opened into the hotel lobby and his blood burned in the arteries of his brain. He sprinted out of the elevator, and charged the *Plexiglas* window. The sleazy man behind the glass barely made it to his feet when Casper jumped through the protective shield. The entire sheet of *Plexiglas* gave way, and sent the greasy man crashing to the floor. Casper picked him up by the collar, and threw him head first over the desk. The man landed on the lobby floor with a grunt. Casper hurdled back over the desk and followed him.

"You think a gun can beat me?" Casper picked the man up by the throat, and drove a knee into his gut. "Nothing...Nobody is more powerful than I am." He bounced the man's head off of the wall several times. The man's face left a bloodstain on the wall with each hit. Casper continued the assault until the greaseball went limp, and finally let him drop to the lobby floor. The man was still breathing, making blood bubbles from his nose.

"I should kill you right now, scumbag!"

Finish him, Cass!

Kill him!
Finish him now!
"No." Casper dusted his hands off, and took a deep breath. "No, not him."

CHAPTER TWENTY TWO
♦♦♦♦♦

An occasional cloud dotted the sapphire blue sky, and the sun was blinding. This weather probably would have been unbearable in August, but the cool autumn wind made the day downright beautiful. Jack squinted as he peered down the sunlit streets. It was mid afternoon, and he had been searching for Casper since early morning. He scoured the parks again, visited the museums, and even walked along the Westside Highway, but Casper was nowhere to be found

The city streets were crowded with the late lunch crowd, and Jack sat down to have a bite to eat at a local Westside pizzeria. He ordered a cheese calzone, and an iced coffee. A poor combination, but the coffee was a necessity, and so was the food. He was halfway through his meal when the beeper went off at his side. It was the office.

"Jeez!" Jack cursed aloud, and threw his napkin onto the paper plate. He had forgotten his cell phone at home.

He looked around the pizzeria for a pay phone, but he didn't see any. He approached the man behind the counter. "Is there a phone here? I'm a doctor."

The small Italian man answered him in broken English. "Pay phone on the corner." He pointed outside. "This phone here not for you..."

"I see." Jack excused himself, and sat back down. There was no such thing as doctor's privilege in this town. He decided to call after he finished his lunch, but moments later, his beeper went off again.

"Christ! Gladys, what the hell is going on?" Jack angrily rose from his seat, finished his iced coffee, and threw the remainder of the calzone into the trash.

He walked to the corner and picked up one of the pay phones. He deposited a quarter, and waited for a dial tone. It never came. He pulled the change lever, but the machine did not return his small investment. He left the receiver hanging by its cord, and went to the adjacent phone. He deposited another quarter, waited for a dial tone, and then called the office. The phone booth was covered in leaflets for a local dance club. Jack picked up one of them, and removed a pen from his shirt pocket.

"Hello, Doctor Benedict's office." Gladys sounded exasperated.

"Gladys it's me, what's going on?"

"Jack I'm not sure. The phones have been ringing off the hook."

"What? Why?" Jack plugged his free ear with a finger.

"I dunno." Gladys said. "It all started with Edna Abramson, she was really upset, crying, hysterical in fact. She said that your partner called her, and told her to hang herself."

"What?!" Jack pressed his palm into his ear, and retreated further into the phone booth to minimize the ambient noise of the city. "Hang herself? My partner? I don't have a partner?"

"That's what I told her, but she was so devastated, she said she is switching psychiatrists."

"You're kidding me?" Jack placed two more quarters in the pay phone.

"I wish I was." Gladys went on. "Then Jodi Ackerman, and Brian Ashton called, and then…"

There was nearly a collision at the corner where Jack was speaking on the phone, and he could not hear Gladys above the commotion in the streets. "Gladys…" Jack screamed into the phone. "I'm having trouble hearing you, could you speak up?" The drivers cursed at one another, and gestured violently.

"Sure." she responded loudly. "I said, Carol Beckman also called for a similar reason. They are all very upset with you."

"Gladys, can you give me their phone numbers?" Jack wedged the phone between his shoulder, and his ear. "Go ahead."

He copied down the phone numbers onto the back of one of the small neon fliers that littered the area, and he thanked Gladys again for all her troubles. "I'm gonna call them right now." he promised her. "I'll straighten things out."

Jack hung up the phone, and dug through his pockets for another quarter, he found only two of them. He carefully laid the small paper on the shelf, and began to dial Edna Abramson. Suddenly a gust of wind carried the piece of paper out of the phone booth, and sent it sailing into the street.

"Shit!" he said, and quickly hung up the phone.

The paper swirled haphazardly between speeding cars and trucks. Jack followed it into the dangerous traffic. Cars and buses screeched to a halt, some of them nearly killed him. The drivers honked their horns, and screamed insults out of their windows, but Jack continued to chase after the flake of neon paper. Just before the other side of the street, Jack snatched the leaflet in mid air, and jumped triumphantly to the sidewalk. He exhaled deeply, and turned the flier over. It was blank. There were no phone numbers on the paper. He looked out onto the street. There were hundreds of these fliers floating in and out of the traffic.

"Damnit!" he said, and crunched the paper between his fingers.

He pulled out his last quarter, and went to a pay phone on a different corner. "How'd you forget your phone Jack?" he mumbled to himself, cursing his dysfunctional brain. He placed another quarter in the slot, and waited for a dial tone. He called the office, and after several rings, Gladys finally picked up.

"Doctor Benedict's office, please hold."

"No! Gladys, don't!" Jack shouted, but it was too late. She had already put him on hold. "Son of a bitch." he cursed, while he listened to the hold music at his own office.

Gladys was taking a long time returning to the phone, and Jack was getting anxious that his quarter would soon run out. "C'mon...C'mon.." he huffed, and looked at his watch. Suddenly a computerized voice chimed in.

"Please deposit fifteen cents for the next one minute...Please deposit..."

"Shit!" Jack frantically patted all of his pockets, but could not find any change. Moments later, there was silence. "Hello?" Jack asked into the receiver, but the line was dead. Jack slammed the receiver into the phone several times. *"Shit! Shit! Shit!"* He kicked and punched the booth out of frustration.

○○○○○○○

Eleanor Kutzman was hysterical, and Casper did not try to comfort her. He was speaking to her on his cellular phone as he walked aimlessly through the city streets. He had been on the phone all afternoon, calling patients that he lifted from Jack's database of depressed patients. He had printed the data from the garage computer before he junked the machine several days ago. He figured it would come in handy. It was a long list but Casper had just about managed to get through half of it.

"It seems that we've exhausted all avenues of therapy at this point..." Casper told her. "And now, suicide may be the only viable option left for us."

Eleanor Kutzman could barely speak because she was so upset, but she managed to blurt out a phrase or two between the sniffles. "Doctor Benedict knows about this?"

"Of course he does." Casper responded. He turned the corner and noticed the commotion at a phone booth across the street. It was Jack, and he was kicking and punching a pay phone. "I'll be damned." Casper said.

Look at him!

He's gone freakin' berserk!

"What next, Doctor?" Misses Kutzman asked Casper. "What should I do?"

Casper stopped on the sidewalk, directly across the street from where Jack was clobbering the phone. "How tall is the building you live in?" he asked her.

"I live in a brownstone. Why?"

"Oh, that's too bad. It's not gonna be high enough."

"You want me to jump?!" she exploded.

"Well, not off a brownstone of course!" Casper waved at Jack, and tried to get his attention. "Ideally we'd like something a little bit higher. Six floors at least. That should do the trick."

"Are you crazy!" Eleanor cried into the phone.

"Maybe, maybe I am." Casper waved and waved. Finally Jack noticed him.

Jack stopped beating the phone booth. He could not believe what he was seeing. Was that Casper standing across the street? Or was it just another illusion? It looked like Casper, but this man was bald, perhaps

201

significantly older, and had a faint beard. He looked homeless. Jack rubbed his eyes, and squinted against the afternoon sun. Casper waved at him with the database print out in one hand, and a cellular phone in the other. He comically modeled his new hair-do and ratty outfit for Jack.

"Casper." Jack mumbled to himself. "Casper!" he shouted across the street, and then ran blindly into the intersection. Cars and trucks screeched around him. Horns blared, and people shouted.

"What should I do now?" Eleanor asked Casper, as Jack recklessly made his way across the street.

"Think hard, think high, and think final." Casper told her. "It's time for you to check out. Gotta go!" And he hung up abruptly.

Jack was almost across the street when Casper ran off. He dropped part of the database onto the sidewalk and darted for the subway station.

"Casper!" Jack shouted as he chased him. Casper was much faster than Jack, and he was easily slipping away.

Casper disappeared down the steps of the subway, and Jack followed him. After jumping the turnstile with ease, Casper slowed himself down to a confident walk. He turned back to look at Jack.

"Casper!" Jack shouted again from the turnstile, drawing the attention of the entire station. "Hold on!"

Casper kept walking away from him. Jack ran to the front of the token booth, ignoring the long line that was waiting to purchase tokens. He threw three-dollars under the window. "Two tokens please, and hurry! It's a matter of life and death."

The token clerk remained expressionless, but slid two tokens under the window. Jack swiped them up, and dropped one in the turnstile. On the platform Jack darted in and out of the thin crowd, and pursued Casper from a short distance. Casper again disappeared down the steps to the express train platform, and Jack jogged after him.

There were only two other passengers on the platform waiting for the Express. Casper walked casually to the very end of the platform, and jumped onto the tracks. Jack shouted to him again.

"Cass! C'mon! It's over Cass! I can help you!" Jack stood on the edge of the platform and watched as Casper disappeared down the dark tunnel. He begged him to return. "Cass!" he shouted after him, his voice echoing down the tracks.

Shit! This is crazy! Jack thought to himself. He sat on the edge of the platform, and carefully lowered himself onto the tracks. "I've gone completely bonkers." he mumbled to himself, and against his better judgement, he followed Casper into the pitch-black passage. He shouted to his friend as he treaded into the darkness. His steps were deliberate and cautious. Each time making sure his footing was sound. Rats squealed and scampered over his feet as he walked further down the tunnel. His attention was focused on Casper, who was now only a vague shadow in front of him. He followed for several frightening yards when Casper suddenly dropped out of sight. There was a turn in the tracks, or an intersection. It was too far, and too dark for Jack to tell. He screamed again. "Cass, come back! This is dangerous." Jack reoriented himself. He could no longer see the tracks below his feet. He believed he was centered, but he could not be sure. He took a few more steps further down the tunnel, and outstretched his arms for balance.

He was about fifty yards from the platform when he stumbled, twisting his ankle between the wooden railroad ties. Pain shot up his leg, and his foot began to throb. Despite the growing soreness, Jack continued to limp in the dark after his friend. "Casper!" He was determined to find him. "Casper?" Only echoes in return, then there was an eerie silence.

The rats in the tunnel began to squeal and scurry. Sheets of them scampered across his feet. Jack stopped in the middle of the tracks, and stood quietly. The ground was vibrating, very faintly. So faint that he could barely feel it through his shoes. It was getting stronger, definitely stronger. Then the metal rails on each side of him started to hum, and a light appeared at the far end of the tunnel.

"Shit!" Jack shouted. "Cass! A train!" Jack turned around and began to limp his way back toward the station. He was about sixty yards away from the platform, and the train was quickly gaining ground. He galloped as fast as he could, but at this rate he wasn't going to make it. *C'mon Jack, Run...Damnit!* The tracks began to vibrate wildly below his feet, and Jack pulled into a full sprint toward the orange glow of the subway station. He stumbled several times, but somehow managed not to fall.

Sparks flew from the undercarriage of the train, igniting the cold darkness of the tunnel. With each blinding flash, Jack's shadow was thrown out of the tunnel in hideous poses as he fled from the on-coming train. The conductor saw Jack in his headlight and instantly pulled the emergency break. The wheels screeched, and the alarm sounded but the train still closed in on Jack. He was almost there, just a few feet away from the platform. Jack's entire body began to vibrate just as he entered the station. He dove headfirst onto the platform and slid on his belly. A fraction of a second later, the train barreled by his body in an explosion of twisting metal and sparks. Finally the train lurched to a stop halfway through the station.

Jack could not catch his breath, and he laid motionless on the platform for several seconds inhaling deeply. A horde of onlookers raced over to him.

"Are you okay?" one of them asked.

Jack nodded, and rolled onto his back. He looked thankfully up at the ceiling. The alarm on the subway rang until the conductor opened the door, and stormed out of the train. He headed straight for the small crowd that surrounded Jack.

"Jesus Christ! What're you trying to do? Get yourself killed? Holy shit! I could have killed you man! What the fuck are you doin'?" The conductor was not so sympathetic to Jack, and he too was having trouble catching his breath.

"I'm sorry." Jack apologized between gasps. "I was following someone."

"Who? I didn't see no one. You're the only asshole that I saw down there."

Jack shrugged, and pushed himself to his feet. He rested his head for a moment between his knees, then straightened up. His ankle was throbbing, and his head was spinning. It all happened so fast, but it definitely happened. This time it was not his imagination. He was following Casper, he was certain of that. "I know what I saw. My friend was down there. He's in that tunnel. I'm not fucking crazy." He looked wild and disoriented, and people assumed he was demented despite this assertion. "I'm not fucking crazy."

Jack pushed his way out of the crowd, and headed for the steps. The conductor was still complaining about Jack as he gingerly limped up the steps. Jack glared at him from above, and gave him the finger.

"Yeah, I should report you, you fuckin' prick!" the conductor shouted up at him as Jack disappeared. "Worthless, crazy piece of shit."

OOOOOOOO

When Jack finally made it to the office, it was nearly five o'clock. Gladys was still on the phone, and had just starting to clean up the workspace when he swung the office door open.

"Oh my God." Her jaw dropped open, and she hung up the phone. "What the hell is going on, Jack? You look terrible!" He was as white as a ghost, and deep skin pockets had formed under his eyes.

Jack came around the desk, and flopped into a chair. "Is there any coffee, Gladys? I really need coffee." He couldn't recall the last good night's sleep he had.

Gladys looked at him queerly. "Sure," she hesitated, "let me get that for you." She went to the automatic coffee maker, and poured a tall cup of black coffee. She handed it to him, and sat down at his side. "What are you mixed up in, Jack?"

"Nothing Gladys. The project did not go according to plan." Jack swallowed a large gulp of coffee. It was extremely bitter, and he nearly barfed. He brushed the unkempt hair from his forehead, and took another sip.

"Someone is trying to sabotage the practice." she told him.

"I know, how far did he get?"

"What do you mean?"

"He's probably been calling my patients alphabetically. Who was the last patient that called today?" Jack looked at the pile of memos on the desk.

"Joanne Lancaster."

"Terrific. Just fuckin' terrific. A through L." he laughed. "He got through nearly half the *fuckin'* alphabet!" Jack's hands shook violently as he brought the cup to his mouth again.

"Jack, what's wrong with you?" She was not used to hearing this type of language from him. She was frightened. Jack shook his head in return, but then giggled inappropriately.

"Is it drugs, Jack?" She waited for his answer.

"I'm not on drugs, Gladys."

"The Mafia?"

"The Mafia? C'mon now, Gladys!"

"Well you've been real peculiar lately, Jack. You go on a surprise vacation for a whole month. I'm sorry, not a vacation, but some big mysterious project that no one seems to know about, and then you show up here looking like all hell broke loose...Not to mention this letter we received today from the Academic Review Committee. I just don't know what's going on anymore. This is not the Jack Benedict I'm familiar with."

"What was that?" Jack asked.

"What was *what?*"

"You said something about a letter?"

"I did?"

"Yes."

Gladys goofed, she was hoping to discuss the matter at a more convenient time. "Today I received this letter from the Academic Review Committee, here..." She searched her desk. "I'll let you see it yourself." She handed the thin envelope to him.

Jack pulled the letter out of the envelope, and unfolded it. It was a notice about a preliminary hearing regarding alleged inappropriate behavior between Jack and several female undergraduate students. There was also mention of his affair with Ellen McCormick. "What the hell?" Jack asked, "Who gave you this?"

"It came through inter-office mail."

"I don't understand."

"I called the committee this afternoon. I hope you don't mind." Gladys told him.

Jack looked at her. "And?"

"It was an anonymous complaint. They're trying to contact the women. Nothing is official yet, but they're treating this matter very seriously, Jack." He rubbed his head. He hadn't done anything. Gladys continued. "Jack, you're suspended with pay until this matter is straightened out. I'm sure it's nothing."

"Holy fuckin' shit!" Jack jumped to his feet, and paced the office. "Suspended? For what? What the hell am I gonna do?" He was furious. "I know who did this Gladys, and let me tell you, there's gonna be hell to pay for this! Believe me! The person responsible for this will pay!" He looked crazed, and delusional.

"Jack, let me help you. Why don't you tell me what's going on?"

Jack ran his fingers through his hair. "I wouldn't know where to start. It's all so complicated."

The phone rang breaking the tension, and Gladys picked up the phone. "Doctor Benedict's office...Yeah...Uh-huh...Yeah...a lot of people have been having that problem today." She closed her eyes and frowned.

"Gladys, who is it?" Jack asked. "Who the hell is it?"

Gladys covered the mouthpiece with the palm of her hand. "It's George McKellar, and he's not happy." Another patient was called.

"Shit." Jack felt queasy. "I'm going home. I'll speak with you tomorrow Gladys." He stormed out of the office talking to himself.

Shortly after Jack left the office, Gladys hung up the phone with George McKellar. Jack's behavior was very disturbing to her. It gnawed at her. Something was very wrong, and she was genuinely concerned for his safety. She picked up the phone again, and without any further hesitation, she dialed Jack's wife.

CHAPTER TWENTY THREE
◆◆◆◆◆

Jack was devastated by this latest news, so he stopped off at a local bar for a couple of stiff drinks before heading home. Did Ellen really file a complaint? And who were the other students he allegedly had sexual relations with? Jack suspected that this too was the work of Casper Lolly, and Casper alone. He mumbled to himself at the bar, occasionally laughing, and then almost crying, but always perseverating on his psychotic colleague. He was also starting to hallucinate again, and people were beginning to notice. He decided to leave before he made a scene, but everywhere he looked, the people around him resembled Casper. He simply could not free his mind of Casper's image, no matter how hard he tried.

It was almost seven thirty when Jack finally shuffled into the brownstone. He turned on the light in the hallway, and hung his trench coat in the closet. Caroline was waiting for him in the kitchen when he walked in. Her face was red and swollen, making it obvious that she had been crying.

"Hey!" Jack greeted her. "So how was your day?"

"What's going on Jack? I spoke to Gladys."

"A little bit of everything it seems."

"Did you go to work today?"

"No." he admitted. "No, work never materialized today. I was experiencing some technical difficulties." He chuckled, knocking on his own head.

"I thought you said you were going to work today."

"No, no I never made it. Let me explain my day to you." He pulled a chair along side the kitchen table and sat next to her. He widely grinned, then began. "This morning, after not sleeping for several days, a policeman called me, and asked me if one of my patients had committed suicide. Later, I was hallucinating that Casper was driving a bus, and riding a bicycle. Can you imagine that? Casper had the whole transit bus uniform on, and everything! Even the hat." Jack made circular motions around his own ear, implying that he was crazy. "Then, I believe the *real* Casper called all of my depressed patients, and told them to commit suicide. These *lunatics* called my office all afternoon and drove Gladys up a wall. Then, I *saw* the *real* Casper on the street! Except that he is now balding, and has a scruffy beard. He looked sort of homeless to tell you the truth." Caroline desperately tried to follow him, but she was getting lost in his ramblings. "So I chased him into the subway station, and followed him onto the tracks. Can you believe that? I followed him onto the freakin' tracks. Into a goddamn subway tunnel. Pitch fuckin' black Caroline! Oh! Then I twisted my ankle in the fuckin' tunnel…" He lifted his foot to the table and showed her his bruised and swollen leg."…And as I ran away with millions of rats, I was almost hit by an on-coming train. Actually I made it only by the skin of my teeth." Jack squealed like a rat, showing his teeth, and then gestured how he dove heroically onto the platform. Caroline looked at him in disbelief, but he continued. "Then, as if there wasn't enough excitement in my day, I returned to the office to find out that I am being investigated by the Academic Review Committee for inappropriate behavior with undergraduate students." Jack closed his eyes, and waited. "They suspended me with pay…So even if I want to go to work tomorrow, I can't."

"Is it true?" Caroline asked.

"Is what true?"

"Are you sleeping with one of your students? Are you wrapped up in something else?"

"Of course not! I promise."

Caroline began to tear up, and Jack went to put his arm around her. She shoved him away. "Promises mean nothing Jack! Actions, actions mean something! And you know what, Jack? You've been acting very strange lately, and I don't know what to think anymore…Gladys called me, she's very concerned too. You're scaring us all, Jack. What is all this shit about rats, and trains, and Casper…Jack? What is this shit? Do you realize how crazy you sound?" She turned away from him.

Jack looked at his wife. "You don't *believe* me?! Do you think I made all of this up? How could you think that? What, you think I'm nuts?"

"I just don't know what, or who, to believe anymore. I'm tired of all this shit. Jack, I think you need help." She began to cry again. "Get help, Jack. Please get help."

"What can I do to prove it to you? Just tell me." He begged, asserting his sanity. "I'll do anything."

Caroline wiped the tears from her face, and sat silently for a moment. Once the tears ceased she answered him. "I want to see the Isolation Chamber. Take me to the garage."

"The garage?" Jack asked. "But…"

"Right now." she demanded.

ооооооо

Caroline did not speak, as Jack tried to explain how Casper had removed everything from the garage, and returned it to its original state.

"There was nothing left! I showed up one day, and all of the stuff was in a pile out on the sidewalk. I swear, people were swarming around, and hauling all of the equipment away." He laughed, trying to put Caroline at ease. "He's made me look like such a schmuck."

Caroline hardly acknowledged him, staring blankly out the taxi's window. The cab turned down Tenth Street, and Jack motioned the driver over towards the alley.

"Pull over right here." Jack said.

The driver stopped and Jack gave the cabby some money through the plastic window. Caroline stepped out of the cab first, and Jack followed her. "It's right over here." he told her, and pointed to the side door.

He led her through the alley, and up to the door. The lock was loosely hanging on the chain, exactly as Jack had left it a few days ago. "See, I smashed the lock off a few days ago with a brick…The day Casper took everything." He pointed at the lock and hinge, but Caroline was not impressed.

Jack pushed the door wide open, and turned on the light. They entered the empty garage together. Caroline stood near the doorway, just a few feet inside the garage. Her face was stone cold. Jack theatrically pointed to where the Isolation Chamber was. He attempted to describe the location of the control panel, the EEG machine, the library, and the monitors. "And this is where the two way mirror was. I would watch him everyday from the console through the mirror." he told her, and outlined the hole in the wall with his hands. "But he removed that too." Caroline was not buying it, and the more Jack tried to convince her of the experiment's existence, the more skeptical she became.

"I'm telling you the truth, Caroline. I swear I'm telling you the truth."

Caroline surveyed the entire garage from the one spot near the door. She fixated on the pile of blue gravel and the two dead goldfish nearby.

"The fish! Those were Casper's fish...I was feeding them during the experiment." He squatted beside them childishly. "The orange one is Pilot, and the more yellow one is Pontious. I hope they didn't suffer. Poor little buggers." He looked up at her.

She looked at him with disbelief. Tears swelled in her eyes, and again flooded onto her cheeks. "Pontious Pilot, that's real cute. Do me a favor Jack, don't plan on coming home tonight." And she ran out of the garage.

"Caroline!" Jack called to her and chased her to the sidewalk. He was slow getting started because of his ankle, but he managed to catch her. He grabbed her by the elbow, and swung her around to face him. "I'm telling you the truth! You have to believe me!"

Caroline tried to wrestle free from him, but he was too strong for her. "Let me go Jack, or I will scream. God help me, I will scream." She wriggled wildly in his arms.

They were already attracting a small crowd, so Jack lowered his voice. "Caroline, listen to me! Be sensible about this." She twisted and twisted.

"Let me go Jack." She kicked and pushed away from him. "Let me go!"

Jack released her, and she ran crying to the street corner. Jack called to her once more but she did not turn around. She hailed a taxi and sped off.

"*Shit! Stupid Jerk.*" Jack cursed himself and retreated to the empty garage.

○○○○○○○○

Ellen McCormick pulled the black jeans over her hips, and tucked in her white silk blouse. She opened the top two buttons, and left the blouse provocatively loose around her neck. Her long blond hair cascaded lazily over her left shoulder and nearly down to her breast. She inspected her body and outfit in a full-length mirror, twisting herself so she can see her own rear. She was pleased with her appearance. She felt casually sexy, and her ass looked great in these pants. She was just meeting some good friends for dinner and maybe a few drinks, but she wanted to look her best anyhow.

Ellen has always had a difficult time dating, especially after her affair with Jack. She found most of the men her age were emotionally immature, and frankly mentally inferior. Her Doctorate in Psychology certainly did not help the situation either. Men were often intimidated by her brilliance, and she refused to play dumb just to get a date. She made a good living, was completely self sufficient, and held a prestigious position at Beth Israel South Medical Center. She needed no one in her life. But as she approached thirty she ironically found herself searching for someone.

It had been almost a year since Jack abruptly ended the relationship with her. She was simply devastated by this, and did not leave the apartment for a long while after the split. She still had a photo of him on her dresser, a constant reminder of a more romantic time in her life. His arms were tightly wrapped around her, and their bodies were entwined in a passionate embrace. It was a taken after a terrific night they spent together at the *Plaza Hotel* last year. She sighed, and lifted the picture to the light.

"Will I ever find another Jack Benedict?" she asked herself, and then carefully placed the picture back on the dresser. "His loss." she said. She said this almost every day.

Unfortunately Jack was the perfect man for Ellen. He was intelligent, witty, athletic, honest and simply sexy to her. Even though he was married, she was extremely attracted to him from the first day they met. This was not a typical May-December romance. Sure, she had been attracted to older men before, but this was something different. This was love. This was pain. In a perfect world they might have had a long and happy life together. But reality was often cruel, and Jack had made certain promises to himself and his wife.

She spread some lipstick over her soft lips, and blotted them on a napkin. She took one last look at herself in the mirror and smiled. "Looking good, Ellie." she told herself. "Eat your heart out, JB!" She picked up her suede jacket, and shrugged it onto her shoulders. She left the brownstone and locked the front door. Skipping down the steps, she headed to a trendy Mexican restaurant on Ninth Street.

Casper followed her from a distance.

OOOOOOOO

Pull yourself together Jack. A voice in his head told him.

Jack was lying on the cement floor in the corner of the Isolation Chamber. His eyes were wide open, but he felt like he was in a sound sleep. His comfortable life had suddenly become a nightmare, and he could not wake up from it. He rubbed his eyes and rolled onto his back.

Casper is still out there, Jack.

Get up.

Jack staggered to his feet. He hadn't slept in days and his legs trembled under the weight of his body. He paced the isolation chamber, and looked at his watch. It was almost eleven o'clock.

"Shit, shit, shit, shit, shit." Jack repeated to himself as he ran his fingers through his hair. "What am I gonna do?"

Tell the police.

"Tell the police? What am I gonna tell them? That my friend is psychotic? That my friend has ruined my career? He's trying to ruin my fucking marriage? Is that what I should tell them?"

It's not a horrible idea.

"It's a ridiculous idea! A fucking ridiculous idea!" he answered the voice.

213

Jack approached the hole in the wall where the mirror once stood and slammed his fist onto the ledge. "Casper you fucking bastard!" He softly pounded his head against the concrete wall. "You stupid, stupid asshole!"

He's made a mockery of us.

He's playing games with us.

"What?" Jack turned to face the empty isolation chamber, and suddenly realized he had been talking to himself. "Christ, I'm going fucking nuts!" He looked into the observation area. "Hello?" Nobody was there. "What the hell is going on?"

Let's get a drink, JB.

"Who's that?" Jack turned several times and looked up at the ceiling. "Who's there?"

A drink will steady the nerves.

Make mine a double.

Jack thought for a moment, and then smiled. "A drink? Yes, Let's get a drink!" The voices cheered in his head. Jack silenced them, and pressed his fingers into his temples. "That's it! *The Sacred Cow!* I haven't checked *The Sacred Cow!*"

He left the garage, and ran through the alley.

○○○○○○○○

The strange good-looking man had been watching her all night, as she laughed and drank with her friends. Ellen noticed him a few hours ago. He stood by the bar and mingled while several women fawned over him. He was somewhat tall with an athletic build. His chiseled face was outlined by a short beard, and decorated with two piercing blue eyes. He lifted a glass to her when their eyes met, and they both smiled and coyly turned away. She continued to watch him out of the corner of her eye. His movements were fluid and confident, like a wild animal. His muscles were stretched tightly around his stone hard body. God, he was sexy. It didn't even bother her that he was nearly bald. Somehow it looked good on him.

When her friends were leaving, she intentionally stayed behind and used the bathroom. She reapplied her makeup in the mirror, and waited until she was certain that her friends had left the restaurant. She went to the bar, and ordered a frozen daiquiri. Casper made eye contact with her several times before he approached her.

She's a piece of ass Casper.

A loser like Jack got her?

"Hi, I'm Casper." He extended his hand to her as he leaned against the bar.

"I'm Ellen." She smiled at him, and was instantly lost in his eyes. There was something feral inside this man, something irresistible.

They talked for over an hour at the bar, without a break in the conversation. She had about four drinks, and she could hardly control herself. She wanted to grab him, rub his thick chest, and feel his arms around her. She felt dangerously young again, and she was drowning in his charm.

"What do you do for a living, Ellen?" he asked her, and she made a face. "What was that face for?" he followed up with a smirk.

"Why is it, that all casual conversations in this city degenerate into a professional interview? If you want to see my resume, place an add in the *Times*." They laughed together.

"All right then, so you're a stripper or something?"

"Ha!" Ellen laughed, and spat part of her drink onto the bar. "Are you kidding me?" She had never heard that before.

Casper looked her up and down, and shrugged. "Nope." He took a long slurp of his beer, and swallowed. "Look like a stripper to me."

Bang the shit out of this one, Cass.

"All right Casper, the not-so-friendly ghost, what do you do for a living? Wait! Let me guess..." She looked him up and down as well. "You're a pornographer."

"Bingo!" Casper acted surprised, pointed at her and laughed. "Actually that's pretty close. I'm a psychiatrist."

"Really?" Ellen was shocked, and she placed a hand to her perky chest. "Where do you work?"

"I'm part of the faculty at New York Hospital."

"Wait a minute." Ellen put her drink on the bar, and grabbed his taught biceps. "What's your last name?"

"Lolly, Casper Lolly."

"Holy shit!" Ellen smacked herself in the head. "You're Casper Lolly? Holy Toledo, I can't believe it." She gasped several times.

"Why? You've heard of me?" Casper feigned humility and surprise.

"Of course! I mean, who hasn't?" She wasn't going to tell him about Jack. She didn't want to ruin anything that may be developing here. "I'm a Clinical Psychologist at B.I. South!"

"Really?" Casper furrowed his eyebrows. "What's *your* last name?"

"You haven't heard of me…I just received my PhD eight months ago. But it's McCormick, Ellen McCormick."

"Doctor Ellen McCormick…" Casper pretended to search his memory. "You did a lot of work with psychotic features in the phobias, right?" Casper knew this from Jack, although he had never formally met her until now.

"Yes!" Ellen was both flattered and shocked. "I wrote my thesis on it! How did you know that?"

Casper thought for a while. "I don't know, I guess all of us head-shrinkers travel in small circles."

Very small circles, you stupid slut!

"Wow! Doctor Casper Lolly has heard of me!" Her smooth skin turned red, and hot. Her ears burned passionately. "I can't wait to tell my colleagues."

"You're too kind." He slapped her hand playfully.

The two talked about their similar professions for a while longer, and then Casper asked her if she felt like going to a dance club.

She slid her hands seductively down his washboard stomach. "If you think you can handle it, Doctor."

CHAPTER TWENTY FOUR
◆◆◆◆◆

The dance floor at the *China Club* was infested with socialites and wannabes. Ellen dragged Casper by the hand off the dance floor and through the sweating crowd. They had been dancing for over an hour without a break, and were both drenched in a thin layer of salt water.

"I need another drink!" Ellen shouted above the vibrations of the house music.

Casper wiped the sweat from his nearly bald scalp. Stubble was starting to grow in and he needed to shave again. He had been hallucinating all night, and the images were becoming more violent and more perverse. He wanted this girl. He wanted her badly. He wanted to do bad things to her. "Me too!" he shouted back. "I'll take a beer!"

At the bar Ellen leaned over and gave the bartender her order. Casper admired her ass from behind, and nonchalantly pressed his pelvis deeply into it. She gently pushed back against him, and they started grinding together slowly while they waited for their drinks. Casper was becoming aroused, and he held her hips tighter as he grew beneath his pants. Ellen found this sudden thickness between her buttocks appetizing. She closed her eyes, bit down on her lower lip, and imagined what it would be like to take him inside of her.

After a few gratifying minutes the drinks arrived and the foreplay ceased. They sat at a table in a corner near the orgiastic crowd that gyrated on the dance floor. The music was deafening with a seductively heavy beat, and the dancers were whipped into a frenzy. Even shouting, Casper and Ellen could hardly hear each other.

"Wanna get out of here?" she shouted to him.

"After this drink!" he responded.

"What?!" She didn't hear him, so she pulled a little closer.

"After this drink, I'm gonna take you home and bang the shit out of you!" He spoke loudly with a straight face. "How does that sound?"

"Oh…" She sat back and attempted to register what he said. "What?!" she asked him again shaking her head. "I can't hear you!"

Casper rolled his eyes flirtatiously, and she smiled back at him. "I'm not sure if I want to strangle you, or knife you to death!" He made comical stabbing and slashing motions with his hands.

Ellen laughed with embarrassment. "Casper, I can't hear you!...You're talking to fast." She wrinkled her face in confusion.

Casper slugged his drink, and placed it down on the table. He took a deep breath and shouted at her. "I'm ready to go! Let's go right now!"

You stupid, stupid slut.

○○○○○○○○

The cab stopped at the corner of First Avenue and St. Mark's Place. Jack stepped out and onto the sidewalk. It was nearly midnight. He quietly walked down the street until he found the little black cow spray painted on the concrete. He descended the steps, and knocked a few times on the door. He waited for several minutes, and finally the slot slid open. A pair of familiar eyeballs appeared, and Jack gave them a quick wave.

"How you doin', Ditch?" he greeted the doorman.

The bushy eyebrows narrowed to a squint. "Freud?"

"Yeah."

"You look like shit." Ditch said bluntly.

"Thank you. Thank you very much."

"What happened to you?"

Jack threw his arms up in frustration. "Can you let me in, Ditch?"

The slot shut abruptly and Ditch disappeared. Jack waited patiently by the door, and it eventually opened. "Thanks Ditch." he said as he entered, and Ditch shut the door behind him. "Can I ask you a question?"

Ditch clapped him on the back and walked with Jack into the bar. "Sure."

"Have you seen my friend lately?"

Ditch frowned. "C'mon Freud, we're all friends here." He slapped Jack softly in the face with one of his monstrous paws. "Get yourself a drink or two."

Jack turned and grabbed the large doorman by the shirt. He was desperate. "Ditch you don't understand." Jack told him eagerly. "My friend and I are in a lot of trouble."

Ditch did not respond. He looked down at Jack's hands, and forcefully removed them from his shirt. He waited for Jack to apologize, and Jack soon did so. "This is a good place to hide from trouble." Ditch reassured him. "Don't worry about anything down here."

"I know, Ditch! But I've been looking for my friend, Doc. Have you seen him?" Jack pleaded. "Have you seen Doc?"

Ditch shook his head. "You know me better than that, Freud. I can't give you that kind of information. It's against our policy. What's with you tonight?"

"Ditch, it's an emergency."

Ditch shook his head disdainfully, and returned to his post at the door without another word. Jack decided not to push him any further, it may be detrimental to his health. He quickly entered the main bar and looked around. As always the place was packed, and the crowd was typically unusual. Jack searched the anonymous faces for his friend, but after two or three laps around the dance floor, he gave up. He settled himself at the bar, and the bartender soon came over to him.

"Hey, how ya doin'?" The bartender recognized him from previous visits. "What can I getcha?"

Jack looked up and down the bar. "Nothing for me yet. Thanks."

The bartender shrugged, and walked away. Jack was exhausted, and his brain was already malfunctioning. He leaned against the bar, and considered his current situation. He had no place to stay, his career was in ruins, his reputation was on the line, and his marriage was on the rocks. One of his dearest friends was now acutely psychotic, and on the loose in the most unforgiving city on Earth.

Fuck it.

Have a few drinks, JB.

Jack motioned for the bartender. The bartender finished pouring a drink, and came over to him. "Change of heart?" he asked Jack, and wiped the bar with a rag.

"Can you make a Mindracer?" Jack asked, and the bartender nodded. "Good then, make it a double."

Double it up!

Jack waited for his drink and carried it to the ledge surrounding the dance floor. He was surveying the crowd when suddenly he saw Casper. He was dancing erotically with another man. Their moves were just short of pornographic. Jack could not believe it, and he took a long sip from his drink before he stepped onto the dance floor.

That's disgusting.

"I never knew." he mumbled to himself as he parted his way through the writhing crowd. "Can't be…"

He approached Casper and his companion cautiously, like a tiger planning to pounce on his prey. Casper began to thrust his pelvis into the other man, and passionately kissed his neck. Jack watched them closely and slowly circled in. The horny couple continued to hump and grope one another. They were completely unaware of Jack's presence. When he got close enough, Jack reached out and pulled Casper by the shoulder.

"What the hell are you doing?" the surprised man said as he spun around. It was certainly not Casper.

What the hell are you doing, Jack?

Jack apologized profusely. "I'm so sorry, I thought you were someone I knew! I'm so sorry. My God, I'm so very sorry."

The two men scowled at him, and angrily left the dance floor. Jack stood motionless and confused in the center of the other dancers for several minutes. He was about to leave the bar when suddenly someone grabbed him by the hand.

"Hey Jack!" the sexy Hispanic woman said. "Remember me? I thought I'd never see you again!" She hugged him warmly.

"Sure." Jack recalled the pretty face, but not the name. She was a stripper, or something like that. She let him go and he looked squarely in her face. She had a distinctive smile, beautiful olive skin, and an unforgettable body. It all came back to him. "Isabella?"

She nodded excitedly. "Hey! You remember me! Where's your friend?"

"My friend?" Jack recalled the night he and Isabella met.

That's what we want to know.

○○○○○○○

Isabella rested her large breasts on the table, and leaned onto Jack. She looked up at him seductively and smiled. "You know Jack, I was so attracted to you the night we met." Her speech was innocently slurred, and Jack was truly tempted. "But you ran home to your stupid wife...Didn't even give me a chance! Me and that pretty pharmacy girl were forced to share your friend."

Jack slurped down his fourth drink, further compromising his fragile mental state. He belched softly. "I can't find him anywhere?" he told her. "You're sure you haven't seen him?"

"Who?" Isabella had been asked this question three times already.

"My friend, Casper, I mean Doc, no Casper."

"For the last time, I haven't seen that prick in a month."

Jack wiggled the ice in his glass, and slid the chips into his mouth. Isabella snuggled closer, and slowly stroked his thigh. She was unbelievably exotic, and Jack could no longer control himself. He slid his arm around her, and cupped her dangling breast. His heart raced as he caressed it slowly in his hand.

"Where's your wife tonight?" With each stroke of his leg, she moved her hand closer to his groin.

"Home." He was getting hot and excited. "She's at home."

Why not, Jack?

We never have fun.

"Isn't it past your bedtime?" she seductively asked him. It was just about three in the morning.

"I can stay up as late as I want...I'm a big boy."

She kissed him softly on the neck, then slowly moved up to his ear. "How big?" she whispered to him, and slid her hand into his crotch.

○○○○○○○

"I'm gonna change out of these jeans." Ellen said, and left Casper out in the living room. "Make yourself at home."

She shut the door only slightly, and began to get undressed. The picture of Jack was sitting on the top of the dresser. She quickly tossed it under the panties in the top drawer, and closed it. She tidied herself in front of the mirror and fixed her makeup. She was very nervous, and was having a considerable amount of difficulty unbuttoning her blouse. She kicked off her shoes, and dropped her jeans around her ankles. Suddenly Casper was at the door, watching her.

"Excuse me!" she said playfully, and attempted to cover herself.

Casper approached her and pulled the blouse off her shoulders. He pressed his lips hungrily into the nape of her neck, and began to kiss her wildly. She twisted her neck in pleasure, and wrapped him in a passionate embrace. Casper removed her bra and began to fondle her full breasts. Ellen was out of control. She pulled Casper's shirt from his pants, and ran her fingers over the bumps on his stomach, then up to his chest. Casper pulled the shirt over his head, and threw it to the ground. Her tongue probed his mouth as he slid his hands down her back, under her panties, and onto her ass. He ripped a jagged hole in the crotch, lifted Ellen into the air and tossed her onto the bed.

"Can I take off my pants, at least?" she asked him, wrestling with the denim shackles around her ankles.

"Absolutely not." He removed his pants and pounced on top of her. He kissed her violently and bit her on the nipples. She arched her back in pain but pulled his mouth closer her chest. He was huge, and she gently stroked him until he was fully aroused. Casper flipped her onto her stomach, lifted her ass into the air by the hips, and tried to penetrate her from behind.

"Wait a minute." Ellen flopped back down to the bed and turned towards him. "I don't think so."

Kill her Casper!

"What are you talking about?" Casper asked.

She waited several seconds, and fondled him playfully. "Not that I don't trust you or anything, but…It's a big dirty city, and I'm a very clean girl."

"Huh?" The sweat was already pouring off of Casper's temples. He was not in the mood for games. "What are you talking about?"

Ellen reached over to her nightstand, and opened the drawer. She pulled out a condom, and gave it to him. "I hope this fits...You should always practice safe-sex."

Fucking prudish bitch!

The condom did not fit completely but he managed to roll it half way down his penis. "Now where were we?" she seductively asked.

He flipped her onto her belly again and whispered in her ear. "Get that ass up in the air, and don't say another word." He warned her, playfully grabbing her buttocks.

She did as he said. "Higher." he demanded, and spanked her lightly. She let out a moan, and Casper continued. "Now put your head down." He slapped her ass again, and tugged her blond hair. Ellen groaned into the pillow. "Don't make me get rough with you, Ellen." he said. "I can be very dangerous."

"Please be dangerous." she begged him. "Spank me."

He slapped her ass several more times until her cheeks turned pink. Then he grabbed her by the hips, and plunged himself deeply inside her. Her legs stiffened in pain and she let out a humiliating cry. He was too large for her and she tried to distance herself from his groin. He continued to thrust himself into her. She placed her head onto the mattress and buried her face in the sheets. Reaching back with both hands she pushed him away from her hips.

"Not so deep, Casper...Oh please, not so deep." she pleaded with him.

Casper slowed himself to a stop. "I'm sorry."

You like that don't you?

You fucking worthless whore.

Casper pulled himself out of her, and the pain subsided. "Hold on a minute." He told her, and picked up the phone from the nightstand. She lowered her pelvis to the bed.

"What are you doing?" she asked. "Who are you calling?" He was such and odd man.

Shut the fuck up, you slut.

"I'm paging someone. Now, get your ass back in the air." Casper hit several buttons, and then hung up the phone.

"Page? Who'd you page?" she asked, as she hesitantly lifted her rear.

"What did I tell you." He was getting angrier. "Now get that ass in the air!" He slapped her on the ass. "Higher!...Higher!"

He plunged himself into her again. This time she resisted him, kicking her legs violently. She could not get out of her jeans. Casper pulled her hips rapidly back and forth against his own. "Casper, stop." Tears filled her eyes. "Please, stop!" She began to cry and yelp with each thrust.

Casper stopped himself fully into her and flattened her onto the bed. She could hardly breathe with him inside of her. "Relax, Ellen." He spoke softly to her while she whimpered. "I want you to enjoy your last few minutes on Earth."

Die you whore!

He wrapped his arm around her neck, and began to strangle her. She kicked and clawed at his muscular arms, frantically gasping for air. Casper tightened his hold on her neck. Her face turned purple, and the veins inflated in her head. Suddenly the phone started ringing. She desperately groped for it, but she was just beyond its reach. After four rings the answering machine would pick up. Ellen fought the unconsciousness, and valiantly struggled for the phone. She fingered the receiver several times, but could not dislodge it. She pulled desperately on the nightstand for the phone, but it would not budge. The person on the other end of the line was her only hope. After four short rings the machine picked up, and this was followed by a long beep. Jack's voice suddenly crackled over the phone.

"Jack!" she gasped, but without air she made no sound. She was on the verge of passing out. "Jack!" she tried to scream again.

"It seems to me that we have a mutual friend, Jack Benedict. Wouldn't you agree?" Casper whispered sadistically into her ear as she struggled, and he tightened his grip on her throat.

"Hi Ellen...It's me, Jack...I dunno, it's very late...Three-thirty?" His voice was slurred and tired. "I don't know what's going on with me...Things are not going too well. Everything is fucked up for me...But then you paged, and I guess that made me happy, considering all that we've been through." Jack was rambling. "I'm at *The Sacred Cow* right now…I'd really like to see you, I got kicked out of my house today…But now you're not home? Wait I'm confused, and a little bit drunk. Didn't you just page me?" Jack belched into the phone. "Forget it! I'm gonna come by, okay? So when you get this message, stay up and answer the door."

Ellen grabbed the phone and flipped it off the hook. It crashed to the carpet with the answering machine but Jack was already gone. Only a dial tone resonated into the bedroom. She would never be able to make it until Jack arrived. Ellen surrendered to the darkness. Reality slowly disintegrated around her as her body fell limp.

When he was finished, Casper gave her neck a sharp twist for good measure, and made certain that she was no longer breathing. He withdrew himself from her, and sat on the edge of the bed. He picked up the phone and answering machine, and placed them back on the nightstand. Jack's message flashed on the machine, waiting to be played.

Stupid ass.

JB is one stupid ass!

Casper pulled the condom off his penis, and shoved it completely in the dead woman's mouth. "There's no such thing as safe sex." he whispered into her ear.

〇〇〇〇〇〇〇〇

Jack hung up the phone, and staggered back to Isabella. God, she was beautiful. She was dancing alone by the table, swaying her hips back and forth. Jack stopped to admire her voluptuous body. She was wearing a tight miniskirt, and a spandex top that accentuated her perfect breasts. Jack embraced her at the table, and kissed her passionately on the mouth. He moved his hands onto her thighs and then between her legs. She was warm and moist already.

"You wanna get out of here?" she asked him.

Jack frowned at her. "I can't."

Isabella pushed him away. "Go home to your fucking wife, you creep." she joked with him, but in reality, she was a little upset. "But

don't expect me to wait for you. This is the last chance I'm giving you."
She turned her ass towards him and slapped it lightly, coaxing him. "Last
chance."

"It's not that, I swear. Believe me. Christ, I would love to." Jack
apologized to her. Isabella was sexy. There was no doubt about it. But
Jack had never met a woman who compared to Ellen McCormick. Not
even Caroline. "I'm sorry," he told the hot Latina. "I have to meet
someone." He kissed her again. "I'm very, very sorry."

"You sure are." she responded and strutted to the dance floor.

CHAPTER TWENTY FIVE
◆◆◆◆◆

Ellen's bedroom window cast a solitary beam of light across the street. It was nearly four o'clock in the morning, when Jack quietly climbed the steps of her brownstone. He rang the doorbell, and waited on the stoop for several minutes, but she never came. He pressed his ear against the door, and rang again. The doorbell was working; he heard it clearly through the door. He listened carefully for noise from inside, but there wasn't any.

Where is she?

That's strange.

"It sure is." he answered, and descended the steps.

He looked at her apartment from the street. He watched her bedroom window for movement or perhaps a shadow. "Ellen!" he shouted quickly, trying to hush his voice.

He ran up the steps and pushed the bell three more times. There was no answer. He went back to the sidewalk, and again looked up to the window. "Ellen!" he yelled more loudly this time. "Ellen! It's Jack!" Still, there was no movement. Jack rang the bell several more times, and returned to the sidewalk. Nothing.

Where the hell is she?

Probably getting laid.

Jack shook his head. "I don't understand." he said, "That's not like her." He picked up an empty soda can from the curb and hurled it at the window. He hit it squarely. When the can fell back down, it bounced down the steps and made quite a racket. Still there was no response.

"Ellen! Open the door! It's Jack!" A light turned on at the brownstone next door. "C'mon babe! Get up! Wake up!" he slurred.

The slut is probably screwing someone right now.

You missed your chance, Jacko.

"Maybe you're right." Jack looked at his watch. It was a few minutes after four. "Where the hell are you?" He banged on the door with his fist.

"Shut the fuck up! You drunk!" Jack had awakened a neighbor from across the street. He shouted at Jack from his front door.

Jack grabbed his crotch, and turned to the man across the street."Eat me!" He was too drunk, and too tired to deal with the neighbors.

Way to go, Jacko!

We're sick of being pushed around!

Another neighbor's voice came from next door. "Buddy, it's four a.m. People are trying to sleep. I'll give you three seconds, and then I'm calling the police..." Jack scowled back at him.

"Ellen!" He screamed, and stumbled down her steps.

"One..."

"Ellen! Your neighbors are assholes!"

"Two..."

"I'm going!" He threw his hands up and staggered underneath the neighbor at his window. "I'm going, I'm going." He turned his face away. "You freakin' prick." he said, under his breath.

○○○○○○○○

The sunlight singed the city landscape, painting the skyscrapers in a devilish orange. It was finally morning. Jack squinted against the glare, and shielded his eyes. He had been walking the barren streets for over two hours while he waited for the alcoholic buzz to leave his head. He felt much better now. He purchased a large coffee at an espresso bar, and he drank it quickly. He still couldn't figure out why Ellen had paged him, and then why she had not answered the phone. He was confused about everything, and he decided to call her later.

A small but rowdy crowd surfaced from the subway, and headed in different directions. Jack was suddenly envious of the normalcy they seemed to enjoy. He finished his coffee and tossed the empty cup in a meshed metallic trashcan. He yawned and stretched his tired body on the sidewalk.

We should go home.

I just want to sleep already.

A few runners jogged past him on the outskirts of Union Square Park, and headed toward the Westside. Jack turned into the park, and headed toward the subway station. He was going home to patch things up with Caroline. He needed sleep. He needed advice. He needed her.

His beeper began to vibrate at his side, and for a moment he assumed it was Caroline. Jack removed it from his belt and depressed the button. He did not recognize the phone number. He tried his cellular phone. It wasn't working well. He dialed the number from a nearby phone booth, and let it ring several times. He was about to hang up when someone picked up.

"Hello?" Jack asked into the silence. "This is Doctor Benedict. Somebody paged me." He was unusually scared.

"Doctor Benedict? I thought you got hit by a train." the voice said. It was Casper. He was calling from the lobby of a different sleazy hotel in the Village.

"Cass, where are you?" Jack looked around the streets, but did not see him. "Cass, I'm gonna call the police. You've left me no alternative. As soon as I go home, I'm calling the cops. I'm sorry."

"I wouldn't call the police if I were you." Casper warned him. "I already spoke with them. They're probably looking for you right now."

"What the hell are you talking about, Casper?" Jack noticed a police cruiser slowly circling Union Square Park. They stopped deliberately several times, and peered into the park. They were clearly looking for someone or something. Jack cautiously ducked himself a little further into the phone booth. "Cass, what did you do?"

"I don't think they're interested in what *I did*…They want to know what *you did*."

"Stop this nonsense, Casper! I've got no time for this bullshit!" he shouted, and the crowd on the sidewalk swerved away from him. "I've done nothing! Why are you trying to ruin my life?"

"You shouldn't have left a message JB."

"What?" Jack kept an eye on the police cruiser.

Casper imitated Jack being drunk. "Hi Ellen, it's Jack…" he was slurring his words intentionally. "…everything's fuck up for me, I got kicked out of my house…Boo, hoo, hoo…"

Jack's heart sank into his stomach. "How do you know about that message Casper?"

"I was there when you called, you drunk, pathetic asshole. I was screwing her brains out while you rambled on, and on, and on. She tried to pick up the phone by I wouldn't let her. She really struggled for a while though."

Jack was nauseated. ·He closed his eyes, and tried not to vomit. "Casper, did you hurt her? Please tell me that you didn't hurt her!"

There was a long silence as Casper swallowed two more pills and washed them down with a can of *Coke*. "Oh yeah, that's where the police come in. They're looking for her killer."

"What?!" Jack shouted. *"You killed her?!"* He started to cry.

"Hmmm, not exactly. I just got off the phone with the police. I told them that an old boyfriend killed her...Older guy, sorta funny looking. Looks like it was a crime of passion or something."

Jack was hyperventilating and could hardly breathe. Another police cruiser pulled around the corner and headed slowly around the park. Jack dropped the phone, and ran towards Ellen's apartment.

"Hello, JB ol'boy?" Casper said into the phone. "Are you there?"

○○○○○○○○

The cold air burned in Jack's chest, and he slowed himself to a jog just a block before Ellen's brownstone. He breathed deeply and tried to catch his breath. The pain in his ribs was excruciating, and he walked the remainder of the way. A small crowd had gathered and several police cars were parked outside her brownstone. A large area around the steps was roped off with plastic yellow tape. CRIME SCENE - DO NOT CROSS.

Three police officers stood outside, and enforced what was written on the tape. Jack approached one of the uniformed police officers that stood behind the tape. "Officer?" He motioned to him, and the policeman came over. "What's going on here?"

The policeman made a face, and waved Jack's breath out of his face. "Whew, you been drinking, Buddy?"

Jack shook his head. "No listen, I'm a doctor and a friend of the woman that lives here. What's going on?" Jack raised his voice. "Is she all right?"

"Calm down, Doc, we're investigating a crime scene. That's all I can tell you. Now go get some sleep…Sleep it off."

A blue sedan weaved between the patrol cars, and stopped short. Some detectives in police windbreakers stepped out and crossed under the tape. Jack continued to press the uniformed officer. "Listen, I know this woman very well! Tell me what's going on!" Jack demanded, and tried to squeeze under the tape. The officer pushed him forcefully backwards.

Another blue *Crown Victoria* pulled up, and parked just behind the other one. Detective John Cavanagh stepped out, and flicked his cigarette to the other side of the street. He nodded at several of the other officers, and ducked underneath the yellow tape. Out of the corner of his eye, he noticed the skirmish between Jack and the uniformed officer. He didn't get a good look Jack's face, but there was something in his posture that seemed vaguely familiar to Cavanagh. He stopped and watched the tussle from the top of the steps.

Jack recognized Detective Cavanagh instantly and quickly turned away from the uniformed officer. He was frightened, and unsure if he wanted to be seen. His heart pounded in his chest as he headed down the street, and ducked around the corner.

The uniformed officer shook his head and laughed as Jack walked away. Detective Cavanagh called to the officer and he met him at the steps.

"What was that about, Bill?" Detective Cavanagh asked him.

"Some nosey drunk guy. Says he's a doctor. Knew the deceased. It was nothing." the officer responded. "Should I have gotten his name?"

"No." Detective Cavanagh watched as Jack disappeared around the corner. "He just looked familiar to me, that's all."

Detective Cavanagh entered the brownstone, and snapped a pair of sterile gloves over his hands. He placed his shoes in surgical booties, and began to survey the apartment. The décor was contemporary and enticingly feminine. There was no sign of forced entry at the front door, and no obvious signs of a struggle outside of the bedroom. He walked into the bedroom as the forensics team flashed their last picture of Ellen's dead body.

"What do we got so far?" he asked Officer Swenson of Homicide.

A short dumpy fellow with a clipboard came over to him. Detective Cavanagh continued to survey the room as he talked to the forensics team. The two officers greeted each other with a brief nod, and then Officer Swenson started. "Her name is Ellen McCormick, we have her license. She is twenty-nine, apparently lives alone. There is no sign of forced entry…"

Detective Cavanagh crouched besides Ellen's body on the bed. She was nearly nude and lying on her stomach. Her skin was a pale gray, and her muscle tone was flaccid. *Rigor mortis* had not set in yet. This murder was only hours old. He lifted her head, and saw the massive bruise that curved around her neck. Her eyes were terrifyingly vacant and her lips were slate blue. Detective Cavanagh removed a tweezers from his shirt pocket.

The officer from homicide continued to update Detective Cavanagh. "The apparent method was asphyxiation by strangulation. It was probably someone she knows. And there may have been a sexual assault. Judging from the torn panties, and vaginal bruises."

Detective Cavanagh parted Ellen's cold lips, and placed the tweezers in her mouth. He pulled out the used condom, and held it up for Officer Swenson. "A sexual assault? You figured that out all by yourself? Wow! That's some real cracker-jack detective work." Detective Cavanagh ribbed Swenson, and dropped the condom into an evidence bag.

"It'll take a few days, but have the boys in the lab lift some fluid off of that." Detective Cavanagh tossed the bag with the condom onto Bob Swenson's clipboard. The officer grimaced, and held the clipboard a safe distance from his fat body.

"Who's the boyfriend?"

"We think it's a guy named Jack." Officer Swenson carefully handed the condom to a uniformed policeman.

Detective Cavanagh looked at Swenson's reflection through mirror on the dresser. "What makes you say that?" He began to open the drawers.

"He left a long message on the machine last night. The answering machine timed it at three thirty-two a.m." Swenson said, pointing to the flashing red dot on the answering machine.

The detective shrugged. "Play it for me. Do we know anything else about this 'Jack' guy?"

Officer Swenson nodded his head. "Some of the neighbors said a drunk man was seen outside the brownstone early this morning, about three-forty-five or four o'clock. But we're not sure if that was Jack. Older guy, middle age, that's all I know right now, but we're getting a full description."

"Got anything else?" Detective Cavanagh sifted through the socks in one of Ellen McCormick's top drawers.

"Just what you're gonna hear." Officer Swenson played the message on the answering machine.

"Hi Ellen...It's me, Jack...I dunno, it's very late...Three-thirty?..." The message rambled on and on. The room fell silent as all the policemen listened to Jack's recorded voice.

The man on the recording was clearly drunk, but the pitch and cadence of the voice seemed familiar to Detective Cavanagh. He listened carefully as he opened Ellen's underwear drawer. He sifted through the pile of silk panties, and discovered a picture frame lying face down on the bottom of the drawer. He removed it, and turned it over.

"I'll be damned!" he said, and turned to face the other officers. "I know this man! I know Jack." He pointed at the picture of the dead woman in the embrace of a distinguished older man. "This is Jack. This is *Doctor* Jack Benedict, and boy is he in a lot of trouble." He tapped Jack's image. "Looks like another psychiatrist has snapped." Cavanagh then took charge of the situation. " Okay, I want all available cars right now. Call reinforcements, send out an APB. He's in the area. I want a clean sweep of the neighborhood including the park. He may be dangerous, so be careful. Officer Swenson, please send your best squad to his home. I'll tell you where it is. I'm gonna gather evidence here."

CHAPTER TWENTY SIX
◆◆◆◆◆

Caroline sat at the kitchen table and stirred the milk into her coffee. She had cried through the night, and spent most of the time on the phone with her family. She was fed up with Jack's behavior and seriously considered leaving him. His affair had virtually destroyed their marriage last year, but against her better judgement she stayed with him. She loved him dearly, and he promised to change for her. He begged for her forgiveness, and she slowly let him back into her life. But now, just one year later, his behavior was more erratic than ever. This was more than lonely nights and empty conversations. This was lunacy. This was madness. She was sure of it. It was the last straw for her. She could not handle much more of it. Something was going to give, and she could no longer sacrifice herself for him. Either things were going to change, or they were going to end.

There was a knock at the door, and then the doorbell rang. She looked at the clock above the sink. It was almost eight o'clock, and Jack still had not returned home. She went to the closet, and threw a robe over her nightgown. There was another knock at the door, this time it was more forceful. Something strange was going on.

"Who is it?" she called from the safety of the hallway. Through the door she saw the shadows of several men on her stoop.

"Open up! Police." someone from outside the door demanded. There was a banging at the door again, and it rattled violently.

Caroline hurried to the door and looked outside. Two squad cars were parked outside of her apartment, and four uniformed policemen were on her stoop. She unlocked the deadbolt, and pulled the door open.

"Is this Doctor Benedict's residence?" a policeman asked her.

Caroline nodded.

"Is he at home?"

Caroline shook her head slowly. "No, no he's not...I'm his wife, is there something wrong? Is he okay?" Her voice quivered.

The policemen looked at one another, and then turned back to Caroline. "We have a warrant for his arrest. Suspicion of murder." The policeman showed her the court order.

"Murder?" Caroline mumbled, and nearly fainted. "I...I...I..." She couldn't believe what she was being told. "Oh God, help me."

Two of the policemen held her up as she nearly passed out.

"Do you mind if we come in?" another policeman asked, removing his hat and helping her stay on her feet. "I'm Officer Charles."

Caroline was in shock. "No, no, of course not."

Officer Charles was a kindly police captain, with a warm smile and comfortable demeanor. He escorted Caroline to the living room and they both sat down on a couch.

"Misses Benedict, the charges against your husband are quite serious. I know this is difficult for you, but do you know where he is right now?"

"No, I haven't seen him since last night."

"Let me ask you this, Misses Benedict..." He took her hand and held it. "Has your husband been acting strange lately?"

She looked up at him, and her eyes filled with tears, telling him everything he needed to know.

○○○○○○○○

The taxi turned slowly around the corner of East Eighty-fifth Street. There was a lot of commotion and the driver tapped instinctively on his break. In the middle of the block, there were two police cruisers double-parked in the road. The hood lights painted the neighborhood in blinding swirls of red and white, and a small crowd of people had gathered outside of his brownstone. Jack slithered down the seat and hid himself from his friends and neighbors. The cab slowed almost to a complete stop in front of the brownstone.

"Don't stop here!" he told the cab driver. "Drop me off on Eighty-sixth Street!"

The cab driver looked at him in the rearview mirror. "You said Eighty-fifth Street." the driver said in broken English. "This Eighty-fifth Street."

Some of the neighbors noticed the cab and looked into the rear seat. Jack turned away from them and pulled his shirt collar in front of his face. "Eighty-sixth Street! Now move this hunk of junk! Eighty-six!" Jack demanded.

The driver pushed on the gas pedal and sped around the corner. "This is good." Jack told the driver and pointed to the sidewalk around the corner from his brownstone. He paid the cabby and stepped outside. He pulled his trench coat tightly around himself, and pulled his collar up. He would be recognized instantly, and he needed a better disguise. He looked at the many shops that lined Eighty-sixth Street. Only convenience stores and coffee bars were open at this hour.

A homeless man in filthy clothing was sleeping on a cardboard box by the subway station. On his head he was wearing an old *Yankees* baseball cap. Jack approached him and crouched beside him on the sidewalk. The smell was almost unbearable.

"Excuse me?" Jack asked the man, but the man did not stir. "Excuse me?" he asked him again. Finally Jack nudged him with his hand. "Buddy."

The homeless man was startled out of a sound sleep. "Who is it?" He looked at Jack ferociously. His fruity breath was laced with a peppermint liquor. "What do you want?" He was missing most of his bottom teeth, and his thick white beard had several dried chunks of puke inside of it. Jack himself was not looking so terrific and the homeless man let him know it.

"This is my corner. I was here first. Find somewhere else you bum!"

Jack looked down at his own attire. He was physically a mess. "I don't want your corner." Jack explained to him, "But I was wondering if I could buy that baseball hat from you?"

The homeless man looked above his head as if he never noticed the cap that was sitting there. "You want this cap?!" He could not believe Jack's odd request. It was old and disgusting.

"Yeah…" Jack removed a small wad of bills from his jacket pocket. "Do you think twenty dollars will cover it?"

The man was homeless, but not stupid. He looked at the wad of cash Jack had in his hand. "Shit man, this is the *New York Yankees!* It's like giving away a piece of my boyhood. It's Lou Gehrig, and Billy Martin..."

"Okay thirty dollars." Jack peeled a twenty and a ten from the wad. He held it out to the scurvy man.

The homeless man acknowledged the money, but continued. "And Yogi Berra, Reggie Jackson, and Tommy Lasorda, and..."

Jack pulled the money away from him, and the homeless man stopped his bartering pitch abruptly. "Tommy Lasorda was not a *Yankee.*" Jack informed him. He was not stupid either.

The homeless man smiled unveiling his bean shaped upper teeth. "Thirty dollars should just about cover it." The man obligingly removed the cap and held it out for Jack.

The cap was worse than Jack had expected, but he had no options. He reluctantly gave the man thirty dollars for the vile headgear, and then placed the wad of money back inside his wallet. The homeless man yelled to him as he walked away.

"Do you need any shoes? Socks? I got plenty of stuff!"

Jack did not turn back around. He dusted the cap off on his side, and then shook it out over a trash can. After examining the interior several times, Jack took a deep breath and pulled it over his head.

Careful Jack.

Jack folded the bill of the cap almost in half, and pulled it snuggly down to cover most of his face. He buttoned his jacket all the way and flipped up the collar. He wanted to know what was going on, so he slowly turned the corner and approached the crowd that stood outside his home. Two of the police officers were now standing on the sidewalk, interviewing several of the neighbors.

Caroline then appeared at the top of the brownstone steps with two additional police officers. She had obviously been crying and one of the officers was comforting her. Jack stopped in his tracks when their eyes met. She recognized him instantly. The police officer noticed him too.

"Who's that?" asked the officer, as Jack casually slipped into a nearby alley.

Caroline was silent for a few seconds. "I don't know." she said.

The police officer did not believe her, and he left Caroline on the steps. He slowly walked down the sidewalk to investigate. He gave some silent hand gestures to the other officers, and they moved the crowd away from the area. Jack hid in the alley and held his breath, leaning against the brick façade of his neighbor's apartment building.

What now, JB?

At the end of the alley there was a large fence. He would have only seconds to climb over it. Indecision gripped him by the throat. Suddenly, he heard the static of the policeman's radio from just around the corner.

"Run Jabes!" Caroline screamed from the stoop, and Jack took off.

OOOOOOOO

The officer drew his gun and sprung around the corner. Jack was already halfway over the fence. "Freeze Police!" the cop shouted, and dropped into a shooter's stance.

Jack looked at him for only a fraction of a second before he tossed himself over the top of the fence. He fell to the concrete below, crashing into trashcans on the other side. Jack scrambled to his feet as the policeman aimed the revolver at his chest.

"Freeze or I'll shoot!" the policeman warned again, but Jack kept running.

The cop never fired his weapon but kept aim on Jack as he ran away. He quickly grabbed the radio that was clipped to his shoulder and spoke into it. "This is one-nineteen! Attention all units! I need backup assistance. The perp is taking flight! He's at Eighty-sixth Street location. I repeat the perp is now on Eighty-sixth Street!"

The officer entered the alley and placed his gun in its holster. He wrapped his hands into the wire holes and began to climb the fence.

"Roger that, One-nineteen. Help is on the way." the radio cracked.

OOOOOOOO

Jack ran through the morning rush-hour crowd. It was now at full force, teeming with businessmen and women. He pushed and shoved several people out of his way as he desperately ran for the subway station. As usual, Vinny was selling floral arrangements from a cart just outside the station. Jack turned the corner too quickly and accidentally slammed himself into the cart of flowers. The impact sent the cart into the stairwell and it bounced wildly down the steps. Flowers flew in all directions.

"I'm sorry Vin!" Jack apologized quickly, and followed the cart down into the station. Vin stood at the top of the steps, speechless.

Get the hell out of here, JB!

Keep running!

The cart crashed at the bottom of the steps, and broke into several pieces. Jack hurdled the floral wreckage, jumped through the turnstile and onto the downtown platform. He ran down the steps further to the express platform and hid amongst the crowd waiting for the train. Nobody on the express platform had apparently witnessed the scene he had just created upstairs, and he moved among the crowd with relative anonymity.

A light appeared in the tunnel. The train was approaching. It sounded its horn and it echoed loudly through the station. People began to file behind one another, and jockey for boarding position. Two uniformed police officers descended the steps. They began searching through the crowd. They were looking for Jack. There was no doubt about it.

Jack watched them cautiously, and buried himself further into the crowd. The train pulled to a stop. He slowly made his way towards the rear car of the subway but the policemen followed. They were still a few cars behind him, and they obviously had not seen him yet.

The doors on the train finally opened and Jack hopped on board one of the middle cars. He sank himself into the dense crowd of straphangers and stood in the corner by the door. He rested his head against the cold steel wall and prayed to wake up from this nightmare. The train crept out of station, picking up speed as it penetrated the darkness further downtown.

Why did you kill that woman? A voice in his head asked him.

Jack looked suspiciously around the subway cabin. "I didn't fucking do anything!" he insisted, and several passengers looked at him. "I didn't fucking do anything." he repeated.

You can't hide forever.

They're gonna catch you.

"I'll figure things out." he said, "Don't worry, I'll figure all of this out." Passengers moved away from him.

You're scaring everyone, JB.

"Screw 'em." Jack scowled, "Screw you all! Don't judge me!"

Jack noticed something in the car ahead of his. The two policemen were searching all of the cars, and they were heading right for him. Jack weaved his way through the crowd away from them. "Excuse me, coming through. Excuse me, coming through."

He parted the crowd until he reached the door between the cars. He opened it and the roar of the subway filled the cabin. He stepped outside and crossed into the next subway car. The police were right behind him. He pushed his way through the full cabin of straphangers, and again crossed into the next adjoining car. The police were gaining ground on him. Jack stepped through the doors and into the next car. The train began to slow as it approached the next station, and there was only one more subway car left. Jack opened the door, and stepped outside between the last two cars as the policemen entered the cabin.

The train stopped, and the doors opened. The policemen angrily searched the last two subway cars and then the busy platform at Fifty-ninth Street. They could not find Jack anywhere.

"He was just here!" one officer complained to the other.

"Did you check the platform?" the other asked. The radio went off at his shoulder, and he spoke into it. "This is One-O-Eight. We've lost him in the subway. Make all units aware. We've lost the suspect in the subway."

The subway doors shut again and the train pulled out of station. Jack was on top of the last car. He spread his arms and desperately clutched the metallic roof as the train sped through the darkness downtown.

CHAPTER TWENTY SEVEN
◆◆◆◆◆

The train slowly pulled into Grand Central Station and crawled to a stop. Jack relaxed his grip on the metal roof of the subway car, and carefully lowered himself between the cars again. He opened the door to one of the cars and stepped into the train. He casually joined the other passengers as they exited onto the platform, and followed them up the steps. He hid himself in a pack of tourists and Chinese women. His filthy attire was conspicuous for this hour however, and it would be extremely difficult for him to remain hidden for any length of time.

The pack turned into the main promenade and Jack stayed with them. He was always awestruck at the magnificence of the cathedral high ceilings and ornate stained glass windows. To Jack, Grand Central Station was truly an oasis of beauty in this otherwise charmless city. Jack ascended the escalator, and surfaced on the streets of Midtown Manhattan.

The streets were teeming with people. Jack immersed himself into the crowd and made his way to a nearby shopping mall. He pushed his way through the revolving doors and headed past the record stores and retail shops. Most of them were not open yet. He rode the escalator up two flights. He grabbed a coffee and a breakfast sandwich from *Burger King*, and sat himself on a bench. He almost regurgitated several times, thinking about Ellen, and what had happened.

He purchased a newspaper at an indoor newsstand, and sat back down on the bench. He pulled his hat down tightly over his head, and held the paper in front of his face as if he were reading. He vigilantly watched the front doors for the next several hours. He needed to think. He needed to regain control of the situation. It was nearly noon when he finally stood back up. He stretched his sore muscles and paced the third floor for a while. He pretended to be browsing.

A mall security guard walked by Jack and eyed him suspiciously. Jack felt uncomfortable. He turned in the other direction and headed for the escalator. He looked over his shoulder. The guard was still watching him. Jack hastened down the steps and stepped off. He turned abruptly again and ducked into in a large department store.

The store was fairly crowded and there were considerably more places to hide than in the mall. Jack took refuge in the men's clothing department. It wasn't long before an annoying sales representative approached him.

"Would you like help with anything?" the salesman asked him, and took a close look at Jack. He was dirty and unkempt.

"No I'm just looking, thanks."

The salesman was clearly repulsed by Jack's appearance, and figured he had no money to spend. "Let me know if you need me." he offered, and left quietly.

Rot in hell, you pretentious bastard.

Jack uselessly fiddled with the racks of clothing. He had the strange sensation that someone was watching him. He felt that telltale uneasiness in the pit of his stomach. He looked around the store but didn't notice anything unusual. Someone was definitely watching him though. He was certain of it.

The salesman stopped to talk with two other salesmen in the sporting goods department. All three men furtively glanced at Jack. He wasn't sure if it was his imagination, but they were watching him too. Perhaps they thought he was homeless. Perhaps they thought he intended to steal something. After all, he looked the part. Jack pretended not to notice them, and moved casually through the housewares department to the electronics.

Get out of here, Jack.

It's not safe for us.

Jack played briefly with the stereo equipment, and moved onto the computer department. Behind the computers was a wall of twenty color televisions. They were all muted and tuned to the local *NBC* affiliate. The news at noon had just started and the anchor greeted the city with a frank sincerity. Jack watched him intently, and wondered what he was so dire about.

He's talking about us, JB.

He knows we're here.

"Don't be ridiculous." Jack said, and turned the volume up on one of the television sets. "He couldn't be."

The anchor continued. "...police at the scene say they are pursuing several leads, and hope to apprehend the suspect soon. Caroline Johnson reports to us now, live from downtown...Caroline?"

The camera scene changed from the anchor inside the studio, to a pretty young woman reporting from the street. "Thanks Chuck...It happened sometime early this morning. A young psychologist, Doctor Ellen McCormick, was found dead in her brownstone apartment, here just above Greenwich Village. An anonymous phone call tipped the police off about six a.m., and the whereabouts of the caller are unknown at this time. Apparently this was a homicide Chuck, and although we are awaiting the official police report, our sources close to the story tell us that this bright young woman may also have been the victim of a brutal sexual assault."

"Oh my God." Jack covered his mouth with his hand.

What did you do Jack?

How could you?

"I didn't touch her, it was Casper." he mumbled. "I wouldn't ever hurt her."

The next video clip was shot from the front of Ellen's brownstone. The police were cautiously removing her corpse in a yellow body bag. The pretty reporter's voice continuously narrated the gruesome scene. "Doctor Ellen McCormick had just received her Ph.D. last spring from New York University and was described by neighbors as being brilliant, compassionate, and selfless." The reporter continued, "Today, the police are pursuing several leads in her tragic murder. Apparently there are several eyewitness accounts of the suspect and some evidence was recovered from the crime scene. No further information is available to us yet, but I will follow this story as it develops. If you have any information regarding this tragic crime, please contact the NYPD at 777-TIPS. Your call will be kept confidential...I'm Caroline Johnson, for *NBC* News."

The anchor returned, and Jack waited to see if he was mentioned. Thankfully he was not. The anchor changed stories and continued.

"There are new developments in the recent allegations of corruption in the Teamsters Union…"

Jack removed the ballcap briefly and wiped the sweat from his forehead. The site of Ellen in a body bag turned his stomach, and now he definitely needed to throw up. He nearly vomited on the floor as he raced to the bathroom. Once inside, the eggs and coffee exploded out of his throat and into the sink. He wretched several times after that, but nothing more came up. He wiped his mouth on his sleeve when he was finished, and washed the puke down the drain.

Jack collected himself for a minute and exited the bathroom. He left the department store and descended the escalator to the ground floor of the mall. Outside on the sidewalk there were several policemen talking to the mall security guard whom Jack had seen earlier. He could not hear what the guard was saying, but judging from his hand gestures it appeared that he was describing Jack's trench coat and hat.

Jack turned away and hurried towards the back door. He removed the *Yankees* cap and tossed it into a trashcan. He unbuttoned his trench coat, pushed through the rear door and stepped outside. He slid his wallet into his pants pocket, and quickly wiggled out of his coat. He draped it over his arm. Suddenly two police sedans rounded the corner ahead of him. Jack put his head down and walked in the opposite direction. He accidentally dropped his coat to the cement but did not turn to pick it up.

Let's get the hell out of the city, Jabes.

Let's go before it's too late!

Jack strongly agreed. He crossed the street against the signal and ducked back into Grand Central Station. The main promenade was covered with police. Most of them were in uniform, while others wore plain clothes. Some of them were showing a picture of Jack to random commuters. Jack turned around and went back onto the street. He walked around the station to a more remote side door, and used it. There were no police present, and Jack easily slipped down onto the uptown Number Six platform.

He boarded the Number Six train and stood by the doors. He rode the train uptown for only one stop, and got off at Fifty-first Street. He began to descend the long crowded escalator when he noticed that someone was following him. It was a white man with a closely cropped hair cut. He looked stereotypically undercover.

Although he could not see it, Jack heard the Number Four train pull into the station ahead of him, at the base of the escalator. He tried to squeeze his way down through the long line of commuters, but the escalator was simply too crowded. After a few tense seconds the warning bells sounded on the Number Four. Jack had just seconds before the doors shut. He would be trapped if he did not catch that train. He impulsively hopped onto the median between the escalators, and slid down the length of it on his buttocks.

Run Jack, Run!

"Freeze! Police!" the cop shouted and drew his gun. He pushed people out of his way, nearly knocking several of them down the moving metal staircase. "Everybody get down!" the policeman shouted, and took aim at Jack. He couldn't get a clean shot with all the commotion so he hopped on the median himself and slid down after Jack.

When Jack hit the concrete, the train had already closed its doors and began moving out of station. Jack sprinted after it as fast as he could.

"Everybody get down!" the policeman screamed again, as he hit the concrete platform. He sprang to his feet and chased after Jack.

It was chaos on the subway platform. People screamed and shouted, and dove under each other for cover. The train was picking up speed, and Jack ran alongside of it on the platform. A shot rang out and ricocheted off of one of the metal pillars just in front of Jack. He ducked his head instinctively but kept running after the subway train.

"Freeze! Police!" Another shot rang out and buzzed by Jack's ear.

Shit that was close!

The train was already more than halfway out of the station, and Jack was nearing the end of the platform. He would have to time his jump perfectly.

Another shot rang out and missed Jack again by only inches. He glanced over his shoulder. The last car was approaching him quickly as the train sped into the tunnel ahead. Jack took several more strides, and jumped off the edge of the platform. He dove for the back of the train, and for a fraction of a second there was nothing but air.

His elbow latched around the chain on the rear end of the car and his body slammed into the back of the train. Jack held on with all his strength, and the subway dragged him off into the dark tunnel. He threw his other arm over the chain, and pulled himself upwards. He was almost there. The speeding train jerked around a corner and nearly tossed Jack to the tracks. His body flew out sideways, and slammed against the wall of the tunnel. But he managed to hang onto the chain. He screamed, pulling his legs under his chest, and swung himself onto the subway car.

OOOOOOOO

Jack knew that the police would probably be waiting for him when the train pulled into its first stop in the Bronx. So as soon as the train began to slow, he jumped off the back of the train and tumbled onto the elevated tracks. He was above the pavement, looking down upon a busy intersection. Cars and trucks crisscrossed underneath him. He stood on the tracks and dusted himself off. The Number Four continued down the track for a couple of miles and finally pulled into station. As Jack suspected, the local precinct was waiting for him.

Jack searched for a way down from the tracks, and finally found a utility ladder. The rails began to shake as he climbed down, and the ladder vibrated violently in his hands. He almost lost his grip. Jack held on tightly, and moments later another train roared over his head.

At the bottom of the ladder he hung by his hands, and dropped to the cement, narrowly escaping the oncoming traffic. Hopping out of the way, he wiped his hands on his pants, and headed down the street.

Ah, the Bronx—A city of suspects.

"You said it."

CHAPTER TWENTY EIGHT
◆◆◆◆◆

Like most of the other suspects in the Bronx, Jack stayed off the streets until the sun set behind the project apartments. It was nearly eight o'clock, and Jack stopped at a nearby bodega and asked for a cup of coffee. He hadn't slept in days and he often fantasized about his warm soft bed at home. After he cleared this mess up, he would sleep, and sleep, and sleep. He promised himself.

"You show me money first!" the Pakistani behind the counter demanded.

"What?!" Jack was not used to this kind of treatment. He inspected his clothing. He was dirty, and now, truly indigent.

"Money first, then you get the coffee!" the Pakistani insisted.

Jack scowled and removed some crumpled bills from his pocket. "How much?"

"Ninety-five cents."

Jack threw a dollar onto the counter, and the man returned with a nickel and a lukewarm cup of coffee. In the typical inner city fashion, there were no niceties exchanged between the two men, and Jack left the store in a hurry.

"Freakin' ungrateful foreigner." he mumbled.

Go back to Pakistan!

He finished his coffee while he walked down One Ninety-seventh Street, and he tossed the empty cup into a dark alley. There were no trashcans anywhere. They disappeared long ago from this particular neighborhood. They were removed because they were being used as battering rams to enter the local stores. The pay phones were also removed due to uncontrolled drug dealing, and the fireboxes were removed due to frequent false alarms. Lawlessness was the only law in this place, and Jack found that comforting tonight.

Hoodlums were beginning to congregate on porches and street corners. Low-riding cars with tinted windows and loud stereos cruised slowly around the neighborhood. Drugs were available on nearly every street corner, and Jack was approached many times. He was scared to death, but he walked with as much conviction as he could fake.

A car pulled along side of him while he walked on the sidewalk. It was an old white *Cadillac* with black tinted windows. It followed him for several steps, and then the rear window slid down. Rap music poured onto the curb, and Jack looked inside. There were five young men inside, mixed races. They were all wearing red bandanas on the top of their heads. Against his better judgement, Jack stopped abruptly and stared back at them. The car stopped also. They stayed this way for several seconds, and Jack would not turn away from them. It was a contest of intimidation, and Jack was in no mood to lose. The man at the window smiled and the window finally rolled back up. Jack breathed deeply as the car peeled around the corner.

Don't fuck with us tonight!

Invincible.

Jack turned down Third Avenue, and suddenly there were flashing red lights and sirens behind him. He froze. Three black and white squad cars tore down the block past him. They screeched around the corner and zoomed away. Jack leaned against the wall, and wiped the sweat from his brow.

That was close.

There were more sirens, and swirling red lights. He again turned his face to the wall. Another squad car and an ambulance whizzed past him towards an obviously grisly scene up ahead.

Once he was certain that the police were a safe distance away, Jack began to walk again. Off in the other direction, there was a distant sound of gunshots. There were many of these little pops. Someone was indeed having a worse day than Jack was.

Misery loves company.

He was wandering aimlessly in a very dangerous neighborhood, and he needed a plan quickly. He needed to recapture his life. He desperately tried to formulate a strategy, but he was so tired that he could do very little thinking. The entire process of thought was failing him.

The white *Cadillac* turned the corner in front of him again. It stopped for a moment, and then slowly rolled towards him. Jack turned around and began walking in the other direction. He didn't want to run yet. It was too early. Another low-rider turned the other corner in front of him. He was sandwiched, and the two *Cadillacs* were closing in on him. Jack stood perfectly still for a split second, and concentrated.

What now, JB?

Just run! Just run!

Jack took off into an alley between two decrepit apartment buildings. He heard the two cars screech to a stop behind him as he darted through the alley. He tripped over an old soiled mattress and fell into a puddle of smelly brown water. He looked back. Eight or nine of the men were coming after him through the alley. He scrambled to his feet, and ran for his life. He ran through a yard and another alley, but ultimately found himself at a dead end. He was trapped. He had to think quickly or he would surely die.

In the corner of the alley there was a pile of large green garbage bags, all filled with trash. Jack quickly grabbed the lightest one, and ripped a hole in the bottom of it. He quietly poured the garbage on the floor and pulled the bag over his head. The stench was appalling. He squatted by the other bags, pulled his feet underneath and held his breath.

The eight men arrived within seconds.

"Where the fuck he go?" one of them asked.

"What the fuck?" another said.

Jack was still. The thugs circled the alley, and looked up at the buildings surrounding it. One of them approached the pile of trash bags. He removed a bag from the top, and looked behind the pile. Jack was not there. "Just more trash." he said, and threw the bag to the ground next to Jack.

"Did anyone see which way he fuckin' went?" he said, turning to his friends.

"If y'all didn't slow me up, I'd caught him! Fuckin' slow as shit. Can't catch a middle aged cracker."

"Aw, Fuck off, man!"

"I was goin' to get him the first time! But you needed your boys! Your fuckin' slow as shit boys!"

The thugs traded insults for several minutes, and then one of them lit a joint. Three of the men stayed behind to smoke it, while the rest of the gang returned to their cars. Jack did not move. He could not move, he was paralyzed by fear. Twenty minutes later, the remaining thugs finished the joint and then finally left the alley. Jack wanted to be cautious however, and he waited several minutes before he removed himself from the pile of trash. When he thought it was safe, he pulled the bag over his head, and shook the crap out of his hair. Bits of food and wet paper fell to the ground. Suddenly one of the thugs reappeared in the alley. He was looking on the ground for something. He must have dropped something. Jack froze, but the man noticed him anyhow.

"Well, well, well. Would ya getta load of this." The gangster drew his gun, and approached Jack. "Hey Michael!" he called to a friend down the alley, but there was no response. The punk shrugged. "Just more money for me, I guess? Hand it over."

"Now, Calm down." Jack tried to bargain with the man. "Calm down."

"Don't fuckin' talk shit to me!" the thug demanded. He wrapped both hands around his pistol, and aimed it squarely at Jack's head. "Give me the fuckin' wallet." He pressed the gun to Jack's temple.

Jack removed the wallet from his pants, and handed it to the man. "Take it all, just don't shoot."

The thug then noticed Jack's *Rolex*. "I'll take that watch too."

Jack frowned, and removed the watch from his wrist. He was getting angry, infuriated.

Kill this fucker, Jack!

That's it! Have no mercy!

"You can't have this watch. It was a gift from my grandfather." Jack told him. "He gave it to me on my eighteenth birthday."

"I don't give a shit who the fuck gave it to you, cause now, your gonna give it to me." The thug nudged Jack in the head with the gun.

Jack continued, "You know, he told me that it could withstand the pressure at the bottom of the ocean. Imagine that! You could swim to the bottom of the ocean with this thing on your wrist, and when you surfaced, it would still work." He shook his head and chuckled.

"Do I look like Jacques Cousteau to you? Is that what you think? Fuckin' Aqua-man bullshit."

"Unfortunately I don't dive either." Jack laughed again, and wrapped the watch firmly around his knuckles.

The thug warned him for the last time, "I want that fuckin' watch!"

Hit him Jabes!

Kill him!

"But I always knew that its durability would come in handy one day!" Jack closed his fist around the watch and belted the thug in the mouth.

The hit was explosive. The gangster's lip split in two, and blood gushed down his chin. The gun dropped to the floor, and Jack kicked it away. He grabbed the gangster by the shirt, and hoisted him up. Jack belted him again in the mouth, dislodging several of his teeth.

"Ooh…That was a gold one!" Jack remarked, as a gold tooth flew out of the thug's head and bounced on the floor. Jack pounded his face over and over again until his fist was blood red. He punched until the thug's mouth became a gaping hole in his head, and his body went limp. Jack's arm had grown tired, so he let the man drop to the floor. He kicked him once in the nuts for good measure.

Goddamn Bastard…Pointing a gun at me!

"You picked the wrong guy tonight, asshole!" Jack spit on the nearly dead man's head.

He picked up the gun and thoroughly examined it. He had never shot a pistol before, but it provided a reasonable security for this neighborhood. Technically it seemed pretty simple to use. Just point, pull the trigger, kill. He carefully placed the gun under his shirt and tucked it into his belt. He picked up his wallet and put it back in his pocket. He held his watch up to the street light, and examined it carefully. He wiped the fresh blood away from the dial. It was very bloody but there were no obvious cracks. He placed it up to his ear and listened. He grinned with intense satisfaction. It was still working.

Jack dragged the thug's body to the pile of trash, and put it where it belonged. He wandered the mean streets for the next several hours, and after a few close calls with the police, he decided to get a bite to eat.

The nighttime crowd was always odd, but the hostess had never seen someone like him come into the diner. He was filthy, and looked possessed. His right hand was bleeding onto the floor, and he smelled like a dumpster. She tried to hide her disgust but her face was brutally honest.

"How many?" She swallowed deeply, and prayed there was no one else with him.

"Just me." Jack said.

And me!

"Would you like a booth? Or perhaps the counter? The counter is sometimes nice." She was hoping he would choose the counter for the sake of the other patrons.

Jack shrugged. "I prefer the booth." He smiled back at her. He knew what she was trying to do. "Booths are nice."

Her expression went momentarily blank. "Okay then." she said, with a forced smile and led him to the booth furthest away from the other patrons.

Jack sat down and opened the menu. The diner was fairly crowded for this hour, and the people stared at him while he waited for service. He was talking to himself, and acting peculiar. He couldn't help it. The evening news played on a color television that hung in the corner, and the mini jukebox at his table was softly playing music. Jack turned the volume up, and quietly mouthed the words, as if he didn't have a care in the world.

Everyone is staring at us.

"I know." Jack said, and looked around the diner. "But I'm fucking starving."

Way to smash that guys face, JB.

"Yeah, my hand is killing me." He lifted his hand into the air, and dripped blood onto the menu. "I'm bleeding too, oh shit." Jack was drunk with fatigue, and his hand throbbed at the end of his arm. A small pool of blood was collecting on the table, and Jack tried to pack the wound on his hand with napkins.

The waitress came over to him, and took his order.

"Can I just get an order of pancakes, and a big, big, big coffee?"

The waitress couldn't hold her breath much longer. "Sure." she said, and tried to escape to the kitchen.

Jack stopped her. "And one more thing, Babe?" He lifted his bloody hand. "Do you have any bandages?" He was beginning to see double. He was exhausted. He was losing himself.

"I'll check…" The waitress grimaced, and retreated to the kitchen.

Go to sleep, Jacko.

Get some sleep.

Jack shut his eyes, and for the first time in several days he slept. It was light but peaceful. He was asleep for only fifteen seconds when he was awakened by the big band sound of Frank Sinatra.

"Start spreading the news…I'm leaving today…I want to be a part of it…New York, New York…"

He was completely disoriented. The music was coming from the jukebox at his table. He frantically flipped through the selections, and there it was. *New York, New York,* by Frank Sinatra. Jack sprang out of the booth. "Casper?"

Casper is here!

"Casper!" he shouted. He was delirious. "Where the fuck are you, Casper?" He was wild and uncontrollable.

Pandemonium broke out in the diner, as Jack drew his pistol and searched from booth to booth. Mothers and fathers pulled their children underneath the diner tables, attempting to shield them from imminent harm. "Don't kill us!" they pleaded.

"These little town shoes…Are longing to stray…"

"Casper! I know you're fucking here somewhere!" Jack started flipping the tables over, and everyone started screaming and scrambling for safety.

"Casper! Come out, come out wherever you are?" He was maniacal.

He's toying with us, Jack!

The hostess ran to the kitchen and dialed 911. Some patrons huddled together and ran for cover, diving from table to table. Others were frozen still. A daring few escaped through the front door.

"Casper? Come out, come out wherever you are?!" Jack sang again and searched for him in vain. "Where the fuck are you, you fucking coward? I got something for you, little buddy. It's not gonna hurt."

The diners ducked as Jack haphazardly waved the gun around. His search for Casper became more fervent. He was crazed.

The song finally ended, and Jack began to regain his orientation.

What the hell are you doing?

He was frightened, and confused. He started to whimper, then cry. Suddenly there was a silence in the diner. There was something unusual on the television set in the corner. It was his brownstone. The news reporter for *NBC* was standing outside of his home.

"Everyone shut the fuck up!" Jack demanded, waving the gun again at the frightened patrons. "Shut the fuck up!"

Holy shit, JB. That's our house!

"I know, I know...Now be quiet. Turn the fucking volume up." Jack pointed the gun at one of the busboys. "Turn it up!" The tremulous busboy turned up the volume.

You're doomed.

A woman's voice on the television reported. "...Police searched the home today of Doctor Jack Benedict, but they could not apprehend the suspect. He has been implicated in the brutal murder and sexual assault of Doctor Ellen McCormick early this morning. He may also be involved with another potential homicide...Another young woman, but authorities have yet to confirm this report. There have been various sightings of him all day in Manhattan, and he may have boarded a subway bound for the Bronx or Upper Manhattan." the reporter continued, "If you come across this man, be very careful and call the local police. He may be armed, and he is considered dangerous. News Channel Four in cooperation with the NYPD has obtained these photographs of the suspect."

Jack's picture appeared on the television screen, and some of the patrons in the diner started screaming.

"Hey mom, that's the man on the TV!" a young boy pointed at Jack.

The room started spinning around him. Jack was going to pass out.

Stay strong Jack, Stay strong.

Jack swung the gun across the crowd again, and they ducked and cowered away from him.

"I didn't do anything!" he cried, "Don't you understand? I didn't do it! I swear, I didn't do it!"

Sirens were approaching from outside. Someone called the police. He darted out the back door and sprinted down the block to the subway station. Moments later the police stormed the diner.

○○○○○○○

The train roared under the East River and arrived at Fifty-first Street shortly after midnight. Some of the passengers got off at this stop, and Jack buried himself in the small crowd. He transferred to the E-train, and rode it for several more stops, and finally got off at Pennsylvania Station. He wanted to check Casper's apartment again. Perhaps he would hide there this time, and set up an ambush for his friend. As he walked the long corridor by the Long Island Rail Road, he fantasized about what he would do to Casper when he found him. He would crush him. He would ruin him. He would harm him.

Redemption, Jacko.

Things have gone too far!

"They certainly have. It's payback time."

As he headed towards the Uptown Seventh Avenue Subway, Jack had a feeling that someone was watching him again. Possibly following him. He tucked the gun deeper into his pants, and tried to disappear.

He bought a token, and dropped it into the turnstile. He descended the steps to the subway platform, and waited for the uptown train. He was searching the crowd on the platform across the tracks, when he noticed a curious looking homeless man in an oversized trench coat. The man was talking to himself, and enjoying quite a good conversation. He was balding, maybe in his forties. His build was sinewy and unusually athletic. His face was deceptively young despite the fact that he nearly had a full beard. He said something to a group of young women, and they all started to laugh.

Jack squinted and rose to his feet. It was Casper. He rubbed his eyes, and Casper was still there. "Casper!" he called out across the tracks. Casper turned and waved at Jack.

"Shouldn't you be in the electric chair by now?" he shouted back. "I saw you on the news, JB...Holy shit, you're gonna fry!"

That's him.

We got him!

Jack ran back up the steps, and crossed over to the downtown platform. Casper ran up the far steps towards the LIRR. Jack sprinted after him, and drew his gun.

"Casper Freeze!" Jack shouted at him, but Casper kept running.

Casper ran down the steps to track nineteen of the LIRR, and Jack followed him closely. The platform was relatively crowded and the people scattered when they saw Jack come barreling through with the pistol.

"Casper! Stop! Or I'll blow your brains out!" he shouted again, creating chaos on the platform.

Casper ran up the steps at the end of the platform and jumped the turnstile to the C-Train. So did Jack. The train was already in station and the doors were open. Casper jumped on board the subway, and Jack boarded the train several cars behind him. Three undercover cops were also in pursuit, and they boarded the car behind Jack. The train pulled out of station, and Jack moved quickly between the cars to close in on Casper.

A pistol goes a long way in this city, Jack.

"It sure fucking does."

Casper opened the door and stepped into the next car. He was running from car to car, but he was quickly running out of space. His only hope was to get off at the next stop. He pulled the door open, and stepped into the last car of the train. There was nowhere else to go. He was trapped.

Jack followed right behind him and soon stepped into the last subway car. Casper stood cornered at the rear end. "Everybody get down!" Jack told the five other passengers in the car. He crossed the car, until he was a few yards away from Casper.

This is between him and us.

Jack cocked his gun, and pointed it squarely at Casper's chest. The train was beginning to slow down as it neared the next station.

"Hey!" Casper taunted him. "C'mon, you're not gonna shoot me! You're a pussy. You got no balls. You wanna shoot me? Just do it already!" He pounded his chest. "I dare you, I'm ready. Pussy!"

"Don't give me a reason to shoot you, Cass!" Jack warned him. The subway door behind Jack opened, and the cops entered.

"Shoot me you coward!"

Jack took aim.

"Freeze police!" one of the policemen shouted.

He fucked us up, Jack!

Shoot him Jack!

Payback's a bitch.

"Please don't shoot me!" Casper begged. "Help me, police!"

"Freeze police! Drop your weapon!"

Kill him Jack!

"I swear, I'll fucking pull this trigger!" Jack's arms started to tremble.

"Drop the weapon Doctor Benedict!"

Do it!

"You must tell the police everything!" Jack demanded.

"I don't know what you're talking about? Help me...Help me! This guy is crazy! I'm homeless, and I don't know what he wants! Oh god help me!" Casper shouted to the police behind Jack.

"Drop your weapon now! Drop the weapon Doctor Benedict!"

Do it, Jack!

Waste him!

"Drop the weapon or we'll shoot!"

"Tell them!"

"You're gonna fry." Casper calmly said.

Waste him!

Blow him away!

"Drop it!"

The train lurched to a stop, and there was a moment of deadly silence. The platform doors slid open.

"Rot in hell, Casper!" Jack said, and pulled the trigger.

The gun fired, and Jack was instantly tackled from behind. The pack of burly men threw him violently to the floor. His face bounced off the subway bench several times, and it left a bloody splotch on the floor.

The undercover police officers bent his arms behind his back, and Jack screamed in pain. Blood poured from his nose.

"What the hell are you doing?" Jack screamed as he struggled. "You want him! He's the killer!"

One of the policemen leaned his elbow into Jack's neck and he snapped handcuffs around his wrists. He spoke quickly and decisively. "Doctor Benedict, I have a warrant for your arrest. Suspicion of murder. You have the right to remain silent. You have the right to have an attorney. If you cannot afford an attorney one will be appointed for you by the court. Anything that you say can, and will, be used against you in a court of law..."

"What the hell is going on?!" Jack screamed again, and tried to break out of the cuffs. "I didn't do anything! It's him! You got the wrong guy!"

Several other police officers arrived on the platform, and boarded the train. Jack struggled on the floor, and began to cry. "I didn't do anything!"

Detective Cavanagh finally walked onto the train and surveyed the scene. He snapped on sterile gloves, and stepped into a pair of surgical booties. As usual, he was meticulous. He picked up the gun that Jack had used, and emptied the clip. "One spent cartridge, and eight unused." He placed the gun and the clip in separate evidence baggies. The suspect was on the floor, and thankfully there was no corpse. The arresting officer explained the events of the apprehension, and Detective Cavanagh listened intently. When the officer finished, Detective Cavanagh shrugged with satisfaction and squatted down by the suspect.

Jack was lying facedown on the floor of the subway car in handcuffs. A puddle of blood collected at his ears. Detective Cavanagh lifted Jack's face from the chin, and looked the suspect in the eyes. They were red and swollen, and blood from his nose dripped onto the detective's powder white gloves.

"Nice to see you again, Doctor." Detective Cavanagh smiled at him. "Looks like you've been having a bad couple of weeks, huh?" He shook his head, and dropped Jack's head back to the floor. "That's our man." He stood and removed his gloves. "Bring him in and lock 'em up."

Jack, the suspect, protested on the floor. "I didn't do anything!" he sobbed. "I swear I didn't do anything! I'm gonna kill you Casper!"

Two uniformed policemen stood him up and led Jack out of the subway. He was a bloody mess, and rambling about some sort of experiment.

Detective Cavanagh slapped the arresting officer on the back. "Good work Lieutenant. Real nice job."

"Thanks." the humble officer responded.

On his way out, Detective Cavanagh noticed that there was a solitary bullet hole in the rear of the subway car. It was warm to the touch, so it must have been new. "Hey Lieutenant?"

"Yeah?"

"Anyone get hurt?" The detective pointed at the hole in the wall.

"Um..." The undercover agent looked around for Casper. "He was right here, some homeless guy. The good doctor tried to finish him. I don't see him now. He must have run off. I guess he didn't want to press his luck any further tonight. The bullet missed him by maybe an inch, probably less."

"Good." Detective Cavanagh nodded. "Excellent work. I'll meet you down at the station. We'll see what Doctor Demento has to say for himself."

The forensics team entered the subway car, and began to take pictures. Jack was lead through Pennsylvania Station in handcuffs, and placed in the back of a black-and-white squad car in front of Madison Square Garden. Back down in the subway, Detective Cavanagh stepped onto the platform, and tapped a cigarette out of the pack he was carrying. He placed it in his mouth, and lit it. He took a long drag, and exhaled a cloud of thick white smoke.

"God, I love this city."

EPILOGUE
◆◆◆◆◆

Detective Cavanagh took another drag from his cigarette and then smashed the flame out in the ashtray. He let the smoke swirl in his mouth before he sucked it into his lungs. He needed a strong hit of nicotine. He was exhausted. They've been at this all night. After nearly a minute, he blew the smoke into the air and it floated towards the ceiling.

"So let's go through this again, Doctor Benedict." They were in the Interrogation Room at the Twenty-Seventh Precinct. "You and this Doctor Lolly, were real good friends. That's how this whole thing started? Am I correct in that?"

Jack was exhausted too, and he could not keep his thoughts linear or coherent. "Yes." he nodded.

"So he had this idea. He set up an experiment in a garage downtown. He volunteered to become psychotic through sleep deprivation, sensory deprivation, and what was the third one?" Detective Cavanagh paced the room as he thought.

"Amphetamine abuse." his partner reminded him.

"Oh yes! The *Primatene*…Sleep deprivation, amphetamine abuse, and sensory deprivation. Is that correct, Doctor Benedict?"

Jack wanted to sleep so badly. "Yes."

Just confess Jack

Tell them you killed her.

"Never." Jack responded, uncertain of whom he was answering.

"Is this the typical type of experiment you're used to conducting? I mean as an academic psychiatrist?"

"Of course not."

The detective pulled his chair closer to Jack. "Okay so what you're telling me now, is that Doctor Lolly went looking for this *Perceptive*

Schizophrenia, a type of psychic mental state in which the subjects can see the future, and all that hocus-pocus...But in reality, this Casper Lolly simply became a Paranoid Schizophrenic. He beat the hell out of you, escaped from the experiment, subsequently ruined your career, ruined your marriage, killed Doctor Ellen McCormick, and then framed you for her murder."

"That's all true." Jack confessed.

"Did Doctor Lolly know Doctor McCormick?"

"Not that I know of." Jack shook his head.

"So, why would he kill her?"

"I dunno. To get at me I guess."

"Oh! I see...And why would he want to harm you?" he sighed. "Do you also see the future?"

Jack looked up at Detective Cavanagh with frustration. "He wanted to destroy me because he's fuckin' crazy! That's it you asshole, he's simply crazy!"

John Cavanagh calmly lit another cigarette and blew smoke into the air. "Tell me about the diner last night, Jack...What happened at the diner? Did Casper do any of that?"

"I'm not sure." Jack was so confused. "The music made me do that...Casper's music. But I don't think he was there now."

"And how about the shooting on the subway? Why did you try to shoot that homeless man? Did Casper Lolly make you do that too?"

"That was Casper Lolly! I've told you that already!"

Hit him, Jack!

Detective Cavanagh furrowed his brow. "Has Casper Lolly always been homeless?"

Fucking patronizing prick!

"Of course not! Just since he's been crazy! He shaved his head bald and grew a beard..." Jack ran his cuffed hands through his own greasy hair.

"Uh-huh." Detective Cavanagh looked at Jack for several minutes without a word. "Well let me tell you how I see things, Doctor." He placed the cigarette in the ashtray and let it burn. "You had an affair with this woman, and you never quite got over it, huh?"

261

There was no response from Jack, and Detective Cavanagh continued. "We have your prints on her doorknob. You left a message on her machine telling her that you were coming over on that night. Ah, she probably wouldn't let you in, right? Just like a woman. She didn't want to see you anymore." Cavanagh was smug, and he winked at Jack looking for a break. "Maybe she found somebody else? And that's why you killed her! Isn't that true, Doctor Benedict?!"

"No, it's not! It's nothing like the truth!" Jack pleaded.

"Her neighbors placed you at the scene around the time she was killed. You left a rambling message on her answering machine on the night she was killed …And in this drunken, jealous rage you simply went berserk! You killed her! Isn't that right Doctor Benedict?"

"No, no way!" Jack started crying again. "I didn't do it, I swear!"

Just tell him what you did, Jack.

Fuck off.

"Have you been hearing any voices, Doctor Benedict?" the detective asked. "C'mon Jack, you can tell me…I just want to help you out. Have you been hearing voices?"

Jack nodded shamefully. "I haven't slept."

"Then in this fragile mental state, you go ballistic in a Bronx diner, threaten the patrons, and then attempt to shoot a homeless man on the subway…That's how I see it!"

"It was an experiment!" Jack snapped. "Listen to me! My friend is out there! He needs help, or he may hurt someone else, or maybe himself. You've got to believe me. Please!"

Detective Cavanagh stood up again, and paced the floor. "Yeah Doctor Benedict, what about that experiment? What about the EEG, the brainwave machine? What about the computers, and the Isolation Chamber? What happened to all of that crap?"

"Gone." Jack looked at the mirror on the wall. He stared hopelessly at the reflection, wondering if anyone sat behind it. He looked so different now. His skin hung loosely on his face, and he was unshaven. Dried clots of blood hung from his nostrils, and his hair was filthy. He not only looked older, he looked dead. "It's all gone." He closed his eyes, and shook his head. "It's all gone."

"No shit!" Cavanagh said. "We've been down there! There was nothing there!" He puffed again on the cigarette. "Doctor Benedict, tell me about the Academic Review Committee. Is that why you killed Doctor McCormick? Because she was pressing charges against you?"

Give up Jabes.

Jack wept. "I didn't kill her! My friend is psychotic, and he did this! I don't think Ellen really pressed charges. She wouldn't have. She couldn't have!"

Detective Cavanagh was fed up. They had been going in circles for hours. He couldn't take anymore of this insanity. It was driving *him* mad. He turned to Jack one last time as he opened the door to leave. "Wanna know what I think?"

Jack was a wreck. He looked up at the detective.

Cavanagh took another long drag of his cigarette, and thoughtfully exhaled. "Maybe it's not Doctor Lolly who's crazy...Maybe it's you?"

He pulled the door open, and let his assistant out of the Interrogation Room. He called to the guards outside when he left. "Send in the shrink! This one is gonna need it."

The psychiatrist had been watching the interrogation from the opposite side of the mirror. He had waited patiently for hours to assess this subject. In fact, he was very excited about it. A psychotic break in a prominent psychiatrist was particularly interesting to him. This would be the most enjoyable D.O.C.I. he has ever done. He rubbed his hands anxiously together, and softly whistled a Frank Sinatra tune while the interrogation progressed.

He carried a large leather satchel that he had laid on the floor by his feet. Like all psychiatrists, there was something strange about this one. He was deceptively fit. He had a distinctly athletic build, giving him a strange youthful appearance. Even his expensive Italian suit could not hide the youthfulness of his muscles. His eyes were a piercing blue, giving the impression of a profound, almost divine intelligence. He stroked his beard pensively while he watched the interrogation come to a conclusion. The suspect, Doctor Jack Benedict, had now been broken. He was a mental jigsaw puzzle, and this psychiatrist was looking forward to playing with the pieces for a while.

He stood, and quickly combed the small rim of hair around his head when he was called. It was time to get this party started. He hoisted the heavy leather satchel over his shoulder. There was something large and metallic inside of it.

"Hey Doc, whatcha got in the bag?" the guards asked him, and started to follow him inside the Interrogation Room. Casper stopped them at the door, and pushed them outside.

"Please guys, I need to be alone with the suspect."

THE END

The Author
◆◆◆◆◆

Sean Kenniff (Doctor Sean) is a physician in Manhattan, New York. An original cast member from the CBS television blockbuster, *Survivor,* he often works in television and radio as a health correspondent. He is affiliated with many charities, and is the national spokesman for the Four Foundation (www.fourfoundation.org), a research and support group for children suffering from brain tumors. He is active on the college and medical school lecture circuit, and maintains a busy health and entertainment website. He is single and enjoys friends, art, coffee, and of course, a good book.

Visit Doctor Sean on the Web at **www.survivorsean.com**

Printed in the United States
2252